Dorset Libraries
Withdrawn Stock

The Broken
KingS

Also by Robert Holdstock:

The Merlin Codex

The Iron Grail
Celtika

Mythgo Cycle

Mythago Wood
Lavondyss
The Hollowing
Gate of Ivory, Gate of Horn

Ancient Echoes
Merlin's Wood
The Fetch

Dorset Libraries
Withdrawn Stock

From the Merlin Codex: Book Three

ROBERT HOLDSTOCK

.ANCZ
NDON

DORSET COUNTY COUNCIL	
Bertrams	06.01.07
	£14.99

Copyright © Robert Holdstock 2006
All rights reserved

The right of Robert Holdstock to be identified as the author of this work has been asserted by him in accordance with the Copyright, Designs and Patents Act 1988.

First published in Great Britain in 2006 by
Gollancz
An imprint of the Orion Publishing Group
Orion House, 5 Upper St Martin's Lane,
London WC2H 9EA

A CIP catalogue record for this book is available from the British Library

ISBN 13 9 780 57507 930 4 (cased)
ISBN 10 0 57507 930 4 (cased)
ISBN 13 9 780 57507 931 1 (trade paperback)
ISBN 10 0 57507 931 2 (trade paperback)

1 3 5 7 9 10 8 6 4 2

Typeset by Deltatype Ltd, Birkenhead, Merseyside

Printed in Great Britain by
Mackays of Chatham Ltd, Chatham Kent

The Orion Publishing Group's policy is to use papers that are natural, renewable and recyclable products and made from wood grown in sustainable forests. The logging and manufacturing processes are expected to conform to the environmental regulations of the country of origin.

www.robertholdstock.com
www.orionbooks.co.uk

For the new Argonauts: Josh, Matilda, Callum, Louis,
Rory & Toby . .

And the three slightly older Argonauts: Kev, Kelly & Ben.
High Seas and Happy Days!

Acknowledgements

My thanks to Abner, Howard, Jo, Malcolm, Patrick, Anne, Darren and Sarah, who all helped keep Argo nosing for safe haven.

Contents

'The unkown *consumes* men like me. We are born in that place.
We can never know its limits. We disappear there.'

Attributed to Jason, son of Aeson, & captain of Argo
from *Argonautika*

Prologue

Unbroken, They Dream Of Kings

Late in the afternoon, the last of five chariots came hurtling through the narrow pass towards the agreed meeting place. The young man who leapt down from the light wicker carriage was tall, dressed in the scarlet and saffron patterned clothing of his class and clan, his cloak edged with purple and embroidered with the image of a snarling wolf. His fair hair was tied into an elaborate plait, wound around his head like a crown. The heavy golden torque around his neck caught the dying of the day in a bright, flashing display.

This was Durandond, eldest son of the High King of the Marcomanni, one of the five federations that drew its strength from the forests north of the great river Rein. He cried out a salute to his foster-brothers, all of whom were drunk by now, then tossed his weapons into the car. The charioteer carefully turned the horses and joined the other drivers where they sat, some way away, eating and drinking and sharing their experiences of the long journey south, into the mountains.

The smell of a wine-laced, fat meat stew was a welcome embrace to this tall prince.

'You're late!' was the admonishing greeting of one of the other four.

'Not too late to help with that Greek Land wine, I hope,' Durandond responded. He embraced his brothers cheek and chin, then tipped the lighter of two slim clay amphorae so that the sharp red wine splashed into his bowl.

'To fate, to discovery – and to the rich lives and noble deaths of our fathers!' he said, and his companions echoed the toast, laughing.

Chunks of goats' meat and a thick slice of dry bread were

passed to Durandond, and he ate the meal with hardly a thought for anything but what he knew as 'satisfaction and the good sigh'. Starvation was at an end. He patted his belly. His journey was at an end. The oracle man, the so-called 'wanderer' who lived a short walk further along the pass, could wait until the bliss of wine had loosened his limbs and sharpened his wits.

This story is not the story of Durandond, nor of his four friends and foster-brothers. Do not become too attached to these brash, boastful characters. They are only ghosts. But their shades haunt the following tale, in particular, the shade of this last arrival at the simple feast: the last braggart, the last charmer, the last of the young men who had sensed, because they had common sense and had seen the death of older men, that their world was about to change.

They walked in single file along the narrow, winding gorge, Durandond in the lead, approaching each twist and turn along the track with caution. A small stream dribbled alongside the path. Bushes of thorn and gorse tugged at their cloaks. The tangled roots of elms, looming above the pass, bulged out like sleeping serpents, greened with fern and scaled in fungus.

For a long while the gorge was dark with an overhanging canopy. Then Durandond led the way into an open area leading up to a dark cave, its low roof jutting out and slung with the russet drapes of deer hides, a curtain door that was now drawn back to admit a view of the interior.

A tall man stepped into the light. It was hard to tell his age through the voluminous black beard that swathed his face and the lank mass of black hair, threaded through with shells and stones that hung around his shoulders. But his eyes were bright and youthful, intensely curious as he let his gaze drift slowly along the line of young princes. He was clothed in filthy buckskin trousers and jacket; a weatherworn bearskin cloak was draped around his shoulders, reaching almost to the ground, the sides tied together with a bronze clasp.

Instead of a staff, he held a short bow and a quiver of arrows. When the five young men unbuckled their sword belts and tossed the weapons to the ground, he threw the bow and arrows back into the cave.

'Are you the wanderer?' Durandond asked.

'Yes.'

'This is the wanderer's cave?' He made it clear he was unimpressed.

'Wanderer.' The man pointed to himself. 'Wanderer's cave. Yes.'

Durandond could not hide his disappointment. 'I'd heard so much about it, I'd expected it to be wider and filled with magic and the oracular acquisitions of your wanderings.'

'I have many caves. I have to. I *wander*. I range very far and very wide. I walk a circular path around the world. I've been doing it for so long I've noticed changes on the face of the moon herself. I'm sorry to disappoint you. Is that why you've come? To talk about my "oracular acquisitions"? To talk about my furnishings?'

'No. Not at all.'

'Then tell me who you are.'

Durandond introduced himself and his companions. The smell of stale animal fat and rank hair was almost offensive to these sons of kings, who were meticulous in their hygiene and were clean and kempt in every detail. But they ignored their repulsion as this young-old man sat down on a three-legged oak stool and leaned forward on his knees, nodding his head to indicate the youths should also sit.

They didn't sit; it would have been undignified. They dropped to one knee and settled back on their haunches. Then, one by one, they placed their simple gifts on the ground before them. The seer eyed the food and drink, the small spear, the bronze knife and the green woollen cloak, then looked up and smiled. His teeth were bone-white and strong. 'Thank you. I shall enjoy the stew and wine. And the rest is very useful. What can I do for you? I must warn you: I don't look far into the past; and I don't help influence change. I look to the future, but in only a simple way. I guide, I warn, I help prepare for change. Nothing more. Anything else is too expensive. Not for you, but for me.'

'Yes,' Durandond retorted. 'We'd heard that you would prefer to guard your talents rather than use them.' He spoke with the arrogant indifference to the consequences of his words appropriate to a champion and future king. 'It doesn't matter. All our questions are the same.'

The wanderer had smiled thinly at the comment. Now he raised his hands, fingers wide, inviting his guests to use him.

The five princes cast lots for the order, and Radagos rose to his feet.

'Rieving bands from the east, each small in number, are gathering together to raid my father's fortress on the Rein. My father and I will ride out at the head of an elite of champions. We will be the first to hurl spear and shield into their cowardly ranks. At the end of the battle, will I be king or still a king's son?'

The wanderer shook his head, meeting Radagos' gaze with cold iron eyes. 'You will be neither,' he said. 'Your land will be ravaged. You will be a whipped dog, terrified and bleeding, running and howling to the west, searching for a rock to hide under, a cave to crawl into, a hollow tree to worm inside, and this will be the way until you reach another country.'

Radagos looked shocked and stunned for a moment. 'I will be none of that! None of what you say. Whether my father lives or dies, I will not be what you see. You are wrong,' he snarled. 'Here. Take your knife!' He kicked the small weapon towards the seated man. The wanderer reached for it and tossed it behind him. Radagos turned and stormed back down the narrow gorge, shouting obscenities.

Vercindond had drawn to place the second question. He stood, his right hand gripping the embroidered edge of his purple cloak. He asked, 'When I win the challenge to succeed my father, and rule the citadel of the Vedilici, for how many years will there be peace with the minor chieftains of my country?'

The seated seer shook his head again. 'Your first act as king of the Vedilici will be to flee westwards, the smoke and ash of your burning citadel on your back, the dead that you hold precious being dragged by ropes. You will be in pain. You will grieve until you reach another country.'

Vercindond stared ahead of him, thinking hard, then glanced back at the old man. 'No. I don't think so. You've seen it wrong. Besides, there is a *geis* on me from birth that says I must only travel to the west in a chariot and with a retinue of five red-haired women. Some would say that's a taboo to be broken! Either that, or at the time of the longest journey of all, at my death, the journey to the Realm of the Shadows of Heroes. No mention of ropes and corpses. No, you've got it wrong. Here, eat your stew anyway. It might help clear your vision.'

He was very calm about it, but very angry. He followed Radagos away from the wanderer's cave.

Cailum glanced at Durandond, frowning slightly, then stood,

holding the fishing spear with its vicious ivory hooks. He stared at the implement for a moment, fingering the sharp teeth. Then he looked at the wanderer. 'I'd intended to ask a different question to the others. But all my instincts, and the embedded wisdom of my druid teachers – what I can remember of it, at least – tells me that the answer will still involve my going to the west, to another country. That seems to be the pattern. So my question is: what can I do to stay in the east?'

'Nothing,' answered the wanderer. 'Your fate is west; your fate is broken. Your lands will burn behind you. Your citadel will become an open space for wild and scavenging animals.'

Cailum stepped over to him and leaned down, wincing with the odour that curled off the man like a rotting elemental force. He placed the fishing spear on the wanderer's lap. The two men's eyes locked.

'Never,' said Cailum softly. 'I will never go to the west in the manner in which you have seen. The fortress is my inheritance, my home, my place of birth, my earthmound for when I die. Not until this salmon spear hooks out the guts of the moon will I leave that hill and its city. By the good strong hand of Belenos and by the hard heart of Rigaduna, I wish your prophecy to be unthreaded and wound around your neck.'

He turned away abruptly. The wanderer felt his neck gingerly, then grinned through his beard.

Durandond had drawn to ask last, so now Orogoth stood up, reaching for the flagon of southern wine. He shook it and smiled, then took it to the seer. 'This will only serve to blur your vision,' he said. 'So I think I'll keep my question unasked. Like my foster-brother, Cailum, I suspect I can already guess the answer. And "west" will feature heavily. By the way, which way *is* west from here? I might as well get started.'

He laughed, tugged his moustaches, an insolent gesture, then walked back along the gully, an expression of wry amusement on his sun-burnished features as he winked at Durandond.

The fifth of the brash princes now stood, holding the short green cloak that he had brought as his gift for a gift. The wanderer watched him without expression. Durandond asked, 'Do you have a name?'

'I'm very old. I've been around a long time. I've had many names.'

'A path around the world, you said. That must take a long time to walk.'

'It does. And I've done it many times. Some parts of it – the North Land in particular – are a tribulation. I do not now, and never have, enjoyed the cold. Sometimes I leave the route to go to interesting places; sometimes I stay in those places for a generation or more. It all serves to break the tedium. I come from a world of forests and plains, the sort of wild hunting you can only imagine, the sort of magic that would be incomprehensible to you, a world in many layers, with spirits and what you call gods in many strange and wonderful forms. It is invisible now, but as I shed lives, so they return there. One day I should go back and visit. But the countries through which I wander become more interesting with every passing century. Old lives must wait while new ones are forged.'

Durandond thought hard about this, perplexed, certainly, but also amused, as if he were enjoying being in the presence of such mystery. After a few moments he shook his head, picked up the gift of the green mantle and placed it in the wanderer's hands. He stepped away, tying his own cloak at the left shoulder and drawing it round to be pinned at his midriff. He bobbed his head in respect then picked up his sheathed sword, winding the belt around it.

It was now the wanderer who was puzzled, surprised by this sudden dismissal. 'No question to ask?'

But Durandond nodded. His pale eyes narrowed. He stroked his chin, head cocked to the side, perhaps listening to the future.

'Yes. I have a question. When I am in that other country ... When I am in the west ...' He hesitated for a moment before adding quietly, 'What is the first thing I will do?'

The wanderer laughed, stood up from his wooden seat. He looked down at the mantle and said, 'You will find a hill as green as the dye on this garment. You will climb it. You will proclaim it as yours. And you will start to build.'

'A fortress?'

'More than that. Much more than that.'

'Much more than that,' the young prince repeated thoughtfully, his gaze distant. 'Much more than that. I like the sound of it.'

His gaze was distant for a moment only. He looked at me, searching. He was curious, caught up in the uncertainty and excitement of what must have sounded a profound prophecy. 'Will I meet you again?' he asked.

How could I answer? I never looked ahead into time to see my own presence. Far too dangerous. That I would be a presence in his world for all of his life was not in doubt. And in his sons' world, and in their sons after them. Not in doubt.

And centuries later I discovered the green hill that I had seen in my vision, and lived for a few years in the great fortress in Alba that the young, cautious, curious man had created out of the ashes of his life. Taurovinda.

When I came to Alba it marked the end for a long while of my walking around the wide Path. Alba embraced me, and the ghost of a future king began to haunt me, and to shape me. That is another story and for another time. I was still attached to my new loves and my first loves: and one of my first loves was beautiful, very beautiful indeed. And this is as much her story as it is of the land to which, one day, she had quietly returned in shame.

One day, during a cool summer …

PART ONE

WATER FROM THE WELL

1

Omens

. . . Argo, Jason's enchanting ship, came back to Taurovinda, Fortress of the White Bull, a year after she had sailed away. She came back along the river known as 'the Winding One'. I had always held a secret suspicion that she would return, but she stayed quiet for a full turn of the seasons, resting below the fortress hill in the subterranean waterways: the springs, streams and hidden tributaries that connected Taurovinda to the otherworldly Realm of the Shadows of Heroes. And so for a while I was unaware of her presence.

Jason and those who were left of his crew of Argonauts slept in her embrace, below decks, close to the Spirit of the Ship, the heart of the vessel. Argo protected them: her captain, her crew drawn from lands across the known world, some from out of time itself. Perhaps she thought of them as her children.

But why had she returned? When I first realised that she was there, she closed herself off from my gentle probing, hull-silent, denying her spirit to me after her first breath of greeting. Why had she returned from the warm seas of the south?

The strange changes in the sanctuaries of the fortress itself should have given me the clues.

Niiv, the enchantress from the North Land, daughter of a *shaman* – bane of my life since I had first encountered her with Jason – had joined the women who guarded the well. Now there were four of them, all young, wild, unkempt, capable of the most astonishing and terrifying shrieks of laughter and amazement, or of horror and despair: all the screams of the 'far-seeing and deep-sensing' that make such guardians of the sacred so disarming, so dissociated from the people who live around them.

Niiv, by this time, had become my lover. She shared my cramped quarters in the fortress, but not my squalid hut in the heart of the evergroves, by the river, a living space among the honoured dead.

In the early hours of each morning, when she crawled across me, seeking me out for satisfaction, she stank of mysteries. The smell of old earth and sour sap filled our small lodge. We lived close to the guarded orchard where the Speakers for Land, Past and Kings – the oak men, as they were known – held their ceremonies. Our own ceremonies were noisier. Niiv was primal and eager. Delight glowed from her. There were times when she was brighter than the moon.

As she scoured my body, her cries of pleasure echoed with recent memory: of the way she had also scoured the world of spirits during her time by the well. When she finally collapsed across me, sighing deeply, the sigh of softening was more to do with her waxing understanding of enchantment than with my own waning presence inside her.

I loved her; I feared her. She had learned to treat me with just enough disdain to draw me closer. She was aware that I knew what she was doing. It made no difference to either of us. Passion flourishes with teasing.

All the signs were that the hill below the fortress of Taurovinda was coming alive in a way that signalled danger from the west, from across the sacred river Nantosuelta – The Winding One – from the realm of the Shadows of Heroes.

To Urtha, High King of the Cornovidi, and to his Speakers and High Women, the signs were sudden and dramatic: sweeping storm-clouds that formed unnatural shapes above the hill before abruptly shattering in all directions; then the thundering of a stampede of cattle, though no cattle were to be seen; other physical manifestations that were frightening and suggestive. But there were subtler marks of the change that was in progress, and I had been aware of them for almost a full cycle of the moon.

The first phenomenon was the backwards movement of creatures. When a flock of birds is swarming in the dusk sky it's easy to see only the shadow movement without noticing that the flock is flying tail-feathers first. Deer seemed to be swallowed by the edge of the woods, pulled back into the green rather than retreating from view. At dawn, as first light cast its faintest glow, the dogs and bigger hounds of Taurovinda all seemed to be cowering, as if at bay, facing some unseen aggressor, walking stiffly, tails first, into the shadows from which they had emerged to scavenge.

As fast as these moments of disorientation occurred, so they ceased, but there was no doubt in my mind that the past and the future were becoming entangled in a deadly weave.

Secondly, there was riddle-speaking. Again, it passed as quickly as it had been manifest. A quick greeting, a passing remark by a black-smith to his apprentice, and the words were meaningless, though spoken meaningfully. To the listening ear they made no sense, a sequence of sounds, guttural gibberish. But the riddle-speakers themselves saw no difficulty. It was as if a forgotten tongue had briefly possessed them – which indeed it had.

This was something I knew well.

As I saw Time begin to play tricks, I looked for its source of entry into the fortress. I went first to the orchard, the grove guarded by Speaker for Kings, tight spinneys of fruit trees, hazel and berry, hidden behind a high fence of tangled wicker and thorn, dense enough to stop even the sleekest animal entering the enclosure. The trees were in blossom, their branches reaching to the setting sun. This was quite natural for the orchard.

Next, I visited the well.

The well was situated at the centre of a high-walled maze of carved stones. At the heart of the maze was a grove of dwarf oaks, green with moss, boughs dripping with fronds of lichen. Within the grove lay the smaller stone enclosure that protected the rising water-source itself.

Around the wide mouth of the well were seats made of a pink, crystalline rock that was familiar to me not from Alba, but from countries in the hotter, drier, more fragrant south: Massila, Crete, Korsa. Those were the lands of the ma'za'rai – the dreamhunters – who prowled the forested hills at night, carrying curses and distributing them. Like the ma'za'rai of those far-off islands, the three women who served the well of Taurovinda were often to be seen racing like hares across the hill in the moonlit darkness, feeding on insects and small animals, leaping in the manner of mad hounds to catch a bird in flight, taking on strange shapes, though by dawn they were once again as mischievously pretty as in their sixteenth year.

When a new woman-at-the-well came, it was always when an

older one had gone, downwards, no doubt, into the waterways below the fortress itself. But one day a fourth woman joined them, and three became four, and there was no disruption to the enchantment.

The new woman was Niiv.

After the first signs that the Shadows of Heroes were active again, I spied on the women every day. They spent most of their time seated on their crystal benches, staring into the open throat of the hill, occasionally casting blood-smeared stones or plaits of grasses and herbs into the mouth, and singing out the insights of what they called the 'glory-vision', *the vision of strangeness, dreams of distance.* When the water responded, it bubbled to the surface, almost playfully, and then the wild celebration started. I took no pleasure in witnessing the activities. Suffice it to say that the women manipulated the water, and drew forms from it. All of that was normal. It had been normal water-magic since long before the citadel had been built upon the hill.

Now, though:

I watched the four women from my hiding place. Were they aware of my presence? Niiv, perhaps, but Niiv trusted me, believing that I trusted her. They were excited, peering into the well shaft, clearly puzzled by something.

This time when the subterranean flow shifted to the surface it came up as a great spout of angry water, roaring from the deep, punching out and knocking over the nymphs who had summoned it. It flexed and shimmered, a creature waiting, watching, liquid muscle swaying like a liquid tree, reaching out and probing the shivering women.

Gradually they found their courage, Niiv most noticeably. They let the fronds of water embrace them, stretching and spreading into its grasp. And when they were entwined with the blood of the earth, so the deep world of the hill began to surface and show itself, to reveal that which was buried there.

Faces from a past older than Taurovinda leered and peered from the water, unblinking gazes that were lost as soon as they had glimpsed the living world.

These once-living forms, these memories of men and women, had become elemental. Their decay in the flesh had left them as mere dreams, shadows haunting the stone below the hill. But now they were released. Some fled, hollow birds breaking from the water, dispersing through the air. Others sank back down, preferring to remain at rest.

Horses emerged, racing from the well, manes flowing, sending the guardians screaming into a crouch as the grey shapes leapt over them, disappearing into the stone maze. Then dogs, hounds of all shapes and sizes, but muzzle-bared and hot for the hunt, backs ridged, bodies flowing with speed as they bounded across the walls, baying fiercely then mournfully as they vanished into the world of men, shades only, but alive again.

Hounds and horses, buried with kings, now seeking the ghost-trails of the wild hunt.

And then I saw for the first time the echo of the ancient man who lay there, the founder of the citadel himself. Durandond.

He rose, naked and unarmed, a water-spectre presenting himself in his middle years, older than when he had listened to my prophecy, so many generations ago, but still years away from the brutal moment of his death.

He looked to the East, to his homeland, then to the skies. Did his gaze catch mine as he turned back to survey the enclosure? I couldn't say.

The expression on Durandond's face was of sadness, then of anger, as if this sprite, this liquid ghost, was aware of what was coming to take his proud fortress once again.

The water dissolved. Durandond returned to the bone-chamber below the hill.

The moment had passed.

2

The Sons of Llew

On the third morning the sun seemed to break at dawn towards the west, a sudden, startling flash of gold against the dark of night. The gleam faded as quickly as it had come, only to sparkle again and again, as if it moved through the forest that separated fortress from sacred river, and the unknown realm beyond.

When the true dawn came, so flocks of birds rose in outrage from the woods, and that firefly kept on coming, finally emerging onto the Plain of MaegCatha – the Battle Crow – in the form of a bright chariot, with two screaming youths driving a pair of red-maned horses.

One of these wild figures leaned forward at the reins; the other straddled the chariot, feet on the sides of the metal car, naked save for a short, scarlet cloak and the torque of gold at his neck and the tight belt around his waist. He held a thin spear in one hand and a bronze horn in the other. As the golden chariot struck a rock and lurched, so he tumbled to the floor of the car, and a furious argument commenced, though the driver, long yellow hair streaming, laughed as he whipped the steeds.

The chariot sped across the plain; the deep horn was sounded; the gathering crowds on the fortress fled around the walls, following the wild riders below as they passed to the north, between hill and evergroves, before turning across the eastern plain to approach the spiralling road with its five massive gates. One by one, as the triumphant youths howled up the steep road, the gates were opened and closed behind them.

They came into Taurovinda, racing in a wide circle three times before the fiery arrival was calmed. They jumped from the chariot, buckled on their kilts and cloaks and unharnessed the panting horses, holding the weary animals by the muzzles and stroking them. They seemed unaware that Urtha and his retinue were standing close by, waiting to greet them.

'Well run!' said one.

'Well driven,' said the other.

The new dawn set a new and blinding fire to the golden-wheeled chariot.

These breathless arrivals were Conan and Gwyrion, sons of the great god Llew. They were stealers of chariots. I had met them before. Half god, half human, they were the world's greatest thieves, and they were constantly being hunted by their father and their angry uncles, most particularly Nodens. Indeed, the grim-eyed, bearded face of Llew himself glared from the side of the vehicle, an image that appeared to writhe with new fury and the silent promise of retribution.

It was the gift of these boys that they were incapable of judgement or fear until harsher judgement invoked semi-mortal dread. And yet they always turned up again, as cheery as before.

They bowed low to Urtha, then Conan saw me and grinned. 'Well, Merlin! As you see, we have escaped from that old bastard our father again. Though this time not without cost.'

He held up his right hand; brother Gwyrion did the same. Their little fingers had been cut away and replaced with wood.

'This is the tinder with which he'll fire our bodies the next time he catches us,' said the eldest of the two. 'But it's a small price to pay for our freedom.'

'For the short while we're free,' added Gwyrion.

'But it will take him a good while to notice the absence of this vehicle, and his two horses. He spends a lot of time sleeping these days. And we can outrun the Sun itself!'

Urtha pointed out that they had been running *into* the sun. The young men looked up into the sky, then to the east, then engaged in a brief and furious row, each blaming the other for stupidity, before pausing, then laughing out loud.

Gwyrion took the horses to the stables; the chariot was hauled into cover, and Conan approached me. He had aged several years. There were lines at the edges of his eyes, and the beard that he shaved so close was hard stubble, its fiery red now tinged with grey; he seemed drawn, yet strong. When I had last encountered this reckless pair they had been ten years younger, even though that encounter was only two years or so in my past. Such was the capricious nature of Ghostland, where they had been trapped.

'Merlin,' he said, 'we crossed at the Ford of the Overwhelming Gift. But there is a *hostel* there now. The hostel has risen again. That hasn't been seen since the plain around Taurovinda was forested. There's something wrong. We entered the place, of course. We waited there briefly, in the room of the Spears of Derga. It's where we were hosted. The hostel is on an island in the middle of the river. It's not a bad place. Plenty of food and gaming. But that's beside the point. There is a man there who says he knows you. He wishes you to come and sit with him at the feast. He says to say "Pendragon", and that you will know him by that name. He says the hostel is safe for the moment, but there are already several hundred men in the various rooms, and many of them are keeping a silent counsel. Gwyrion and I were hastened on our way before we could investigate further. It's all very suspicious.'

'Suspicious in what way?' I asked him.

Glancing round, he murmured, 'They are crossing from the wrong side.' (It was not wise to talk too openly of the hostels, not even for a semi-mortal.) 'Either that,' he added, 'or they are the wrong patrons. Gwyrion and I can cross in either direction. The Shadow Heroes cannot.'

I began to see what he meant: some hostels at the river – including the one under discussion – had been constructed to admit travellers *from* the realm of the living into that of the dead. This was the ordinary way of things. Others, though, were meeting places to evict those from the realm of the dead back into the lands of the living. These were to be feared. Conan was suggesting that the Hostel of the Overwhelming Gift was being compromised.

I realised suddenly that Conan's hand was on my shoulder, the young man's face etched with query. I had been dream-drifting and he was calling me back.

'Thank you for the information,' I said to him, but he shook his head, still quizzical.

'This Pendragon. A king-in-waiting if ever I saw one. He knows you. And yet he's of the Unborn. Are you aware of that?'

'Thank you,' I repeated. 'Yes. I'm aware of it.'

'He knows more about you than can yet have occurred. Are you aware of *that*?'

'I'm not surprised by it.'

The intensity in his gaze relaxed, and he was reckless and wild again, green eyes sparkling with potential mischief. He had given up the pursuit of the answer to his question. 'You're a strange man, Merlin. I don't think I'll ever understand who you are until the time comes for me to grow up, to become the Lord in place of my father, Llew.'

'The same could be said for me,' I replied.

'Yes! But you won't have to fight your brother.' His features darkened. 'I don't relish the far-to-come, Merlin, when brother and brother must fight for the chariot without stealing it.'

He turned away and went to find lodgings and rest in the king's enclosure.

3

The Rising of the Hostels

It is the privilege of the human offspring of inhuman gods to run or ride, on horseback or in chariot, through the world of transient shadows, the world of men, with blithe indifference to their encounters with the otherworldly. To Conan, the existence of a hostel on the river Nantosuelta was just one more stop for a feast, a good sleep and a few days of gambling, perhaps, or games, perhaps an adventure along a path that had, and would, lead him to many such locations in this world or that. To the Cornovidi, the people who farmed the lands around the fortress, those simple people who maintained the vast, high-walled enclosure, the appearance of the hostel would have been terrifying.

It was more than five generations, I understood, since the Hostel at the Ford of the Overwhelming Gift had last shown itself.

I decided to keep quiet about Conan's conversation with me; for the moment at least.

But even as I made my preparations to travel to the river, to investigate the presence of the Unborn horse-lord, Pendragon, so – later in the same day – a cry came from the watch tower on the west wall that the king's children were coming back from their hunt, and they were riding in the wild fashion, as if running from danger!

As they came within hailing distance of the Bull Gate, the *uthiin* warriors who were their guardians broke away and returned to the fortress; Kymon and Munda stood up on the saddles, arms stretched, searching the high walls above for a sign of the man they wished to speak to.

That man was me.

Munda caught sight of me and made a beckoning gesture, then

she and her brother rode quietly along the hidden path across the wild plain, to the evergroves, by the nearest curve of the river Nantosuelta.

I followed them and found them arguing. There was a fierce debate. Kymon was looking browbeaten and angry. The girl sparkled, her face glowing both with the heat of the dispute and the heat of the ride.

As I approached between the stones, between the low mounds that covered the dead, I took a moment to watch them from a distance. Kymon paced, a little king, in his hunting colours, short cloak and tight bronze crown-band. He was not yet allowed to wear a torque, but about his thickening neck he wore a small symbol of Taranis, 'Thunder of the Land', on a bull-leather thread.

He was growing up fast. He could hardly have been ten years old. Ten in years, yet fifteen in posture and manner. He still wore his hair loose, and had painted small twirls of red on the ends of his lips, to signify the moustache that would soon be his to grow and wear with pride. He loved to hunt, to race, and was adept at the games, maybe not the finest player of ball or board in the fortress, but a young man to be remarked upon.

He was extremely serious. He had inherited much from his father, Urtha, but not that quiet man's sense of humour.

The girl, too, was older than her years. She was not yet – as the High Women so charmingly put it – 'in the flow of the moon'. It wouldn't be long. She copied the clothing and hairstyle of her stepmother, the Scythian huntress Ullanna who had become Urtha's wife after the death of his beloved Aylamunda. The hairstyle necessitated three long tails, tied at the tips, the central tail being longer than the others. She shaved her temples high, and streaked them with ochre. She wore a loose shirt, tied at the waist, a colourful patchwork affair, and calf-length britches, split to the knee. When she shared a meal with her father and stepmother she wore a pale green dress, more suitable for the girl who would become a High Woman in the family.

Munda was determined to learn everything about the lore and history of the fortress. But she was first forced to learn five of the champion's feats before she reached a certain age. In the same way, Kymon was required to learn five of the tasks of Farsight. He was no natural scholar, but had found he could memorise tracts of poetry, and the lineage of kings. He was less successful when it came to medicinal lore; and he refused to dance; he had turned to me for assistance in understanding the deeper movements of the earth itself, the spirit tracks that lie below us and can sometimes be encountered.

Munda's first achievement was to steer a chariot and run along its short yoke, calling to the horses to stay running in a straight line. That was a good feat. She had learned spear-play and shield-play. Lately, she had been acquiring the skill of the hunt. And it was from a boar hunt that the band – *uthiin* entourage and king's children – had been returning in the wild way. Kymon had a small pig tied to his horse; Munda, a brace of wild fowl, presumably snared as she failed to chase down the other beast. It didn't matter. These were just the special tasks imposed upon the children of the warlord, and when she did, eventually, manage to turn her pig at bay, and had speared it, she would probably never think of the act again – exactly as Kymon, once he had recited the lines of the epic of the Cornovidi during the time it took for a mid-winter moon to move across the night sky, would probably forget every stanza and every declamation that had been forced upon him.

When Kymon spotted me, he raised a fist before him, eyes blazing. 'Merlin! This is a *bad* encounter. I feel it.'

'It is not bad at all!' Munda riposted, her hands outstretched. She met my gaze. 'The hostels are returning. Why should that be bad? We've waited more generations than my grandfather's to feel the heat from their fires and learn from the men passing through them.'

'It's wrong! It's dangerous,' the youth insisted. He was almost spitting. 'It's the Hostel at the Ford of the Red Shield Riders, Merlin. Ask anyone. That hostel only lets the dead through to our world. Ask anyone. If the dead are coming ... we are not yet strong enough.'

'The dead are *not* coming,' insisted Munda. She watched me, seeking acknowledgement, perhaps, and was not pleased to see how I frowned. But I didn't know much about the hostels.

Kymon shouted, 'There is a man there who does not belong in this land. He's waiting. He calls himself *King of Killers* ...'

For the first time I was shocked. The boy saw it and seemed triumphant, a small smile on his face. His sister shook her head dismissively. 'There are always ghosts when the hostels surface. We're taught this. Anyway, it's only *one* hostel ...'

'Two!' I said quietly, and she seemed startled.

I told them about the Hostel of the Overwhelming Gift.

'I told you so,' Kymon whispered, more to himself. He gave his sister what the druids called 'the grim look'. 'I told you. *I told you.*'

'How do you know this man was called *King of Killers*?' I asked them softly.

There were tears in the girl's eyes as she looked up at me. Kymon stared at me too, for the first time, perhaps, a little alarmed himself.

'He's a son of Jason,' Munda said in a whisper. 'Jason! Your wild friend. But he's only the shadow of the son. And he's waiting.'

'Waiting?'

She shivered. 'For the blood-bone-brother who can release him.'

'How do you know this?' I asked, knowing full well why she had become suddenly so distressed.

She crossed her arms over her chest, looked down.

'I went inside,' she said in a tiny voice. 'I broke taboo. I went inside.' She looked up tearfully. 'Merlin, it's not a dreadful place. Not at all. But I should not have gone inside. I'm sorry. What do I tell my father?'

Her anguish was scorned by her brother, but by look only, not words. That was unfair. If she had broken taboo, then as a king's daughter she would be obliged to pay tribute of some kind, and sometimes the paying of tribute was a very great hardship.

But what had she meant by 'the blood-bone-brother'?

I asked Kymon in a whisper what he understood by that expression. He scratched his hairless chin as he stared at me, thoughtful. 'I suppose,' he said, 'the shadow is the shadow of a man who is still alive.'

'Yes. I believe you're right.'

Thesokorus! Jason's eldest son, a young man displaced in time, who had taken the name *Orgetorix*, 'King of Killers' (or sometimes, 'King among Killers'), and who had tried to kill his own father under the menacing influence of his mother, Medea. The ghost of Thesokorus! Was the flesh and blood son himself in the land? If so, it could only mean that he was searching for his father, Jason.

There was more than a storm of heavenly proportions gathering around these westernmost lands of the Cornovidi. Something darker was about to break loose.

I consoled Munda by promising that I would speak to Urtha on her behalf, and accept the burden of any reprisal. The girl seemed astonished at the offer and I reminded her that I was an outsider in the fortress, a man who walked a different path to her and to her kin, and that Urtha was deeply in my debt for saving his life on numerous occasions.

Kymon snorted disparagingly. 'On one occasion! Don't brag. One occasion only. I've heard my father talk of your time with him.'

'One occasion still lends itself to a favour, to a kingly favour. Don't you agree?'

He shrugged, nodding grudgingly.

'What's the matter with you, lad? Why are you behaving as if you've been wolf-bitten?'

His look was sharp, angry. The wolf-bite had struck him in his pride. His words were as sharp as his look. 'My name is Kymon. I'm the king's son! You should remember that! The manner of your question is not appropriate.'

'Yes, you are. You are indeed the king's son. And I'm the king's friend.'

'No friend of a king is closer than a king's son. The manner of your question is *not* appropriate.'

His glare was furious. He was hiding more than just a childish need to be addressed as a man. I was curious. I would have taken a quick look into that aura of ferocity, to see the demons that harassed him, but I wanted to grow along with this fretting, fierce-tempered youth. One day he would lead the Cornovidi; and one day, when he was older than me, he would probably have need to call on me: Merlin; Antiokus; the man of a hundred names; the unchanging man in his life, and a greater friend to him than his closest foster-brother.

If my long experience was anything to go by, he would soon find that to be the son of a king would make him no friend of his father!

'I've asked you a simple question,' I said quietly. 'What is the matter between us?'

He gave me the 'hound's eye': narrowed, menacing. 'I don't trust you. That is the matter between us. That is all of it. My father ages, you don't. My sister turns to you when she should be turning to my father. I find that a strange turn of events. In short, I repeat: I don't trust you. You are compromising us.'

Munda stared at me. Her brother's words had shocked her into a colder state of mind. She watched me cautiously. How easily a brother could influence a sister!

I was not compromising anyone, but I was not certain of my place in these young adventurers' hearts. I took the only option available, short of using charm and thus truly betraying my relationship with them, and answered, 'You have always known I come from a different time, a different world. How is it that you had the wits to understand that as children, yet now, as youths, you deny your own memory?'

'I have heard the older men speak about you,' the proud boy declaimed. 'You could do wonderful things for our family and our clan. Yet you refuse to use the *ten charms* because it weakens you. You put yourself above the needs of others.'

It was true. He was absolutely right.

I had never denied the fact that I harboured my skills carefully – the use of enchantment, of what he called the *ten charms*, is the only way that I seem to age – and I rationed my talents very carefully indeed. But I was disturbed that 'older men were speaking of me'. It suggested a growing resentment. Even that was curious, however, since for a very long time now there had been nothing but contentment in the fortress, nothing but the normal round of trophy-raiding, cattle-raiding, horse-rearing, competition, hunting and the 'Three Delights of the Feast': the making of laughter, love and the young – also known as the Three Exhausting Desires.

I would ask Urtha about this, but the question would be raised in due course, not at once.

I was intrigued by this sudden rising of the hostels. I had questions to ask. And the druid Cathabach, Urtha's close friend and Speaker for Kings, would be certain to have an understanding of what was happening. He would have answers.

Cathabach had been born to the priesthood, but had renounced his courses of learning and training after an incident in his youth – he never spoke about it – and become a member of Urtha's elite warrior entourage, the *uthiin*. As a champion, he was among the best. But after nineteen years he had cut through the marks on his body that showed his champion's status. He had taken up the hazel staff and the cloak-of-dreams. He had become an oak man: not so much a priest as a visionary and a rememberer. He was now in an intimate, moon-driven relationship with the High Woman Rianata, though they were forbidden from allowing their offspring to survive at birth, should a birth occur.

Cathabach guarded the orchard that lay at the heart of Taurovinda. Protected by a high fence of thorn and clay, it contained the burial shafts of kings and queens, the relics of the first builders of Taurovinda, as well as a multitude of sour-apple trees, hawthorn and hazel scrub and thickets of tiny oaks, their trunks and branches laden with bright green moss. Two men were appointed gardeners of this area, both mute. Cathabach lived just inside the enclosure, in a small shelter, but was frequently to be found standing, staring at the sky, just outside the gate.

He carried a short, highly polished, well-honed sword, the instrument of sacrifice and vengeance, and he was strong and determined enough to use it. Even if Urtha himself tried to enter the orchard he would use it. Cathabach was entitled to kill even a king, should he attempt to enter the sanctuary grove outside of the allowed days or nights.

And he would kill me too. (He would fail, of course.) But he and I had a certain understanding; nothing more than sharing the experience of being reckless in our younger days (though my own younger days had lasted several millennia), and the simple pleasure of being able to talk about a greater, wider world of nature and secret than our noble compatriots who inhabited the hill fort so briefly, causing havoc and hilarity with their mayfly spirits.

Cathabach was a friend of the mind as well as of the heart.

I found him, surly as ever, leaning on his staff. He was waiting for me, watching me without expression. As I entered the outer enclosure, he stepped back into the orchard, inviting me to follow him. As soon as I was inside the grove, he closed the heavy gate. The apples were in blossom; the ground was a carpet of flowers. The long briars of the berry bushes were all tied into shapes, waiting for the fruit to form. The gnarly oaks spread wide canopies, making shade and shelter in the thickets. It was a wood for crouching, but we descended into a dell, away from the sun, and in doing so came to the small hut that was Cathabach's resting place. No wider than a tall man, no higher than the same, it contained a circular wooden bench, was hung with wolf-skins and the desiccated remains of crows. It had no hearth, no fire. It was empty of convenience. It was the sitting place of a man who came here for no other purpose than to rest after his thoughts, after the telling of the ritual of the kings, after all the ceremonies that the Speaker for Kings was required to conduct.

It smelled of the man's sweat, and the unmistakeable odour of animal fat that had been burned, though not in the hut; it was burned fat that he had used on his body.

It was a home from home: my wanderer's cave, only slightly less spartan.

'I'm aware that the hostels are rising again,' he said without preamble. 'Tell me what the king's children have experienced. And those other two idiots.'

I told him everything I knew.

When he had thought for a while, he told me about the hostels.

'When I was training, during those eighteen years I learned that there are many rivers, such as Nantosuelta, which carve the land between men and the dead. We think of Nantosuelta as the greatest, but there is no great and no small: all the rivers are connected through what you've told me you call a "hollowing".'

I had told him a great deal about my life walking the Path around the world.

'The ways under. Yes. I move through them all the time. The rivers flowing there are very strange, mostly very dangerous. But I'd never encountered tales of the hostels before coming to Alba.'

He was surprised by that, frowning and thinking hard for a moment before continuing, 'According to the Declamations of Wisdom, which we learn in the groves, every one of those rivers has five hostels, though they are dedicated in different and incomprehensible ways according to the people who live along their eastern banks. One part of the Declamation suggests that each hostel hides the heart of a broken king. Some of them are welcoming, some not. All of them are full of rooms, some full of traps, all of them potentially deadly. Most of the rooms are empty, or appear to be. Others open into one of the Seven Wildernesses.'

'And the Dead have their own hostels. And the Unborn theirs. And they rise at the fords where these ghosts cross the river. Is that right?'

'Yes. Ours are the Hostel of the Overwhelming Gift; the Hostel of the Red Shield Riders; the Hostel of the Bier of Spears; the Hostel of the Miscast Spear, and the Chariot Hostel of Balor.'

'The Dead and the Unborn cross between worlds when there are no hostels present. So what does this rising mean?'

'I don't know.'

'And which are the dangerous ones?'

'Balor and Red Riders, certainly. And one of the others. But if I remember correctly: all hostels can be compromised. Something greater is happening than the raid of a few summers ago.'

The raid of a few summers ago. The forces of the Otherworld had scoured Taurovinda and possessed it in its entirety: killed the king's wife and youngest son; sent the king's other son and daughter into hiding; destroyed the land, and occupied Taurovinda until forcibly removed by young Kymon and his father, with just a little help from an underworld bull ... and a young-old traveller of the Path around the world.

If that had been just a raid, what was brewing now?

Cathabach's concern and ignorance of potential events showed in his creased face. I noticed he was stroking one of the purple tattoos that adorned his body: it was the one over his throat, which showed two salmon leaping. The salmon: spirit of Wisdom.

Cathabach – absent of wisdom at the moment – was unthinkingly summoning the spirit of an older memory.

4

Battle Arm and the Strong Shield

Not for the first time, either here in Taurovinda or in the past, I found myself at the centre of events, both searching and diplomatic. Munda had led her grey colt quietly through the gates and retired to the women's quarters, to wait in silent vigil until her father summoned her after I had spoken to him. Kymon was still somewhere by the river, exercising his right as the king's son to prowl the evergroves (his ancestors were buried there, after all) and – when I took a quick look at him through the eyes of a wren, hopping from branch to branch of a willow – I saw him staring moodily at the flow of Nantosuelta. Fish were shoaling, taking insects; dusk was falling and the riverside was alive with feeding. The young man was feeding only on his angry thoughts, however.

Urtha himself, and his *uthiin*, were still somewhere to the south, hunting the thick forests for deer, wild pigs – even wild horses, which sometimes could be found in the glades. They would certainly be looking for meat, but as likely were also taking the chance to assess the strength of the clans that lived beyond the woods. There had been too many reports of small bands of armed hunters being seen along the banks of the several rivers that flowed south from Urtha's stronghold.

He was increasingly attentive to the borders of his realm, as was his Scythian wife, Ullanna, a descendant of the great Atalanta.

Ullanna and her own retinue were hunting to the north, across the river from the evergroves.

A long night passed, then at dawn a horn sounded from the walls. Distantly, through the early mist, a group of riders came trotting slowly across the plain from the south, leading pack ponies draped with the tethered forms of two deer, and the carcases of three dark-skinned pigs.

As his comrades dispersed to other tasks, Urtha was joined by two armed and shield-bearing riders who accompanied him as he rode towards the double gates of his royal enclosure. Catching my eye and frowning as he passed, he beckoned me to follow him into the warmth of his shield-lined house.

In the three winters that had numbed the land, Urtha had changed very little, though his beard was quite grey now, and his face horribly scarred where he had taken the glancing blow of an axe during a skirmish with a band of *dhiiv arrigi*, exiled, vengeful warriors, outcasts from the tribal lands, who existed like lice upon the skin of the world. Their numbers were growing. The blow had missed his left eye, however, and his eyes were as keen and knowing as ever.

We entered the main part of the lodge, where a good log fire burned, and light streamed from the open roof. 'For all your skills with enchantment, Merlin, I can always tell when there's something troubling you,' he said as he discarded cloak and sword belt and sprawled out in his stout, oaken chair, staring at me. 'More omens?'

'The strangest yet,' I agreed, and he leaned forward as I took a seat on one of the benches that lined the hall.

When I had finished my account he scratched the stubble on his chin. Leaning back again – a weary man – he reached for his beaker, draining the contents in a single gulp. 'When I was growing up,' he mused, staring at nothing, 'the hostels were part of the adventure of storytelling. In this very hall I sat with other boys and listened to the Speaker for the Past tell witty and wonderful tales of the land since the first fortress was built here. All very thrilling. But I never gave the hostels much thought after that. Something to scare your children with. The ways across to the Shadow Hero Land are by certain fords across the winding river, but even then, no one went near the winding river. Not, at least, until *you* came into my life. And you say that Speaker for Kings doesn't understand the significance?'

'No.'

'And the Speaker for the Past?'

'Lost in the groves, engaged in training his successor.'

'But Cathabach thinks they signal a greater danger than we can imagine.'

'He seems to think so.'

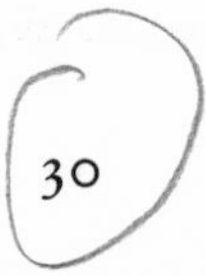

Urtha nodded sagely, though it was clear that he was hiding a complete and utter incomprehension. 'We must certainly strengthen the fortress, and the defences to the west. We need dove-watchers within sight of the hostels ...'

He meant signallers, doves being the new way of signalling to Taurovinda, as they always flew home to their small cages.

'I will need to discuss support in arms from Vortingoros. The High King of the Coritani will exact a high price in oxen and favours in arms. But I think I can persuade him to take more in horses after any event that might occur. We are not under-burdened with horses!'

His sudden gaze on me was bright and fierce. 'I will need you and Cathabach ... Manandoun as well, and perhaps your lively lover—'

'Niiv?'

'Why not? She's reaping your knowledge while you sleep.' His grin was taunting. 'She'll soon be as wise as you!'

I smiled, but it was a bitter gesture. Yes, Niiv was still trying to extract my powers of enchantment. It was in her nature. Who – born the daughter of a northern 'magic man', as she had been – would not seek to enhance experience by using the illusion of curiosity to cover a dedicated determination to scour the signs and symbols of power from one who carried them on his bones? If Urtha thought that Niiv was being successful it was only because I had not revealed to him, nor to any other, that I was constantly displacing the girl's focus and thoughts to less viable areas of the strength in enchantment that I carried within me.

I let her nowhere near the *ten charms*.

'If you insist.' I added, 'But she has a habit of getting in the way, rather than helping.'

'Well then: I'll leave that to you. But you must investigate what is happening at the fords on Nantosuelta.' He gave me a long, hard look. 'Yes, I think I'd trust your vision even more than that of Cathabach, wise though he is. In the meantime, I'll get "battle-arm and the strong shield" from Vortingoros.'

He sighed. He was indeed tired. He was at a turning point in his life between hungering for the fight and longing for the peace. 'Omens to the right ... omens to the left,' he murmured. 'What in the name of the gods are we riding into, Merlin?'

'Whatever we are riding into, whatever is riding against us, it would be a good idea, I think, to make an offering to the Thunderer. Get him on your side before he is persuaded to help the enemy.'

He waved his hand. '*Taraun*? I don't deal with gods. That's for the priests in their flesh-stinking groves.'

'I would freshen the groves, if I were you; and make a point of being there.'

He scowled. 'That means taking heads. I've taken enough in my time. The pleasure has become a chore.'

'Time for Kymon, then. Time for a great test for your son.'

For a moment, as he stared at me, eyes blazing, I thought he would kill me for the suggestion, but in fact, the expression was one of delight.

'Yes!' he said, slapping the arms of his chair. 'I should have thought of that myself. Time for Kymon's great test! Two wildfowl with one slingshot. The boy becomes a man, and we gather both gods and the forces of Vortingoros to us in the same action. Well suggested, Merlin. Not even Manandoun, my wise council, would have thought of suggesting that. What a moment that will be for him. For us all. I'll talk to the lad later.' Then he paused, face darkening. 'Now, I suppose, I should go and speak with my disobedient daughter.'

His whole demeanour suggested that he would find this a harder task than anything he had undertaken in the last few days.

5
The Wren on the Rafter

Wrens, tiny birds, highly revered, had the capacity to flit back to their own territory if removed to a distance. They reappeared suddenly, without visible signs of having flown. They were held in high regard by druid and High Woman alike. They had been a favourite form of travel and watching for far longer, however. As a boy, one of my first lessons had been in the possession and control of the spirit of the wren.

A wren now bobbed onto the rafters of the long hall where the High Women gathered, and where Munda had gone to wait with them until her father had returned from his latest skirmish against the *dhiiv arrigi*, a large band of whom had been seen riding from the south, towards the river. He was tired and dirty, but he had gone straight to the hall.

All the women but Rianata had left. Munda's mother, Aylamunda, would in ordinary circumstances have been here as well, but Aylamunda was dead and travelling below her mound. Ullanna, despite being bonded to the king, had been forbidden from entering the women's hall. Ullanna – huntress and bright spirit – was never to be seen complaining about the fact.

Urtha was sitting down on a grey wolf-skin, facing Munda, who knelt on a similar rug, her hands clasped in her lap. She was both worried and moody, waiting for her father to get comfortable. I could imagine what he was thinking as he eased himself into position.

His right lower leg was now tucked under his left thigh. His left leg was extended towards the girl, crooked slightly across her. Leaning forward, his right elbow rested on the knee of his right leg. His left arm reached behind him as support.

This was one of the Three Positions of Friendly Encounter: the one for family and friends. The other two were, first, for enemies who might plead a good case to keep their heads; and second, for animals that might be possessed by one of the Dead and wished to be heard concerning their treatment at the hands of the *druids*.

Urtha had never had to adopt the difficult posture of this last, and was privately very relieved about the fact. He had confided to me that in any case he had no idea what he would do under the circumstances.

The Three positions were alternatively known as The Positions Designed to Kill a King through Discomfort. It was a joke to anyone who had never had to adopt them. The joke did not amuse Urtha.

'I was told today,' father said to daughter, 'that you have achieved the feat of saddle-spinning.'

'Yes. It took me several tries. But I managed.'

Saddle-spinning was where, retreating at the gallop from an enemy, you turned round in the saddle, threw a spear or unleashed slingshot, before turning again to the front, the whole feat to be in a single movement without pause.

'I used to be able to do it. Now I find it hard enough to look back, let alone spin back. I get a pain in my joints. I suppose I'm getting older than I feel.'

Silence.

'Well. Today,' said the father, 'I came back from the Forest of Singing Caves. I chased off seven vultures that had been hiding there. Desperate men. Vengeful outcasts. Seven escaped. Seven did not. They fought furiously.'

Still silence. Urtha shifted uncomfortably.

'I've brought you a small gift. Nothing that you can touch, or eat, or see. But yours nevertheless.'

The girl looked up. 'Tell me?'

Urtha warmed to his subject. 'While we were moving very quietly through a bright, open expanse of wood, we came to a wide glade. Two horses were there, a mother and her foal. The mother was a strange dappled russet and grey. I'd never seen colour like it. The foal was russet, with a black mane and a splash of white at his throat. He was lame in one of his hind legs, and very distressed. The mare circled him furiously, watching us constantly, flaring and snorting. I swear by Taraun that she was trying to grow bull's horns in order to charge us.'

Munda watched her father in silence, wide-eyed.

Urtha said, 'I left them there, of course. I believe the place is an old shrine. But I found a piece of beech bark and marked on the smooth side the symbols for *Succellos riana nemata*—'

Munda smiled, nodding her head. 'The grove of the healing horse …'

'I don't know if you will ever find it. But if you do, I think it will be a place of healing for more than horses. A place of protection too. That is my small gift to you.'

Again silence. Urtha broke it after a moment: 'What two *gessa* were placed upon you in your eighth year?'

Munda was momentarily startled, then said, 'That I must never swim in the Winding One to the west, even if I see my brother, or any friend, drowning and crying for help. And that if I see a hound in distress, whether lame or starving, or boar-savaged, I must cease whatever I'm doing to come to its aid.'

'More or less,' Urtha acknowledged. The High Woman shook her head, smiling faintly. There was always more to these rules than was implied in the simple words that described them.

'Do you know why these bindings were placed on you?'

Munda nodded soberly. 'I was rescued from raiders by your hound, Maglerd, and taken to safety across the river. Kymon was rescued too. My brother Urien was killed and dismembered by the raiders, and the hound that tried to protect him was slaughtered alongside him. I was protected just across the river, and my grandfather came and took me back, but it was a gift from the *Matronae*, the Mothers of the Dead, that saved my life. I entered the Otherworld before my time, and I am forbidden from entering it again until it is truly my time.'

'Well remembered. So now you must explain to me: why did you choose to ignore the *geis*?'

Silence. Father and daughter engaged each other in a long moment of visual inquisition. Finally Munda lowered her head. 'I was curious. I felt drawn to the doors of the hostel. When I entered, I became afraid. By then, I had stepped across the bridge to the place itself. It is in the middle of the winding river.'

'What drew you? Why were you curious?'

'A dream voice. Singing. I remembered the happy times under the protection of the Mothers, when I was being hidden on the other side of the river. When our fortress was being attacked that time.

I thought they were calling me. I wanted to go there. I felt as if I belonged there. And for a while I thought I was wrong. The hostel was a vile place, and the faces that looked at me, and the smells, and the sounds, that laughter ... it was a bad place. I was terrified and fled. But I fled from what was strange, and beyond my experience. My brother was more afraid than me. When we were back in our own land, I realised that I'd had nothing to fear.'

The wren on the rafter took careful note of all of this.

Silence.

Urtha then said, 'How I wish your mother was here. She would be proud of you.'

'Proud of me?'

'Proud of your courage. You have had an unpleasant experience. But who knows? Perhaps a valuable one. You think you have made a great mistake, and here you are, mournful and woebegotten. But why? You have had a moment of inspiration, of encouragement, not of warning. And you haven't broken your *geis*.'

She looked perplexed. Urtha shrugged, awkwardly from his position of friendly encounter. 'A *geis* cannot be half broken. I'll have to ask Cathabach about this, but I'm sure I'm right. Fully broken, yes, but not half. Not like a golden crescent moon, a *lunula* that can be cut in half, like the half of a lunula that hangs around your neck, the other half on your brother's.'

Munda reached to touch the amulet on its leather tie. The sun-metal gleamed in the light. The fragment, cut from an amulet older than time, was her prized possession, a gift from her father, half of an emblem that had been part of this family since the time of Durandond. It was her tie to her brother. It was a precious thing, a connection between Urtha's surviving children which the king himself hoped would always keep his family united.

'When I cut that piece of gold in two,' he said quietly, 'I was both breaking and making a bond between the two of you. Halving gold is easy. Halving a taboo is not. And that is my decision. The hostel was in the middle of the river, you said. Halfway across. Well, halfway is neither here nor there, if you follow my judgement, daughter. You have broken nothing.'

Munda flung herself upon her father, wailing with delight. Urtha collapsed backwards, looked up at the High Woman, who merely shrugged. She should have had her say, but there hardly seemed a point in it.

'Get off me, girl! You're too heavy.'

Munda stood and made a sign of respect to the sprawled king, then turned and ran gleefully from the women's lodge.

The wren on the rafters noticed that High Woman Rianata was involved in helping Urtha back to his feet.

6

The Unborn King

It was a relief to realise that Urtha hadn't believed a word his daughter had told him. He loved the girl, of course, and was aware that her account was influenced by darker forces. He had spared her. He was aware that she had been possessed.

He at once consulted with his commanders, and with the Speakers, on how best to divide his own forces to address what he discerned as the growing threat from across the river. It was agreed that herdsmen should be constantly on stand-by to bring in the cattle and horses in the event of a raid, and many of the smiths, tanners and potters should fall into that role if necessary. Meanwhile, the production of long, oval shields, covered with thick bull's hide, would be increased, as would the production of short stabbing spears, crudely made to be disposable. Stone workers would be set to practising the timeless skill of fashioning long, thin flint blades, often more effective than iron, though iron could have a terrible effect on the more ancient of the Dead.

Urtha himself would take a retinue to Vortingoros of the Coritani and hire a hundred swift-shields. The Parisianii in the north would be more difficult to persuade, but since their territory was further from the edge of Ghostland, they might co-operate, though they would exact a heavy price in compensation. To the south, the mercenary bands of the *dhiiv arrigi* would be sure to add an extra danger to whatever might come across the winding Nantosuelta.

The Speakers would attend to the more mystical defences, the wood figures and carved columns, the straw-and-bone animals and masked trees that would form a barrier against certain of the Dead. It was the Unborn who were most troublesome when it came to such elements of repulsion: many of them didn't recognise the protection for what it was and rode straight through. But the Unborn were usually less hostile than their ancestors, and it was necessary to count upon that small fact.

It was my lot to ride to the river, accompanied by Niiv, a personal guard of four men, and Ullanna, with her own squad of youthful riders-at-arms as protection. I was glad of her company. Her personally trained retinue, drawn from the women of Taurovinda, were a match for any of Urtha's *uthiin*.

Nantosuelta flowed out of the west, out of the deep woods, flowing away from the permanent glow of the setting sun. She wound through rocky valleys and hazy marshes, through crowded forests and steep, wooded hills; occasionally, along her sinuous length, could be found the stone remains of buildings and time-worn statues. Several tributaries joined her from the shadow realm, waters that foamed red as they mixed with the main stream of the sacred river. Where Nantosuelta rose was a mystery, hidden in the Realm of the Shadow Heroes.

When she finally disappeared, at the northern extreme of Urtha's tribal kingdom, it was into the forest known as 'the trackless wood of visions', to a hidden fall which could be heard as it roared to unseen rocks, but not seen. When she reappeared, she was running east to the distant sea, now fully in the realm of the Cornovidi. She passed the evergroves, still magical, but no longer impenetrable, though her waters were still dangerous to enter. She bounded the land of the Coritani, embracing the kingdom, protecting it and nourishing it, and she was as much the spiritual strength of that nation as she was of Urtha's. Her banks there were heavy with the shrines and sanctuaries of past people, past encounters with the gods.

The five fords that crossed the river were all in the west, however, and at each of them now stood a hostel, its doors open, seemingly inviting.

I went first to the Hostel at the Ford of the Overwhelming Gift.

Ullanna at once pulled back, as frightened as her mare. Despite its name, the hostel was a grim place, fashioned of oak, a great heavy lintel above the low door. The pillars that stood to each side of the entrance were carved into the grimacing features of goats, standing on their hind legs, heads locked together at the horns, seemingly impaling the image of a woman's scowling face. A rickety walkway reached from the nearer bank to the muddy island on which the eerie building had risen. Broken swords hung from the eaves, clattering in the brisk breeze. The roof was high, made of poles, unthatched. Smoke drifted from the gaps between these crudely fashioned struts.

A deep howling noise came from the open door. It set the horses to a nervous disposition and managed even to raise the hairs on the back of my own neck.

Niiv huddled in the saddle, hood drawn low over her face, keeping close to me.

On the bridge, watching us, was a tall man in a dark red cloak, fair hair hanging to his shoulders. His face was clean-shaven. He was young, bright-eyed, carried no weapon, but held the reins of a powerful black horse.

I recognised the form of Pendragon. He was a ghost who haunted my dreams. He was a man, as yet unborn, who had visited my life on several occasions, though only fleetingly.

He beckoned to me and I dismounted, entrusting the reins to Niiv. As I stepped across the narrow bridge, keeping my balance carefully, Pendragon turned, tethered his own steed and ducked to enter the moaning inn.

I followed him.

The moment I stooped through the door into the hostel, I felt the disorientating effect of Ghostland. The narrow corridor seemed to widen and stretch away from me a vast distance. The moaning resolved into the low din of voices, the unearthly sound of laughter. The inn seemed to rock below my feet. The air was heavy with wood-smoke and the smells of roasting meats. The resonating sounds of metal on metal, like the beating of the vast bronze bells I had heard in the east, became recognisable as the striking of iron blades. There was feasting and competition at work in this hostel.

Rooms opened on both sides of the corridor. Pendragon had disappeared into the belly of the inn.

I searched the rooms.

In the first room I saw seven men in plaid cloaks, seated moodily and watching me. Each had balanced a broad-bladed axe across his knees. A copper cauldron was settled over a smouldering fire between them, and I could see the wood and bone hafts of weapons rising above the lip. They scowled at me as I peered into their chamber.

In another room I saw four much-scarred-faced men, naked to the waist, their chests marked in green dye with the features of wolves. Each had a silver torque around his neck and a circlet of boar's tusks around his head, tying back fair hair. They seemed afraid and confused, watching me with a curious expression, but making no move to beckon me to join them. They were seated around a large chequered board, across which were scattered small figures carved from bone and dark wood. Each in turn moved a figure with the point of his sword. There seemed to be no reason, no rule to the game, but at each move the others cried out in despair, angrily watching for the next prod of the blade.

In a third room there was a great open fire, and the carcase of a small ox being slowly turned on a spit by an old man, who turned his toothless face towards me, revealing that his eyes were as empty as his mouth. He grinned and nodded as he sensed me standing there. Two young men, wearing plaid kilts and bone breastplates, were leaping across the roasting animal from opposite directions, and clashing short swords as they somersaulted in mid-air. The action was not a fight, merely a game, and their bare arms were spotted red from the spitting fat. *There was something disturbingly familiar about this, I remember thinking.*

In a fourth room, more of a hall than a room, I found Pendragon again, and his small retinue, and here I ceased my exploration of the hostel.

This was a wide hall, with benches and tables and a host of men of all types, some bearing weapons, some not, some cloaked, some not, some with cropped hair, others with the high horse-tail style, others with their heads half-shaven here, a quarter-shaven there; and such a tapestry of tattoos, in such a palette of colours, that it was hard to distinguish man from pattern. The noise was a din; the throng was at ease. There were clay jars of wine, and wooden barrels of honeyed ale at each table, and the men ladled the liquor into horns or cups and were very drunk. Six or seven heavily cloaked figures carried wide trays of pink-roasted pig joints and spitted fowl.

Only Pendragon and his four men were sober and without food at their table.

I sat with them, but having ridden for some time was hungry and thirsty, so availed myself of flesh and wine, a sour brew with a strong after-taste of pine resin: a Greek Land fermentation, I was sure.

Even the Dead, it seemed, sent to the south for their pleasures.

'Drink that and you might stay here for ever,' Pendragon growled at me.

'I've been to Ghostland before and escaped,' I replied. 'And I've been to Greek Land taverns and wondered if I'd ever see the next day, let alone the end of the world.'

'Eat that, and the underworld pigs will claim you for your own,' murmured one of his companions as I tooth-stripped a cut of loin.

'I've eaten in a thousand forbidden places,' I retorted. 'Nothing can hold me, except the need for more.'

'You expect to see the end of the world?' asked a second man. He was young, lightly bearded. He seemed genuinely curious about me, as did a third man, seated next to him, who might have been his twin.

'My world has ended a thousand times,' I told him enigmatically. 'A broken heart, a broken hope, a broken joy. But if you yourself have the same capacity for forgetting as I can summon, then thank whichever god protects you. Memory lost is a life begun again.'

'That's a sour and very sorry way to live,' said the fourth of Pendragon's retinue critically, an older man, his eyes bloodshot, his breathing laboured. 'But who I am to say a word against you? I haven't yet lived. My time is to come. I just hope it comes soon.'

I asked him his name. Like Pendragon, he had only heard his name in dreams: Morndryd. The name sent a shiver through me. I was puzzled why he should appear in full mature years, rather than youthful like the rest of his band. But this was a curiosity to which, at the moment, I had no time to devote.

Hunger and thirst satisfied, I asked Pendragon about the hostel, and the men I had seen in the other rooms.

'There are seven in one, very unhappy men ...'

'Unhappy indeed. And for good reason. They are seven cousins, all sons of a king and his brothers who will resist an armed invasion from the east. The eastern army will be a formidable threat, legions of men equipped with weapons beyond imagining. In order to set an example, they will slaughter those seven men when they are still *children*. The reason they brood and are angry is because they are aware, in their dreams, that they will never become the men whose bodies they inhabit as they wait for life.'

'And who are the four men playing at the chequerboard?'

'They are the four sons of Bricriu, who will possess their own land within two generations. They are compulsive gamblers. They have fallen foul of a druid, also waiting for his birth, who might have foretold their fate, and he has set them the task that you see: to play the game nineteen times nineteen times nineteen moon cycles. The result of the last game will declare their future, but they have lost count. To play too many games, or too few, will be devastating for them.'

'That's a complicated number of moons.'

'Indeed.'

'And who are the combatants leaping across the roasting ox?'

Pendragon shrugged. 'They are a mystery to me. To everyone here. They don't seem to belong. They are possessed by the youthful spirit of a different age. The leaping is compulsive. When they are exhausted they sleep for several days; they then feed voraciously on the ox. When the carcase is stripped, a new ox is put on the spit and the leaping begins again. They carry a secret; that at least is my suspicion. But not even they are aware from where that secret originates.'

I didn't tell him that their activity seemed very familiar to *me*. They were bull-leaping, but in a place where such a practice did not belong.

Then I told Pendragon that I had heard he was waiting for me. I asked him what he expected of me. His answer surprised me. I had not expected so depressed a response. He spoke in the formal way, as if he were a Speaker for the Future, rather than a king in waiting.

'We are aware, we who will one day ride, roam and rule the land, that we are in a place of waiting. We are all aware that our dreams mean nothing. We have never been born, we are simply the spirits of life and lives that will one day occupy this territory, the forests and plains, the gorges, valleys, the sea channels, the rivers, that high hill with its ancient escarpments, its fallen walls ready to reconstruct.

'And we will build on the dead, and on what the dead have left behind.

'We are shadows without history. We live among shadows which brood, breed and bewail the unfairness of their ancestors. We are hostages, we Unborn, in the Realm of Revenge. To you, those of you who live with your druid tales of how wonderful the world after death will be, be aware, there is nothing comforting about the land of ghosts. Life is as brutal after death as it is before. I do not say to you that the pleasures of forgotten life no longer exist. They do. But when both Dead and yet-to-be-born are ageless, there is no compassion. We have no change in life, no ageing, no testing-ground on which to develop the satisfaction and fulfilment that leads to eventual calm, to that moment which we envy – as we watch the world beyond the river – that moment of passing-on. The moment of sublime release.

'The short life of a man, ending his days of hunting, leads to the long life of the ghost, endlessly hunting.'

His companions nodded as he spoke, all of them sharing the sudden melancholy.

After a moment I prompted him: 'And you were waiting to see me ... because—?'

'I intend to part company with this hostel, which might be a dangerous thing. But I sense that you are in danger, as is that king you work for, and his family and his nobles.'

'Are you trying to tell me that the Realm of Shadow Heroes plans to raid the fortress for a second time?'

Pendragon looked confused. 'It's strange to say this, but it doesn't feel like it. And yet it has to be the case. When Taurovinda was raided before, the armies gathered at the fords, practised at arms, made themselves fit for the fight, exercised the horses and gathered provisions. This time we are summoned to gather in these grim hostels, but there is no mention of armed conflict. We are simply waiting, though Morndryd has scouted the land behind and there are forces of men moving through the valleys. But they are not coming to the river.

'This inn is where the Unborn are gathering. We are all very uncertain, some more than others. We were content on our island, the Island at the Edge of Dawn. Good plains for the wild hunt; good forests for the tangled hunt. Good valleys and hills. Good water. Groves where the vision of magic was comforting and sometimes enthralling. When the level of the sea drops occasionally, it reveals a causeway, and at those times I have taken the opportunity to cross and enter the realm of Taurovinda. It is the privilege of the Unborn to be able to tour the land in which they will live. You have seen me on several occasions when that privilege was granted. But always, the word from the whispering shrine at the heart of the Island was to ride abroad and hear and listen to the wind and rain, and note the concerns of the living. To make the journey brief. To come home again.

'This time we were urged to come to these inns and wait. Boats came to take us from the Edge of Dawn. Our questions, usually answered clearly, are simply ignored. This is a not a raid. This is something different, something greater, sinister, not at all noble. An invasion? If so, it will be of an unexpected nature.'

I became aware of the clamour in the hall again, the noisy jollity, the angry exchanges, the coughing and choking of men indulging too fiercely in this waiting time.

'Is there a source behind this sinister, not noble, action? Does the danger come from a single person?'

Pendragon shook his head. His companions seemed equally uncertain. 'The answer to that lies beyond this shadow land. Which is why I wish to cross from this place. But if I lose you in the effort ... Merlin—'

He used my name with a hesitancy that suggested it meant more to him than just the fact of remembering how I had introduced myself. From the first moment I had encountered this bright-spirited, bright-eyed warlord we had both known that we would meet again, though in a more solid, more earthly way, and a long time in the future.

Indeed, Pendragon went on to conclude: 'If I lose you at this time, look for me in the years to come. Look ahead if you can, if you dare risk it. There is an unsettled feeling in the land where your good king rules. One day that world will pass to another king.' He leaned forward and gave me a smile, saying quietly, 'And when I take it, I would like it to be free of what corrupts it.'

I left the hostel and joined Ullanna and Niiv. A while later, Pendragon and his four companions thundered across the bridge, heads low, cloaks flying. The ghostly grey cloud that seemed to reach for them might have been the smoke from the fires, but I saw an angry face there, and five wide-winged birds rose above the riders, beating their way east, following the fleeing Unborn.

7

The Shade of Jason's Son

The Hostel of the Red Shield Riders was two days' ride away, through difficult country. The river at the ford here was wild; we approached through a narrow defile, clattering over loose rocks, stumbling on the driftwood that had been deposited there when the river had flooded. A boulder-littered bank faced the rapids and the grim lodge that stretched from the scrubby woodland that crowded the far bank.

The entrance was a double door in the shape of a woman, her arms outstretched, hands resting on the heads of two rearing hounds. Each entry was between a hound and the woman. She was carved from dark wood, was bare-breasted, her legs covered with a long skirt. Her eyes were gaping holes, dark as night. The hounds seemed to be reaching to rip her, but she held them away from her.

'An unusual door,' Ullanna observed dryly. 'But it reminds me of something.'

I had had the same feeling. An older image was represented by this sophisticated carving, and it had nothing to do with the world of Urtha, or any world that had preceded him. But which?

This was the hostel from which the careless daughter of the king had fled in confusion as she realised she had broken taboo, but had also been filled with a sense of change for the good.

There were guards here. As I left Ullanna on the shore to ride across the shallows, picking my way carefully through the weed-slick boulders, they emerged from the gloom, two men of mean eye, heavily built. They wore loose mail shirts and patchwork trousers. Kirtles stitched from strips of leather protected their loins. They carried oval shields, unmarked and heavy, and a brace of javelins.

As I clambered onto dry land, one came forward and casually took the bridle of my horse. He muttered a few words to me, watching me carefully. He repeated them, frowning. I entered the spirit of the language for a few moments, and recognised a northern dialect. He was asking me if I was 'newly dead' or 'another bloody ghost waiting for its flesh'.

I replied that I was neither, but that a man was waiting for me inside the hostel. His question, though, suggested that traffic through this inn was two-way.

They allowed me passage into the gloomy interior, and again I found myself in a maze of corridors, with small, miserable rooms opening on either side. Distantly, the sounds were of chaos, the clamour of voices and the din of argument. I followed one of the guards towards the light. I led my horse, which tugged nervously as we walked through the narrow corridor towards the open garden at the heart of the hostel. Here, to my surprise, I found a sunlit square that belonged in Greek Land, not in Alba, a place of olive and pine trees, and small houses, whitened with lime, roofed with red clay tiles. The air buzzed and hummed with a different summer. The chaos was behind us. Groups of men and women sat in the shade, drowsily talking, some drinking, a few tending to fires. In the shade of an apple tree, his shield leaning against his knees as he sat, was a young man I recognised, older now by several years and very hard of look. His right eye had taken a slashing blow, and the hair above the scar was white. He was missing a finger of his left hand. His legs and arms were ridged with veins. His clothing was simple, a loose, patterned shirt, knee-length trousers, sandals. But behind him, as he sat ill-at-ease, were stacked his weapons.

He was expecting me, that much was certain. The moment I entered the square he saw me, half smiled, then waited for me to tether my horse, and come and sit in the shade.

And talking of 'shades', Orgetorix had hardly greeted me before he said, 'Yes, you're right. I'm only the shade of the man you knew. You, I'm sure, are Antiokus. You were present when I tried to kill my father. The event is like a dream to me. I see everything through a dark dream. That's because the living man of whom I'm the shadow communicates to me. I feel his pain. I feel his scars. I feel how lost he is. I grow with him, and change with him, but I'm the shade. I call him my bone-blood-brother. I exist only as long as he is lost.'

Orgetorix in spirit shape, it seemed, was as melancholy as the young warrior who had roamed the hills and valleys of Greek Land.

I should perhaps write a few words about what had happened to Orgetorix. He was the eldest of Jason's two sons by Medea, many centuries before, born after the quest for the Golden Fleece. Named Thesokorus, he was nicknamed 'little bull leaper'. His brother Kinos was nicknamed 'little dreamer'. When Jason betrayed Medea for another woman, Medea – an enchantress of savage power – slaughtered her two sons in front of her lover. Jason was devastated, never recovered, and eventually died of grief because of the loss. In fact, Medea had used trickery and illusion to present only an apparent execution. The two boys were spirited away into Greek Land. And then – and this was the ingenious part – she spirited them away into Time itself: into the future; into the very time in which this tale is set. The boys were separated, but Medea created a 'ghost brother' for each of them, though this cost her dearly in life and power. Eventually the ghosts went their own ways. Kinos died under tragic circumstances, but Thesokorus, now known as King of Killers, after he had fallen in with Celtic mercenaries prowling the lands around the river Daan, was found by his father. They fought in the shadow of the oracle at Dodona, in Greek Land, and Orgetorix rejected the older man, having horribly wounded him.

And how had Jason himself returned to life so far in the future that he could meet his time-flung sons?

Well, a conspiracy between old lovers saw to that: a ship (Argo of course) and me. And it was when I helped resurrect the Greek hero from his resting place, below Argo's decks, at the bottom of a Northland lake, that I met the divine and dreadful Niiv, the persistent presence in my life, in my mind, and below my furs. (And under my skin!) But enough of that for the moment.

On the subject of Jason's flesh-and-blood son: now, it seemed, he was having doubts about his decision – to abandon his father – and this shade was a party to that anguish.

At this time I had no idea where the living Orgetorix was. Somewhere in Alba, though.

'*Are* you Antiokus?' the shade asked again.

'Yes I am,' I confirmed. 'I'm also known as Merlin, my nickname from childhood. I've had many names.'

'I seem to recall that you are very old. You don't look old.'

'I've left more than a few traces, certainly. Wind and rain will have obscured them by now.'

He seemed amused by this, though only for a moment. 'My bone-blood-brother is doing very much the same. His traces, unlike yours, still haunt the wind. He is hound-harassed; he is watched by eagles. He's close. It won't be long before he finds you. This place ...' He looked around him at the small square, the low, cool houses. 'I – *he* – waited here to visit a shrine. In a hot country. I sat below this tree. I was with companions. Rough men, but proud men. And that was when I saw you.' The shade looked hard at me. The memory was strong for him; and yet the memory was coming from elsewhere. I was intrigued to know where.

I wondered, as we sat there, how much of this illusory place might be extended beyond the hostel. When I had indeed first set eyes upon Jason's eldest son, he had been in Makedonia, waiting to ascend the hills with his small troupe of comrades, to consult an oracle where he would learn his true past. There were always truths and lies in shrines and oracles. Medea, his mother, had inhabited that oracle in Makedonia. Perhaps, again, she was watching over her son, waiting for him, waiting for me, waiting to guide him yet again.

What did we stand to lose by trying?

I said to him, 'If this place is a true reflection of where I first saw you ... the human you, I mean ... then there is an oracle in the hills behind us.'

'I know. I was sent to take you there. I've been waiting for some time.'

'Take me there? To meet—?'

'My mother.'

'Ah.'

I was right.

As we untethered the horses, Thesokorus asked me, 'Is the girl all right? She seemed upset, entering the hostel. But my mother's influence is very strong. She came all the way through to this square. I tried to make her comfortable as I gave her the message to take to you.'

'The girl is fine. She's the daughter of the king. She has a great deal of courage.'

Medea had created this hot and dry, heavenly scented piece of theatre, I was sure of it now. Orgetorix rode slowly up the winding path into the hills, stooping below the low hanging branches of gnarled olives, clattering through the dry defiles, squeezing between the rocks with their intricately woven carvings, the clear signs that we were approaching an oracle.

Behind and below us, the small square shimmered in the lazy heat, the whitewashed walls of the buildings blurring into uniformity, though beyond them was the sprawling stretch of the hostel, a wide lodge bordering an almost unrecognisable river and the misty world of Urtha beyond. The hostel took on a different form when seen from Ghostland. It welcomed, it comforted.

As if he had been here before – and in his dreams he had – Orgetorix rode slowly and without mistake to the outer enclosure of the oracle, following the wooded paths to the craggy wall of grey rock where the speaking cave could be found, behind its screen of heat-twisted oaks and olives. This was in every way a reflection of the Oracle in Makedonia, north of Greek Land. It had been called 'the caught breath of time'. The wind whispered and called from the clefts in the rocks. I can think of no better way of putting the sound that summoned from the earth. Orgetorix seemed to enter a dream, passing me the reins of his horse and pushing me slightly away from him. 'Go and hide in the rocks. Let me make the encounter. Quickly!'

He waited, still in a state of trance, as I withdrew to the overhang where, years before, I had listened to him ask about his fate, unaware that it was Medea who was answering him.

I tethered the horses and watched from the shadows. Orgetorix stepped towards the widest of the caves, leaning slightly as he peered into the darkness, his arms hanging limply and unthreateningly at his sides.

'Mother?'

He stood there for a long time, unmoving, the breeze catching his hair. I had expected he would repeat the call, but he stayed silent, unnervingly so, as if frozen, a creature caught suddenly by torchlight in the night, unable to make sense of the sudden brightness, mute-muscled with indecision.

Then he called again, almost a whisper, and this time I heard him say quietly, 'He's come. I found him and he's come. Mother?'

The breeze stiffened. He straightened. The air seemed to silence him. A moment later the face of a ram, curled-horned and fierce, glared from the wide cleft. The horns were black, the face the colour of blood, the eyes wide and unblinking. The creature was monstrous. It came through from the earth in two bounds, towering over the young man before butting him to the ground and thrusting a hoof to his chest. The head lowered. The animal's screech was angry, protective. It tipped its head and plunged a horn into the sprawled man's belly, ripping it open in an instant. Orgetorix screamed, eyes streaming with fear and confusion. The second horn went into his throat, throwing him over, leaving him twisted in a death throe, one arm raised behind his back as if to reach for help. The creature urinated on the dying man, turned to stare at my hiding place, then bellowed and bounded towards the scrub oak that bordered the oracle.

I could sense it moving there, prowling, steaming, rubbing its horns against the trees, scraping off the blood. The priestess of the Ram, the murderess from Colchis; Jason's wife. In *familiar* form.

Waiting for me, for the man who, when the world was raw, had been her first love.

Medea had always liked to play this game of animal disguise. I thought of following her in wolf form, but she – especially as a ram – would be a match for any such creature. A bear? She would be quicker. A rival ram? There had always been something ungiving about Medea, and I doubted I would win such a contest. It was the game she played, and as I realised and remembered this, so it occurred to me that she was not setting out to hurt me, just – my first instinct – just to see me again.

But I could play a good game too, though it would cost me. When I entered the open woodland, following her spoor, I went in the shallow illusory disguise of Jason, carrying a bow like that of Odysseus, bone-strengthened and double-strung.

When she saw me coming, a crouching, careful hunter, she struck the ground in irritation, snorting and backing further into the rocks and the over-arching trunks of oaks.

Her eyes gleamed, menacing in that blood-red face.

Illusion is cheap enchantment; to have fired a shot would have been expensive; the best shot was the shock of her suddenly seeing her hated husband, Jason, from those long-gone days in Iolkos, after Argo's voyage to Colchis.

The ram disappeared. I approached the cave with caution, stooping to enter and letting my eyes adjust to the gloom.

Medea herself now sat against the cold rock, wrapped in the skin of the ram, watching me with fierce eyes.

'That was unnecessary. That was cruel.'

I almost laughed at her gall. 'Not as cruel as the gore you've just inflicted on your melancholy son.'

'That? That was not my son, and you know it. Just the toy I made to keep his brother happy.'

'A toy that breathed. A toy that felt. A toy that was frightened. A toy that was lost.'

'We were taught to do it. We were made to do it. Don't you remember? It was a long time ago, Merlin. We were taught to do some harsh things. We were told that our very bones were scarred with the codes and secrets that could make us stronger than rock. We were told we would never rest, that we should conserve the gifts that had been given to us, this charm, this magic. We were told to "walk a Path". But one by one – do you remember the others? There were others – one by one we fell to the wayside. Fell to the flesh. Fell into love. One by one. All except you. Toys? We are all toys. You have done far worse than me, when it comes to *malice*. I had two sons by Jason. I saved two sons from that monster, your friend, that same Jason. I gave each son a 'toy' ... the ghost of his brother. The toys were my sign of love for my sons. I had to hide my sons from that monster, your *friend*, Jason! I had to separate them. But they could not bear to be apart, so I made a toy for each of them: a brother-from-the-shade, a shadow-boy, the image of their needs. The comfort of familiar company. The toys don't matter, as well you know. Only the sons matter. And one of them is already dead. The other ... alive. And that is why I wanted you here. We must talk about Thesokorus. I need your help. And we must discuss that other man. Your friend. Jason.'

There was such a mix of intensity, uncertainty, anger and regret in Medea's voice and manner that for a while I couldn't respond. We sat in silence. She gazed at first into the distance, then more fondly at me.

The ram's fleece had loosened and I suspected she was deliberately letting me see the body within.

I found my voice again. 'Why are you doing this?'

'Doing what?' she asked with a frown

'Why are you sitting here, taunting me? Dressed in a ram's hide?'

'Ah. Perhaps I want to show you my scars.'

She shifted and came towards me, holding the fleece more carefully about her naked body. She leaned towards me, watching me with amusement. 'My scars, Merlin. The scars of a hard, long, desperate life. Would you like to see them?'

'Why would you want me to see them?'

She settled back, crossing her legs, adjusting the ram's skin to cover her. 'You've lived long, but you've not lived enough. Do you know why I say that? Because you forget the damage you've done. I have never, ever forgotten the damage that I've done. And my body has the scars to show it. There are men here,' she taunted, stabbing a finger against her chest and belly. 'Many men. Many Jasons, though he was the one that left the deepest scar. Your own scratch?' She gave a little laugh. 'It's somewhere here, below the fleece, if you want to be reminded. You were the first, Merlin. The little boy grown big, who still couldn't tie the thongs that held his shoes in place. Isn't that what "merlin" means? "Can't tie his laces". But your mark is on me. How many marks on you?'

'My marks are deeper. I hide them.'

'Of course you do,' she sneered. Then she seemed to soften. 'Or perhaps they fade, like nettle rash and briar-scratch. Like that little northern snow-rose you fuck for your pleasure. How many snow-roses, Merlin? How many roses, bloom-lost because they met a man who couldn't fall to the wayside; couldn't fall in love; kept walking, shaking off the touch of life as a dog shakes off the touch of rain? I pity you.'

'And I pity you. Your great love, your sons, the remnants of your children, all of that so-precious touch of life has come to this.'

'Come to what?'

'Lost, alone, abandoned, all forsaken. Miserable in your melancholy, hopeless in your harrowing, dreadful in your dance with dying. You *are* dying, Medea. You've used your strength too much. It costs little to paint a fresh face. You cannot bring back a fresh heart.'

'My, my,' she murmured slowly, shaking her head. 'What failed poet has been whispering to *you*, I wonder?'

We were silent for a while, each huddled in our own way, each remembering. The mood seemed to have softened. Medea's sharp words brought back a passionate past, and the land where we had shared it, if only briefly.

I said something that would have best been left unspoken. 'There was a time when I would have dragged you from the burial mound itself. For a final act of love.'

'Really?'

'Yes. Perhaps nothing has changed.'

'Then I'll be sure to be cremated!' Her laugh was a crow's laugh. 'You can make my shape in ashes on your bed.'

'You're cruel.'

Her sigh was of despair, as she cradled her head in her hands. 'Oh, not that again! No, Merlin. Not cruel. I'm tired.' And she looked it as she suddenly gazed at me. 'That's what living does to you. It's *you*, Merlin, who are dead. Not me. And you've been dead a long time. Since you were a boy, in fact. No snow-rose, squeezing you with her clever hands, putting the morning and evening sap into you so that she can *sap* it out at her whim, no clinging *ice*-whore can change the fact that you died when you made that silly little boat—'

'What silly little boat?'

'You called it *Voyager*. You set it to float along the river where we grew up, when we were children. You said that it would come back because all rivers came back to their source. Don't you remember? You must remember, Merlin. Even the Dead have memories. That little boat meant everything to you. When you let it float away ... your heart went with it. The rest of us practised our skills, learned our lessons, played our games, passed the tests, and went on our way according to what was written inside us. But you: oh Merlin, do try and remember. You yourself floated away with that silly little boat. You are the only one of us who never grasped at the chances we'd been given.'

I remembered Voyager as if in a dream. It had taken me a long time to build it. One day the model ship had slipped away from me, caught by a current in the river, lost for ever into the forest wilderness among the mountains. What did Medea know that I had forgotten?

I saw her more clearly now. She crouched before me, an ageing woman, hair grey, cheeks drawn, fierce-eyed, certainly, and strong in aroma and presence. She knelt before me as if subservient, but this was no position of humility or begging; I sat shivering and uncertain, aroused and dry-mouthed. She had me in a gaze that was both willing me to be gentle, and willing me to be strong.

'Do you want me, Merlin? Do you want me as you used to want me? Or have you forgotten how you used to want me?'

'I've forgotten,' I said bluntly – and noticed the quick frown of disappointment on her face, quick as the beat of a wing, but noticeable nonetheless. How quickly her mood could change. 'But I've not forgotten that we've played this out before.'

'Played out? Are we back to toys?'

'Played out this seduction. You've done this to me before. A hundred times.'

'A hundred times,' she echoed, shrinking back into the fleece. 'A hundred times before. You remember all one hundred, I suppose.'

'I know that you've tricked me before.'

'You're so easy to trick. It's hard to resist you. But there's more to a trick than just the trick. That's the tease. After the tease comes the pleasure. You seem to have remembered the tricks and not the passion. What an odd man you are, Merlin. You are as old as me, despite your youthful looks. But you are as old as time. As fruit, we are ripe and sweet. In fact, we're so damned old we should be rotting on the vine. But you are still sour. Youth has kept you sour. And that puzzles me. I remember when you were young, and you were as sweet as honeyed fish. You said the same to me. And you should know. I've never tasted myself in the way you tasted me. But you have grown so bitter.'

'I would have expected no more from you.'

'No more than what?'

'No more than the same tricks. We've been here before. You know it. Nothing you say can hide the fact that you're up to something.'

'I confess that I've tricked you before. But not this time.'

'I remember those same words. From before.'

'I have changed my mind about many things, Merlin. I won't say I've grown wise. I'm tired. Tired of summoning anger and aggression towards a man who once was brutal, and now is just as lost as I am. And no, I don't mean you. I mean Jason. I had two sons, Merlin, two that I kept. I let many go before they had breathed their first air. I had to. They were too full of the man. But I kept two, and I loved them. A little dreamer, and a little bull-leaper; a quiet boy and an active boy. Each, in his own way, a delight to me – and, of course, to Jason. When I stole them from Jason I killed him there and then, killed everything he had known, every hunger in his heart, every dream of peace in his mind. Now I realise I wounded myself in the same way. Thesokorus is alive and searching for us. I mean it truly, Merlin. The boy – the man – deserves to be with both his parents.'

I said nothing. Medea was exhausted, every movement of face and limbs testifying to frailness and fragility. I was helpless to explore the extent to which this was an act; on this side of the river my abilities in insight were cramped, closed down.

I was suspicious of her, and it was certainly the case that she had lied to me in a very similar and persuasive way, the last time in this very land of the dead, on this side of the river, in a valley that echoed and appeared to be the image of our place of growing up. How badly I had fallen under her spell! But of course, it had happened before. With each new encounter with Medea, so I remembered a little more of those early centuries, when we had been close as friends, as lovers, and as seekers, prowling the Path around the world in awe and wonder at what we were discovering.

It was an uncomfortable thought. I was bound to Medea because she, having squandered her enchantment, ageing rapidly, could remember so much more than I could. I, who had hoarded my magic and stayed young, was paying the cost by being denied my own long life.

Only by ageing would I understand and experience the pain and pleasure of the encounters and experiences, the adventures and wild pursuits that had been my life for several thousands of years. Like a head-damaged veteran of some terrible war, able to remember only a few years, sometimes only a few days at a time, I was closed off from myself. In some remote part of the eastern world, where clay tablets were used to record the actions of kings and the deeds of heroes, the sentences of criminals and the wealth of brides, perhaps there was more being written about my life than I could dream in a hundred years. My life was clay. I remembered so little.

Medea knew this, and there was a look about her, enticing and seductive, that told me she was aware of that knowledge.

'Help me, Merlin. Will you help me?'

'What exactly is it you want, Medea?'

'To have Thesokorus reconciled with his father. To have reconciliation between Jason and me. Hard, I know. A hard thing to do. Which is why I can't do it alone.'

I watched her for a while. She was so difficult to read. I wished

I could entice her across the river where she would need stronger defences to stop me searching her spirit.

'Of the two proposals, which is the more important?'

It was worth a try, but Medea could have seen that obvious question from the Moon itself. 'Thesokorus to be reconciled with Jason,' she said. 'But I will try with every sinew in my body to become part of the family again. But first: father and son.'

'Where is Thesokorus now? The real man.'

'I don't know. Close. Not in Ghostland. But hiding. If you find him, you may tell him everything I've said.'

After a moment, I agreed. Then I asked her to help me in return. 'What is happening along this river? Why have these hostels appeared? They signal some dramatic change. The priests in Taurovinda are in no doubt of it.'

'I don't know. And that is the truth. But there's no denying that something is about to happen. It's been coming for some time, now. The islands are deserted. The ocean is obscured by mist, but strange ships can sometimes be seen. The deep forests are in winter. There are immense storms over the mountains. Something is shaping the land. There is a shaping force at work. I feel it's "old", Merlin – old like us. If I can find out more, I promise on my son's life I'll tell you.'

She saw my cynical look, smiled and shrugged. 'I have nothing else with which to swear to you, so take it or leave it. I *will* help you. Please help me.'

I am neither strong nor wise. Neither now, as I write this, nor then, when Medea watched me with eyes that never aged, and thought of me with a mind that remembered our time together as lovers. She must have seen that I wanted her, but that I was frightened of renewed intimacy. But I was unable to resist.

When the ram's fleece slipped from her shoulders I entered a dream. We held each other for a long time. I remember crying. I remember her soothing words. We were playful. We made love to each other in the Greeklanders' way. I thought my heart would burst with the strain.

Later, when I surfaced from shallow sleep, in great discomfort, I expected to find that all had been a trick, that she had teased me and stolen from me, as Niiv was always attempting to tease and steal from me. I expected to wake cold, alone, and once again the fool that is the man who won't give into the natural tide of Time.

But there she was, a small, sagging, sad figure, curled in her skin, sleeping gently. There were dried tears on her cheeks. She was murmuring as she breathed. She was drawn in on herself like a frightened child.

I tried to wake her, but she mumbled through her drowsiness, tightening her body further.

Though sleep helps solve riddles it is also a haven from despair. Except at dawn. At dawn, dogs fly into the dream, ravaging the peace.

I kissed her very gently. Would she wake now? No. She was lost. I left the cave, riding down through the quickening light, back to the hostel and then away.

I came quickly back to Ullanna and her band of shaven-scalped companions. It was dawn, the air was fresh. Three of the retinue were sitting on their ponies, arms crossed, eyes closed, snatching a moment of sleep. Two others were crouched at the bank of the river, backsides over the water, chatting and laughing. Ullanna herself was slumped over the back of her oak-brown mare, head on the animal's neck, flicking the reins from side to side. When she saw me approach she straightened up, kicked the mare into a canter and came over to me.

She was not happy.

'Niiv has gone back to the fort. I sent two of my riders with her. Something upset her.'

'That was foolish of her.'

Ullanna was more angry than I'd realised: 'Do you know how long we've been waiting for you?'

'No.'

'Three days! Do you know what we've been eating?'

'Wild geese? Salmon?'

She slapped the leather reins across her legs, a furious gesture that suggested more frustration than anger.

'We've eaten nothing! The hunting here is dead. No birds, no fish, no game, and the grass stinks! There is something wrong, Merlin. Everything looks the same, but it's not. It's dead. And for a long way back towards the hill. I agreed to wait for you, but you've returned now. So come or stay, that's up to you. But we're off! Riders! To horseback!' she shouted.

Sleepers awoke, others mounted up, and with a flurry of hooves, a bird screech of cries – they seemed less anguished than their leader – the wild band had begun their gallop to the east, looking behind them all the time, as if careful to watch for what might be following, or perhaps to watch what they were leaving behind.

I followed in their tracks, but kept a slower pace.

When I caught up with them, later that night, they were camped among ruins, a fire burning. A nearby spring flowed gently into a well and Ullanna was crouched there, scooping the water, filling a make-shift trough for the horses.

The women were singing; small game was turning on the spits. Perhaps we had reached the edge of the dead zone.

Ullanna saw me and beckoned me over, motioning me to crouch. She scooped a bowl of fresh water, but held it before her, staring at it. 'What's going on, Merlin? What's happening?'

'I don't know.'

She sighed, a weary sound, a sad breath. 'I haven't been in his life for very long; I don't want to lose him. I haven't been in this country very long; I don't want to lose it. If I seemed angry, it's because of just that: I don't want to lose what I've come to love. Urtha. This country.' She looked round at me. 'What have you been seeing in the last season or so? Nothing is right.'

'Echoes of a past,' I replied truthfully. 'Faces out of the well. Memories. And not all of them belong here.'

'Something is shaping change,' she murmured grimly.

I was startled as she used similar words to Medea.

'Yes.'

'What do you think it might be? What do your faces from the well tell you?'

'Clues. Observations. No answers. But I'm coming to believe that it has a lot to do with Jason. I can't explain it, just a feeling in the human part of my gut.'

'Jason,' she repeated, shaking her head. 'Time is askew. But then: hasn't it always been? Here—' she passed me a filled leather cup, then scooped from the spring herself. 'In my country, to drink water from the well is a sign of welcome to strangers, since water tastes the same everywhere. And we drink it also to remember a good life, and old and new friends.' She sat back on her haunches. 'It seems to me you've been encountering a few old friends. I have too. Here!' She tapped her head. 'But the new is more important.'

Her eyes shone in the firelight as she looked at me, and there was a thin but welcome smile on her lips. We touched the edges of our crude cups together.

I didn't know what was going through Ullanna's mind. She was Scythian. I was Ancient.

But together, we drank water from the well.

PART TWO

GREATER, MORE NOBLE, MORE TERRIBLE

8

Night Hunting

While I was investigating the rumours from the hostels, Urtha and a retinue that included his proud son, Kymon, made their way east through the forest, to the land of the Coritani. Here, close to the river Nantosuelta as she approached the wide sea, rose the high-walled fortress of the king, Vortingoros, a smaller hill than Taurovinda, but still prominent and austere.

The Coritani had been at peace with their neighbour in the west for several years. Vortingoros had, as a child, been fostered for a time in Taurovinda, with Urtha's father. He was two years older than Urtha, and over those seasons they had shared in the king's enclosure, and hunting at the edge of the Plain of the Battle Crow, they had 'counted coup' equally, which meant touching the opponent in otherwise potentially deadly combat, rather than inflicting a wound. Despite this likely humiliation for the older boy, they had found a close friendship that survived into their adult lives. It was lost over a dispute concerning cattle found grazing loose along the river that linked their territories, and which might have belonged to either kingdom. The war, no more than a series of skirmishes, had continued for two years and cost several lives. But the friendship was won again, after a settlement by combat of champions and the exchange of shields, horses and slaves of equal value. This time it had lasted.

Now, however, the country of the Coritani was in a state of apprehension verging on fear.

When the warlord Brennos had called for the finest warriors of the clan kingdoms to come and assist in a great vengeance raid on the oracle at Delphi, in Greek Land, Vortingoros's champions had responded almost to the man, as had many of Urtha's. They had crossed the sea to find the gathering of the army on the river Daan, ready to move south, scourging and scouring all the lands they found on their way. The Great Quest, as it had been known, had eventually triumphed, only to discover that Delphi was barren of the treasure they had anticipated plundering. Most had returned home disillusioned, and damaged by fighting.

But their initial departure, when hope was a song of joy, led to changes in both lands that were frightening and confusing, in Urtha's case, tragic.

Urtha returned to find his country blighted: deserted, ravaged and destroyed, his fortress sacked and burned, many of his friends – and one of his sons – dead.

For the Coritani, the change had been as bleak, but far more strange. All wildlife vanished from the woods, all fish from the rivers and streams, only the birds remained, in increasingly dense flocks. The taste of crow is foul, but even a child could soon shoot an arrow and strike this carrion-seeker on its wing. This abandonment by nature was curious enough on its own.

But then, after the champions and lesser warriors had ridden or rowed to the east, to cross the ocean and land near the mouth of the river Rein, so wooden images of the departed began to appear in the groves. They howled for a few nights, terrible sounds that kept the Speakers from entering those sacred places, after which, they dispersed, in the darkness, across the territory, some to the water's edge, some to the fringes of the woods, some to narrow gorges, others to the heights of cliffs. There they knelt on one knee, oak weapons clutched against their bodies, and became cold, hard tree once again.

Each effigy was perfect in its representation of the man who had gone to the raid on Delphi.

Urtha had known a little of this, and had been intrigued by it. Now, as he and his group emerged to within sight of the steep western rise of the fortress, his curiosity was teased again.

The effigies that peered from the undergrowth, ivy-clad by now, and some half toppled, had been daubed and cut with crosses or spirals, decked with wreaths of dead flowers, or covered with ragged red shawls. Following along the willow-fringed river, the same thing was true. There were fewer statues here, and the crows and others birds had daubed them in their own particular way, great white streaks running down the once-proud features.

Even so, these kneeling men had been fashioned further by frantic, clumsy hands.

Urtha's first thought was that they had been turned into memorials of the dead men, and that families came to remember them.

He was only half-right. Vortingoros gave him a fuller picture after he had welcomed his guests, fed them, given them strong, sweet wine, salvaged from the wreck of an eastern trading ship driven ashore on the rough sea-coast of his kingdom, and treated them to songs and poetry from his oldest and most respected bard, a shaven-headed, clean-cheeked man called Talienze. Talienze was from across the grey sea, from somewhere south, and was a prisoner of Vortingoros's who had traded death at the turning of winter for his talents, which were varied and often amusing.

Talienze took a place on the bench behind Vortingoros, with the chieftain's counsellors and the High Woman. Urtha noticed that as Vortingoros spoke, so the bard's eyes were half-closed, his lips moving almost imperceptibly; he was perhaps memorising the conversation.

'You have a fine son,' Vortingoros said, raising his wine bowl to the boy. 'His eyes tell me that he has seen death, and also courted it. And won the courtship, of course, since here he is.'

Urtha raised his own bowl. 'The boy has had a hard time of it—'

'I can speak for myself,' Kymon suddenly interjected, rising to his feet and glaring at his father. Though Urtha was surprised by this rudeness, he calmly looked up at his stiff-bodied son.

'No. You cannot!'

Torn between youthful anger and an understanding of his place, Kymon was unable to speak for a moment. At last he said, 'I know I still have to face the challenge, but surely I have done enough, in the winning back of our own fortress, to be able to speak ...'

'No! You have not. Sit down.'

Kymon hesitated just long enough to signal his disapproval of his father's words, then sat, crossing his legs and leaning forward, his gaze on the sleeping mastiff at Vortingoros's feet. Vortingoros contemplated Kymon for a moment, then nodded his head.

'I am very keen to hear you speak for yourself, Kymon. But your father, my good friend, is right. Keep your counsel. You have a lot to say, I can see that, and no doubt a lot to offer. But at the right time, and in the right way.'

'You are very courteous,' Kymon murmured.

'Yes. And I have a nephew who is as blood-headed as you. He's not here now, but you'll be meeting him soon enough.' He leaned back in his chair. 'I lost my own sons, all three of them. They were older than you, but not by much. They were killed when your brother Urien was killed. Do you remember him?'

'Urien? Of course. He fought like a man and was hacked down; I was dragged to safety, whimpering, by dogs.'

'Thank the Good God you were,' said Vortingoros. 'You'll have a long life, now.'

'Not as a dog!'

'Those dogs,' Urtha reprimanded his son, 'were my favourite hounds. One died trying to protect your brother from the killers; the other two saved you and your sister. Dogs? How dare you call them dogs. Hounds, boy! And brave as any champion. If I die tomorrow, those hounds become yours.'

'I'll welcome them,' Kymon agreed in a disgruntled tone. 'They're old, but I'll welcome them.'

There was a moment's pause as father and son stared at each other.

Kymon said, 'I'll be a hound as good and as fast and as fearless as your hound Maglerd, who saved me; and Uglerd, who saved Munda. I'll be my father's hound and I'll be proud of it.'

Then Urtha said, with his own proud smile, 'You'll have your moment, Kymon. Too many moments. Long after I've gone.'

'I *long* for that moment. Of *having* moments,' he quickly corrected. 'Not of having you gone.'

Vortingoros laughed, spilling wine from his bowl. 'All this way – such a long journey – to have a family argument and reconciliation? Well, if that's all you've come about, Urtha ...'

Peace was restored.

The discussion turned to the portents of change: those from the past, those being currently manifest.

Vortingoros turned to one of his advisors, murmured something, and the man left the king's lodge, returning moments later, dragging, with help, a low cart with a wooden effigy sprawled and twisted upon it. The figure was screaming in death, one hand clutching at its chest, the other bunched into a fist. It was the very image of a dying warrior in his death throes: eyes half opened, mouth gaping, head thrown back, weapons still hanging from his belt and shoulders.

'This is Morvran,' Vortingoros said in a low voice.

'One of your dead?'

'No. One of our living. Morvran came back from Greek Land, from that deserted oracle at Delphi.'

Kymon was staring at the figure with childish awe. Urtha ran his hand over the polished wood of the effigy's face. 'This is the face and posture of a man fallen in combat. Are you sure Morvran is the man who left?'

Vortingoros then described the events following the raid on Delphi, and the return of his sword and spearmen.

They had come back in small groups, anything from four men to forty, rowing up the river, or riding on stolen horses. Many returned on foot. They were all exhausted, many angry, a few triumphant, though only with the mercenary spoils of war that could be gained during retreat.

Families welcomed the men. Vortingoros set ten fires burning around the perimeter of his stronghold, each with roasting oxen and pig, and stone jars of sharp, scented ale.

Vortingoros was never short of surprises and delights, and never backward in sharing them.

A few days later, the howling from the forests began again, this time at dawn.

Wrapped in their cloaks, a few men and two of the Speakers rode towards the river, through the early mist. Several shapes moved ahead of them, shields held above heads, swords stretched out to the right. When the riders caught up with them they saw they were the effigies of those living who had returned. They howled like wolves, a sound that rose to a sort of keening as the oak-warriors reached the river and stepped into the water. There they at once became shapeless, simple cuts from the trunk of a tree, the gloss of their skin turning to the deep, winding grooves of oak bark.

The dead wood floated away towards the sea. The sudden silence was welcome.

Day after day the same apparitions occurred, the same wailing. There had been a form of life in the oak men. Perhaps they were mourning their return to the shadows.

Then, out of curiosity, and in the hope of learning something about the life of oak, the druid who was the Speaker of the Land, persuaded Morvran – lately returned from the quest – to let him ambush his own effigy as it stalked to the river. Morvran, informed by ignorance, agreed readily. The statue struggled with Morvran and four others, but eventually succumbed with a terrifying scream of anguish and fell, frozen in the position in which it was now preserved.

Morvran was at first delighted with the trophy. He helped haul it to the stone and thorn enclosure where it would be kept, dressed it in his own battle-harness and war kilt, and spent a great deal of time using the curiosity of visitors to explain his combat deeds in Greek Land.

Vortingoros and Speaker for the Land tolerated the man's blustering and bragging until, during the feasting for the day of fire, celebrating the first sowing of corn, he claimed that the effigy demonstrated 'triumph over the tricks of the Otherworld'.

The moment he used these words, the king condemned him. Speaker for the Land cursed Morvran roundly before leaving the feasting bench to return to the apple orchard, to consult with skulls on what had occurred.

'A little after this,' Vortingoros told Urtha, 'the man began to behave very strangely. His wife would wake to find him gone from the bed. But a short while later he would be back, stinking of the night forest. There would be blood on his mouth and sometimes wolf-stench on his back. He would be asleep, but then would wake in tears. He often said a name, someone in the town, and would avoid them. It became noticeable that the person whose name he had cried out in despair would fall ill, or break a limb, or die. Four men died quite unexpectedly after he had called their names. All of them were those who had returned from the raid on the oracle in Greek Land.

'I'm sure I remember that you, like us, practise night-hunting under the Wolf Moon ...'

'We do,' Urtha agreed. 'And under the Stag Moon as well. Strange deer can surface at that time. Strangely coloured.'

'It's a common practice, then. A night-hunt went out as the Wolf Moon was rising. A pack of wolves had been seen hiding among the stones of the long-mound groves. The runs and traps were set, the hides built and covered, the scents prepared, the torches ready for the confusion as the family broke cover.

'We were waiting at the crouch, faces blackened, keeping our eyes away from the reflection of the Moon, when a proud, grey wolf, a big male, suddenly bounded from the woodland edge, stopped and sniffed the air. This was a fine foe, and would be a fine spoil, a fine skin. But even as we thought this so we became sweaty with excitement and the brute smelled us and turned on us. Teeth bared, we could see that his canines were as long as daggers, silvery-white in the moonlight. We would have to attack fast, and risk a savaging.

'At that moment a figure appeared out of nowhere, a man, cloak flying, eyes gleaming. The wolf turned to face him, howled angrily and charged. The figure of the man *somersaulted* over the brute's back, landing on his feet and turning to face the return charge. Those teeth could sever two heads with one quick flick of the neck. Again, the apparition of the man ran towards the animal and somersaulted across its back.

'This time, when the brute wolf ran at him, he dealt it a massive blow on the head, killing it at once. Then he straddled the wolf's carcase and turned it over, peering down into its features, holding the limp head by its jowls. And he cried out, the cry of a man who has committed a dreadful deed.

'As fast as he had appeared, the cloaked man ran from the scene of the killing and was lost in shadows. We approached the dead creature carefully; the wood beside us was heavy with the breathing of the rest of the pack, and a sudden charge would overwhelm us. We had not struck the torches. By moonlight alone we looked at the dead face, with its black and white markings and glazed eyes. And for a moment we saw a human face there, just an instant. And we all agreed that we recognised the man.'

'And shortly after that the man fell ill.'

'The man died in the night. He had been a champion in the field, and in the games. He was a well-liked and well-known man. We all mourned him.'

'And the cloaked man … Morvran?'

Vortingoros nodded gravely. 'He cried out in his bed, he cried the name of the man who would die. He reeked of the night and of the musk of the wolf. He didn't deny what he had done, though he claimed only to have been dreaming. When our friend died, the Speakers and priests called for a trial and judgement. They took him to the groves for five days and nights. They couldn't decide on what he was, what he had become, or what possessed him. So they consigned him. And that was that.'

Consigned him! That meant he had been hung head down, gagged and bound tightly, suspended from a cross-beam at the bottom of a narrow shaft, dug to the depth of a deep well; then closed off from the world above by a thick round of oak, with stones on top, earth and offerings of meat and drink, berries and marrow-bones on top of that, all to satisfy the hunger of any 'descending spirit' that might be curious as to the corpse below; an encouragement to leave it alone. And charms in metal and stone placed at the top of the shaft, to seal it. Earth piled high over the seal.

And Morvran was gone for good.

These events had rapidly become known in the towns and villages of the tribal territory of the Coritani. The Coritani had become a people afraid of their own dreams. The events were incomprehensible to them, and to the seers and to the druids and to the Speakers. The High Women, with their powers of *imbas forasnai*, the light of foresight, had no answers either.

Urtha watched his old friend closely; Vortingoros seemed disturbed just at the memory of the story he had told. 'Why didn't you come to Taurovinda before, when these things were happening? Perhaps we could have helped.'

The other man was mildly scornful. 'Do you think I didn't think of asking? But *how* could you have helped? Bearing in mind the location of your own stronghold, I imagine you have problems enough on your hands.'

'Problems indeed. And puzzles. Which is why I'm here, to ask to borrow some of your best men. I've brought my counsel and Speaker for Kings, to negotiate a fair tribute in return.'

From Urtha's experience before the raid on Greek Land, Vortingoros would normally have cocked an ear to that and asked: what exactly are you offering: horses? Cattle? The loan of a bull? Chariot wheels?

But to Urtha's dismay, Vortingoros shook his head. 'Your puzzles are with the Shadows of Heroes? With Ghostland?'

'Aren't they always?'

'Then even if I could spare them, I doubt that they would want to enter your land. This is a frightened nation, Urtha. I've just made that plain enough, surely?'

'But if the threat against us is as great as our Speakers think it may turn out to be, then your territory is unsafe as well. You helped me once before, Vortingoros. The sight of a hundred of your horsemen bounding from the woods at the edge of the Plain of MaegCatha, as we struggled to take back Taurovinda from the occupying army, is a sight that has gone into many poems and songs within our walls. It was a heroic moment. My son here fought alongside your own champions.'

'I remember,' Vortingoros murmured with a fond glance at Kymon. 'It was a good piece of chariot work. You kept control of the horses well. But things were different then.'

Kymon rose to his feet stiffly, resting his right hand on the ivory grip of the small iron sword hanging at his waist. His was the only sword that had been allowed into the king's enclosure. Urtha caught the whiff of irritation in the boy, but the action was so swift, Kymon's tongue loosed like an arrow, that he was helpless to silence the reckless lad.

'Maybe men were braver then. So if not the men to our assistance, then what about the boys? I could lead them.'

Now Urtha too rose to his feet, fuming and red-faced. He loosened the golden brooch that held his cloak at his shoulder and let the robe fall, a sign of apology to his host. He fixed his gaze on his son, who returned it coldly. 'You will pay dearly for that remark. And the choice of debt will be at Vortingoros's whim. Now leave the hall.'

Vortingoros said quickly, 'Urtha, I would like him to stay. I am not insulted by his words. Discourtesy in a comment does not necessarily mean that the comment is untrue. Kymon is right. It isn't just fear that afflicts us. It is a lack of courage. The forests are beginning to smell of *dhiiv arrigi*, the outcasts of generations coming back for vengeance. They seem to know that we are weak.'

'The *dhiiv arrigi* are becoming a nuisance in my land too. It's part of the puzzle.'

Vortingoros tugged at one of the long curls of his moustache. 'The Dead are raising a new army?'

'I suspect so. The Wanderer is at the river even as we speak, assessing their strength. The Five Hostels have reappeared. We believe this signals a greater invasion than previously.'

'The Wanderer? That enchanter friend of yours?'

'Merlin, yes.'

'Well, that's useful. He can cross the river and gain insight and farsight.'

Urtha shook his head. 'His powers are curtailed once he crosses Nantosuelta. Besides, he shares his powers of enchantment like an old man shares his ale: grudgingly.'

'Unlike a king's wife shares her favours,' Vortingoros sighed.

Urtha, startled by the un-kingly indiscretion, noted the comment but showed no response. Aylamunda, his own wife, had been impeccable in her manners towards her husband before her death; Ullanna, his wild accomplice in the royal lodge, would kill any man who tried to touch her in an intimate way, or try to charm her. Vortingoros seemed aware that he had overstepped the mark and with a quick cough returned to the subject.

'The Five Hostels,' he repeated. 'It's been a long time since I've heard talk of *them*.' He turned slightly to his bard, Talienze, who leaned forward and whispered in his ear for a few moments. Talienze's gaze never left Urtha's as he spoke to his own king. Urtha was curious that Talienze should know of the Hostels, since he was from another country. But then: all bards had prodigious memories. It was almost certain that the ex-prisoner had absorbed the history of the land to which he had been brought, and of the kingdoms around.

'I need to give some thought to the matter,' Vortingoros finally said. 'I can agree with you that the situation is serious; I will offer you what help I can. First, I must discuss the matter with my counsel.'

'This is appreciated.'

'And I must introduce Kymon to my nephew. I have a feeling the two young men will get along very well.'

Kymon smiled and bowed his head. Was he aware of the murmur of humour in the ranks of champions in the king's hall?

'At least, before the chin-cut,' the host king added, to more mirth.

Vortingoros rose and gripped wrists with Urtha. 'By the way, despite all I've told you, we still practise the Moon hunt. Its time is nearly here, and if the Speaker for the Land agrees, we could hunt the night after tomorrow, after moonrise.'

'For boar?'

'For a stag, whose belling tells us that he's a prize on four legs.'

'After what you've described to me, are you sure it's wise?'

'Wise? No. But the hunt is still in our blood. You and your son must join us. I will present you with the best portion of the flesh, though we must go to convivial combat together if you wish to secure the velvet and the horn.' He laughed. 'What do you say?'

'I say yes.'

An owl, dark-faced, tawny-feathered, suddenly swooped through the hall and rose into the stream of light from the smoke-hole in the roof.

Frowning at the bird, which had startled him, and with the quiet comment, 'Do you watch *everything* I do?' Urtha retired to the guest hall with his son and retinue, weary, apprehensive, unable to sleep.

I would have to be careful how I answered his question, when it came to the moment.

9

The Chin-Cut

The evening before the Moon Hunt, by arrangement and agreement between the two kings, Kymon and Vortingoros's nephew Colcu met in the circle where the game was to be held, a wide space, defined by feathered posts and filled with a scatter of rusting weapons, wooden swords, bent-shafted spears, ropes and 'leaping' points, the cut trunks of trees and carefully positioned flat-topped blocks of grey stone. A few thorn bushes had been allowed to grow there, and a central oak, sufficiently battered and broken as to suggest the hazardous and limb-damaging use to which it had often been put.

Kymon inspected the circle and was contemptuous. 'Nothing bright. No bright iron. No sharp-edged bronze. No shields. This is a child's playground.'

Urtha picked up one of the discarded blades and bent it until it snapped. He had seen at once what this circle represented. Not a playground for children but an echo of the crow-ground after battle. These weapons, even the wooden batons, had been taken from a skirmish field. Urtha glanced into the fading light above him. Sure enough, a bird was hovering there, swooping and disappearing as it eyed the ground. One of the *Morrigan*'s daughters, given a small role as she herself grew to become a retriever of souls when blood-tempered iron was dipped again into the life-forge.

There would be no killing today. The bird was young, her presence in the clouds simply to watch and learn.

Colcu had been out with the group setting traps for the coming Moon Hunt. Now he trotted through the main gate into the hill on a white pony, which was decked with red and black feathers above its bright bronze eye-covers. His feet almost touched the ground.

He rode straight to the games circle with his uncle leading him and swung down from the narrow saddle to confront Kymon. The two youths engaged each other's gaze coldly while their guardians talked and laughed. Colcu was a full head taller than Urtha's son and he seemed to be in distress at having to 'prove' himself with this Cornovidian 'child'.

Although Kymon kept wisely quiet, he was alarmed to see the purple 'torque heads' tattooed on each side of Colcu's throat, a mark that always preceded the fitting of a golden torque, the mark of royalty but also of having taken a life. Colcu saw the slightly nervous glance from his opponent and let a smile touch at his lips.

Fair-faced, pale-eyed, Colcu looked like the warrior he was determined to become, his hair limed white and stiff for that form of conflict that would most likely lead to death. He wore a loose, leather battle harness, a grey and green kirtle with red-embroidered edges, and black bull's-hide ankle boots. The sword at his right hip had an ivory and onyx grip, wound around with white leather. Colcu drew the weapon slowly, with his right hand of course, and presented it to Kymon.

No word had been spoken, but Colcu's amused yet moody gaze had remained unblinking.

Kymon passed over his own sword. The guardians received them and the parties withdrew to their benches, for refreshment and instruction.

The boy was anxious. 'He has the marks of a torque on his neck,' he said to his father. 'What does that mean exactly?'

Urtha had already spoken to Vortingoros. 'There was a raid on a hunting party in the wolf-glen, south of the hill. A while ago, now. Several of Vortingoros's horsemen were surprised by a band of *dhiiv arrigi*. Colcu and two companions were among the party, and though they withdrew when the attack came, Colcu launched a sling-stone that killed the leader of the vengeful outcasts. It was a timely shot, and he is promoted in the order.'

'Then why the contest with me?'

'He still needs to go through the formality of the youth game. This is a good opportunity for you, Kymon, should you win the contest.'

In the brief, shocked silence that followed, Kymon's face turned from astonishment to outrage as he stared at his father. Urtha tugged nervously at his greying moustaches.

'A formality?' Kymon said in a thin voice, and then at full volume, 'A *formality*? I am not a *formality*! I am nobody's *formality*. This is an intolerable insult.'

'Not at all,' Urtha retorted. 'It's an excellent opportunity. How many times must I remind you: to keep your anger for when it can be used to full advantage. And always look for the opportunity in any situation.'

Some way distant, there was laughter. Colcu and his escort of pale-featured youths had heard Kymon's outburst and were mocking him. It had the effect of cooling the boy's blood, concentrating his fury.

'He's tall and looks very strong,' Kymon murmured. 'This will be a hard game. Hard to put the chin-cut on him from the vantage point of victory.'

Urtha glanced at the tall, chalk-haired youth, now parading barefoot and in his battle harness. 'Yes. You are up against the odds. But remember: what to Colcu is a formality to you is a challenge that will earn you a line in the history of the year. There's a bard watching us. He's quite young, probably looking for some good verses, some good sneers and jibes. To be mocked or praised? That's up to you, now. Make an opportunity out of a formality. Whatever happens, you will have received your chin-cut. Then the game can begin in earnest. And then – never forget – there will always be other bards!'

Urtha embraced his son before helping the youth dress for the contest.

The cut on Urtha's chin was so clean, so healed, that I had only noticed it when the faint scar caught bright moonlight, at a time when we had been in the snow-covered North Land together. Even then, I had assumed it was a battle-taken wound. In fact, he had received it when younger than Kymon, though he had made the cut on his opponent first.

Both Colcu and Kymon would receive the cut, each from the other, but to place the mark as the winner – the first to cut – would be remembered. It would also be remembered who had placed the second wound, the loser's strike: Colcu would swagger through the final years of his youth, by all the signs, and Kymon's appetite for age and honour would be severely blunted.

Urtha could tell this. Kymon was taking his anxiety out in no uncertain terms with his father, criticising this, growling at that, becoming heated and wet-eyed in anticipation.

Urtha drew away from him, hardening his attitude, making a slight mockery of the boy himself. But he added: 'Colcu won't crow for long. His swagger will be his downfall. Any man who makes such a wolf's kill of meeting his opponent will soon find himself howling.'

A wolf's kill. A mess. A badly performed action.

Kymon spat into his left hand, and clenched the fist. Urtha enclosed his son's hand with his own, then looked up at the sky; it was darkening, and the clouds were moving fast from the west. The breeze was strong, bringing the scent of his own land.

'Cut him cleanly,' was all he said, still staring at the heavens. 'Make him remember you. Tomorrow we'll hunt this bellowing stag; then we'll get back to the business of persuading them to help us.'

A ring of champions, old and young, stood leaning on their shields, a fence around the circle where the contest would be played out. There was no favouritism; the ring of solemn men was silent, appraising the two boys as they met in the centre and embraced, then returned to their horses.

From the moment they rode at each other, through the watching circle and into the weapons arena, Urtha's heart sank a little; it was clear that his son was outclassed.

The two youths charged each other down, voices shrill, then each bent down from the saddle to scoop up a weapon: Colcu grasped a broken spear, Kymon a blunted iron sword. The first furious meeting was inconclusive, but Colcu was lithe, twisting and stooping, flicking up sharp stones, using lengths of frayed rope to snare and snag his opponent's struggling mount.

In every way, Colcu outwitted and outrode the Cornovidian youth. Though Kymon managed a savage strike, playing on Colcu's faulty use of the left-hand back-strike, Colcu at once acknowledged his weakness, covered it and compensated for it.

When the two of them faced each other on foot, the horses being tired and fleeing the arena when freed, Colcu surprised Kymon with a double leap, and though Kymon leapt back, Colcu caught his opponent's calves with a broken spear shaft. He brought the boy down, placed the shaft across his throat and knelt on it, pinning Kymon into submission.

The son of Vortingoros drew his bronze blade and made the triumphant cut along the angle of Kymon's jaw. He let Kymon up, stood facing him as Kymon made the mark upon his opponent's chin.

The chin-cut was done.

The two young men then embraced three times, solemn and silent, unbothered by the flow of blood from their skin, one of them deeply unhappy indeed.

As Kymon left the arena, passing through the silent ranks of older men, his blood flushed as he heard the spontaneous laughter of Colcu's comrades.

He made his way to the guest lodgings, where Urtha was in conference with his advisors. The king had not stayed to watch his son's humiliation, slipping away after the first few rounds of the contest. Kymon had seen this and been startled by it.

'I have a question,' Kymon said boldly to his father, though he was shaking.

Urtha glanced round at him. 'Yes?'

'Was your own chin-mark obtained in triumph, or on the losing end? I've never thought to ask this before.'

'In triumph.'

'Mine was not.'

'I know.'

'Should I feel ashamed? Angry? Humiliated? What should I feel?'

'What do you feel?'

'Angry. Warped and angry. Hugely angry. I will burst through my skin at any moment.'

The retinue laughed quietly, though they were tapping their knives on wood, a sure sign that they were not mocking the boy. Urtha turned back to the issue at hand, adding only, 'There's nothing wrong with that. I pity the stag in the hunt tomorrow night.' He glanced at his men. 'I expect you'll see Colcu's face even in its backside as it runs from us. I'd hate to be that stag.'

More gentle, appreciative laughter. Kymon retreated in confusion, slumped into a small corner of the lodge, glared for a while, then cried as softly as he could.

I did not witness the Moon Hunt. I had withdrawn by that point, attending to other matters. I heard about it from Kymon, later, and what he told me astonished me. If only I had had the wit to understand the significance of the event.

10

Moon Hunting, Oldest Animal

The sounding of bronze bells summoned the hunters. Urtha and Kymon, in the king's hall, had finished their preparations. Their faces were streaked with a dark dye and the fleeces of black sheep were tied around their shoulders. When they stepped outside, they found their horses waiting for them; the horse-handlers had replaced the metal harnessing with leather. The moon was low, and not quite full, flaring and darkening as clouds moved across her face.

Twenty men had gathered for the Moon Hunt. They formed a circle around the Speaker for the Land, who was cloaked in black crows' feathers and crouching on the ground. He seemed disturbed, as did Vortingoros, who acknowledged Urtha then returned his attention to the agonised activities of the druid.

Colcu had led his own horse to the circle and glanced briefly and sourly at Kymon, but he was now on his best behaviour. A quick, mocking touch to his scarred chin and he looked away.

The Speaker for the Land listened at the earth, then slapped his palm seven times on the dry grass. Urtha whispered a question to the hunter who stood next to him. He learned that the druid was confused as to the size and nature of the stag. The sound it made was familiar, but the way it was running was not. It was at the edge of the wood, directly towards the moon, and was moving steadily towards the fortress. But the land was not responding as it should have been to the presence of the creature. There was something not right.

The Speaker for the Land rose to his feet and addressed Vortingoros. The hunt should be abandoned, he counselled. The stag had *got wind* of the impending hunt and was gathering elemental forces to protect it. This was something he should have been able to see more clearly, but was failing in the task. Abandon the hunt.

Nonsense, was the king's reply. We have guests. The hunt may bring home a beast ten times larger or ten times smaller than expected, but the Moon Hunt would proceed.

There was some dispute about this among the king's entourage, to which Vortingoros listened with visible irritation.

The druid spread his cloak of crows' feathers on the ground and lay down upon it, to remain there in shame until the hunters returned.

'Are we going, or are we staying?' Kymon muttered impatiently. He felt his father's gentle grip upon his shoulder.

'Going, I think. Stand quietly. Don't forget we're guests.'

'I haven't forgotten how I was treated,' the boy responded grimly, eyeing Colcu. 'My spear will pierce the stag's hide before his, I promise you.'

'Make sure his spear doesn't pierce *yours* in the darkness.'

'Thank you for the advice.'

'By the breath of Hernos ... I think a decision has been made!'

Vortingoros had hauled himself onto his horse and turned for the gate. The rest of the hunt mounted, settled, and rode in some disorder down onto the plain, turning towards the moon and the far forest.

The moment they left the fortress, Kymon felt himself become detached from the rest of the hunt. The land whispered to him. The moon seemed to swell. His horse, cantering on the hard ground, became softly fluid, rocking like the wooden model on which he had played when very young. The other riders moved dreamily away from him in the darkness, spreading out to face the forest. The sounds of hooves diminished. Kymon felt enveloped. He looked for his father, but he had been drawn into distance and gloom.

This surreal sensation was abruptly snapped when Colcu rode up beside him, spear held above his head, dye-smeared face grinning.

'My cut is already healed. You should have cut deeper. Or used a sharper blade!'

He kicked away, spear now lowered, head down, riding in the direction of the moon itself. The insult – the reference to the blade – infuriated Kymon, as it had been intended to do. His first instinct was to hunt in a different direction to his tormentor, but after a moment's pause, he followed Colcu at a gallop.

As at Taurovinda, the land around the Coritani fortress had been cleared to the distance of a spear thrown five times. The edge of the wood rose like a wall, cut clean, shimmering in the three-quarter moon. The hunters now prowled along that edge.

The language of the hunt was a series of brief horn calls and owl sounds. Messages rippled along the line, confusing to Kymon – and no doubt to his father – but meaningful to the Coritani.

There was sudden movement; the line turned to the north and rode swiftly, again spreading out, but this time wheeling round abruptly and entering the forest, slouched low in the saddle, working their way between the trees. There were no hounds on this hunt, no baying, no snarling, just the crash of horses, the chatter and drone of the signals. Birds flew skywards, alarmed. Creatures snuffled and fled through the underbrush. Kymon became lost in the darkness, forcing himself to follow the sounds ahead of him. Colcu passed in front of him at one point, recognisable by the darting, bright-eyed and insulting glance, then he too was gone.

The earth shuddered, then; the sensation was of something gigantic beginning to run. The hunt turned south, through the woods, men streaming past the confused form of Kymon. Urtha recognised his son – Hernos alone knew how – and urged him to follow.

'Is it the stag?'

'It's something,' his father agreed. 'Though how it's managing to run in these woods is a mystery to me.'

Again, Kymon was lost. He could hear the sounds of the hunt all around him, but he himself had broken cover. He was not back on the plain but in a clearing. A ridge of bare land rose before him, the moon half concealed by the escarpment. The earth shook again. His horse became nervous, trying to back away from the ridge, despite Kymon's attempts to urge it on.

A flurry of startled night-wings told Kymon everything he needed to know: the earth-shaker was on the other side of the ridge, approaching.

Spear held high and ready, he waited for the rise of antlers against the moon. Instead, a horseman galloped along the ridge, stopped, turned about and reared up. Colcu raised his own spear at the oncoming beast, then cried out in alarm.

No antlers rose against the moon. The shape that loomed suddenly and hugely, small eyes sparkling, white tusks gleaming, was a boar of monstrous proportion. It charged swiftly onto the ridge and with a toss of its head had savaged the horse, throwing Colcu to the ground. The youth rolled out of the first lunging strike of those tusks, tried to fling his javelin but had no angle to make a good throw and the weapon glanced harmlessly off the great boar's flank.

The animal growled deeply in its lungs and straddled the nephew of Vortingoros, who screeched as the beast placed a foot on his chest and turned its head for the slashing kill.

Kymon shouted a nonsense word, a distracting cry, a fury sound. He kicked his horse towards the fray and flung his own javelin with all his might. The blade struck the animal in the ear, and it straightened up, furious and howling. Kymon, standing on the saddle now, leapt at the raised face, narrowly avoiding the tusks as they tried to catch him, and somersaulted onto the boar's back, his hands making the lightest of touches with the spine-sharp brow.

He turned and pushed his sword into the tender flesh behind the creature's ear, his legs wrapped around the neck, his left hand gripping the razor-edged tusk. As the blade sawed and sank, so the boar shook and screamed, then was very still.

It growled again. There was pain in the sound.

'Not the ear! Take the blade out!' it said, its voice a deep rumble of pleading. 'Not the ear. It hurts too much.'

Startled, Kymon released his grip, and in that instant was shaken to the ground. As he sprawled, so the animal leapt upon him, leaning down to push its earth-stinking mouth close to the boy's face. Kymon's heart raced and he cried out to Avernus, thinking he was about to die, asking for a good walk to Ghostland.

But the killing blow never came. The boar suddenly rose onto its hind legs, a massive silhouette against the gleaming moon. With human hands it plucked the javelin from its cheek, looked at it, made to snap it in two, then changed its mind, tossing the weapon onto the earth. Bright eyes regarded Kymon. The beast's belly grumbled.

'That was a fine leap and a good throw,' the boar said. 'I'll be in pain until this time tomorrow. Perhaps longer.'

'What are you?' Kymon asked nervously, getting carefully to his feet. 'Man or boar?'

'I am *Urskumug*. I am both. Old animal. One of the many. Something has woken us and we are looking around. Freedom is a luxury that doesn't last for us. A good leap. A good cast.' The towering form again stepped closer to Kymon. Rank breath and fear made the boy recoil. He stepped back until he came up against a tree and felt frozen there. The boar's nostrils flared, the brow furrowed. The face of the creature was almost human, marked out by chalk, the sketch of a man on the face of a beast.

Urskumug said, 'You stink of possession. Inhabited. There is more in you than just boy. You are dangerous. Killing you would make my life easier. But so would making you a promise. Which do you prefer?'

Pinned against the tree, Kymon had no hesitation in answering, 'The promise.'

'I can't promise much, but say my name in any of my sanctuaries and I'll growl at you. I don't have many, but they're well concealed.'

'What good is there in growling?'

'What good is there in leaping?' Urskumug retorted, rubbing his bloody ear. Then Urskumug raised his snout and sniffed the air hard. 'Sour scent. The scent of other lands. Do you smell it? There is something extraordinary in this blighted land. Something at large. Oldest animals waking up. Old ghosts too. Something shaping. Be careful.'

The beast turned away, dropped back on all fours, growled, tusked the earth and was gone.

A while later, a horse whinnied with a moment's pain, and died, released from the agony of disembowelment. The sound snapped Kymon from his daze. At the bottom of the ridge, Colcu rose from the grim task, cleaning his blade and murmuring an invocation to Rhiannon, gatherer of battle horses. Then he walked over to the tree and faced Kymon squarely.

'I was not frightened of you in the combat ring, and I was not in awe of you. I am not frightened of you now. But I *am* in awe of you. That creature could have killed us both. I am alive because of your well-thrown spear and that fine leap. You are alive because the beast spared you. I understand very little of what has happened ... Kymon.'

'Neither do I. Colcu.'

'Then again, understanding is for druids. Action is for the rest of us. I have twenty good horse-riders, all of my age, all well-experienced with the feats. I will bring them to your father. I lead them. Do you understand? You can join us if you wish. But I lead them.'

'That is an acceptable condition,' Kymon said in the formal manner.

Colcu hesitated, meeting the other's gaze hard. 'That creature … it said you were possessed.'

'I know.'

'What did it mean, do you think?'

'I don't know.'

'Do you feel possessed?'

Kymon looked up at the ridge, then towards the darkness of the woodland where Urskumug had disappeared. After a moment he answered: 'I don't know.'

The talk was uneasy. Colcu smiled for the first time without the expression being a mocking one. 'No wonder our poor Speaker for the Land was so confused,' he said. 'I think we should call to the rest of the hunt. Call it off. It was the wrong moon.'

'I agree.'

Colcu was not quite finished. There was sweat on his face and apprehension in his eyes. He said, 'I will be High King when my uncle, Vortingoros, passes on. I have sown the land with charms to make sure this happens. Will you be High King when your father crosses the river?'

'I expect so. But in due course. Not yet. And I have no charms to sow.'

'Your accession is safer. You are a son, not a nephew. Will we be friends, I wonder? Or enemies? What does the possessed man think?'

Colcu was a powerful, subduing presence. Though Kymon had not been in fear of this older boy in the combat ring, he was anxious now. There was a sudden deadness in Colcu, the insensate staring of a beast. Kymon chose to respond as he imagined his father would respond to such a challenge. 'Friends now,' he said in an even tone. 'That is certainly the case. In the future? I don't know. I don't know.'

'That is an acceptable answer,' Colcu said quietly. And in the formal way.

11

Oestranna's Child

At the same time that Kymon was encountering the man-boar, his sister Munda was undergoing a transformation of her own.

Her own new blood on her hands, a strange fury of excitement glowing from her, she escaped from the women's lodge and ran to the high wall of the fortress, climbed the ladder and stood there, staring out towards the west. She was wearing only the woman's robe that had been given to her, her first, not to be her last. The two women who had been guarding her ran behind, but were too slow to catch the fleet-footed child. Though they summoned her back, Munda ignored them. She was in a state of despair, it seemed.

The moon was low; a three-quarter moon. The west was dark, Ghostland seemingly asleep, though everyone in Taurovinda knew better.

The two guardians were intercepted by the High Woman, Rianata, also known as the Thoughtful Woman.

'Leave her alone.'

'She is in our charge.'

'Leave her alone,' Rianata insisted. 'She has the light of foresight. It will either stay with her or slip away. This is either a dying or a growing time for the king's daughter.'

Munda screamed and wailed from the wall.

'I see it dark,

'I see it drowning.

'I see it moonless and with winter eyes.

'I see the night-surge of the dead.

'My brother opposes this gathering of old land, old life.'

Then, with an almost childish tone of voice, she called, 'But I can still see! I can still see!'

She had spread her arms wide, as if welcoming everything she could envision in the darkness.

She cried out then; with pain, with fear. After a time she came down from the ramparts and huddled into Rianata's maternal embrace.

'My brother will destroy us,' she whispered. 'He will act to stop them coming. I must stop him acting. Somehow I must stop him.'

She saw me, then, standing in the shadows, and brightened up. She ran to me and hugged me around the waist. Almost at once she realised the state she was in and stepped back sheepishly, holding her bloody hands out as if they were dead rats.

'I'm Oestranna's child, now. I'll be like this for a long time.'

'Yes. You will.'

'Life will form in me. Raw, rough life.'

'It will.'

'But I can still *see*, Merlin,' she whispered delightedly. 'Most of the women thought the sight would have gone. The farsight. The light itself. Even Rianata. Will I have it for ever, I wonder?'

'Come with me,' I suggested. 'To the well. You can clean your hands there and I'll show you something.'

The three women who guarded the well looked up as we approached. Their initial outrage at the uninvited intrusion subsided as they saw my companion. They each sat by a torch, which illuminated both their pale faces and the deeper gleam of the water. Niiv was not with them – up to her own form of mischief, no doubt.

When Munda was clean, which is to say, as clean as decorum and company would allow, I made her look down at the shimmering surface.

'What can you see there? In the deep.'

She peered hard, but shook her head. 'Nothing. What *is* there to be seen?' Then she added, glancing up at me, 'What can *you* see?'

'An old friend,' I told her. 'Quite a few things, in fact, not just the old friend. There's a world down there, an amazing place, spreading out through the streams below the land, all leading to and from the Winding One. Your dear Nantosuelta.'

Again, Munda stared hard, leaning out so far across the stone wall around the well that there was a murmur of warning from one of the three.

'Nothing,' the girl repeated in frustration. 'What point are you making, beyond that you've got the eyes of both a hawk and a fish?' The three women laughed at that.

'When she first looked down, Niiv, who has a great many strengths in charm and enchantment, could see a great deal too. Not as much as me, but a great deal. Now she can't, not unless she expends a great deal of her energy.'

'You're saying it will fade, then. The sight will fade.'

'I'm saying that it *might*. It might not. I'm saying that it is a talent to be used wisely, a gift and a commodity not to be squandered. Act as if it might cease at any moment! In the time that I've been in Alba, I've learned that it is rare for there to be *two* women with the *imbas forasnai*. As has been happening to me for a *very* long time, the gift wanes with usage.'

Munda looked at me with mischief in her eyes. 'Everybody says you're very mean with your gifts.'

'Been saying so for centuries.'

'You could make my father High King of High Kings if you wanted to.'

'I couldn't. That's the truth. And even if I could, I wouldn't. And Urtha wouldn't want it either. Don't listen to the teasing talk of Urtha's *uthiin*. They're bigger mischief-makers than Niiv. Or you, for that matter.'

Then she asked me quickly, 'Who's the old friend down there?' The question was so sudden I hadn't expected it, and I had answered before considering the wisdom of answering. 'Argo.'

'Argo? That beautiful ship?' The thought delighted her. Once more she searched the deep well for a sign of the mast, the deck, the oars, anything, but drew back disappointed.

'What exactly can she be doing down there, I wonder?'

I led the girl away from the careful listening of the three women at the well. Munda went on quietly, 'Right down there? Immediately below us?'

'No. Hiding somewhere along the waterways. She's angry and upset about something. I think she's gathering her wits about her – as much as a ship can gather her wits.'

The girl slapped her hands together three times, thinking hard. 'To sail back all this way, just to hide. She has a secret. A *bad* secret.'

'I think you're right.'

'Are you going to tell my father?'

'I'll have to, now that I've blurted it out in front of those women. But not until I've found Argo herself, and asked her some questions.'

'I'll keep quiet too. On my sight!' she added with a mischievous smile.

'Thank you.'

Transformation was in the air, a potent presence, invisible, intangible but unmistakeable. Its source was not confined to the west. The whole of Taurovinda was enveloped by it, and yet all remained normal in the fortress. At dawn, dogs and cockerels made their sounds. The furnaces started to puff and wheeze, the hammering of iron ringing through the hill at first light, unearthly bells, striking in disordered fashion.

Around the hill, the plain shifted and heaved, stretched away from the fort, then narrowed again. Or was that just an illusion of the growing light of dawn? The dark forest to the east seemed closer than was usual, but as the sun brightened and the green began to show, so it could be seen to be in its rightful place.

I had spent the night in the eastern watchtower, brooding over Munda's words:

My brother will destroy us.

What had she meant by that? What had she seen?

I see it dark, I see it drowning.

My brother is opposed to this.

He will act to stop them. I must stop him acting.

I could not fathom those words and no insight could allow me to experience what *she* had experienced. That she argued with her brother was undeniable. That they were moving along different paths was quite obvious. But why *destroy*?

When the two of them had returned, frantic and bemused, from the far west after their encounter at the Hostel of the Red Shield Riders, it had been *Munda* who declared that Ghostland was not threatening her father's country. Kymon had been angry, fearful of the risk. But he had helped to drive them back once, and he would do it again. That much was clear from his posturing. Taurovinda was his and his alone to inherit. He was arrogant, proud, and at great risk to himself, of course, but the attitude was there, if not the strength in terms of numbers of defenders. He had no intention of destroying his stronghold.

I was distracted by the sound of riders below, and the call to open the eastern gate. Looking down I saw Munda and two spearmen for guards, riding out of the fortress. She must have known I was in the tower since she glanced up and gave me a half-smile.

She too was transformed. Her hair was braided in the complex way that I had seen worn by her late mother, Aylamunda, when I had helped bring the shade of that great woman back from the underworld, a long time ago now. And the girl wore her mother's riding clothes, shortened and tightened to fit the smaller, thinner frame: trousers and split-sided tunic of bright green, richly embroidered at the edges, and a short, dark-red cloak, pinned at shoulder and waist. Her guards carried a clutch of short spears, and their oval shields were slung on their backs. They were looking unhappy, exchanging anxious glances as they followed Munda down the road, through the lower gate and out onto the plain. Here, they turned along the hidden track, towards the evergroves.

What was going on?

I was tempted to send a hawk to sit on her shoulder and peck at her thoughts, but instead I slipped and slid down the tower's ladder and made my way through the clusters of houses to the centre of the hill, where the orchards, sanctuaries and the sacred well were concealed behind their high walls. Just as I started to skirt to the north, so Rianata came running round to the south, saw me and shouted across the distance.

'Merlin! The girl has gone moon-sick. She's endangering her life!'

Rianata told me that Munda planned to enter the evergroves and bathe in the river. 'She said she dreamed the need to do it. A "water-whisper" will tell her how to defend Taurovinda against her brother. What does this mean, Merlin? What has got into her?'

'Your guess? As good as my guess.'

Though this was not strictly true. Water whisper?

Water *whisperer*, more likely.

Cathabach, the Speaker for Kings, was not pleased when I found him and told him that the king's daughter was again about to break taboo.

'The little fool!'

He fetched his cloak and a staff of twisted rowan, made fiercer with thin blades of flint at its striking end. There were many times when Cathabach eschewed metal for the incorruptibility of stone. Our horses were brought to us and we rode in pursuit of the reckless girl, intending to stop her. But we were too late. We met the horsemen who had accompanied her at the edge of the groves. Forbidden to enter, they found themselves unable to stop Munda. She had ridden into the trees and disappeared behind the lines of deeply incised grey stones that rose within the woodland. They were anxious and upset, but Cathabach ignored them.

'Wait for us,' I said, and they dismounted, watching as I followed the druid.

To enter the evergroves was to pass from the harsh, wind-bitten reality of the present into a sanctuary that almost shimmered with past and future. For someone like me, attuned to Time should I allow myself to stop and listen, the voices of the long-gone and the long-to-come echoed and wailed, distant cries, faint chatter, the laughter and pain of many ages, blowing through this place of stones and silent thorns and oaks, many of which had been growing here, unchanging, elemental despite their solid appearance, for many millennia.

I loved the evergroves. I was used to such sanctuaries, touching, as they did, the reaches of both kronos and kthon, Time and the Deep. They were indeed my 'touching' places, and one day it would be through just such a wooded circle as this that I would re-explore my origins.

For the moment, though, I heard briefly a familiar and comforting song from the more ancient of my days and passed on to the river, where, too late, we tried to stop Munda from entering Nantosuelta, the river that flowed from Ghostland, and in whose waters she would be in danger.

She had cast off her clothes and was swimming like a fish, darting down into the depths, almost singing with delight as she surfaced, eyes closed, head thrown back.

I called to her to come ashore.

'Oh Merlin, Merlin!' she called back, 'if you could only hear what I can hear!'

'Come ashore!'

She plunged again, kicking deeply, disappearing for a breathtakingly long time. When she reappeared it was so far upriver, towards Ghostland, that Cathabach and I were astonished. She must have swum like an eel to go such a distance. The flow brought her back to us, a pale form, floating gently in the middle of the stream.

'Come *ashore*!' I urged again.

'There is no threat from them, Merlin. We have been mistaken.

She assures me we are mistaken. We have misunderstood everything about the hostels and what is happening there. Something wonderful is about to happen, Merlin. Something bright. The future is so bright.'

She was certainly being seduced. But by whom?

Before I could call for a third time, Munda had again plunged down. Cathabach and I watched anxiously upriver, but the girl had swum to the bank behind us, crept to her clothes and dressed. She was teasing us, laughing as she caught us by surprise, standing, hair dripping with river water, smiling as she squeezed it from her braids, breathing hard.

'Will you punish me, Cathabach?'

'This place is forbidden to you, unless access is granted, and only a Speaker can grant it.'

'I know. I entered the evergroves with you when Taurovinda was in the hands of the Dead.'

'I remember,' the Speaker for Kings said. 'You and your brother rode to the gates and challenged the occupying force. You nearly died for your efforts. You were reckless then, you are reckless now.'

'Reckless then, reckless now, but successful on both occasions. You are my father's friend, Cathabach. You must persuade him that we have been wrong about the Dead and the Unborn. They are looking for nothing other than to be our allies in the land, to share the land, not to possess it.'

I exchanged a glance with Cathabach. The look said it all. Possession? It's the girl that is possessed.

A voice had whispered to her, changed her, occupied her reason and twisted her vision. Though the Unborn, those waiting to cross the river into new life, were neither friend nor enemy, nothing that the country of the Cornovidi had experienced in the last many generations suggested anything other than that the Dead were most emphatically at war with their human neighbours.

Munda smiled thinly as she saw our expressions. 'Merlin,' she said quietly. 'You and I should talk about this. You know so much. But you don't know everything.'

It was a confident, authoritative suggestion, and she turned from us quickly and left the evergroves.

*

Transformation. In the air.

It was a cold embrace, a sinister caress. I was not alone in feeling it. The hounds and horses were agitated and unhappy. The children in Taurovinda, who earlier had fought and frolicked in their own simple festival of flowers and masks, were subdued now. They kept to their houses; the younger ones cried frequently. The joy had gone from them, and was replaced by apprehension.

The otherworldly storm clouds returned; the wind was cool and restless. At dusk, the sun slid into the Realm of the Shadows of Heroes, holding still for a while, a fire without flame, glowing and glowering.

Munda declined the invitation to wait until her father's return before facing the Speakers. A Council of Speakers was convened the following day, in the shrine sanctuary of Nodons, inside the central orchard of Taurovinda. It was the first time Munda had stepped inside the high wicker walls around the plantation and she was apprehensive and alert, but quite determined. She was clad in a simple dress and short, plain cloak, a braided belt around her waist and her precious golden relic – moon sign in sun metal – round her neck.

The shrine of Nodons was a simple thatched building, stone-walled, with wide windows. There was no altar. What few sacrifices were made here were placed in a covered pit before the niches where the images of the gods were placed, to rot down or to give off the charred odours of their burning.

Four niches in the wall were aligned next to that of the bearded Nodons himself, who peered out through narrowed, sinister eyes at the assembly in the small space. To his right was the wooden figure of Nantosuelta, her hands clutching the small house with which she was associated, her hair carved to represent the river. She seemed benign. On Nodons' left was her consort Sucellus, a brooding figure, shaped roughly from oak, holding a mallet and a small bowl, the blood bowl from which he could draw life or return it. He was known as the Good Striker. Only Nantosuelta was decked with flowers, small purple columbine around her neck, twisted ivy around her body to symbolise waterweed.

As I sat in the shadows of the sanctuary, I noticed that the small house she held was very like the hostels that had appeared along the river; it made sense to me: Nantosuelta was part of both worlds, a 'watcher' of hearth and home, and gateway to the land of spectres.

Was it this goddess, this spirit who had been whispering to Munda?

The girl underwent a brief interrogation by the three Speakers, a protocol called by an old name and which meant *the justice of the law of taboo*. It was a tedious process, reflective of many such inquisitions where those who mediate between the world of flesh and the world beyond use their frail insight, sometimes their sharp and luminous dreaming, to establish a truth. Each Speaker had a small wicker cage before him containing a wren. As the girl spoke, so the men watched the darting, hopping movements of the birds. Munda spoke easily and without fear. It surprised me slightly to learn that she had felt compelled to pass through the evergroves by the presence, in her sleep, of her grandmother, Riamunda, buried within the stones. A silver owl with hazel wings had called to her, the spectre of the woman. Munda had taken the presence of the night bird as a sign that all was well, and that she was safe.

No, it was not the river that had whispered to her as she'd swum, but someone whose voice was carried by the stream. Nantosuelta was merely the messenger, but the message was clear to her.

Taurovinda was not in danger from Ghostland; the two worlds should unite, and this should be done when the king was back and in his proper place, within the walls.

At the end of the interrogation, all three druids were profoundly disturbed by what the girl had said to them. They remained in Nodons' sanctuary to engage in the *wren talk*, which would involve the sacrifice of the birds and an inspection of their innards. Knowing Cathabach as I did, a practical and sober-headed man who had been a champion warrior and member of Urtha's *uthiin* for nineteen years before returning to the priesthood, I found it hard to equate the gritty realist with this bird-augury. Nothing could be read in the splayed guts of a wren!

Then again, across the world, all around the Path I walked, the supernatural in nature could be seen to work and be effective when conditions and the minds of priests and enchanters were fully attuned – albeit to a tiny extent – to the shifting edge of the underworld.

Munda's small but vibrant skill was deluding her now. I lost her for a while, then discovered her at the western end of the hill. She had instructed the daubing of symbols in red ochre on the three tall gates. Her work was being carried out with puzzled amusement, though the Thoughtful Woman, Rianata, was not amused at all as she watched from a distance.

'Is she aware that red is the colour of the dead? She must be. She is painting signs of welcome. And what is she building?'

Some way from the inner gate, straddling the rough road that led to the centre of Taurovinda, Munda was herself helping to construct a rickety hut. Five men were doing the heavy work. Two of Urtha's champions watched curiously, leaning on their shields. No one knew whether she had the right to do this, nor could they understand the reason. The structure was so flimsy that a brisk breeze would blow it down, so any sense of disobedience to the laws of the fortress were easily dismissed.

It was only as I wandered across to the busy girl – busy binding poles together to make angled supports for the roof – that I realised she was making a model of one of the hostels by the river. It would have a double entrance, the central pillar already crudely painted to suggest the form of a woman, her arms outstretched and resting on thin pillars of elm, stripped of their bark and ready to be patterned as animals.

'What is this for?'

'It's a place of welcome. For the representatives of Ghostland.'

'It's small. Not many representatives could fit inside.'

'They won't have to stay here. This is just the welcoming place.' She looked up at me and smiled.

'I can't imagine that your father will welcome them. Have you forgotten Urien? It was the Shadows of Heroes who killed him.'

'I haven't forgotten Urien – of course I haven't. But don't you understand, Merlin? The mood has changed. I've seen it and I've heard it. The voice is urgent. We must not be alarmed by what is happening at the river. We must prepare for a great event. A union between worlds. And my father's country will become a greater country than all the others put together.'

She bustled and busied herself with her toy. The words that came from her lips were spoken in her voice, but they were not her words. Everything to the west was still, but the skies streamed towards us, silently, without breeze or gusting wind, a storm seen in the still surface of a pool.

I watched her and wondered. Curiosity got the better of me and I summoned a little charm, glancing into the girl as she concentrated on what she was doing.

Innocence and pre-occupation were all I saw for a moment, but then – as I risked probing a little deeper – an older presence loomed before me, barring the way, a storm-shrouded figure of power and life-draining fury. I was shocked and drew back quickly, but not before I had caught a glimpse of the flash of eyes – fierce eyes, angry eyes.

It was only later that I realised I had glimpsed not an old enemy, but an old friend. And it was time to see her.

Niiv helped me pack supplies. She had been persuaded to stay behind and help look after Munda. 'She needs a knowing eye on her,' was my way of stopping my vivacious lover from insisting on accompanying me.

The encounter I was facing was one I wished to make on my own.

As usual, I begged two good horses from the small herd of travel ponies. I selected animals that would be adept at negotiating forest and marsh. Fighting horses were no good for that. And then I left Taurovinda, Munda watching me with hawk's eyes from one of the gate towers, Niiv, on the walkway of another, making the usual motions of a swan in flight. She had put on her cloak of white feathers, and as I left at dawn, so the rising sun transformed her into a slowly moving bird, waving to me, calling to me. My swan girl.

I rode north and east, and entered the forest. After a few days, I recognised that I was leaving the tribal lands of the Cornovidi. The markings on the trees, and the patterns on the tall stones, began to change. I was close to Nantosuelta, but Argo was hiding from me.

She sent her emissary to fetch me, a *fetch* himself, a living spirit. He didn't speak, he didn't acknowledge me; he appeared suddenly at the other side of a glade and beckoned to me.

I didn't hesitate. I followed my old friend Jason, knowing that he would lead me to where I wished to go.

12

So Old, So Beautiful a Ship

Argo had hidden herself in a little patch of late summer. She was nestling in a creek, among thick rushes and dense willows. The air was misty and warm, the sounds those of very early morning, combining a certain restlessness, a certain stillness.

Jason's dark form loomed ahead of me as he wound along a hidden track, keeping close to the river's edge, his feet sinking in mud. Two black-crested cranes flew up before us, alarmed, and winged their way into the gloom of the wider river. Then I saw Argo for the first time, just the eyes painted on her prow. They seemed to watch me forlornly as I approached, pushing the tall rushes aside.

Jason glanced at me before he walked away from the ship. As I watched him disappear, so I saw the imposing shape of my old friend and fellow argonaut Rubobostes, a Dacian of girth and strength, but a man who now stared at me, half-hidden by the high grasses, with an expression of blank ignorance as to my nature. He looked gaunt, eyes rimmed and dark, beard and hair no longer the lustrous black of our first meeting, our first adventure, but grizzled and unkempt. He slowly sank down to a crouch, wrapped in his heavy cloak.

When I raised my hand towards him, he made no response.

I was consumed by the atmosphere of desolation and despair. What had happened to the bright ship, this beautiful ship of other years, the vibrant shell of oak and birch that had sailed over seas and along the narrowest of streams, even crawling over the land between the headwaters of rivers, shimmering with magic, set apart from ordinary eyes, transformed according to older laws of nature? And what had happened to her crew?

Argo was listing slightly towards the bank. A rope ladder dangled from her rail. The once-vivid decorations along her hull, the symbolic echoes of her past – medusae, harpies, cyclopes, other, stranger creatures – were faded, as frail to the eye as was the ship's life-spirit to the senses.

'May I come aboard?' I whispered, my words almost lost in the susurration of the rushes.

For a moment there was silence. Then the ship's guardian goddess, Mielikki, Northland's Lady, answered: 'This is a sad ship, Merlin. This is a damaged ship. This is a ship in shame. But, yes. You may come aboard.'

I swung up the rope ladder. Argo shifted slightly with my weight. Everything about her felt precarious. When I peered over the low rail, I saw the fierce features of the Northland's Lady at the stern, the goddess of the ever-winter or ever-summer of the north, of Pohjola – where Niiv had been spawned. The Pohjolon forest spirit stared hard at me through slanting, trickster eyes, a birch-carved figurehead that leered towards me. The flowing locks of her hair, intricately patterned by the people who had constructed her, were tangled with ivy, draped with the bright yellow fronds of willow. She, and the ship, were both being drawn back to the wood.

The bilges stank of stagnant water and rotting food. Barrels, ropes, bales of cloth and the bones of animals were scattered, as if she had been wrecked against this fronded bank, not moored here.

Argo, my precious ship, my precious friend, was in a very sorry shape.

I waded through the filth on her lower deck and approached the narrowing of the stern, where I knew the 'Spirit of the Ship' was hidden. Mielikki – 'birch and bitch' as Rubobostes called her – loomed above me. I heard the slightest sound of creaking wood as she angled her head to keep an eye on me, but she knew that I was no threat to Argo; and besides, she was as fond of me as it was possible for the Northland's Lady to be fond of anyone. Cold-hearted she may have been in her homeland, among the frozen forests, amid the snow wastes, by the deep, icy lakes, but she – like Argo, her mistress – favoured the captains, whether old or new.

I had been Argo's first captain.

Something told me – an intuition, nothing at all to do with enchantment – that Argo needed me, now; that I was a guest she had craved for, but had been reluctant to summon.

The Spirit of the Ship is a threshold between the world of the lower deck and a world out of time, an all-world, a place where all seas are being sailed, all shores raided, all sanctuaries violated or acknowledged, all summers the same, though the celebration of summer is a different feast in different worlds. I stepped across the threshold and into a swirl of ship's memory.

Mielikki, now in her gauzy veil and clothing, was standing among summer trees; in her youthful guise, slender and serene, she raised a hand to me in greeting. The sinister trickster was gone. The pricked-eared lynx that was her companion crouched in front of her, eyes wide and watching, fur hackled along its spine.

Mielikki beckoned me forward. I stepped deeper into Argo's spirit, and:

A wave broke across the bow, throwing the crude ship towards the rocks.

The sky glowered, the wind howled, the cold sea raged at us. Ropes flailed, planks creaked, the tarred knots that bound this simple craft together screeched as the strain tore at them. The small sail was shredded. A few oars had not been smashed against the rocks in this narrow passage, and they heaved against the swell, while the captain and another man hung onto the steering oar with all their might. This was not Jason; this was not his Argo as I had known her. This was an older ship, on an adventure that was part of the ship's memory, not mine. The captain, hailed by one of his men, was Acrathonas; the name was familiar. An adventurer of the highest calibre, a Jason before Jason.

In this sea-dream, I saw the white shapes of creatures in the cliffs; creatures in the form of bones, creatures of enormous size. This was the sea-passage of Petros, and I knew now where Argo was going, though why she was dreaming this particular storm was not clear to me.

Through Argo's eyes I saw those bones take on flesh, then colour, the iridescent greens and reds of sea monsters; they bulged from the high stone walls, slipped and slithered into the ocean, and began to snap and tear at Argo with impossible jaws, staring at their prey with lifeless, unblinking eyes.

Harpoons were slung and hauled back. Men were whipped overboard, snatched in the toothed jaws of the leviathans and dragged, bloodily, into the roiling sea.

Only when an immense, lizard-like head rose above the ocean behind Argo, a head the size of a house, eyes the size of a giant's shield, did the ship begin its long, sea-slide to safety, running from the skeletal jaws of fate, borne forward by the sea wave that resulted from the rising of that behemoth.

A new sail was hauled quickly to the mast head, and the west wind, amused by the narrow escape, blew a gust in favour of the flimsy craft, which leaned dangerously close to a capsize, but turned to grab that saving breath and ploughed with the storm, towards the east, towards an island, a strange and mysterious stretch of mountainous land, that I would one day come to know well. Acrathonas, like Jason after, would pillage that island, though I knew this from tale-telling alone.

I had had no time to try and understand the significance of Argo sharing this fragment of dream with me – and there was surely a significance in the act. Argo, for all that a human heart seemed to reside in her, was not given to senseless nostalgia. Shortly after, I was back with the ship in the world of the present.

The woodland shimmered; the cave mouth behind me in the crumbling façade of rock, formed from petrified wood, blew gently. The tall grass that separated cave from woodland blew in that breeze. The lynx prowled restlessly and Mielikki drifted towards me, eyes bright behind the thin white veil, mouth solemn.

When she embraced me, I was consumed by her, but we seemed to fall slightly, and though I was grasped by a woman's arms, I was embraced by the sea-racked wood of Argo's staunch hull.

I smelled salt-breeze and bitumen, rotting rope and hewn wood.

The Spirit of the Ship, the old sentience, spoke to me through her guardian.

'She is ashamed and frightened, Merlin. She was responsible for a great betrayal in her past, and the shadow of Nemesis is close. This ship is more than wood and rigging ...'

'I know. Why remind me? I built her!'

'You built her out of innocence, and set her loose on the world's waters with pride. As you grew to become a man, slowly, over many ages, so Argo grew to become the fine ship that Jason sailed. A snake sheds skins to grow; Argo shed wood. Shipwrights and builders have taken the craft and re-shaped her across the years. She is stronger, faster, sleeker and trickier than the coracle that you constructed, but that infant's heart, the sliver of oak, remains embedded.'

I was puzzled. I knew well enough that Argo contained a splinter of every vessel she had been, a fragment of the heart of every captain who had directed her course along rivers or across the oceans. And I was aware that my childish efforts in boat-building, under the watchful eye of ten masked figures, ten thousand years before, or more, had been the beginning of this sea-going life-form, this world upon the waves.

Why was she going to such lengths to remind me?

Sadness and anxiety were a rich taste in my dry mouth, as I let Mielikki pass on the feelings and the dreams of the vessel.

And I was suddenly in the world of my childhood, and all about me was the roar of water.

It was a moment of exhilaration, a flash of memory so powerful, so real, that it stunned me. This revisit was not of my own doing. It was Argo, spending her own life-force to send me back, to give me a glimpse of the moment when I had put enchantment and life into the boat.

I was waist-deep in the wide pool, below the high rocky overhangs of the sanctuary, watching the water fall in cascades on two sides. The pool boiled where the fall struck the surface. The sky above was a brilliant circle of azure, framed by the arms of summer trees. Where the pool was not framed by the silver cascades, the undergrowth was a tight mass of wood and fern, and ten faces watched me as I marked my creation.

Ten *rajathuks*, my guardians, my inspiration, all waiting for me to finalise the building of my boat.

I painted eyes on the round craft; Silvering: the eyes of a fish, to take her up rivers safely; Falkenna: the eyes of a hawk, because I wished the boat to *fly* across the water; Cunhaval the hound, because she would nose her way into hidden lands and secret waters.

My *Voyager* was also made under the watchful gaze of *Skogen*, the shadow of forests, and I had been inspired by *Sinisalo*: the child in the land. I had summoned *Gaberlungi* to put adventure into the craft, great stories, a fate of adventure waiting for her. And the greatest of the *rajathuks*, Hollower, set a charm on the vessel that would allow her to move through unseen rivers, and to go deep into the world, downwards into the earth itself, to become a craft of many realms.

For myself, I carved a small image of a man out of wood, my own captain, and hid the crude figure behind one of the wicker struts.

I remembered clambering aboard and taking up the paddle, turning several times, laughing as I fought to get control of the skin-covered frame. Then the deep current reached up a hand and tugged me, drawing me away from the pool, over the shallows and into the stream that wound away from my valley.

As I spun one last time, still unsure of the balance of the vessel, I saw that seven of the rajathuks had vanished. Three remained, their bark masks long and mournful, watching me through narrowed eyes.

'You were not necessary!' I called to them. 'I'll come back when I need you.'

Lament was the first to withdraw, then Moondream. Last of all, the skull-mask of Morndun: the ghost in the land.

'I don't need you,' I called again, but now, looking back, I felt that moment of uncertainty.

You must mark your boat with all the masks. That way, protection will be with you always.

My mother's words. The words of all the mothers who were saying farewell to their children. Did the others obey, I wondered now? Did the others find a way to bring sorrow, the moon and death into their vessels?

You were not necessary. I'll come back when I need you ...

Arrogance! Pure arrogance. And yet I had meant the words genuinely. I could not see the point of Death and Lamentation at this early time, let alone the Dreaming of the Moon, but I had not intended to dismiss their importance. I was full of life, and my spinning coracle had a life of its own, and was testing me severely as I struggled to control her, the river gripping the hollow craft, the overhanging willow and alder branches acting like flails as I picked up speed, plunging into the embrace of their fronds, pushing away from the mud, laughing as the land took me, as I was carried away from my home, to begin my life on the Path.

How could I have known that I was fated to lose the vessel, wandering aimlessly for years before finding the Path and taking to my new life on foot and the backs of whatever animals could support me? I was unprepared.

The intensity of the memory passed away, and again I was in the Spirit of the Ship, smelling summer and North Land's winter mixed together, the warm, still presence of the Lady of the northern forests both a comforting and disconcerting presence beside me. Her lynx was purring, but ever attentive, ever alert.

But though the stark visual images faded, an echo of despair and fear remained, constructed perhaps by my own mind, a mind inadvertently and unwelcomely opened to its origins.

I had never been able to control that simple boat, that bowl in wicker, oak and leather that had run the rivers despite my efforts, and obeyed me only in the still waters of the shallows and pools that we encountered on our journey.

A storm had struck, a winter nightmare, ice blowing in the air, leafless trees showing that they were anything but lifeless as they thrashed the river, reached to grab my frightened, freezing form in its vulnerable, spinning bowl.

I heaved to the shore and tethered the coracle, crouching in the lee of an overhang, crying, huddled, watching a dark wall of snow approach on the wind from the west, always trying to see through the darkness, back to the north, where my mother's fire burned in the valley that was my home, and my father's paintings, deep in the womb of the gorge, would be as fresh and vibrant as the day he had made them, before he himself had entered the earth, along the winding guts of that other mother, never to return.

The snow began to swirl, innocent and gentle at first, then like insects, frozen insects, creatures from story-lore, the memories of the older people who had explored the land around our valley.

The little vessel was bobbing violently on the river. I had not tied it with a knot, merely wound the tether round a trunk and wedged the free end into the split between two branches. She would not hold against the storm.

Now I struggled with the laces on my boots, but my fingers were clumsy, the leather strings slipped and coiled away from me. In frustration I began to cry; then my fingers were so numbed that I gave up the effort and lay back, my cloak over my face, my tears turning from desperation to anger, from loneliness to fear.

I heard the movement close to me and froze, thinking that an animal was nosing towards me. Then – the gentle fumbling of knowing hands at my skin boots; deft fingers laced me up, tugged the leather tight. I uncovered my face and looked down, and saw a cowled shape, a small shape, and when the cowl was lifted, two fierce and wonderful eyes met my gaze.

And a smile that mocked as well as welcomed.

'You really should have paid more attention,' Fierce Eyes said.

'I cannot tie knots. I can *not* tie knots. I will not be ashamed of the fact. I will fashion shoes that don't need them.'

She snuggled up to me, drawing her cloak tightly around her body, but reaching quickly to squeeze my hand. The snow raged at us, settling on our noses.

'I didn't expect this,' she said.

'Neither did I. What are you doing here?'

'What are you?'

'I drew the boat to shore. The river is too high.'

'I lost mine. It turned over and threw me into the water. I tried to hold her, but she was taken from me. So now I walk.'

I looked at the small boat and thought of trying to row it with two of us, but the thought was not sustained. Our lives had been suddenly taken away from us; everything we had known was now gone. Fierce Eyes and I were not the only ones. There were others. I had begun to forget about them. I had begun to forget about this girl, who had teased and tormented me, loved me and amused me for so many years, the slow years in the valley, when time passed around us, but not within us. That long, playful and challenging childhood that filled our heads with dreams of what was to come, and carved powers as yet untested on the bones that cranked and worked our cold, pale bodies.

Her presence here was like the best of gifts, and I leaned into her warmth. Again our fingers entwined. I felt her shaking. I thought she was nervous of this tentative touch, but after a moment I realised she was crying, and I remained silent, stiff ... still touching.

Then the bough broke!

The winter alder cracked along its central trunk, and my ineffective tethering began to unravel.

'My boat!' I yelled, scrambling to my feet. Fierce Eyes saw the problem, and as I flung myself towards the unwinding rope, she slipped down the bank to try and hold the coracle itself.

She screamed and tumbled, shocking me for a moment. In that instant the rope withdrew from the tree, like a snake slithering effortlessly into its hole in the grassland. Fierce Eyes had plunged into the river. Her head was under the water, her hand above it. Through the snow it was hard to see what was happening, but the coracle spun suddenly into the middle of the water, winding the tether around itself. I saw my friend's hand grab the end of the rope, then rise like a nymph from the depths, soaked and shrieking. She grasped the edge of the vessel and clung onto it, turning a pale, terrified face towards me as the river, the storm, the night and unseen hands drew her away from me again, allowing distance and snow-battered darkness to take her, leaving me with nothing but her cry on the wind, a cry that might have been my name.

In such simple dramas, on such cold, insignificant nights, are great histories set in motion, fates set on their path. How could I have known it? All I knew, for a long time after that dreadful loss, was the sound of my own terror and abandonment.

Now, too, there was something terrified and abandoned about Argo. She was a miserable ship. She was living with a secret, and holding that secret embedded in her hull of oak and birch. The secret was a guilty one. And like a child she was as keen to let the fact be known as she was to keep the fact concealed.

I struggled to disentangle myself from the close embrace of Mielikki. The Lady of the North Land drew back; the spell of communication was broken. Her lynx crouched and hissed at me; its breath was foul. Mielikki hushed it and it backed away from me at a crouch; disturbed, protective, wild.

Mielikki drew back the veil that covered her face. This was the first time I had seen her uncovered, except as the fierce crone carved in wood that oversaw the ship. A face of astounding beauty regarded me with interest and sympathy. Her eyes were elfin, as I'd expected, but her skin was as pallid as milk, just the finest blush at her cheeks. Her features could have been shaped from snow, even her lips, full and sensuous, were bloodless, yet ripe with life.

'I was carved differently,' she said, with an amused nod towards the entrance to this spirit land, beyond which the wooden effigy scowled. 'The people who wanted a figurehead for their boat carved me from fear, not love.'

'Yes. Clearly.'

'I am not the strongest of Argo's guardians. Before me there was a Greek Land goddess—'

'Hera. Yes.'

'One of her names. One of her names only. And her daughter, Athena, too. She casts a long shadow back through time, and the time of the ship. She drowned with Jason after that long voyage, after his death from despair. A part of her, anyway. A small part, a fragment of life, a fragment of his protecting spirit, drowned in the Northlands with her favourite captain. Both ship and guardian can have favourites, and Jason was certainly the one she favoured most. She had others. Before Jason, a man called Acrathonas; before him, in raw times, rough times, a man of great courage, great fury called Argeo Kottus; before him, a woman of pale countenance but strong will. She is remembered as Gean'anandora. There were many in between. The first was you, the boy captain, the inspired shaper. The first shaper. The first shaper of many.'

Shaper. That word again. That name again.

'Argo is disturbed,' I said. 'She's a very strong ship. She is not letting me know exactly what it is that is distressing her.'

'You could use your talents and crack her hull, her protection; like a seagull cracks a shell.'

'I could. I won't. It would be too costly and too dangerous for me. Besides, I will not ask for anything she doesn't wish to tell me.'

'A betrayal is catching up with her,' Mielikki said quietly. 'A moment in her life when she acted against the instructions, and loyalties, of the man who made her the ship she has become, the great ship founded on the small boat that you once fashioned from wicker and skin.'

'Who was that?'

'I don't know. She is not ready to reveal it. But she is here, in Alba, because of what she did. And I am certain that she wishes you to sail with her again. You are not safe in Taurovinda. No one is safe in Taurovinda. You are all looking in the wrong place for the source of the trouble that will soon swamp the land.'

This cryptic conversation was infuriating. I tried to slip into Mielikki's mind, but a lynx bared its teeth, and the ephemeral form of the beauty from the ice wastes of Pohjola proved to be an empty vessel. Most of this goddess, this tree and snow spirit, was still close to the northern lights where she had been born from the frozen earth. There was very little to unfurl in the spirit guardians that accompanied Argo.

Mielikki was not amused by my probing, but not angry. 'I can't help you,' she insisted. 'I can be Argo's voice – that's all I can be – but this ship is in mourning.'

I could understand. Argo would reveal the source of her distress slowly. But for the moment, she was keen to warn me away from Taurovinda.

'I know you have been here for a long time,' I said to her through the Northland's Lady. 'So you know that Ghostland is rising across the river; there are places, hostels, where the Dead are gathering to feast before the fight. Tell me anything, anything at all you can to help us protect ourselves. There are Unborn in that gathering, but they have always been less aggressive than the Dead. What is happening, Argo? What can you tell me? Anything that will help.'

After a while Mielikki whispered, 'No one is safe in Urtha's land. The Broken Kings made sure of that. Urtha's land is set to slip into twilight. There is nothing you can do.'

'The *broken kings*?'

'Each of them innocent. Each of them guilty. I can only tell you one name: Durandond. He was the founder of Taurovinda. Argo is aware of him, below the hill. She thinks that you remember him.'

Durandond! And his companions.

How quickly memory came back. How simple the opening of inner eyes that had been closed, not for reasons of fear, but for reasons of boredom. Why, with all that had happened to me over the ages, would I remember five reckless youths, five simple gifts, five disappointed and angry young men? Why would I bother with the snarls, sneers and complaints of brash champions, offended and wounded at the blunt predictions of their futures?

I had made a living telling the truth by foresight; and been skinned on many occasions when my physical reaction had been slower than my wit, escaping wrath. But those five boys, visiting me in my home 'close to home', the small cave and clearing where I often relaxed and recuperated after walking the Path for two or three generations ... they had vanished from memory as swiftly as their chariots had carried them home to disaster.

But I had always remembered Durandond. A broken King? I would have to find out more about him.

It was clear to me that I had engaged with the shuddering ship as much as she would allow for the moment. I reminded her, through her protectress, that Urtha and his son were returning from the eastern tribal lands of the Coritani. A final, charged response came through from my old friend.

Keep them there! Don't let them return. Abandon the fortress.

I didn't hesitate. Though I wished to ask a hundred questions, I drew back from this hinterland, this summer threshold within the ship. I waded back through the rain-rotting bilges, climbed up to the oar-deck and over the side, slipping back into the reedy mud and stepping to the firm earth of the bank.

Argo watched me forlornly. It was late in the day, growing dark, the air heavy with moisture. The river, further away, rippled with movement, nothing more than ducks.

I called for Jason and was answered by the wind rustling the reeds. As I came closer to the woods, I called again. Argo was behind me now, and hidden in the shadows. Had her crew somehow crept back on board the listless ship?

A sudden movement caught my eye and Jason appeared. He was still standing like a living corpse, lank, blank, sallow of countenance and incurious, even though his gaze was on mine. Behind him, I could see Rubobostes, the Dacian. I wanted so much to see those scowling features break into his famous laugh. But he was inanimate of mood, just alive in the flesh.

A further surprise followed: stepping towards me, lean and dark, his eyes bright, was the Cretan Tairon, another of Jason's second crew of Argonauts, from the time of the raid on Delphi.

Tairon was a hunter of labyrinths. He had been born on Crete, the very home of labyrinths. He was strange in ways that made me believe he was older than his age. He, like Jason and the others, had the same air of detachment from reality about him; he was distant in mind, though clearly present in physical form. It was just ... those eyes! He was closer to waking than the others.

I had seen it before, of course. There is a brightness that suggests awareness, even in a corpse. There is a sparkle that tells of 'watching'. Though Tairon was asleep, like the rest of the crew, there was a spirit within him that was motivating him to contact me.

I said to him, 'I thought you'd gone home after the adventure at Delphi.'

'So did I,' the bright-eyed man answered solemnly.

'Then why are you here?'

'I became lost again. Argo found me. Argo asked me back. I can help in the events that need to be accomplished.'

He was silent for a moment, frowning as he stared at me, as if trying to remember something. Then he continued: 'I can advise on the events that were once accomplished.'

'Events?'

'Argo's past is a maze equal to any maze. I think that's why she wants me here. A terrible event occurred to her. Don't ask me what it was. I don't know, though I have a suspicion. When I wake, you will have to remind me of this conversation. A small part of me remembers you, Merlin. I'm glad to see you. I'd thought time would have swept you into the future.'

'I've found a rock. I'm hanging on.'

'Cling fast. I'll see you shortly.'

The spirit flew from his gaze, then, and he became as blank as Jason and the others. They stood there, these several sorry figures, ragged and hollow, waiting for me to leave.

I left.

I got my bearings and paced back towards the forest. The horses were not tethered where I had left them. It seemed I had lost my horses. But my skills permitted me access to the animal world, and I could fly, swim, prowl or gallop with a creature of my choice.

I found one of the animals by flying to it as a crow. I turned the beast around with swooping aggression. It came back to me, harness drooping, mouth moist at the bit, eyes shameful.

I forgave it at once.

Whilst flying, however, I had seen Urtha, his retinue and many others making their way back towards his tribal lands. They were following the trails to the dry river that separated Coritani from Cornovidi, to the two huge boulders known as the Stones of the Single Leap. So I knew where to go to intercept him. As soon as the horse was rested and fed, I would make haste to meet him.

13
Kryptoii

I kept to higher ground whenever I could, using a little insight to locate old and hidden tracks when the forest deepened. In two days I knew I was close to Urtha. I was also aware of being followed at a distance.

Suspecting it was Jason who was shadowing me, perhaps on the horse I'd lost, I sent a winged spy to catch a glance. But as bird and pursuer encountered each other, so the woodland drew around the rider like a cloak, embracing and swallowing the figure, hiding him completely. The action was so sudden it caught me by surprise, an alarming twisting of nature that I associated with those who possessed shape-changing talents rather than grizzled ex-mariners. Whoever pursued me, then, was someone more like me, but they approached from north and west, where Argo lay brooding.

I put the puzzle from my mind. Argo's words – *stop them going back* – were restless in my head. That sense of impending transformation was everywhere, and there were too many oddities and uncertainties in this otherwise ordinary world of sparring and warring tribes, for me to embrace at this time.

I was weary. I was forced to acknowledge the fact to myself. The call of the Path was becoming stronger. It would soon be time to move on my way, to pick up that old track again, to journey out of one world and into a new, a stranger one, a step back into the broader and deeper Time that governed my existence.

I was reluctant to embrace that call.

Niiv was in my blood, now; thoughts of her, and feelings of comfort with her, were pre-occupying forces. And there was Medea too, that memory of love in my childhood. If I were to abandon Alba, I might abandon this renewed, if painful, encounter with the woman who had once been so important in my life.

I rode on, confused and harried by uncertainty, not resting for my own sake, only for that of the animal.

I caught up with Urtha within a day or so, at dusk. I was riding, with the half moon behind me, coming from Coritanian territory into Urtha's own land. Crossing a bare ridge, freed for a moment from the wildwood, I saw the spread of fires below me. Urtha had camped for the night in the dried river course that separated the two kingdoms. The fires burned between boulders and ragged trees, and tents were slung everywhere, twenty or more, in a wide circle around a broader enclosure, which I took to be that of the king and his retinue.

I could hear, distantly, the raucous laughter of resting men, and the cheerful teasing of youths. If there was a scent of cooking on the air, the wind was denying me that pleasure.

One of Urtha's *uthiin* intercepted me, recognised me and led me to the camp. Urtha came out to greet me. 'Merlin! Casting a moon shadow, I see. I hope that's a good omen. Come into my fortress!'

I ducked below the skins of the tent. Several men sat there, some of whom I recognised. The rough ground was strewn with blankets. Urtha passed me a clay flagon of cold wine, his expression curious.

'From the North? What have you been up to, old friend?'

'From the North?'

'Yes. I left you at Taurovinda, but here you are, riding from the North.'

'Well, I move fast when I move. I've been trying to talk to Argo. She's in the land, and she's a very disturbed ship.'

The men in the king's enclosure looked on, uncomprehending, and Urtha waved me quiet. 'Later, then. We'll talk about this later. In the meantime, I've roused this rabble into support ... here they are ... the champions of my good friend Vortingoros, though the king himself must stay and guard his own land.'

I was briefly introduced to the top men of the Coritani, and then Urtha told me of his encounter in that kingdom.

Most importantly: he had brought nearly a hundred good fighters with him.

'Men against the Shadows of Heroes?'

'It has worked before. What else can I fall back on?'

He whispered the words. I understood why. Everything he did, every act, every deed, every challenge to the Otherworld that bordered his land was made with defiance. Determination and desire could often be stronger than iron and chariot.

His account of the wooden effigies, their return to life or their forlorn and final walk to the river, was intriguing, however. Once again, small thoughts, fragments and abandoned memories, niggled at the hidden nests of my experience.

A more intriguing story was to come.

Hearing that I was in the camp, Kymon left the small shelter that he shared with the seven youths of the Coritani and came to his father's tent. In fact, he didn't come alone. A gangly, pallid young man came with him, a boy whose face showed the scars of anticipated triumph, a gaze that was hungry, a mouth that disdained. But when he saw me, he frowned, and settled quietly at the edge of the covered ground, sitting cross-legged and patient.

Kymon greeted me, tilting his head to show the raw scar on his chin.

'I have my chin-cut!' he said. 'That boy there gave it to me. I gave it in return. His name is Colcu, and I have come to an arrangement with him concerning leadership and honour.'

'Good for you. I haven't understood a word you've just said.'

Kymon was briefly aware of his father's quiet laugh, but he was too full of himself to care. He gave me a detailed account of his combat with Colcu, and the winning of the chin-cut. I noticed Colcu shake his head on two occasions, and clench his fist several times. Kymon's account was not as true as the full moon, then. But Colcu, for whatever reason, was allowing the story to be told at his own expense.

He and Kymon had come to a 'champion's' agreement, that for two seasons Colcu would be master of the group of fifteen youths, five of them Cornovidi, ten of them Coritani. And then for two seasons, Kymon would command. After that, they would contest the leadership. This agreement was as uneasy as a heifer faced with the bull for the first time, but it was clearly working, the terms agreed, the terms accepted, terms to be born, even with discomfort.

I was introduced to Colcu, then, and I found that I liked him. I had a strong feeling that he and Kymon, opposites in many ways, would one day become strong in alliance, strong in friendship. These meagre years, their shallow age, were a challenge to their experience, and they bristled with each other. And yet everything was in place for a future of unity and power.

Only the Shadow Realm stood between them now, a fact that they acknowledged without fully understanding it. Kymon had been torn from his heartland in his own childhood, and remembered the pain of the tribulation. Colcu, unburdened with such memory, nevertheless seemed inclined to accept his companion's experience as having been real, and was committed.

Colcu and Kymon and the other youths had formed themselves into a band similar in concept to Urtha's *uthiin*. They called themselves *kryptoii*.

'Is that a Greek Land name?'

Kymon frowned, but Colcu smiled. 'Older than Greek Land,' he said. 'I've heard of it, and dreamed of it; dreams flow freely in this Island, did you know that?'

'No.'

The freckled youth smiled again and nodded in a conspiratorial way. 'But they do. This is an island of dreams. They fly from all over, but where can they fly further? There is nothing but the setting sun beyond Ghostland. I've heard of cliffs and a raging sea, and islands that appear and disappear. But so what? This is the edge of the world, and dreams can fly no further than birds. We are living in a dreaming pool, and words and lives come here and stop here, and there are some of us who can catch them, and I caught a dream, a boy's dream, from an older land than Greek Land, and he said he was *kryptoii*.'

Colcu was speaking as if in a dream, or as if someone were speaking through him.

And what did he mean by *kryptoii*?'

'Good question. I think he meant: *concealer*. I think he meant: *I know yet I don't reveal*. I think he meant: *I contain a secret*.

'In the dream,' he went on, 'I saw a nut, still intact, but there was no food inside the nut, just something waiting to be known. The wood of the nut must age and grow brittle, and then the secret will emerge. Now there,' he said with a confident grin, 'is everything that is a boy for you!'

'Nuts waiting to age?'

'Ready to reveal all when they mature.'

'Then why not call yourself "the nuts"?'

The men laughed, but the boy remained focused and intense. 'Odd words, odd language, old languages ... You should know about this, from what Kymon tells me. They ring better in the telling. In the poet's telling. Old words. Older meanings.'

'*Kryptoii*? Yes. It rings well.'

Kymon said, 'We are bound, now. Bound by an unknown truth, and an unknown outcome.' He looked towards his father. Urtha was watching his son with great interest.

The boy pulled the gold half-lunula from inside his shirt.

'This binds me to you, and to the fortress. Never forget that, Father.'

'How could I ever forget it? Munda has the other half.'

'Yes,' Kymon said with a frown. 'I hope she values it.'

Taking a chance, breaking through this moment of revelation and union: between father and son, between brother and foster-brother – that being the relationship between Colcu and Kymon that I believed was occurring – I reached to lift the half-moon symbol where it hung from the boy's neck. Urtha had cut this ancient decorative disc into two unequal halves. I had never really looked at it before. I had seen so many such chest ornaments. But Kymon's protective gesture towards it, and the sudden glint of firelight on the beaten, battered gold, made me intrigued.

Here was a test of trust: would the boy let the enchanter examine his inheritance?

'I'd like to look more closely,' I said. 'Take it off for me.'

Kymon glanced at his father, then looked down at the frail gold. In a moment, hardly pausing to think, he had unhooked the amulet and passed it to me. I was pleased. The tie of trust still existed.

Here in my hands now, was a quarter-moon in gold, a winter symbol, cast in sun metal, beaten out with the patterns of stars, the cluster of seven, the sun in partial eclipse, the moon shown in some phases, the strike of light that was the falling of sky fire. Munda's half would contain other aspects of the sky, of course. It had not occurred to me before, but this old disc, this heirloom, handed down across the generations, had been fashioned with a skill and message that might have meaning.

I felt, at that moment in the river course, in the wild night, in that quiet evening before the storm that was just about to break, I felt like an open hearth: the doorway at which all visitors come knocking.

Everything was gathering, more than just storm. There was a

prickle in the air. What was it Colcu had said? Odd words; old language.

The old and the odd. The secret about to break. A truth about to be revealed. And yet I couldn't see it.

The fires burned; wildfowl sizzled. Sour wine slaked tired throats; old jokes still raised a laugh. Old men dreamed of youthful triumphs. Youths dreamed of triumphs yet to come, triumphs that would be remembered with tired wine and sour minds.

We had gathered. We were caught. The trap was set.

And even as I began to become concerned, so Kymon began to whisper to me of his strangest encounter, the encounter with the boar man, with Urskumug, with the oldest animal.

'... I stopped it killing Colcu; I stabbed it. I thought I was a dead man, the beast was so huge. But it stood up, wrenched the spear from its chest and threw it down. It was like a man who has been surprised and doesn't know what to do next. It said, "That was a good throw". Then it leaned down and said "There is something extraordinary in this blighted land. Something at large. Oldest animals waking up. Old ghosts too. Be careful." Then it walked off.'

'Were you frightened?'

'For a moment,' Kymon conceded. 'But then: no. Not at all. The boar was my friend. It seemed confused by being out that night. As confused as I was at fighting a boar in the shape of a man.'

'Part of being *kryptoii*, perhaps.'

The thought was too large for him. He and his new band of proto-champions had created the word more as a game than with any serious intent. But the name had come from somewhere; the name shaped the boy and his friends, not the other way round, and I wondered if the man-boar was linked to that shaping.

Kymon shrugged as he answered my question. 'Perhaps. Yes. Should I try to understand further? Can you help me? Could you look for me?'

'Look for you? You mean, look to see what really happened?'

He nodded. 'Well?'

'If I look to see what truly happened I would see you, tussling with a creature from the old earth, rolling down a bank, stabbing, thrusting, cowering ... and then surviving. And listening to a foul-breathed observation from a creature from your nightmares. Everything, in other words, that you experienced yourself.'

Kymon watched me closely as he digested this, then asked quietly,

'But it said it was in the world without a reason. You could look for the reason.'

'And get hauled into the underworld by my hair and beard! There are ways of looking in the land that can be of advantage. That's my skill. To look into the wrong realm can be as dangerous for me as for you or your father. So no: I shan't enquire too closely as to the reasons for Urskumug rearing his tusked and tousled head.'

'It doesn't matter,' Kymon said with a shrug. 'I won the skirmish. And the beast indicated that it respected my actions. I'm not afraid of Urskumug, now. I was just asking ...'

Kymon left me. Which other of the Oldest Animals was rising, I wondered? First the hostels, now these. Who or what was calling them?

Urtha wanted to talk, matters relating to his wife and daughter, whom he had not seen for some time now. There was discussion of strategy, the deployment of the scant forces of men, chariots and champions when the forces of the Shadows of Heroes crossed Nantosuelta, at the fords, coming against Taurovinda.

I listened. I was detached. I could feel the jaws of the trap around me, the bite closing. Nothing was right, and Kymon's strange and affectionate encounter with Urskumug was simply setting the seal on the simplest of facts:

The Otherworld had tricked us, misdirected our vision; caught us unawares.

I went outside the cold enclosure and stood, staring at the moon above the bare ridge. A figure suddenly stepped into view there, leading a horse, a man dwarfed by the silver gleam. He called, 'Merlin. Get out of the river. Get out now! All of you. The river is in full flood. You have moments only. RUN!'

'Jason?' I called, recognising the haunted voice. The cloaked figure raised an arm to the south, then again that urgent instruction: 'You are in its path. Get to high ground!'

The earth below me shook. I looked south, through the night, and saw the clouds swirling in an unnatural way. The scent of fresh water was suddenly strong. Urtha had heard the shouting, and now I added my own alarm:

'Get the horses. Leave everything else and ride up through the trees.'

'What's happening?'

As if in answer, the flooding river, still hidden by trees and scant distance, broke against boulders. I saw the spray of the wave as it rose and fell. The roar of the flood suddenly boomed like a groan from the underworld.

The whole camp was alive now. Horses panicked and scattered. Men and boys fled in all directions, some scampering towards the figure on the ridge, others back towards the land of the Coritani. Jason, I noticed, began to descend to the dry bed.

There was no time to engage my talents in enchantment. Besides, what might I do? Block the river? Possible, but unlikely. Almost without thinking, however, I had thrown my farsight to the rolling waters and grasped the essential truth: Nantosuelta had once flowed here, and was flowing here again! When this dry, abandoned tributary was flooded anew, and had connected with the main river to the sea, Urtha's kingdom would be cut off, as it had been isolated once before.

Cathabach had told me this years before. I had forgotten.

The Otherworld was not attacking Taurovinda with men; it was changing the shape of the land itself!

I ran east, scrambling through the rocks, struggling up the wooded slope, aware of Urtha and his son close by, of Kymon calling for Colcu, his vanquisher and now his fellow rider, of horses whinnying and slipping, hauled to safety by grunting men, fighting with harnessing in one hand and holding arms and shields in the other.

And to the west, a few men running in the wrong direction, crying out in fear, lost and confused.

The river surged into view, then, glowing like a beast, curling up and around the trees and boulders, embracing the old course, consuming it, drowning it, reclaiming it.

I see it dark ... I see it drowning ...

I see the night surge of the dead ...

Munda's prophetic words called to me as if in a dream. A girl controlled by her small vision had seen an event that had only eluded me because I had failed to think to search for it.

I heard Kymon shout out in alarm and anguish. The tall boy, the freckled and arrogant youth Colcu, had lost his footing, grabbing at the branch of a tree but losing the grip. A surging wave had struck him and turned his path to mud. He flailed, turned on his back, slid towards the river. A second curving limb of Nantosuelta reached up and wound around him, thrusting him into the foam as the water roared past below us.

To my horror, then, and certainly to his father's, Kymon deliberately threw himself down the slope after the nephew of Vortingoros. He had wound a length of harness around his waist, for his own use, and I saw him unravel the leather as the flood took him and drove him below the surface.

'The little fool!' Urtha cried out. One of his *uthiin*, a burly man called Bollullos, thrust the king back and began the descent in pursuit of the two boys, but I caught Bollullos's arm and shook my head.

I had summoned a small piece of charm, swimming fish-like through these enchanted waters, and seen Kymon and Colcu embraced in the moment of drowning: a moment only, because both lads were kicking strongly, grasping the harness. They surfaced, out of sight in the darkness, forced hard against an oak that had been half-wrenched from its bed, but was still clinging fast to the earth.

They were breathing, alive, and full of the furious will to survive.

Their chins, recently cut, bled into the water as the wounds broke.

'Which way?' I heard Colcu gasp.

'Back to your own land,' Kymon spluttered. 'There's something wrong in mine.'

They remained stuck there as the Winding One tried to force their frail carcases from the failing tree.

Then oak of a different cut came into sight. She shone with life. She listed, waterlogged and swamped, but afloat still, greater in strength than this raging, carving stream, moving *against* the flood, passing the boys. Turning in the river, she bore in upon the stranded youths, patterned hull looming above them, crushing against them. Kymon flailed in the water, grasped the saturated rigging that was dangling from the deck. Colcu did the same. As the oak tree released its grip upon the earth and tumbled into the river, so Argo straightened, bearing her burden of young spirits. She moved by her own magic to the eastern bank, coming hard ashore and trembling as a third surge of Nantosuelta struck at her with icy fury, a roaring and foaming attack on the small ship that failed to dislodge Argo from her berth.

Kymon had never smelled so sweet, I imagined. The oil and lime in his hair was stripped away. Even the dye on his skin, which could last for seasons, was scoured from him.

I noticed that he glanced at Colcu. And the two boys laughed: in amazement and relief. They had a sense of danger, but no thoughts of death. Such luxurious ignorance; two lives already marked by the pain of loss, cut by pride, but not yet shaped by the harsh howl of years.

The river took them, took the ship, spinning her, sweeping her away. Her soft glow, the watching eyes on her prow – sly and knowing, no longer sad – slid into the distance, tumbling in the rushing water. But she was equal to Ghostland's unexpected and furious grip and quickly turned her keel to ride the flood.

I abandoned my presence in the river to find Urtha struck with fear and tears.

'Argo has them safely!' I reassured him.

'The ship is lost.'

'No. Not lost. Never lost.'

'In those waters? She'll be swamped.'

'Not Argo. She has sailed in wilder waters than these.'

He seemed calmed by the words, but only briefly. A strange light illuminated his face, reflecting from eyes that were widening with astonishment.

I have often had cause to doubt my insight, but never more than at that moment, then, when the final stages of the invasion from Ghostland were made manifest to those who had escaped to the wooded eastern hill and safety.

As Nantosuelta, coursing through her ancient bed, cut the land of the Cornovidi from the mortal world, so the edge of that land became the edge of the Realm of the Shadows of Heroes. The forest loomed large, thickening and strengthening, becoming darker and more entangling. Then light began to shimmer and shine from the glades and narrow gullies that led deeper. Creatures howled and bayed, taunting calls. The evening sky was dark with crows, streaming flocks that split and circled as hawks stooped and hovered, not preying on others of their kind, but watching the frantic, daunted host that was now in retreat. They were the sharp eyes of those who were overwhelming Urtha's land.

And still the river rose! It was a living creature, breaking through the wooded slopes, snapping at our heels, driving us further in to the forest on the eastern hill. Eventually it calmed, flowing strongly, silver in the moon, deceptively beautiful.

Then the sun seemed to rise in the west. The forests were woven with fire. A mournful gale howled at us, carrying the distant sounds of a myriad human voices, a tiny clamour of triumph, growing ever louder, under-sung by the thunder of horses and chariots. The fire and the forest were shaped before us; one of the hostels took form there, light spilling from its double doors. The Hostel of the Red Shield Riders. To right and left as our eyes scoured the river, the otherworldly inns were appearing, grotesquely carved with the leering faces of creatures out of Avernus's scowling underworld dreams. It was as if they had come to watch us.

I dreaded what would emerge from the gaping doors of the hostel across the river from where we clung to the hill, stunned by transformation. Urtha was murmuring words that at first I found hard to discern, but then heard more clearly than I wished:

'Munda ... Munda ... she's gone. Great God, don't take her. Not Munda. Not my little world ...'

Bollullos was bullish, and had gathered ten of the *uthiin* and several of the Coritani. They crowded towards the king, swords unsheathed but held with tangs pointed towards the earth.

'We have ropes, Urtha. We can haul ourselves across this muddy brook—' he waved his blade cockily at the wide river '—and take that place, take it with force. There is no point in just sitting here enjoying the view!'

'Do you have any idea at all what is happening?' I shouted at the king's champion, attempting to warn him of the danger.

'None whatsoever!' was his response. 'What's that got to do with anything?'

'That river is the Winding One, as you call it. She has broken through the old dams that were once raised to block her and she's claiming back part of the world that belongs to the Shadow Realm. You cannot cross her. Only the Dead can cross her.'

'Only the Dead?'

'Only the Dead.'

'Then I'll die trying!' Bollullos riposted loudly, dismissing me as the charlatan he no doubt considered me to be.

Not all men trusted the wisdom of druids. Bollullos was one of those men who trusted only their own common sense and awareness of their physical limitations. And like all such men, he acted on neither.

'Hide the blade,' Urtha said to him grimly, an instruction to sheath his weapon.

The champion glared at him. 'I'll follow the king, or stand to protect the king; but the king must act!'

The words of the angry, battle-hardened *uthiin* were a stark and pointed reminder of events when Urtha's children had been far younger, and the fortress of Taurovinda had fallen, albeit for a few seasons only. Bollullos had used those words then, a kick to the flanks to break through Urtha's mourning for his wife of the time and gather his wits for battle.

Urtha grabbed a handful of leaf mould from the ground where he stood, clenched it hard as he peered across the river. 'The act will happen when this nightmare is finished. I will want you by my side, Bollullos. These dead leaves will scatter over corpses as we take the land back.'

He might have said more, there might have been further protest, but the edge of the Otherworld now began to blaze with daylight, a false dawn, a western dawn, eerily bright skies over the hills and forests around Taurovinda, though we who watched were still in the night.

This was impressive enchantment!

Into the new light, rising above the forested slopes, came the shapes of giants. Their leashed hounds bayed wildly. Each man held five of the bronze beasts. Each man – three times the height of Bollullos – was cast from bronze himself. I counted twenty of these *talosoi*, these guardians from an older age. They were century-worn and combat-broken. They had seen many fights. They bled green copper from deep wounds in their armoured bodies. Their faces were masked behind helmets that were shaped from images of the spirits of the damned, shedding their nightmares before dying and giving up their horrors to whoever had created these dreadful machines.

On the ridge of the hill they stood tall, holding back the feral, heat-forged hounds. How they longed to cross Nantosuelta and wreak havoc among us.

'I know these creatures,' a familiar voice behind me whispered.

'So do I,' I replied.

Jason's breathing was heavy; his breath was foul. I glanced at him and saw a stronger light in the vacancy of his eyes, though he was still dishevelled and waxy-skinned, almost as if dead. His gaze was fixed on the other side of the river.

'They don't belong here.'

'No. They don't.'

Urtha glanced at him, then stared at me for a moment, frowning. 'You know them from where?'

'From a land in the southern seas. An island. They walked around the edge of that island, guardians, destroying the ships of invaders, or mercenaries – like Jason here – punishing traitors, carving caves into the walls of deep gorges, a spirit land for fleeing gods. Zeus himself was reborn there, after one of his early deaths. The island was a hiding place for all manner of strange visitors: the mountains are riddled with labyrinths. And the *talosoi* are not earth-born but man-made. Which is to say: a man made them. An inventor. A Shaper ...'

'Though he himself is not of this world or any world we know,' Jason breathed behind me. 'Daidalos. His name was Daidalos. I remember something about him. But Daidalos is long gone. Long dead. What brings his monsters here?'

'Has the world gone to the moon?' Urtha suddenly hissed. He was angry. His face was flushed. Behind him, Bollullos and two others were watching me with a furious gaze. 'My son is lost!' the king went on. 'My daughter is over there. Over *there*! My wife is over *there*! And my closest advisor is talking in a dying druid's riddles. Inventors? Long dead? Machines? What does it all mean?'

It was Jason who replied to Urtha's question. 'Vengeance,' he breathed softly. 'The consequences of piracy. The consequences of enchantment. A long wait for vengeance.'

Though his words baffled the king, they sent a shudder of recognition through my own, slowly wakening mind. Echoes of the past began to sound; and yet ... not strongly enough that they seemed a part of my own past (much of which was hidden from me). His words reminded me of something I had heard, perhaps, some story told to me, an encounter with legend, rather than with the fact behind the legend.

I wanted to know more, but Jason was still only half under Psyche's wakening care. He still roamed the dream.

'In the pitying name of the Quick Forest Father!' Urtha suddenly cried. He was pointing at the hostel, and the bright maw of its doors, the openings below the reaching limbs of the carved beasts, their rearing forms held apart by the tall, masked woman.

A girl was standing there, a small shape, fair hair streaming, arms at her sides, plain robe billowing in the wind. Her face was twisted into a smile of triumph. Her eyes glowed with fire and pleasure. Round her neck her fragment of the golden lunula shimmered. It was so bright that I saw a reflection of it in the river itself.

Slowly she raised her hands, as if to say: you see?

She called out loudly, 'They have taken back what was theirs. Everything is returned to its natural state. My brother has lost the battle for the land. Father! Father! Come back to us. You can cross safely. You have nothing to be afraid of.'

Bollullos declared, 'You see? Come on!'

Urtha drew his sword – a swift movement with his right hand tugging the blade from the sheath on his right hip – and flung the weapon at the ground in front of the other man, where it stuck, barring the *uthiin*'s way forward. It would have been unthinkable for the warrior to disobey that order.

'We have everything to be afraid of,' Urtha insisted. Then he settled to a crouching position and stared forlornly at the smiling girl as she stood on the threshold of the land of the Dead and the Unborn, part of a world that she should not have embraced for many years, and yet in which she now seemed to belong.

14
Argonauts

We did a count of those of us who had escaped to the east. More than half of us had run in the wrong direction, and now languished alive in the new land of the Dead. This included many of the youthful *kryptoii* that Colcu had brought with him, seven in number, and ten of the fifty Coritani horsemen that Vortingoros had allowed Urtha. And of Urtha's *uthiin*, only Bollullos, Morvodumnos, and an exile from the North, Caiwain, remained. The other five had run for their land and were now lost to us.

Argo's call was a mournful drone in my head, but Urtha insisted that we regroup away from sight of the hostel. The *talosoi* had withdrawn, though the bronze hounds bayed in the distance. The doors to the hostel were closed, claiming Munda with them. An unnatural peace had encompassed the far side of the river, though still the earth rumbled with war-wagons and the gathering of forces.

The Coritani had had enough of events, even though they had done nothing. All but a hooded and cloaked horseman withdrew, going home, finding horses where they could, leaving us most of their supplies, riding or running back to their stronghold. Four of the boys went too. And when they had gone, the hooded man revealed himself.

He was gaunt and pale, his head shaved, his eyes green and bright. He caught my glance and smiled thinly, nodding slightly, a greeting as pale as his features.

'You?' said Urtha.

'The king released me to be of help to you,' said this man.

'I've forgotten your name.'

'Talienze. But I'm no champion. Not with weapons. Which isn't to say I can't add a good throw of the spear or fire an accurate arrow.'

'You're the druid,' Urtha muttered.

'Speaker for the Past,' corrected Talienze. 'We make the distinction.'

'Then I'm glad to have you. My own Speakers are on the other side of the river. Including the best, Speaker for Kings.'

'Cathabach. Yes. I know him. When we were training we talked in the groves.'

'Which groves?' Urtha asked.

'The evergroves of your territory. The whispergroves of the Coritani. Other groves in other places. We were allowed there. We met frequently.'

'I hope you'll be able to meet him again,' Urtha said pointedly, then turned to me. 'I'm at a loss, Merlin. What do we do? I'll listen to all advice, including the brash bull's.'

I supposed by that he meant Bollullos. Urtha was drawn and tired. He seemed more of an old man than the fighting king I knew him to be. Talienze watched me carefully. The man had a similar gift of enchantment as Niiv. He could protect himself, frustrate the 'easy look'; he had a little more control over nature than Cathabach, but this was not the time to probe too deeply.

Jason's living ghost stood nearby, waiting for full resurrection. The boys chattered and shouted, nervous and ignorant, lost without Colcu, uncertain of their fate, yet not prepared to abandon the adventure on which they had embarked. Colcu was alive; this was a fact I knew. But they would not have believed me, not words alone. They needed to see their friend. And soon they would.

Everything had to do with Argo. This thought had grown and matured in me, had nagged and nipped at me, had prompted memory in me, had engaged me with recollections of our first years together. My simple ship was now telling me, as Argo no doubt intended, that she needed my help. I had been her first captain. She had controlled her world as she had grown. Her eyes had seen the worlds of Ocean and the rising springs of rivers. The eyes on her deck – the men, rough-cut and rowing for their lives – had experienced wonders. But now the ship needed me, though the nature of that need was elusive.

'What do we *do*?' Urtha said again. He had probably asked the question several times as I had had crouched there, staring wistfully into the past.

'Find the ship. Board the ship. Repair the ship. Sail the ship. Talk to the ship.'

'Argo?'

'Well, yes. Unless you know another ship?'

Urtha looked at me despairingly. 'She can't have survived that flood.'

'She did. And so did Kymon. And his friend. She has been swept away, but not out of reach. Don't you agree?' I addressed this last remark to the gaunt enchanter.

Talienze cocked his head and shrugged. 'I wouldn't know.'

I couldn't work him out. He didn't belong. But the very fact that he was here, among us, among the survivors of the flood, that very fact suggested to me – I was confused, I'll admit it, but grasping at straws myself – it suggested that he should come along. I thought this because it seemed to me that he knew more than he was letting on.

Argo herself might answer my doubts.

Our sorry little band now headed north, keeping out of sight of Nantosuelta, following the ridges, moving to where the river had a more friendly prospect, flowing into the sea that separated Alba from the broader lands beyond. I led the way. We had five horses and used them to carry what weaponry and supplies had been dragged from the camp before the Winding One had rushed in to claim back her ancient path.

We numbered fourteen, and five of these were boys. And of the other nine, three were walking as if in a dream, lagging behind, but not unwelcomingly so. I visited each of them – Jason, Tairon, Rubobostes – and whispered gentle words. They were sleepers, walking, and soon their eyes would open.

Argo called to me and we found her soon enough, moored in a shallow creek, disguised with rushes and willow fronds. Colcu stood at her stern, his arm resting lightly on the figure of Mielikki, perhaps unaware as yet of the angry nature of the Northland's Lady. Kymon was on the bank, kneeling before a small crude wooden figure, a roughly hewn depiction of a girl – his sister, I intuited – which was encircled by glowing ashes. Several shards of broken iron had been hammered into the effigy's breast.

As our group of men and boys emerged through the trees, he stood up and shouted a greeting to his father. He looked a little guilty for a moment, glancing at the figurine, but then found a new resolve.

'She won't take the land!' he declared.

Urtha walked down to the shrine and kicked out the fire, then flung the statuette into the water. 'You little fool. Don't tear the family open before we've had a chance to weave it back together.'

'She won't take the fort,' Kymon whispered, his voice, his manner almost feral. He was challenging the older man and the two exchanged a dangerous look.

'No she won't,' Urtha said. 'The question is: does she really want to?'

'She's on the other side of the river.'

'So is my wife! So are the Speakers! So is my closest friend! So are a legion of Dead and Unborn. And shapers we can't know about. Don't let your anger rule your wits, you little fool.'

'Don't let a daughter steal yours!' Kymon responded furiously. Urtha struck him. The boy accepted and considered the blow, but his gaze never left the older man's.

'Someone is speaking through you,' Urtha murmured, and his son laughed.

'Yes!' he challenged again. 'I hear the voice of my grandfather. I hear the voice of his father before him! The voice of *his* father. As far back as the voice of Durandond himself! Don't you?'

Urtha could not resist the laugh of appreciation. 'If that's so, then it's admirable. I'm glad to find you alive. We could do with Durandond's advice.'

Kymon touched the cheek where his father's hand had struck him. His gaze was hard, probing. 'I'm glad to find myself alive as well. But then, I have a lot to live for. I have the ship to thank for it.'

Then he looked at me with a frown. 'When I crawled onto her deck, I felt safe. But the ship feels angry. I know Argo has feelings, like a man or woman has feelings. But I was surprised by the fury. I just thought you should know.'

I acknowledged the words.

Angry? She had been in despair before. Had something changed?

I had noticed also that Colcu and Talienze were in quiet discussion, the Speaker holding onto the youth's hand as Colcu leaned down to hear the man's words. They exchanged finger signals and chin touches, and drew apart.

*

A warning was shouted – by Bollullos, I believe. There was danger approaching from the direction of Taurovinda. Indeed, we could hear the controlled growling of the Shaper's hounds. Somewhere beyond the ridge the new guardians of the edge of the Otherworld were creeping towards us.

Argo whispered to me to get everyone aboard. She fought at her moorings, twisting in the creek, a vessel alive with impatience. Colcu was thrown off balance, complaining loudly, but when I informed Urtha he issued orders at once. Men and boys scurried to the muddy shore, pushing through the reed beds, throwing their belongings over the deck rail and hauling themselves into Argo's clutches. Bollullos tethered the horses to the stern. They would have to swim behind us until we could find a place to let them step into the hull. Urtha and I untied the mooring ropes and were the last to scramble into the small ship. It seemed half the mud of this quiet backwater came with us.

Silently, Argo began to move across the creek. She turned, listed, caught the stronger current and began to run towards the sea.

Behind us, the woods became crowded with fast-moving shapes, still slick from the river crossing – their tentative invasion – loping towards us. We were a good way downstream when these strange creatures formed up along the shore, watching us depart. They were not all hounds. I saw goats and wild pigs, bulls and bird-faced animals that did not belong in Urtha's world. And they did not gleam bronze. They were fashioned from polished wood.

Jason was right. He knew who had come to occupy Ghostland. I had seen all the signs, hints that had been obvious from the moment the hostels had begun to reappear. I had simply not put them together.

But how had it been achieved?

What was the Beast Island's great inventor doing so far from his warm-ocean home, many days' sail from Greek Land, and so many centuries after his disappearance?

Mielikki drew me from the chaos of my thoughts: a simple whisper.

'Argo will take you to where the answer lies. To the island itself. But she is reluctant. The sea journey will not be difficult. It will be a hardship when you arrive at the shores and have to find the right haven. Take one of the *dri'dakon* with you. There is one that is out of place.'

I waited quietly, attempting to place the word. 'Wood and spirit', I sensed: a very old word. Then I grasped what she meant: one of the oak effigies that lay scattered among the woods of the Coritani.

Mielikki's voice came again, suddenly more urgent, warning me: 'Someone is coming who has need of you. She is running, frightened and fawn-like. We must wait for her. Accept her. Then you must enter the Spirit of the Ship again. Encourage your own little creation to confront her past, and to journey back in time. This will be hard.'

Very hard indeed, was my sour thought. My 'own little creation' – Argo herself – was probably as vulnerable as was I to the strains of reaching from one time into another, of taking on such enchantment.

The longer I spent in Alba, the older I seemed to get. Ageing was wearying, and I was not used to it, and I did not like it.

And I was about to be aged further, though only by the return to my life of enthusiasm and the fire of youth. It was Niiv who was pursuing us. Could there be any doubt about it? I could not think of anyone better able than the Northland nymph to cross from the world of the dead to the world of the warm-blooded. Pure desire, pure determination, would have propelled her across Nantosuelta even in the shadow of those bronze monstrosities and their cruel ways of defending and abducting those who broke the borders that they guarded.

Argo was in control, her crew in confusion. We cleaned the mud from our bodies and clothes and trusted to the ship's intentions. Kymon, Colcu and the *kryptoii* sorted out what provisions we had, made sense of the ropes, the torn sail, the splintered oars, made space for living as well as voyaging. Urtha and Talienze kept a wary eye on each other, standing at the prow of the ship. The three argonauts of old sat huddled and grim-eyed, still in the dream, not yet with us.

A woman's scream from the forest, a trumpet shrill of high anger, brought us all to our feet. It was a screech worthy of Medusa's when she had seen the blade, wielded by Perseus, that – too late to avoid – would strike her off at the neck: a howl of desperation; a lung-powered, throat-scarring plea to stop.

Argo became motionless in the water, defying the flood. We crossed to the rail and the forest was ripped apart by Niiv as she strode towards us, furious and breathless, clearing a path by use of charm. Her dark hair was plastered to her face. Her eyes were wide, defying exhaustion; mouth grim, muttering. She was muttering, *bastards, bastards … why couldn't they have waited? Bastards …*

She was on the point of collapse. She had certainly run on enchantment rather than natural energy. She clutched a small leather sack at her side, holding it for grim life. Strands of briar and ivy were caught in the wool of her simple black dress. And she was *barefoot*!

Her feet had seemed clad in red shoes. But it was her own blood that caked her, dried and thicker than leather.

She waded out into the river, stumbled, lost her footing and started to splash. She cursed fit for a champion. She found her balance again and swam towards us, her eyes fixed on mine, her face telling of irritation.

'Throw up the bag!' I shouted down.

'Just help me up! Why couldn't you have waited?'

Bollullos and I hauled her aboard. She snatched herself away from my consoling touch and went to where Jason was watching us. She sat down beside him – still muttering – and started to wring the water from her hair and clothes. She was talking to Jason, quietly animated, but after a moment, when she had received no response, she peered at him more closely. She ceased her chatter and leaned back, frowning, disturbed by what she had come to realise.

The ship had already slipped her invisible moorings and drifted quickly back into the stream.

We got three of the horses on board, not without difficulty, and each small animal was made to lie down, to be tended by one of the boys. Argo felt very crowded. We put out four oars and kept the ship in centre stream; they were only needed when the river curved sharply and we needed to avoid the mud banks. We found what comfort we could in the cramped hull; no one spoke.

Niiv, after a while, moved away from Jason and found a small space in the prow, where she huddled down, still damp, still clutching her simple possessions. She was in a very strange mood, but used her left foot to tickle the flaring nostrils of the horse that lay, with its *kryptoii* handler, just in front of her. The beast snorted and seemed amused and a moment's brightness flashed over the Northland girl.

The smile evaporated as I crept round to crouch beside her.

'Go away. I need to sleep. And I'll catch my death of fever in these damp clothes.'

'What have you got in the sack?' I asked her.

'Nothing that concerns you,' she replied with a scowl.

'If you've food in the sack, it concerns us all. Hand it over.'

She swore softly, opened the leather bag and drew out fruit, dried pig meat and mouldy, hard oatcakes. She tossed these meagre items at me then drew the cord tight again.

'What else have you got in the bag?'

'Nothing! Nothing that concerns you.'

'If you have magic in there, objects ... talismans, anything like that—'

'Nothing like that.' She tapped her head pointedly, her eyes wide with annoyance again. 'Everything's here. Or left behind in my home, below the snow, looked after by Old Forest Lady. Leave me alone.'

'You have *something* in the sack.'

'What do you want me to do? Produce a dead swan, swing it round my head and watch it fly away? Leave me alone. There's only one thing in here and it's personal. And if you look – if you *look*—' she challenged me, threatened me '—then you're a worse lover than I ever realised.'

She hunched up over the bag, cold, wet and under the influence of pique, muttering away, something like: '... which isn't saying much ... old men ... no stamina ... minds always on other things ...'

But I took a look anyway, stole a glance, smiling all the time. There was a small copper disc in the sack, and that was all. It had no meaning, told me nothing, conveyed nothing, engaged with no emotion, natural or charmed. It was just a souvenir, I imagined.

'Did you look?' she asked suddenly, catching me off-guard.

'You asked me not to.'

'So you didn't look.'

'No.'

She sighed. She had mellowed. 'What liars we both are. You just got older by one grey hair.' Her glance at me was sad yet fond. 'It doesn't stop me loving you.'

'You've got older too,' I replied. 'Around the eyes, around the mouth.'

'It wasn't easy, crossing that river,' she said very quietly. 'And other things ...'

'What other things?'

'Never mind. Nothing that concerns you.'

She lay down, then, curling up and drifting into sleep, the bag with its cold, empty disc clutched to her breast.

'You seem to think that *nothing* ever concerns me.'

'I'm sure it does,' she murmured cryptically. 'When it suits you. Before it's time to move on.'

She seemed to be asleep but I knew she was awake. I sat by her for a long time, watching her. I was only forced to move when a horse started to nip my feet.

As we drifted down the river, I spent a while thinking about Daidalos.

In the long-gone I had heard him referred to on many occasions. The stories of his creations were carried by mariners along all the coasts of all the known lands of his time.

He had created creatures of bronze and stone, and the labyrinths to which the likes of Tairon – a labyrinth hunter – were dispatched, to explore the inner realm and bring back their vision – or not to come back at all! (Tairon was one of those: he had become lost in labyrinthine time, else he would not have been here, in Urtha's world.)

Daidalos had also learned how to animate oak, the sacred tree. He could fashion the wood into almost living creatures. He had learned the craft at one of the sanctuaries in Greek Land. Indeed, the kings of the people who had inhabited Greek Land during this time had paid well for such strange and entertaining products of that otherworldly man.

Now, some part of him was in Ghostland.

The rising of Urskumug, and others of the Oldest Animals, didn't sit well with the skills of Daidalos, however. And yet – the events must certainly have been linked. Who controlled the Oldest Animals? Was there a second Shaper of the land at work?

Argo was taking us to the island – Beast Island, Maze Island – the place had so many names. Mino'ana was another. And *Crete*.

To Crete, then. To find a forgotten past.

After a while – a day or more – we arrived at the river jetties that serviced the stronghold of Vortingoros, beyond the forest, huge on its hill in the distance, outlined with the flames of watch-fires. It was night by now, and several men stood guard at the landing places, leaning on their shields, shadowy in the torchlight. They called to each other as we approached, a horn was sounded, and there was a scramble of activity, but when Urtha hailed them they settled down and even helped us to tie up.

Two small ships were moored here already, both traders. One was from Greek Land. Her crew sat huddled in the shadows, watching us suspiciously. She had traded wine and honey, by all the signs. Several clay jars were still stacked on the narrow wharf. This was a long way upriver to have come for so meagre an exchange, but she was perhaps part of a bigger convoy. Vortingoros had a second stronghold that watched the estuary.

We let the horses off here, intending that they be looked after until our return. It had become clear that it was impractical to sail with them. But we ended up trading two, one with the Greeklanders for preserved fruits, wine and healing herbs.

The other vessel was a Northlander, shallow and wide, its deck covered by a tent of stitched hides. She was trading dried meat and skins, and we bargained a second horse for two barrels of deer meat and hides enough to make a shelter from the rain. Argo was in a poor state of repair for the moment.

These provisions would have to suffice until we could find an easy haven on the southern shores.

Fourteen in number, then, and five of us boys. Not enough to row Argo if hard rowing would be needed.

Argo whispered, through her goddess, 'Hurry. Don't delay. It is a long journey, longer than you realise.'

Before dawn, when the ship was quiet and even the old argonauts seemed to be resting, I went ashore, passing through the riverside defences and prowling the forest for the wooden effigies of the Coritani that had been left here, so long ago. They were scarce now. The living had returned, or the dead had passed by, on their way to Ghostland, and released their images from their carved and frozen duty. Only a handful remained, crouched, spears held firmly, resting on their shields. They were all empty of the ghost – except for one, and I found him, crouched well apart from the others. It was the image of a man called Segomos. It took a small exercising of charm to find this out.

I was growing greyer by the day!

'I know you can move, because I know who created you.'

The light was beginning to illuminate the east. The woods were frantic with birds, noisy with activity and song. The day freshened the air, quickened the blood. The oak surface of the statue began to gleam, the jutting head casting a deep shadow on the armoured breast. A whisper of human memory remained in the deeper grain of the carving.

'Talk to me,' I urged the effigy. 'I know you can. I know who made you.'

After a while the wooden sheen seemed to fade, the hardwood softened. The figure seemed to settle back, the spear lowering, the shield moving to one side. His face turned to look at me, nose wrinkling above the heavy moustache, eyes narrowing.

'Where am I?' Segomos asked.

'Dead. Dead and lost.'

'I'd thought as much. I dream of living, but I never leave the dream. I was in a hot place, fighting furiously. It was a good day, a savage encounter. I was one of thousands. We were facing a gorge, with the sea to our left. The Hot Gates. I remember thinking: these are the Hot Gates ... but the sea is to our left. I remember the sea swell, the salt air, the gull shadow, the fine, fierce, forcing march forward, the full-on attack, the fist-fighting, shield-pushing, the dismembering progress, the blood smell, the glazed eyed look that signals triumph, the grip that weakens, the blood-splattering moan of fear-filled final fury, and then ... the swallowing feel, the crushed feel, lung-bursting, the pain-loaded numbing, dream-drifting, the drift into darkness.'

Again the wooden eyes took in my gaze. 'But why am I lost?'

'I can't answer that. You died in Greek Land. Others died there and have come home. For some reason you didn't.'

'I'd hardly known about the place before I went there.'

'You were not alone in that.'

'But where am I? Where is my heart?'

There was a sudden moment of despair in the wooden voice. The trapped spirit of the man who had gone to raid the oracle at Delphi was struggling to retrieve a memory that other gods than his had decided to retain. He would never know his fate. He was caught in the tidal zone, neither open sea nor on land. He would founder there for ever, drawn down by the mud of the nothing-place.

'Help me understand,' the crouched warrior whispered. 'Can you help me understand?'

'I will get you back if I can. Not alive, not for your family ... but back ... back to the proper crossing place to the Realm of the Shadows of Heroes. To do so, you must come with me now, come aboard Argo.'

'I will never live again,' Segomos said mournfully.

'No. That time for you is gone. A Greeklander's sword saw to that; and a Greek Land priest who dragged you from the *Morrigan's* crow-gathering and *Bathaab's* bone-scouring to service his own shrine.'

I knew enough of Greek Land to know that this was most likely the case. The remains of Segomos were probably encased in marble. His hide would have been tanned and worn as priest's clothing.

'We'll bring you back. I promise. And you will cross Nantosuelta to the Island of your choice. Everyone you love will join you there, not all at once, but in time.'

'Did they come with us? Soul-gatherer, bone-scavenger? Was the Morrigan there? The scald? The screech? Were they there?'

'They were there. They did their best.'

'Then why was I left behind?'

'I don't know,' I repeated patiently. 'Help me if you will, and I'll help you back.'

The shard of Segomos's mind that remained changed from mournful to puzzled. Help you? he seemed to be asking. How can I help you?

It was a question I couldn't answer. Argo seemed to think he was important. Perhaps Segomos would not be able to help at all. But I wanted him with us when we arrived at the Shaper's Island.

Segomos rose to his feet. The sound was like a tree bending slowly in the wind. He cast aside his shield and spear. I led him to Argo. We threw down a ramp for him and when he was on board he went to a secure place in the prow, away from the glowering effigy of Mielikki, crouched down, curled up, his arms crossed over his chest, head bowed towards the glowering face at the stern. He became a part of the hull, though he gleamed, an echo of invention, where Argo was dull with wear and stained with salt and bitumen.

It was time to leave Alba again, time to embrace the wider world. We were under-provisioned and under-crewed, but the river would be with us until the sea, and then we would use the strong winds that played along the coast and recruit along the way when we reached the milder, gentler climate of the south. Our only fear was attack by mercenaries, ship-pillagers who lay in wait in deep coves, watching for traders.

But we would have the small Greeklander ship for company, and her crew were keen-eyed and knew the dangerous routes. The earlier mistrust had been banished after the trade, and we would sail with her and her four companion vessels, waiting, we now learned, at the mouth of the channel, back to the Southern Sea, where they would make harbour to take on fish and oil and oranges. Trading networks were complex; they always had been; I had never bothered to give them much thought.

We would be a small fleet, then, and there was protection in numbers.

But it was time to leave Alba: and I was sad at the thought, because I was certain that I would never return here. Though Niiv was with me, she was burning out like the fiery ember she was. Medea was behind me, no doubt planning her own next move, now that one of her sons was dead, and the other lost in a Ghostland of his own. If our paths were to cross again – something I deeply wished for – I hoped it would be after Niiv had gone. The girl had already lost her fury and stood beside me, quiet and concentrating, watching as the river slipped behind us, saying her own farewell to Taurovinda and the life she had known there.

She would not be coming back, I was sure. She was only on loan from the North Land. The goddess that protected Argo also protected her own impetuous child; and though Mielikki gazed at us with snow-cold fury, she was a kind mother, and Niiv was her child. When this was over, Argo would be seeking a new protector; and I would be looking for a new lover.

When this was over! How easily the words come now, so long after events, so long after the resolution. I tell of those events by looking back, and I record by remembering how it was, how we felt, the fear and the sadness, the anticipation, the hope and the confusion that had gathered around this small band from two large kingdoms who were being threatened by their own past and future, the living spirits of ancestor and descendant who had gathered at their frontiers, blood-thrilling and land-gathering, and all under an influence they could never hope to comprehend, and for reasons that they could never have known in a hundred generations.

I didn't know those reasons either. I wasn't prepared to scan the future. I had an inkling that a great challenge was ahead of us, and that resolution was possible, or devastation inevitable. Either would free me from the bind to Alba.

When this was over!

When *what* was over? We were to start seeking answers in a place that Argo knew well, an island that I, for my part, remembered vaguely, and where – for reasons that Argo denied me – Jason could not be permitted to go, not in any fully sentient state. She was taking him there as a ghost.

We were all in a web, a maze. Finding the thread that would lead us out would be our challenge.

Meanwhile, I was not alone in my sadness at leaving the greater island of Alba. Urtha and his son stood, arms around each other, faces set grim, watching their neighbour's land pass into the distance, swallowed by every lazy bend in the river and the woodland that gathered at every curve, branches reflected in the water, as still as the hearts aboard the ship. Father and son, no doubt, were thinking of two women who remained beyond that now-threatening hinterland of bronze hounds and ghost-swarming hostels.

Ullanna and Munda: two women with very different sympathies to the circumstances that had overtaken them.

PART THREE
KRYPTAEA

15
Awakening

Rubobostes the Dacian was on the steering oar, braced against the storm. He seemed immovable, even as Argo listed violently and juddered as massive waves swept across her deck. Jason, cloaked, hooded and haunted, stood at the rail, holding a lantern, signalling to the Greeklander vessels, keeping in touch by a code that he had contrived with them as soon as we had reached the open sea. Tairon – the exile from the very island to which our sea path now took us – clung to the rising prow, soaked by the bow-waves that flushed our poor ship, seeking a way through the mountainous waters. Tairon was an expert on labyrinths, and this ocean, south of Alba, close to Gaul, was a maze more complex than the tombs that burrowed below the great white-crystal pyramids of Egypt.

These three old argonauts had at last begun to wake from the dream. Yet though they went about their business, they were still uncommunicative; they recognised me, but not in the human way, as if we regarded each other as reflections in a dark mirror. Argo was not yet ready to give them a full release from the silence she had imposed upon them. Their voices were functional only.

In the late afternoon, in storm-darkened weather, one of the Greeklander traders began to take on water, listing heavily, signalling her distress. The coast in the gloomy distance was high and craggy, no obvious haven or cove. Her companion vessels were some way ahead of us. The storm had caught us by surprise, and in the wrong part of the ocean.

Jason shouted, 'She's asking for help. For four of her crew to come aboard Argo, and as much cargo as we can manage.'

'How many crew on board?' Urtha shouted across the noise of the sea.

Jason called back, 'Four that are important, he says! And fourteen pairs of hands at the oars.'

Urtha struggled towards me, slipping on the wet planking. 'Four pairs of those hands should see us at full capacity, if I remember the last voyage well enough. But who is to decide, Merlin? Who is captain on Argo?'

'Hardly the time to discuss rank, Lord Urtha,' I replied. He frowned at my use of the formality. 'Jason will be captain when Argo wills it. Not until then. For the moment, you must take command. I agree with you. Four or six can be saved – from the galley! – and no cargo.'

'I agree.'

Rubobostes leaned his great bulk on the steering oar. Bollullos and Caiwain stood ready to grapple the trader. Argo leaned and lurched towards the other vessel. Four fat and sea-swept faces watched us anxiously. Each of those men carried a large pack, tied to his back.

Bollullos flung ropes and the four grasped the ends, leaping into the heaving ocean and beginning to drag themselves towards us. The waves broke over them, but they clung on desperately. Behind them, saturated faces watched us from the deck in despair.

Bollullos let go of the ropes. Four white, screaming faces rapidly disappeared astern.

We sea-shifted as close as was safe to the trader, which was now beginning to list dangerously, sea swamped, the mast threatening to strike our own ship. The oarsmen jumped – where else could they go? We heaved seven of them aboard. The rest foundered along with their ship, sucked down with its cargo of clay jars, its skins, its horse – our traded horse, poor creature – and its plums in spiced wine.

Niiv took my arm as the craft disappeared below the waves. 'I don't know what gods live down below, but they'll be feasting well tonight.'

The storm abated towards dawn and we caught up with the other merchantmen. We were all ragged from the rough ocean and at first light made for a shallow haven to effect repairs. We were still some way from the cliffs of the Iberian peninsular, and found a sandy bay, backed by reedy marshes. There was a good supply of wildfowl here, slow and easily brought down by slingshot, but no fresh water and no sign of a village.

Three of the seven souls we had saved returned to the small convoy from Greek Land. The other four remained on Argo, glad to use their muscle for an adventure a little more inspiring than bartering figs for pigs.

We sailed on.

Two of the trading ships left us at Gades, on the Iberian coast, the others catching the wind to follow the peninsular as far as the Gates of Herakles. Here, they too left us, one to scour the bays of Numida, the other cutting south and east across the ocean to Carthago. We anchored with our companion in the Iberian bay of Erradura, a small town that stank from the stone vats of rotting fish, a delicacy in many lands and highly prized, but which also supplied us with aromatic fruits and preserved meats. There were several Cymbrii here, exiles from their tribal lands in Alba, excellent storytellers. We passed a pleasant day in this gentle company.

Argo then passed the Isles of Balearis and was rowed powerfully to the harbour at Massil and the marshes of the Rhone delta before making a crossing in open sea to the primitive island of Korsa, and the tomb-lined harbour of Lystrana, with its half-drowned skeletal ships and black-cowled guardians. It was here, where once he had sailed on the quest of the fleece, that the full light of reason re-kindled in Jason's eyes, and in Rubobostes' too, who came awake with a huge yawn and then – when he saw me – a huge grin.

Tairon was busy tidying himself, checking the ragged nature of his beard, examining the salt-encrusted skin of his arms and legs. He was a thin, fastidious man, but a man with great ability.

I suspected that Tairon had been in a higher state of alertness for some time, but he gave nothing away.

Jason strode about the ship, inspecting the supplies, the state of the oars, the sail, the damage to the mast. He cast a quizzical glance over all of the new Argonauts, nodding politely. He seemed impressed by Bollullos, perhaps recognising strength and determination, two useful assets. He seemed bemused by the five youths, though of course he recognised Kymon. He playfully tried to tip Niiv over the side – she was not amused – then came over to me, tugging at his lank beard, eyes bright, teeth stained as he grinned at me.

'You keep a sloppy ship, Merlin.'

'We've made it halfway to Crete, sloppy or otherwise.'

'Ah!' Jason looked at the surrounding white cliffs, then grasped where we were. 'Korsa! I recognise the place. We harboured here with the fleece, with the Colchean witch, had to fight off the Lysistarians. Gruesome creatures; brained two of my crew with clubs the size of a bull's backside and dropped rocks on us from the foreland. No sign of them now, thank Hades. When did we arrive here?'

'Not long ago. You *have* been in a dream.'

'Yes,' he said with a grim glance at the figurehead of Mielikki. 'Something went wrong, soon after we left Alba the last time. Argo's mood changed. She held us prisoner. I'm not even aware of where she took us, but it was dark, and cold, and she made us row like madmen, and then suddenly we shipped oars, hunkered down, and that was that. I knew I was sleeping, but I couldn't rouse myself. But here I am. And Rubo and Tairon too! Is that all of us? What happened to the rest?'

'This is all of you. I don't know what happened to the rest. I believe they were abandoned.'

Jason was clearly unhappy with that answer. 'There are some questions to be asked. But the first of them is: what are we doing here? And why are we going back to that dreadful country?'

I suppose that I wasn't paying attention. It took several moments for his words to affect me. *Back* to that dreadful country?

'When were you there before?' I asked him. But before he could answer, the ship began to move on a sudden swell. The sea seemed to rise around us. A flowing wave poured through the narrow straits from the open sea to the enclosed harbour. The bole of water broke over everything in its path, Argo included, ramming the vessel against the crumbling stone jetty. We were all thrown off our feet.

The swell subsided as quickly as it had struck. Jason got back to his feet, touching a finger to his lips (be quiet about the matter) and went to help stack the strewn jars of supplies.

Tairon, with a nervous glance at Mielikki, whispered to me: 'You would think Poseidon had caused the wave. Yes? But no. The wave came from the ship. I could see the pattern in the water. A deep wave flowing away from Argo, then returning to cause the havoc.'

'Are you certain of that?'

'As certain as I can be. This is an unhappy ship.'

Tairon's words hardly surprised me. But later, he asked to accompany me ashore, into a narrow valley where Colcu had discovered a spring. Spring water was considered almost magical to the Celts, even though we had an ample supply of fresh water from streams running into the harbour. So each of us carried two large, leather pouches, to be filled with as much as we could manage, such water to be restricted in its use.

I asked no questions about this. Tairon wanted to escape the heart of Argo.

'She abandoned all but the three of us,' he said to me quietly, as we rested after our walk into the valley. Our water sacks were full, our faces freshened from the spring, our bellies satisfied with almonds and the rich berries we had gathered along the way. Distantly, over high mountains, storm clouds loomed ominously, but here, facing south to the bright sun, we felt at peace. Argo was a small vessel in a narrow harbour, surrounded by wrecks. The white gleam of the chalk cliffs that enclosed the bay were almost homely.

'Left them by the water's edge; in Alba. It was a cruel act. They have no way home, those others. But she abandoned them because she is no longer the ship that she was. Something is rotten at her heart. Or something has buried itself there, and is dying, causing that corruption. She has brought us the long, northern coastal route. I don't know these seas well, but Jason does, and he has raised the question: why didn't we sail south, along the coast of Numida, to Carthago, then to Sicila? It would have been quicker, and far safer.'

I was certain I understood the answer to the question: Argo was retracing her sea path from that previous voyage, when Jason had managed to bring her overland from the headwaters of the Daan, to the Rhone river that flowed south through Liguria and emptied into the ocean near to where Massil would one day become a haven. And then to this open sea.

Perhaps Argo was picking up echoes of that greater, happier time. Perhaps she was gathering little shards of her life, cast off in previous centuries as I knew she was capable of doing, small ships, faint echoes of her own early years that could sail or be rowed into the hidden realms of shades and shadowy magic.

It was time to return to the harbour. Tairon shrugged the water-laden bladders over his shoulders, clearly struggling with the weight – he was very slightly built – and we set off down the path.

'When did you leave Crete?' I asked him, aware that I knew very little about this man.

He staggered a little as he tried to turn, then kept on pacing. 'A few years ago,' he replied. 'We met in the far North, by the frozen lake. Where you met Niiv and rebuilt Argo. You surely remember.'

'Very clearly. You came out of nowhere in the middle of that long winter night. You said you'd been wandering through a maze for some time. You were surprised to find yourself so far north, so cold.'

'Yes. I got lost.'

'Who was the ruler in Crete when you left?'

There were many. He told me a name. It meant nothing. Then I asked him about the great painted palaces that had been built before the Greeklanders had conquered the island. They had been in ruins, he told me. The centre of the island had been shrouded in a permanent cloud. Every fortified town now displayed the double axe, the *labrys*, the island's symbol of power, but the mazes had become forbidden places.

That was why and how he had come to be lost. A few boys were born into every generation with some of the old skills in maze-running. This was a strictly controlled practice. But the temptation to break taboo was usually too great. Those lads who maze-ran before they had received the necessary instruction mostly disappeared into the earth for ever. The few who returned were mindless, gabbling, and were quickly sacrificed, though not to a deity but to a wild woman known as 'Queller'.

Tairon was one of the lost.

My memory was vague; too many centuries of learning to recollect everything that came my way by way of story, action or legend. But it seemed to me that Tairon was not just a few years out of his time, rather, nearly a thousand.

And Argo wanted him on board. My curiosity was keened. The more I heard about Crete, the more intrigued I was by the island, and by what had passed there in the long-gone.

From the white harbour we continued our way south, through the Tyrrhen Sea, then through the narrow straits of Mesna before catching the trade route across the ocean known as Cerauna towards Greek Land itself, to the southern peninsular, which Jason called Achaea, wary for warships and the swirling waters that could suck even a large vessel to the sea bed in instants, and which were common off these shores. Charybdis was the most renowned.

We saw sails in the distance only once, some twenty or so, highly coloured, billowing in a strong wind. We could make out the faint beat of drums as the ships signalled to each other. They were Greeklander, and sailing on a parallel course to our own, but sea haze and a rising swell had soon taken them from view. Rubobostes heaved at the steering oar and altered our course just enough to make sure we put even greater distance between ourselves and that unpredictable fleet.

Rubobostes was in low mood; he was sad, grieving. I had hardly spoken to the man since he had shed the ghost, in the mouth of the Rhone, but now – with Bollullos taking over at the oar – the Dacian's heavy hand grasped my shoulder, and his foul-breathed grin greeted me as memory of our previous encounters returned. 'It's good to see you again.'

'And you.'

'Where are we going?' he asked.

'To Crete.'

'And where's that?'

'South. A long, thin island, full of mystery.'

'Why are we going there?'

'To find answers.'

'Answers, eh?' The big man looked knowledgeably thoughtful. He reached for a small jar of wine as we sat in the hold. 'Then I hope we find them. But for the moment, I'm too tired to even think of *questions*. And I miss Ruvio. Ruvio haunts my sleep. Whatever happened to Ruvio? I will die with his name on my lips, I'm sure of it.'

Ruvio was his horse.

'Ruvio is roaming free, somewhere on Alba, fertilising everything that gallops in front of him.'

'I'm glad of that,' the Dacian murmured, then drew heavily on the jar. 'That horse and I are part of the same life. Did you know that, Merlin? Not just inseparable, though we are separated now, but part of the same being.'

'I know you loved the creature very much. You were two of a kind.'

'We were one and the same,' the big man corrected. 'We came from the same womb. Did I ever tell you that? The same mother gave birth to us both.'

'I didn't know that,' I assured him uncomfortably, surprised by what he was telling me. 'And perhaps the less said at this time the better.'

But the Dacian shook his head. 'One mother, two children. You've heard of centaurs?'

'Centaurs? Yes. They once existed in Greek Land. Dead now, destroyed by Titans.'

'They exist everywhere. They've learned to hide. The lessons from Greek Land were not ignored. Man-chested, horse-bellied, the limb-supple grasp of a man, the swift-striding speed of an equine. I was destined to be *centaur*, but the womb split the two parts of me. It happens, apparently. So we were born brothers, one to ride and one to carry. So I was told.'

'You are part horse?'

'No. The horse part of me was separated. As I've just explained.'

'But your mother gave birth to an infant and a foal at the same time. Quite a woman.'

'Quite a labour,' Rubobostes added.

'Did she survive it?'

'The foal-mother died. Ruvio was huge, I'm told. My own suckling mother lived, though not for long.'

Dacians!

I began to grasp a more naturalistic situation, one based on the intense worship of the horse among Rubobostes' clan. A woman, about to deliver a chieftain's child, would be walled up in a cave – the mother womb – with a mare about to foal. The child and the horse would thereafter be reared together; the horse would be the child's first horse, the bond would be maintained until the horse died. References to 'centaurs' were symbolic, remembering a stranger time of myth.

Rubobostes was in his twenty-fifth summer, though he looked older because of his size and hirsute wildness. Ruvio had been the same age, then, until he was lost. An astonishing age. Dacians bred beasts to last, it seemed.

'I'm sorry about your mother. Your suckling mother.'

'I never knew her,' Rubobostes said with a shrug. 'Her face was tattooed on Ruvio's right flank. Sometimes I would cut away the hair to see that face. She was in profile. She looked very strong. That is all I had of her. I'm sorry to have lost the horse.'

We were in open water, dangerous waters. There was scant breeze and though the sail was up, we had eight at the oars, rowing lazily and carefully over a sea that caught the full fire of the setting sun. There were islands to the east, but they were no more than black smears on the horizon. Talienze was at the prow, his youthful familiar, Colcu, with him. I had noticed that the closer we came to Crete, the more tense were the muscles in the Speaker's face, the more anxious his glances. Kymon seemed relaxed, playing game after game of chance with the other *kryptoii* (occasionally including Colcu). In fact, these were not so much games as a sort of training. They were making rules of silence, laws of secrecy, plans of silent campaign. It was boyish, but it suggested stronger motives.

Talienze intrigued me, though. He and Jason had not spoken a word together, not in all the long days of the voyage. Everyone else had at least exchanged a greeting, or offered to share a task. Not those two.

In fact, just once Jason referred to the exile from Armorica who had become so important at the hall of Vortingoros.

'What do you make of him, Merlin?'

'Very hidden. Very quiet. He's becoming anxious.'

'He's coming close to home, I think. It's just a feeling. But he has closer ties with this part of the world than the rest of us. Except for Tairon.'

'And yourself, of course.'

'Me? I'm from Achaea. Greek Land.'

'*Are* you going home?' I asked quickly, and the mercenary frowned. I was thinking of his earlier comment that he was astonished we were going 'back' to that island.

'No. Not at all. Not home. But I'm returning. I can't deny that.' He paused for a long time, staring out to sea, clutching the rigging, riding the shifting of the ship. Then said, 'But why, how, when, whatever … the memory has gone. The memory is stolen.' And then he looked at me sharply, a half smile of irony on his lips. 'At least: it is being denied me for the moment. Argo is ensuring that.'

'You and Argo have a past that goes a lot deeper, a lot closer, than I'd realised.'

'I think you're right,' was Jason's final comment before he moved to his oar-station to relieve Tairon.

The glow of the sun split the sea horizon to the east. A flock of dark-headed gulls chose to settle and fuss about our mast and rails, spreading their wings and rising as if without effort before landing again, with screeching interest at this solitary vessel. A dark mass rose before us, mountains still in night, though they began to catch the fire of the dawn. A great arm of land was reaching out to embrace us to the left. And Talienze shouted, 'The land is here! Steer east, steer round the headland.'

Bollullos was instantly at the rail and flinging in the sounding rope. 'Rocks! Rising fast. Back oar!'

Activity, mayhem. Argo was slowed. (She could have slowed herself! She was fickle when it came to sailing with men on board.) As the light grew stronger we saw the shadow of the ship on the ocean floor, the movement of sea creatures, and the strewn shapes of sunken masonry.

We were in the shallows, and close to breaking on the hidden reef.

Jason reminded us all, by his actions, of what a great captain he had once been. He spat instructions to the oarsmen, took a hand at the steering oar, whilst using Rubobostes' great strength, and with Talienze and Tairon scouring the water for hazards, seen and unseen, he guided us round and back to safety, then steered a course about the headland, in the lee of the towering cliffs, and into the safer harbour, below what Tairon instantly recognised as the Cave of Akirotiri.

We flung down the sea anchor, shipped oars, and waited for the full of the day to make our situation clear.

16

Queller

From the cave above the harbour, Queller watched the arrival of the painted ship and its strange crew. She stepped back into the shadows, hugged the cold stone wall, nervous now, and trying to remember. *Remember!* There was something familiar about the ship.

Something so familiar about the ship.

It couldn't be. It can't be. So long ago ... so long ago ...

There was something familiar about the ship. But that ship—

No! It can't be!

—was long lost, long gone. Time, tide and the turning of stars and sun and moon, surely by now they had swallowed her up, made reef-wrack of her planks, sea-rot of her decks, and mast, and sail, and that hideous, hateful, grinning, smiling, bitch-headed, bitch-breasted siren-singing guardian!

No!

Not that ship, not now, not after so many turns of the sky. Not after so many turns of triumph.

She crept forward, trying to quell her fear. The ship bobbed in the bay among the skeletons of other ships. The tide rushed and faded, the hulk moved on the swell, her small and pitiful crew gazing upwards, scouring the cliffs, pink, blank faces, curious and fear-filled, uncertain, but anxious to be ashore.

Queller caught the stink of one of them and again drew back into the shadows.

Not him. Not again. It can't be him. Fawn and Vine! Quell the beat of my heart! Not him. Long dead. Long dead. Not him. Not him.

Again she invoked Fawn and Vine, the Bull and the *Labra*,

but there was no answer from these old forces, though they lay throughout the island, quietly aware.

She pulled back from the cave, ran briskly through the labyrinth, emerging in the storm-cave in the mountains, among the broken statues and scattered bronzes that had been brought here to appease the storm in the time of the Shaper. She looked out across the woods and the fields; she listened to the rushing of water, the flutter of wings, the rustle of the vines as they spread and reached, snagging and tugging at each other in their urge to grow more densely. She listened to the bees. She smelled the potency of the herbs and flowers on which they gorged. She trembled as the earth itself slowly swallowed all that was rotten: a snake ingesting its prey.

Again she passed below the earth, this time coming to the southern shore, high on the hill, looking out across the vast expanse of aquamarine, sensing only the surge and swell of the great ocean.

And back through the earth once more, emerging this time at the head of a dark valley. There were always storm clouds here, swirling silently. The bleak valley threatened her, even though its occupant had long since disappeared. The water that flowed from the valley was ice-cold and sour. The trees that grew from the steep sides of the gorge were mangled, blackened, living on the stone-wood, the petrified remains of the forest that had once grown here. Shaper's valley.

Now Queller's valley. She had fought hard for the place. She hurried to the nearby stone ruins.

The honey child was still in her sanctuary. Queller ran quickly around the crumbling walls, glancing inside to see the girl. Her heart calmed a little. The honey child was watching her. Everything was safe here. Nothing had been disturbed. Nothing had passed up the valley.

The honey child was smiling. She was so pretty. Queller waved to her and called, 'I can't talk now. But I'll come soon.'

She slipped back into the cave, traversed the labyrinth, closing rock, opening rock, and came again to the cliff mouth overlooking the northern haven.

The ship was moored, men finding their footing on the weed-slick rocks, offloading equipment. A small group were threading their way up one of the old paths, their eyes on the slippery slope, their attention directed towards safety.

Three others were coming towards the wide, low cave. One of

them looked shifty, brighter-eyed and more canny than the others. He looked wrong. He was young, but he was heavy with age. Terrible with age.

Queller slipped back into the darkness. This was very bad. Very bad indeed.

She would have to think. There was only one place to go to think this through, and so, like a silver shade, she slipped into the underworld, abandoning the cold cavern.

But she had left an echo there, an echo of her fear and surprise, of her concern and her loneliness, an echo inaudible to a man like Urtha, who was with me as we entered the cavern, but an echo that rang in the head of a man 'terrible with age' louder than one of the huge bronze timbals that had sounded in Medea's skinning-fleshing sanctuary.

I drank that echo and digested it. I could not see the woman's face, but her silent chatter and her restless, nervous flutter were as distinct as the paintings on the cavern's walls.

17

Raptor Rising

Before that, however, for a long while we stood on Argo's nervous deck, away from the quays, riding the swell, examining the harbour. Tairon was puzzled.

'This is certainly the harbour at Akirotiri,' he said, 'but it's deserted. This is one of the great harbours of the island. You can see that just by looking around you.'

Enclosed by rising cliffs, protected by a double barrier of sea walls, the quays themselves lined by a tumble of buildings, from sprawling warehouses to clustered dwellings, all painted in vivid colours, the place indeed seemed rich.

Those colours! Vibrant greens, blues of every hue, from aquamarine to lavender, rosy pinks, and dawn-blushing orange ... the exotic brilliance that surrounded the choppy waters was in stark contrast to the brooding mountain that clasped the haven.

'That is the Akirotirian Cave,' Tairon reminded us, pointing to the low, wide mouth, halfway up one of the steep slopes. 'It's the cave where Kronos shot the arrow that struck Zeus as he swam towards Greek Land. Zeus used the arrow as a mast, tying his shirt to it as a sail. There are more caves on Crete than can be imagined, and all were created to celebrate or begin a life. Dyctea is the greatest of them all, deep inland, almost impossible to find. That same Zeus was first formed there, spilling from its womb covered with hair, but already fully shaped as a man.'

The maze-runner stared around him, uncomprehending and disturbed. 'This place should not be so abandoned. What's going on?' he mused.

'We won't find out just by sitting here,' Jason said loudly from behind us. He had been listening to the conversation. 'Let's berth, sort out the ship, find what supplies we can, and get a team or two up to the high ground. Pretty colours, and freshly painted, too. Deserted? Then there's a reason. I think we'll find food supplies if we look carefully.'

There was general agreement. Everyone was hungry, but the rationing of fresh water was a greater incentive to strike land. The mast was lowered into place, and the starboard oars run out. The sea anchor was hauled aboard and with deft, gentle strokes, and with Bollullos at the steering oar, the crew brought Argo into the curling grasp of the double wall.

We turned the ship and moored her so that she faced the open sea, at the very edge of the town. If we needed a fast escape, this would be the only place from which to effect the manoeuvre.

The boys were given the task of cleaning the vessel. The Greeklanders attended to repairs, to the cracked oars, the ripped sail, and the torn and cracked hands of those of us who had become callused as we had heaved across the ocean, from Alba to this warm, unwelcoming place.

Jason led a small group up to the westernmost edge of the cliffs, to survey the lie of the land. With Urtha and Tairon, I ascended the steep path to the cave.

And it was here, crouched below the confusion of images painted and scratched upon the rough walls, that I caught the echo from the woman who had been watching us all along.

A torch held before him, Urtha was staring at the decorations. They showed birds in flight, and other animals, stretched out as if being wind-dried; and there were odd designs related to ships and sails, and symbols that might have represented engineering structures. The walls were awash with them, overlapping and disordered.

'These are all very strange,' Urtha observed, somewhat unnecessarily. 'I've seen nothing like them. They're human, but not quite. Animal, but not quite. Very strange faces. So strange in the face, so striking in the eyes, almost canine. And so long and thin. They don't seem to be proportioned right. Though that said, when I look at Rubobostes, more horse than man, I'm not sure that there is anything that can't be achieved in the womb.'

He prowled about the deeper part of the cave, stooping occasionally to peer along the narrow shaft that led away from the mouth. Tairon watched him from the entrance. The maze-runner was very disturbed by something, but in answer to my gentle question he remained impassive, motionless, staring not into the shadows but into his own past, I suspected.

'It's gloomy down there,' Urtha said. 'But I see glinting: metal perhaps, or that stuff that glows in dark, that funny stone. I saw it on the way to Delphi.'

'Phosphor.'

'The tunnel goes a long way, by the looks of it. But it's narrow. Too narrow for a grown man.'

The echo of the woman-like but not wholly human creature that had recently been here was still strong. I followed it through the shaft and Urtha was quite right. The tunnel became no more than a crawling space, winding and branching, a network that curved around, knotted in and about its own dimensions, spreading out into the subterranean gloom. The walls closed in on me and my breath caught in my lungs, suffocating me with a sudden panic.

I broke the connection with the strong yet elusive memory, came back to find Urtha settling down on one knee, leaning back on his haunches, the flaring torch dipped before him. He was still staring into the bowels of the cavern.

'Tairon went down the passage. I could hear him for a while, but now he's vanished. Shall we go after him?'

I didn't think that would be a good idea. Tairon was a labyrinth-runner and if *he* could get lost – as he had done before – then even I could become dislocated if I wasn't careful.

But it would be a great loss to us if Tairon failed to come back.

We needn't have worried. No sooner had Urtha and I returned to the deserted harbour, meeting up with the other groups that had set off to explore the immediate hinterland around the cove, than Tairon appeared, walking over the ridge of the cliff, clutching his small bag. He came to the path and joined us.

The water was brisk, a swell beginning to form before a breeze from the west. Dusk was not far off. We exchanged information and observations, nothing much of consequence, certainly nothing that was more important than Tairon's and my own feeling of entering a cave from which we had been watched, though Tairon was clearly holding something back.

It was only when Urtha looked around for his son that he asked the question, what happened to the *Kryptoii*?

Rubobostes answered, 'They went up there, along that narrow path, strung out like insects walking along a twig. That bald man, Talneeze, was leading them.'

The path that he indicated would have taken them over the highest point of the hill overshadowing the harbour.

'Talienze?'

'That's the one. Said he wanted to get the lie of the land. Said that the boys' eyes were sharper than ours.'

'I don't trust him,' Niiv whispered in my ear. Her fingers gripped my arm meaningfully. 'I don't know who he is, that Speaker, I don't know where he came from. And I don't trust him.'

Urtha heard these murmured words and agreed. 'He behaved very strangely in the hall where Vortingoros made us welcome. He said he was from Armorica, an exile. The shade of his skin is more like Tairon's.'

'I was thinking the same thing myself,' the displaced Cretan offered, 'but his eyes are green and slightly yellow. A very unusual colour for this part of the world. That said,' the maze-runner added carefully, 'from the moment we approached the sea channel to this island, the man seemed at home.'

All of this took some understanding, but for the moment, Urtha was more concerned for his son. He sent Bollullos and Caiwain to climb the same path. They armed themselves and set off.

We were hailed from a distance by one of the Greeklanders. Two others were rolling a fat clay pithos out from one of the buildings. When they reached us and hauled the vessel upright they cut through the thick wax seal to reveal what looked like congealed yellow fat.

It was solid honey.

If several of the argonauts looked a little disappointed that the treasure was not of a more liquid nature, the truth was this was an excellent addition to our occasional meals. Peering into the jar, Niiv added: 'There are dark objects at the bottom. Could be fruit.'

Better still.

I noticed that she concentrated in that way signifying the rash use of her powers of charm. As she saw more deeply into the jar she suddenly jerked back, frowning quickly.

'Is it fruit?' I asked her.

'Nuts,' she replied as she moved to sit down on the quayside, slightly shaky.

'What sort of nuts?' one of the Greeklanders asked.

'Large ones,' was all she said, and the Greeklander suddenly understood.

Better news was to come. A loud hail from the cliff top, towards dusk, announced the return of Bollullos and Caiwain. They were in the company of three of the young *kryptoii*. As they began to descend the treacherous path, Tairon noticed that the big man was carrying something around his shoulders. It was soon revealed to be a goat, still alive, tethered by the hooves. It was an odd-looking animal indeed, with horns that spiralled in strange ways, and a colour to its coat that seemed more in keeping with the bright hues of flowers than the dull disguise of a grazing animal.

Kymon and Colcu were not with this party. They appeared above the Akirotirian Cave in the company of Talienze. Urtha was disturbed by this.

I flew up to the cave, watching closely, hovering before them in the form of a humming bird as they helped each other down the craggy face of the cliff and onto the narrow ledge at the mouth of the cave itself.

They explored the interior, wondering at the paintings, then descended to the harbour.

Bollullos had made his own report.

'The land is enchanting. From the top of the cliff you can see there are valleys stretching away into the interior, and a mountainous region in the distance. Some of the valleys are obscured by clouds, others are heavily wooded. But there are open spaces where all manner of creatures are running and grazing. To the east, I can see a plain, and a wide river. What looks like storm clouds in the distance must be more mountains. This place is wide, wild and shrouded.'

'Are there signs of people?' Tairon asked.

'Hard to tell. There are patterns on the land, and structures that might be the ruins of buildings.'

'But no living person,' Urtha prompted.

'Only goats and creatures that must be special to this place.'

When Colcu arrived, he confirmed what Bollullos and the other boys had said, but added, 'There are certainly buildings; they seemed to me to be in the process of being swallowed by the earth, half here, half in the rock. And another thing: I saw smoke in the distance.'

Kymon added, 'There is movement in the distance, on the dawn side of the land. Flashing light, reflection, apparent movement, a little like people running into hiding.'

'This is certainly not the land I left,' Tairon said to me cryptically. I had been watching him as he listened to these various reports, and he was clearly disturbed and perplexed by what he was hearing.

'It was a long time ago that you left in your maze-wandering,' I reminded him.

'I know. But this change – the hint of it, at least – is very odd. It's almost as if this is not the same island. Just a *form* of it. I'm puzzled, but I need to think.'

He moved away from me; a while later I saw him board Argo and creep cautiously into the stern, below the goddess. He stayed there for some time, talking occasionally – he was quite animated when he talked – mostly crouching quietly, perhaps listening, perhaps contemplating this return to his old land.

At the other end of the ship, the motionless oaken figure of Segomos stared back at him.

The goat was skinned and gutted, stretched out to hang for a day or so. We made a meal of its liver, lungs and stomach. The Greeklanders knew just what to do, and the food was delicious, if a little sweet.

Tairon came walking down the ramp from Argo and returned to us, but he was distracted; he sat brooding, moody, his attention often drawn to the dark mouth on the cliff above us. He suddenly sat upright and attentive when Urtha reached into his belt and drew out several coils of bronze.

'I found these in the cave,' Urtha said. 'Beautifully wrought, very intricate. This piece has the small head of a hawk.'

The metalwork was indeed fine, several broken lengths of twisted bronze, very strong; and two pieces of a softer metal mix that was flexible. Urtha demonstrated this by twisting it several times. 'You'd expect it to snap, but it doesn't. It's like rope, but stronger. It's not all metal. There's animal sinew in here as well. And I can see thin strands of gold.'

Now Tairon emptied the contents of a small cloth pouch onto the floor in front of us. 'I've been collecting too,' he said. 'These were very deep in the cave, along the narrow passage, scattered. I think they've been torn in anger. Creative anger.'

His own treasure was similar to Urtha's. Urtha picked up a length of the entwined bronze strands. It had a dove's head on the end. 'Made by a true craftsman. But what are they?'

'Bits of rigging,' Tairon said quietly.

'For a ship?' someone asked.

'Not for a ship.'

'If not for a ship, then what?' Jason asked irritably, growing tired of Tairon's cryptic behaviour.

The thin man looked up at the sky, at the first gleam of stars. 'For two boys,' he said. 'And a journey that may even now be still underway.'

'I realise now the significance of this particular cave,' Tairon said, pointing up to the cliff. 'I knew the story, but like everyone of my age and time on this island, I was never sure where the final events had occurred. I'm certain of it, now. This is the most remote of his Shaping Chambers. He had a hundred such chambers, hidden on the island. And it was from this harbour that the Shaper's sons made their final, fatal flight. Somewhere to the north of us, one found the end of life, either in the sea or on the rocks. These are the trimmed struts and rigging of their earlier wings, I imagine. Perhaps not strong enough.

'You see? He has shaped the ends of each main wire into the heads of the two birds that symbolised his sons. His two lost sons.'

Niiv, paying close attention to Tairon's words, nevertheless found a moment to squeeze my arm. 'More lost sons? This is becoming a habit. Are there any lost sons in your own life, Merlin?'

'None. Be quiet.'

'I don't think I believe you,' she teased, with a sly glance. 'I don't think I believe you at all. And now I'll be quiet.'

It was now that Tairon told us one of the hundreds of tales from his homeland, an ancient event: of how a father, a man with the talent for what he called 'machines', had created wings for his two sons.

The tale contained a shadow of familiarity for me, though Tairon's Island was not on my Path. It had been preserved in the memory of the Greeklanders, though in a much changed form. The father was Daidalos, of course, in one of whose many labyrinths Tairon had run as a youth and become lost, before finding me, Jason and Argo.

And it seemed that Argo had now asked Jason to recount the legend.

Raptor rising:
The wings (Tairon told us) were like a mix of swans' and hawks' wings, sewn deeply into the bodies of the boys, one set of white and one of black, waterproofed with wax, sewn to the muscles with bronze and gold-threaded bull sinew. When the boys flexed their shoulders, the wings moved.

Their father believed that between the harsh, storm-scoured realm of earth and the unchanging and glittering vault of the heavens there was a world, invisible to the eye: a hinterland. That which changed in the heavens changed here, in this middle realm, and only darkness stopped the land being seen. He had become aware of it whilst studying the stars from one of his Shaping Chambers, at the centre of a maze that ran inside a hill whose summit was open to the sky.

But how to reach that place? How to fly that high and understand all that might be seen? A mechanical bird was of no use. But his sons were light-bodied and athletic, and were keen to do their father's work.

He set his sons, white-winged Icarus and black-winged Raptor, the task of flying higher and higher every day, and every day they came back exhausted, with tales of how the very air itself seemed to thin, how despite the Sun, the air was colder. How, despite the Sun, the stars began to show from the vault, as if night were coming. How their eyes seemed to see with crystal clearness. But they could not see the middle land.

Daidalos strengthened the metalled tendons in their spines, ran threads of twisted bronze across their flesh, girth-lashed them with ivy roots, trimmed the flight feathers of the wings, coated their bodies in oil to make them slip more easily through the aether. He gave them masks, with narrowed eyes and sharpened noses, to refine what they could smell and see to a higher degree. He launched them from a cliff towering over the western sea – this same cliff – and the boys swooped, caught the rising thermal wind, ascending out of sight.

Day after day, each day flying higher.

'Did you see light on the hidden land?' Daidalos asked impatiently.

'No, but the darkness is brighter than we have ever seen,' said Icarus.

'If our wings would carry us, we could fly on for ever,' said Raptor. 'Father, that vault is vaster than any land you might dream of.'

Clipped in places, extra feathers glued, more harnessing, more cables in the flesh, even their food became the food of birds, intended to keep them light, to hollow out their bones.

'No middle land, but the vault is ablaze with stars!'

'To look down, the earth is like a lake, a perfect lake, so blue, so white, like a dish of crystal water. Our land floats in it like a great ship lying on its side.'

'Go higher!'

On the last day, Raptor saved his energy whilst Icarus strove strongly to rise. Raptor fell behind. His brother was a small, white speck in the darkening sky above. Already, the sheen of star-glitter was brighter than the other flier's broad, white wings.

Raptor now used his strength, leaving the rising heat, stretching every feather to find this thinning air.

After a while he saw a bright star gleaming. Coming closer, he saw it was Icarus, hanging at the edge of destruction, exhausted, wings moving, head turned up in wonder. Mars glared at them, fierce and red. They could both see the long roads and sturdy fortresses that covered the heavenly land of the War God. And Luna herself, half in shadow to the earthbound, showed her dark face clearly to these young men's eyes.

'There is no middle land but wasteland,' Icarus murmured with almost his last breath. 'Just wasteland!'

Then he fell, wings collapsed.

Horrified, Raptor swooped down to catch him, caught him, holding him above the clouds, but Icarus shouted, 'Go higher! You can't stop my fall! I'm finished, brother, but you can go higher.'

Raptor's fingers, struggling to hold his brother, tore away his brother's wings; struggling to catch him again, tore open his brother's chest; struggling to retrieve him, tore open his brother's throat.

Icarus plummeted. Raptor, grieving and frightened for what he had done, struck up to the vault, crying, 'I *will* see what our father dreamed for us!'

He was never seen again. There are those who say that wind came from the Sun and helped him through the wasteland, where there are no paths, where the air is ghostly-thin, where no spirit beckons to you, no guide to lead the way. With father's love and brother's blood, Raptor came at last among the stars. Some believe he hides in what the Greeklanders call *Cassiopeia*. If you look closely, you can see the shape of wings.

Tairon had told the story in a strangely formal way, as if reciting from the memory of an older storytelling. His eyes had been focused elsewhere. His hands had shaken slightly as he gesticulated in a theatrical way to accompany the events he described.

Now he returned to normal and looked around for a response from his listeners.

Most of us were quietly bemused. Kymon said, 'If one brother was dead, and the other lost, how do you know what was said between them?'

Tairon just smiled.

'What was the point of the story?' Bollullos asked. 'I liked the story, don't get me wrong. Very unearthly. But – its point?'

There followed a long and confusing discussion on the meaning of Tairon's tale, everything from the true nature of birds to the nature of wastelands, from the cruelty of fathers towards their sons, to the search for knowledge, and the necessity of sacrifice. Everything was nonsense.

'I'll tell you what the story means,' Niiv said suddenly. I hadn't seen her getting to her feet. She stood, half in shadow, only the bare skin of her folded arms catching the firelight; and her eyes, bright like crystal as she stared at me. 'It means that when two people strive for the same thing they should succeed together or fail together. Raptor could have gone on but he tried to help Icarus when he fell. Icarus begged Raptor to abandon him and try alone for the middle realm. These were both good motives. But Icarus broke on rocks, and Raptor was lost against the vault. Nothing was achieved. If Raptor had helped Icarus, if one bird had helped the other safely back to earth! If they had *flown together*! Then both would have lived to try another day.'

Urtha nudged me, whispering with a little laugh, 'I'm not sure, but I think she's talking about you. You've been neglecting her.'

The argument ceased. All eyes turned to Tairon.

'I told you the story because Argo asked me to,' he said quietly.

'Whether there is a point to it remains to be seen. But if I understand Niiv correctly, then she has come closest. There has been a conflict here, on this island, between two minds that see the world in different ways. Argo asked me to tell the story. She must have had a reason.

'By the way,' he glanced at me. 'She has asked to see you. I think she wants us to sail along the northern shore and find Ak-Gnossos.'

'The old city?'

'She's taking us into the heart of the island. I don't know why. But I think we should follow her instructions.'

18

Maze of Echoes

I boarded Argo and climbed down into the prow, to the threshold of the Spirit of the Ship. I'd expected that Argo would allow me in, but she turned me back.

Mielikki whispered, 'Not yet. She doesn't wish to speak to you at the moment. But she has told me to tell you to sail east, to the Bull Palace. There is a hidden river there that will take you deeper into the island, to a city close to the Chamber of Discs. She asks you not to enquire too closely at this moment. This is difficult for Argo.'

I reported this to Jason and to Tairon. The Bull Palace, Tairon told us, was famous for its labyrinth and sat at the heart of Ak-Gnossos, a high-walled city. After a brief discussion, it was decided that there was no real alternative than to obey Argo, unenlightening though her instruction was. We had arrived here in confusion, sailed here in obscurity, at the whim of an old and beautiful ship, worked at the oars by painful memories that had yet to be revealed.

We prepared the ship, took the huge pithos of honey with us, and rowed from the colourful harbour, catching the wind and sailing along the northern coast to the legendary and labyrinthine palace at Ak-Gnossos.

We kept as close to the cliffs as was safe. Tairon surveyed them constantly as we steered our way through the heaving waters. Rubobostes was at the stern oar, Bollullos drummed out the rhythm when we were forced to row. It was dangerously rocky here and the swell surged back against the ship, a booming resonance that rocked the vessel. The cliffs were over-looming, sheer, encrusted with gnarled growth, occasionally shimmering with outcrops of crystal, or with the fall of streams of water draining from mountains beyond our view.

The cliffs never fully dropped away, but occasionally receded slightly to expose steep beaches and the narrow mouths of widening valleys, revealing cloud-obscured hills in the distance. Bright colour and illusory movement, in those misty regions, told of villages and small havens, but everything was drowned in silence, a land that was smothering life.

A day later we reached the bleaker, ruined harbour that guarded the river leading to the Bull Palace.

Once, the river-approach from the sea to the great palace had been awe-inspiring. Towering figures had lined the banks. The tombs and shrines of the kings of the land and their powerful consorts had shone white and gold. Guard stations and trading stations, sprawling forges and tanning sheds had mixed with pleasure gardens and the beckoning fragrances of honey-traps, where music played and the sounds of revelry were a delight to the sea-worn ears of the traveller.

Most impressively, four great bulls had once bestrode the river, one of bronze, one formed from accretions of obsidian, one carved from cedar wood and one shaped from gleaming marble. Their massive heads had been lowered, the horns horizontal, a clever mechanism in each of the heads making the huge tongue lap slowly up and down into the water, so that each ship that sailed to Ak-Gnossos had to adjust its stroke to miss these dangerous rhythms.

It was part of the bull game, Tairon remembered, part of the private humour of the sea-lords and kings who had owned the surface of the land for generations, co-existing mostly peacefully with the two primal forces that had warred with each other for possession of the island's deeper realms.

Tairon had been a child during that fabulous time, and memory was now an echo; now, however, he stared at the bleak remains as Argo moved against the flow of the crystal waters, between the corrupt and fading edifices of that age.

Of the obsidian bull bridge, only the curved horns remained, rising forlornly from the river. We passed through them without interruption. Of the wood bull, a charred mass on the western shore suggested its fate. The marble creature was recognisable only by its eyes, the horns broken off, the once-savage features smoothed and shaped by wind and rain.

The bronze bull was drowning, its muzzle above the river, greened and corroded, a great hoof stretched onto one of the banks, a twisted horn rammed into the trees on the other side. Argo's keel scraped the dead metal as we crossed the statue, a scream, an echo, a despairing cry of memory. And at that moment we saw the palace, and were astonished at the sight.

The land was sucking it down, reclaiming the shaped clay as it was reclaiming the whole of the created world of men. The high walls were sloping towards the south, half consumed, the foundations, close to us, being torn from the earth. Away from us, the buildings and chambers, the courtyards and watchtowers, all had already been wrapped about by the folds of rock and soil. Trees of all kinds were growing up the angled walls, branches clutching at every nook and cranny, helping to drag the vast royal residence back to nature.

Birds flocked and wheeled over the silent structure. The sun caught the brilliance of the painted walls, as if the consuming earth was pleased at least to allow these vibrant hues, these flower colours, to remain intact as the snake swallowed her prey.

Ak-Gnossos was vast and wide, but the mouth of the island was wider. Even as Argo was moored and the argonauts leapt ashore to explore the passages and chambers of the sinking palace, so the ground trembled below our feet and stones fell from on high; a further swallowing; the prey dragged deeper in that gulping moment between the long, quiet periods of breathing.

I descended a steep, stepped ramp into the gloom of a chamber that had always been deep, and was now deeper in the earth. The clever construction of the building allowed for shafts of light to pick out details on the walls, small pools of illumination in the otherwise complete dark. Everywhere was the *labrys*, the double-headed axe, some carved in the wall, some carved from stone, a few of corrupting bronze. Sea creatures of all descriptions were painted in these passages and hollow rooms, and the profiled heads of youths and girls watched by the staring eyes of land creatures, their features incomplete. Sometimes I could hear the calls of other argonauts, heralding their finds, calling out in awe. Their voices carried along the gloomy corridors, echoing through the wells of light.

The smell of rank stone suddenly gave way to the sharp odour of the ocean. We were a long way inland, but the salt air was unmistakeable, as was the sound of surf surging against a beach. That sound excited me. I began to understand the nature of Ak-Gnossos and hurried towards the hidden sea.

As I did so, I became aware of someone running ahead of me.

The way to the beach was blocked by a massive gate, its central column a double axe of immense height and breadth, the blades curling down to the floor to allow a double entrance inside the sharpened edges. The haft was a tree, twisted many times around its own core. Within the dulled bronze of the blades I could see the patterns of the night sky, the stars and constellations picked out in detail, now greened by the tarnish and fading.

I passed through the gate. The ocean heaved against a bleak, stony shore, where marble statues leaned or had already fallen. A three-quarter moon was bright in the night, moonshadow everywhere.

'Where are you?' I called.

'I'm here,' Niiv replied, slipping from behind a statue, almost invisible save for her pale features. She approached me tentatively, then scampered close and put her arms round me.

She was breathless with excitement.

'This place doesn't exist,' she said in a voice charged with understanding. 'It's all illusion.'

'Of sorts. Yes. But how do you know? What have you been doing?' I felt my pulse race.

'I *looked*. There was no harm in it, was there? I wasn't looking at *you*.'

'You silly little fool!' I grabbed her again, turned her head in the moonlight. Silver light softened her features, but her hair glinted grey. She had aged. She had spent her precious life on establishing a truth that she should have known I would already have discerned.

'Don't waste what you have!' I said to her for the hundredth time. She was an exasperating lover!

Indignantly, she pulled away. 'When my father died, in the North, in the snow, cold, alone, abandoned by his spirits, he bequeathed his charm to me. He meant me to *use* it, Merlin. Why else leave it to me?'

She had done this so often before. I could almost have cried for her. It was so unnecessary for her to squander life simply because she had a talent for the Otherworld and for vision.

'You are half a year older, Niiv. Because of what you looked at!'

'I don't feel it,' she argued.

'Half a year that I won't have with you.' *Added to all the other lost days, lost moons.*

'Nonsense. You will have me to the end.'

'Why are you so stubborn?'

'Why are *you* so ungrateful?'

I hugged her. She was still consumed with pleasure at having broken the wall of unreality.

'What do you think has happened here?' she asked after a moment. I had used a little of my own power to touch in the details, but little was needed. Though *we* rowed, Argo was setting the course. She had brought us here for a purpose. No doubt she was waiting to surface from this subterranean dream of an ocean. I was certain now that Argo was ready to take us to where the tragedy had begun. She was taking us on a tour of her past, and Time would flow differently whilst we were in the embrace of the island.

But I said this to Niiv:

'Will you promise me not to "look" until I ask you to? It isn't necessary. If I need your help I'll always ask for it.'

'You say that,' she pouted, beginning to argue again. 'But you never do.'

'Not true. I've asked you for help many times.'

'Not for anything serious. You don't use me, you don't *teach* me.' It always came back to that: teach me, let me touch the 'charm' that's carved on your bones. 'When my father died, he didn't leave me his spirit just to *live* with it and then *die* with it. He expected me to be practical.'

'But you're not strong with it, Niiv. It wastes you too much, especially if you waste the skill. You once looked into my own future, remember? I can mark the wrinkles around your eyes; I can pinch the softening skin on your arms – all the result of *that* stupidity. I never expected to love you like I do ...'

'Love me? Hah! You fight me off all the time.'

This was not true. She knew it in her heart, so I didn't argue the point. I wondered, though, how much she understood the nagging pain I was feeling, a pain that was growing. In the moonlight she was fresh; she was alluring; I wanted us to make love right there and then. This is what I always adored about the woman, these times of anger and the times of joy that followed the anger, without the interruption of the world around us; most particularly without Urtha entering our small house unannounced and cheerfully apologising as he drew back, loudly joking with his *uthiin* outside as he waited for me to emerge and blister his ears with irritation.

Oh yes, Niiv was in my heart. She was not the first – Medea had been the first, though memory was misty – and she would not be the last. But she was the only woman I had ever known whom I wished to keep distant from me because I couldn't bear the thought of losing her.

She dabbed at my eyes with a finger, looked curiously at the glisten. 'Well, well. The man bleeds salty love.' She quickly licked the finger. 'Magic,' she teased. 'Even in your tears there must be magic, so I'll thank you for my daily feast. Here's my own contribution.'

She reached up and kissed me. Then, with astonishing strength, she drew me to the cold beach, close to the night surge of the water. Her hands were like imps, her fingers the sharp thorns of their weapons. I bled beneath her loving touch. She found a way to press our bodies close inside a tent of our own clothes.

I could hear Urtha calling for me, Jason too. But Niiv's strenuous breathing was a balm to those unwanted and searching cries from above, from the halls and staterooms of the swallowed palace.

Suddenly, in the night as we lay quietly, half asleep, there was the smell of honey. Someone slipped across the beach and peered down at us. Ephemeral and elemental, the woman cocked her head this way and that, touching ghostly fingers to our faces, withdrawing like a sudden breeze as we both stirred to take a closer look.

'Who was that?' Niiv asked, shivering slightly.

'I don't know. But she was watching us when we came into the harbour.'

'The illusory harbour,' Niiv said pointedly. 'An illusion within an illusion?'

'I don't think so.'

'Why don't you look? I'm not allowed to! Makes me too flabby and old,' she mocked.

'Shut up.'

'You should look!'

I was watching the shadows, but the elemental had slipped away. Her scent trail led into a cleft in the rocks on the shore, and I suspected that a labyrinth wound its serpentine way from that small entrance place.

'I recognise the smell, but can't place it,' the girl said.

'Honey.'

'Oh yes. Honey. Like the smell in the jar, but sweeter; the jar with the ... things at the bottom.'

'The heads. You know they were heads.'

'Four of them!' She shuddered then looked up at me. 'Why would anybody want to keep heads in honey?'

'It makes them last longer. I'll keep *all* of you in honey when you're dead, if you like; take you out for a lick every new moon. Honey keeps a body supple too.'

She didn't like the tease. She was staring out across the brightening ocean. Dawn was rising, the stars fading. The new light caught the unexpected anguish on her face. 'When I *am* gone,' she said, 'I want to go home.' She looked at me, suddenly melancholy. Home to where my father lies. You *will* make sure that happens ... Won't you?'

'It won't be for a long time yet.'

'But it will happen.' She hunched up, throwing a pebble into the foaming surge of the ocean on the dark beach. 'And you said it yourself: I squander time as if it were water from the well. When I go, I want to sit next to my father, and his father, in Tapiola's Cold Cave. It's my right as *shamanka*. Don't let anyone prevent it, just because I'm a woman.'

I put my arm around her. 'Nobody will argue with me. And meanwhile, I'll squander for us both. You must simply resist the temptation to show how strong you are.'

The moment of sadness passed. Dawn began to glow. Niiv sniffed the air. The smell of honey had gone. Now there was the pervading odour of a man's sweat. We looked round to see Urtha, Jason and Rubobostes standing behind us, all of them grinning hugely.

'Don't mind us,' Urtha said. 'But when you're dressed you might explain what's happening.'

The spectral encounter with the honey sprite, and the unexpected moment of reflection on death, had made us forget that were sitting by the water's edge, naked and cool in the rising light. If it bothered Niiv, she didn't show it. She stood and stretched, magnificent, slim and as pale as the Moon, save for the dark hair that framed her face and shoulders. She turned, then, and stepped into the cold water, shivering as she entered more deeply and stooped to freshen her skin.

'I hope this is safe,' she called to her four admirers, before launching herself into the waves.

So do I, I thought, but she swam safely and came to shore, and by that time most of the other argonauts had slipped and probed their way through the strange palace, and found the beach and the buried sea.

'You're talking in riddles again!' Urtha protested as I briefly paused for breath during my attempt to explain my understanding of our situation. 'Riddles! This is the third or fourth time. Don't get me wrong, I'm glad you're here, glad of your knowledge ...' he tapped me on the shoulder with the haft of his eating knife. He had been stabbing impatiently at the stony beach as I'd talked. 'But nothing you say makes sense. Oolering men? Hollowings? Echonian Lands? Does anyone else understand this drivel?'

Bollullos and Rubobostes shrugged, shaking their heads. Niiv chuckled. 'I do.'

'You would,' Urtha growled.

'I have an idea about it,' Tairon confirmed. Again, Urtha muttered, 'You would.'

Tairon had listened carefully, and with a rare half-smile on his face, dark eyes absorbing me as he absorbed my words. Close behind him, Talienze had listened with equal intrigue.

The youthful *kryptoii* were playing beach games in the unnatural light of the unnatural dawn, some sort of touch game, with much precocious somersaulting and leaping. It reminded me of the bull-leaping for which Greek Land and Crete were famous. And I had seen such leaping in the Hostel of the Overwhelming Gift, though the bull in that case was being roasted.

We were missing two of the Greeklanders and Caiwain the Exile, left at the harbour with Argo.

'I'm sorry, Merlin. Please continue.'

Urtha's outburst had relieved his growing frustration. My words had been as alien to him as this island itself. He looked abashed, but interested again, resuming his stabbing of the beach, though when I stared pointedly at him for a moment he stopped and sheathed the small knife.

Cloak around his body, he was crouching on one knee, as was Bollullos. The rest were either crouched on haunches, or sprawled back on elbows, as if basking in a sun that – though present on the far horizon – was giving off no heat at all.

There are parts of the world – they exist in great numbers – where the land has echoes. These might be valleys, small islands, plains, forests or mountains. These echo lands – I had used an expression, Echonian, which I had heard from a storyteller by the name of Homer – existed below the earth as it could be perceived. Importantly, they were not Otherworlds, or Ghostlands, or any sort of place where the Dead might journey to seek rest or rebirth.

They were simply echoes. And they had not all been formed when the world was formed, though it was believed there were ten that had. Most of them had been brought into creation by anguish, or dreams, and the intervention of creatures such as me.

They were, to put it bluntly, the leftovers of play, the fragmented remains of exercises in charm, enchantment, magic and manipulation. Once formed, they were very hard to discard. They lived on – as Echo, fading slowly but never completely, as persistent as memory.

And we were inside such an echo.

During my own extended childhood, these discarded echo realms had been guarded by 'oolering men', who maintained a lifetime's vigil at the entrances to the false lands, preventing the inadvertent straying into non-existence. Later, these entrances had become places of pilgrimage, and the guardianship of what were now called 'hollowings' – as often enough the source of oracles – had passed into a more powerful form of government: that of priests, priestesses and those who could benefit from the attractive power of such situations.

Poor Delphi itself, that poverty-stricken hole in the rocks, its temples purloined of all richness by various nations, exploited by profiteers disguised as prophets, had almost certainly been the remnants of such a hollowing.

I liked to call them 'ways under'. I was afraid of them. They were unpredictable because they were substantially the product of unpredictable minds. Young minds, usually, but sometimes mad ones. One day, some time in ages to come, there would be secrets to be discovered in the 'mining' of them. But such endeavours had never particularly interested me.

I was interested now, however, because not only were Jason and his companions sitting silently in the centre of such a 'way under', but everything about it stank of deliberate construction.

Tairon had referred to 'Shaping Chambers'. The island was covered with the Shaper's 'Shaping Chambers'. Could these have been the entrances to the largest Echonian land that I could imagine – an echo of the whole island of Crete itself? Were we now crouched on a beach that was one of those entrances, and a large one at that: the labyrinthine Ak-Gnossian palace? It was an intriguing thought.

If my feeling was right, then who exactly had made this place? Who had turned this long, thin island into a maze of echoes? And if this was all echo – where was the real island?

Honey had visited Niiv and me in the night. The honey smell, the honey spell, the elemental presence of something that was most certainly not of Shaper's invention. Was *she* the anguished dreamer who had created the devouring dream?

I rambled on, thoughts tumbling, oblivious of the dark frowns of the ignorant, aware of Tairon's gleam, Talienze's smile.

'At some point,' I concluded, 'at some moment along our journey from Alba to the harbour at Akirotiri, we passed from the familiar world to the echo world that now surrounds us.'

'At Korsa!' Tairon exclaimed. 'I knew there was something wrong there. It was there, I'm certain of it now. Remember that strange tide? The way the sea surged, the way Argo threw herself against the wall of the quay? That was the moment! And it was not you nor I, Merlin, who was spinning the thread of that change.'

'Argo herself,' I concluded for him. This Cretan was clever.

'Argo herself,' Tairon agreed.

'Talking of whom ... here she comes,' Jason murmured, rising to his feet and pointing into the rising sun. '*Is* it her?'

There was a look in his eyes, I noticed, an expression that was not so much joyous as apprehensive. He watched what he thought was his ship, a small shape in the gleam of sea, but he was anxious now.

Niiv whispered, 'Look at your brutal bastard friend. Well, well, well.'

'What do you see?' I asked her. 'With your eyes and intuition, I mean. Nothing else.'

'The same as you. He's frightened. And he doesn't know why. This is the moment!' She grasped my arm. Her voice was soft, malign: 'Soon we'll hear the sound of chickens flapping home to roost. This should be good.'

I pushed her away from me. She was outraged, wide-eyed, her hands on her hips in that most obvious of poses; a moment later, devious, pretending she was not upset.

I ignored her. All I could see was Jason. I have seen elementals in many forms, but those that clouded his head now were like the marsh insects that swarm around men and cattle alike at dusk. Fury and memory, fear and fire were shaped in that ethereal miasma, a past being drawn from a man who had long believed it buried.

Approaching the beach was not a ship but a wave. It loomed larger, a bow wave, cascading in silver foam from a prow that slowly rose above the water.

Argo surfaced like Leviathan, surging from the sea-wrack, painted eyes watching us as her keel found the land and her prow ploughed onto the pebbled shore as we scattered from her sudden, shocking arrival.

Rage and regret dripped from her hull, as potent and tangible as the water that drained from her deck. Jason stepped forward. He pushed me roughly aside. He was being summoned. I risked a moment of eavesdropping and heard the harsh, hoarse voice of the ship, mournfully bidding him aboard. The rest of us were discouraged from approaching, and Jason alone entered Argo, passing into the Spirit of the Ship.

He appeared a while later, ashen and haunted, in a very bad mood. He called out, 'The others are here. Wet, but alive. Time to sail. Push this rank old barge off from the beach.'

We did as we were told, using brute strength and what ropes we could find, to drag the ship back into the ocean. Once we were all aboard, Argo turned her bow to the middle of nowhere and caught a current that only she could sense. She crossed the sea and eventually entered the channel of a river.

Now oars were pushed through, backs put into action, and we struck the ship out of the underworld and into the centre of the island.

19
Ephemera

Later, we emerged from the gloom as if from a dream, finding ourselves suddenly surrounded by mountains. The sun was bright. A colourful city sprawled away from us on each side of the river. There was not just fragrance in the air, and the passing sour whiff of tanning leather, but sound. The sound of life. The noise of bustling activity and the sharp cries of curiosity as a small crowd gathered to stare in amused confusion at our vessel, our Argo, as she banged and butted against the quay, while Rubobostes and the Greek Land mariners struggled to find mooring ropes and hold the old ship still.

'Much more like it,' Urtha approved, looking round. 'A civilised town at last! A place I can understand.'

This was indeed a wonderful place. High-decked barges drifted past us, their crews watching us cautiously; smaller boats were rowed not to the beat of drums but to the rhythmic blast of small bronze horns. Narrow-necked pithoi were stacked on the quays. Crates of fruit were being hauled on carts pulled by oxen. Dark-coated goats bleated as they were herded into pens; away from the harbour and somewhere behind the purple-and-rose coloured houses a festival was taking place. The jangle of tambourines punctuated the severe thump of a drumbeat with accompanying wailing horns. Occasionally there were cheers. Occasionally groans. Sometimes a scream.

Light sparkled on the hills around, and by looking carefully we could make out processions of children, all dressed in white tunics, all carrying small reflective shields. They wove their way along the paths, higher and higher towards the sky.

'Where *is* this shit-hole?' Jason suddenly shouted. He was in a foul mood. 'Where have we come? Does anybody know?'

Tairon turned to him and called, 'Yes. Home.'

'Whose home?'

'*My* home!' bellowed the Cretan, but he grinned as Jason frowned.

'You were born here? In this beautiful city?' Urtha asked. Compared with the muddy, forge-ringing, fire-burning chaos of Taurovinda, I could see why he was impressed.

'Right there,' said Tairon, pointing into the press of buildings. 'In the Street of the Bee.'

The name, once they understood it, had Urtha's *uthiin* roaring with laughter. They discussed briefly possible names for some of the streets of their own city; nothing was quite so delicate.

Tairon ignored them. He stared into the distance for a few moments, absorbing the colour and confusion, then cast me a glance. 'It hasn't changed much. I wonder how long I've been gone.'

'Easy enough to find out.'

While Jason negotiated mooring fees with the bureaucratic entourage who had appeared almost as soon as we'd reached the quays, Tairon and I walked into the town. The noise of the festival grew louder, the sense of gaiety more intense. I asked Tairon what the festival might have been and he looked uncomfortable.

'I'm not sure. But if it's what I think it is, best not to go there.'

In fact, he left me for a while to go to the area of the celebration. When he came back he immediately beckoned me back towards the Street of the Bee, continuing our exploration.

'Well? The festival?'

'Do you have a strong stomach?'

'Yes. Usually.'

He told me what was happening in the ring. It wasn't particularly festive. As the crowd groaned, then broke into a magnificent roar of pleasure, I thought of the cruelty of populations, but also of the kindness of a man like Tairon who wished to spare me outrages.

He was a quiet and deep man; he was, of course, a lost man. But here he was, home again, and he exuded anxiety and nerves like a child awaiting punishment. The city was so familiar to him that it must have felt as if he'd traversed the ages, coming back to the place at the true time of his childhood.

And that indeed is almost what had happened.

A familiar voice shouted my name from behind us. I sighed

and turned and Niiv came gasping up to us, but smiling. She had somehow found a loose dress, coloured green and decorated with leaping dolphins. I suspected she had stolen it from the market.

'Isn't this a wonderful place?' she enthused. 'Just breathe that air!'

She was right.

We had passed into the honey quarter – the scent was intense, the different flowers and herbs with which the liquid honey was being aromatised caused a heady sensation. There was much incense in the brew, I suspected.

We walked on and came to a small square. Here, Tairon pointed with astonishment to an old man sitting quietly in the shade of a chestnut tree. The man was blind, and one arm was cut off at the elbow. He held a strange stringed instrument in the surviving hand, and his thumb occasionally stroked the strings, making a meaningful and melancholy tune.

'By the Bull! I know that man. Thalofonus, a freed slave. He was once a fine musician. The king did that to him, took away his playing hand, because he once sang an inappropriate song. It was shortly after the trial when I was tested in the labyrinth for the first time, before I became lost in the maze. I was here, in this place, this street, just a few years ago then.'

What are you up to, Argo? I thought to myself.

Tairon went over to Thalofonus and took the man's hand, whispering something in his ear. Thalofonus seemed to hesitate for a moment, then brighten and reach up to touch Tairon's cheek. He whispered something back. Tairon kissed the old man's hand, strummed the strings playfully, then came back to me. He was puzzled, but bright-eyed with anticipation.

'My mother is still alive, it seems. Still alive!' Then he frowned. 'This will be difficult. You should wait here, the two of you.'

'If that's what you want, then of course I'll wait here. But I'd rather come with you. I shan't interfere.'

'Nor will I,' Niiv promised.

Tairon thought for a moment, then nodded. 'Come on, then.'

But as we walked away from the small square, a youth, naked but for the stubs of bull's horn tied about his head, his belly and back blackened with dye, came racing past us, breathless and terrified, truly terrified. He flung himself against the wall of a house as he saw us, eyes wild and gleaming, lips slack as he gasped for breath.

He edged past us cautiously, then broke into a run again. Sweat sprayed from him as he moved; the stink of his bowels lingered long after he had disappeared.

Somewhere, a few streets away, several tambourines were shaken for a few moments, then fell silent, to be replaced by the whispering of human voices.

Tairon had watched this, and listened to the sounds, in silence. Now he started to walk quickly, pointing up the street, to a house painted green and blue and decorated with the images of octopi and nymph-like sea sirens.

'That's my mother's house. I was born there. It has a large garden, and a deep cellar. My father was confined there for the season after my birth. The whole place is bigger than it seems. My family are – *were* – wealthy in wool and hives.'

Niiv was astonished. 'Your father was confined after your birth? Why?'

I tried to silence the girl, but Tairon was in an understanding mood. 'All creatures, when born, are the gifts of Lady of Wild Creatures. She dictates their time; she dictates their numbers; she attaches life force, or death force, according to her whim. Whenever a male child is born, we placate Lady of Wild Creatures by confining the father for a season. He is gardened and fed, fed and gardened by Lady's servants. Three are assigned to a house where the male child is born.'

'You can garden a man?' Niiv asked.

Tairon and I stared at the girl. Tairon said, 'For the seeds. For Lady.'

Niiv looked between us then smiled nervously. 'Oh yes. I see.'

There was no time to indulge her. Tairon had walked to the shuttered door and was touching the wood with his fingers, shaping words in the air, finally touching two hands to his heart, then opening the door and peering into the interior. He beckoned me to follow.

The outer door led into a cool receiving area, a light-well filling the space, which was furnished with empty pots and a small shrine with the clay figure of a goddess, her arms raised up, each hand clutching a serpent. Lady of the Threshold.

A tall wooden door, more screen than door, opened into a courtyard lush with greenery, stifling and still. Two women in vibrant red-and-blue patterned skirts, short, black open jackets drawn tightly around rouged breasts, and high hats coiled about with strings of shells, rose from where they were sitting and came towards us. One was younger than the other, but one was certainly the mother and the other the daughter. 'This is the house of Artemenesia.'

'I am Artemenesia's son,' Tairon replied.

'Impossible,' the older woman stated strongly. 'Tairon entered the labyrinth at Canaeente and was drawn away for ever. He was twelve years old. If he had survived, he would have returned through the earth mouth at Diktaea within the year. He is long lost, long dead. Drawn far away.' She appraised Tairon with suspicion in her hard-set face. The younger woman seemed nervous.

'He was,' Tairon responded, 'drawn far away. Everything you say is true. Something has drawn me back. Is my mother willing to receive me?'

There was a brief glance between the women, an uncomfortable and insecure look. Then the younger one said, 'Your mother is with the honey children.'

Tairon seemed to sag a little. After a long moment he asked, 'Am I too late?'

Again, there seemed to be confusion between the two assistants to Artemenesia. The younger woman was dispatched across the courtyard, running to the cloisters and disappearing into the shadows.

Tairon was all gloom.

'Is she dead?' I asked him.

'It seems so. I am just too late. And the strange thing is: I didn't even know I had the opportunity to be here. Someone is laughing at me, Merlin.'

His dejection was profound, but he braced up and looked about him, remembering this old home of his. A small bird, some sort of finch, was hopping about on a fig tree. I harnessed it quickly and flew it into the far chamber, where Artemenesia was with her honey children.

What a strange sight greeted my small bird eyes!

Artemenesia, very old and naked, lay spread-eagled on a bed of lambswool. Her body was opened in many places, small cuts with cane tubes pressed into them. The children were filling the carcase with honey. They were all boys, tiny lads with blue hair and oddly swollen heads. Their limbs were as thin as sticks and they scrambled around, scooping liquid honey from clay jars, a bustle of activity in the name of preservation.

Artemenesia shifted slightly, sighed softly. The younger Lady was whispering to her. The children seemed irritated by the woman's intrusion. There were ten children, but their faces were drawn and skull-like, I noticed, though the eyes were bright.

They were very argumentative. They all kept dipping fingers into the honey and eating it. Sugar gave them the rage and the active limbs to make the room spin dizzily with their constant fussing at the old woman's body.

When Artemenesia slowly sat up, these honey killers scattered, complaining loudly, 'Not finished. Not finished.'

'Finish later,' the woman said.

Honey oozed from her wounds.

She was cloaked, covered, made ready to receive her son.

The finch hopped away. No one had noticed me.

Niiv was made to stay in the courtyard. Tairon and I were ushered into a small, fresh receiving room. There were three small couches, some fragrant flowers, a dish of sparkling water, a single window through which the sunlight illuminated the image of Lady of Wild Creatures, constructed out of mosaic tiles on the floor, and coloured green.

Artemenesia sat hunched on one of the couches. Tairon and I occupied the others.

The woman stared at her son for a long time, then asked, 'If you are Tairon, then you'll know who caught the apple.'

'My sister. It fell out of nowhere. She ate it at once. That was the last we saw of her.'

'Which branch broke?'

'The third. It was too small for the small weight of the boy who lay on it.'

'Who caught the boy?'

'You caught the boy. The branch cut your cheek. That cut, the cut I can see below your ear.'

Artemenesia sighed and shook her head, never taking her gaze from the man. 'Tairon,' she whispered, repeating the name. And after a while, 'What made you stay away so long?'

'I took a wrong turning,' he said sadly, looking down and sighing. 'When the rock closed behind me I was terrified. But fear made me learn the maze. I found exits to the world, and entrances for the return. Eventually I found a way home.'

'Tairon,' the old woman whispered again. 'At least I have the pleasure of seeing you for a few moments before Lady leads me into the hills, to the forest, and turns me free and wild.'

There was something very heavy, very difficult in the air. I realised suddenly it was the feeling of repressed tears. Mother and son watched each other with affection, but from a distance. Tairon's lips quivered, his brow furrowed, but he remained steady.

'I've caught you in time to stop you dying. You can get rid of those embalmers.'

Artemenesia shook her head. 'I wish that was true, Tairon. I'm sorry. You've come a few minutes too late. But for as long as you're here, we can talk.' She looked at me, searched my face with her gaze, then seemed to recognise me.

'This is Merlin,' Tairon said quietly. 'He wanders, he's wise, he has a gift with spells, enchantment, charm; he even understands labyrinths. Or so he tells me.'

'I see you, but I don't see you,' the woman said. 'You're dead. Yet alive. I see you as bones, not flesh. But you have a nice smile. Is my son happy?'

For a moment her words had taken me surprise. Tairon seemed to be unaware of what had passed between Artemenesia and myself. I grasped it at once, of course, well ... just as soon as I'd glimpsed the fact that she was in fact dead, and still in that short shadow time between death and parting, when the breath has not yet gone stale.

'This moment will mean a lot to him,' I said. Tairon glanced at me, frowning. I ignored him. Artemenesia smiled. I went on, 'As he said, he took a wrong turning. He has found himself among friends, new friends. His life is as dangerous as it is fulfilling. When he comes back to his home he will be a stranger. But—'

'All strangers can settle,' the woman finished for me, as she saw me hesitating. 'I was a stranger here once. I know about strangers. I know about the struggle to make the land embrace you. Tairon will settle. I hope you'll help him.'

I had to be honest with the dead woman. 'I'll help until I have to leave, which won't be long. There is something waiting for me in the years to come. I'm not allowed to know what ...'

'Are you curious about it?'

'I'm terrified at times.'

'You deny it.'

'I have to. If I embraced it, Tairon would pass through my life in the blink of an eye.'

'I've heard of people like you. I never believed you existed. You are a trail-walker. You circle the world and shed lives like skins.'

'Yes. How do you recognise me?'

'One of you walked through this land and left a skin behind. That was a long time ago. But the story is remembered. My son will ask me a question, now. And I will answer it. I will tell him what I know, and he can explain to you later.'

I understood what she was hinting.

'You want me to go.'

'I would ask that you go. I have only a few heartbeats left with which to remember; a few heartbeats to give Tairon a memory that will sustain him. Lady of Wild Creatures is at the head of the valley, and she is impatient. Everything that has happened here is to do with her, and her anger. But still, I can't deny her. Wild Creature Lady thinks she has gained the island. The war has been difficult and destructive. You cannot see it, but you can surely sense it, smell it, hear it. These have been dreadful and terrifying years. The Daidalon is gone, stolen. It was taken by pirates. Tairon is here because he has been sent – or rather, *brought* – here.'

'By whom?'

'By one who wishes the truth to be known.'

'And how do you know all this?'

She laughed. 'I have a foot in both worlds. Don't you? It is a brief moment of enlightened vision. A vision of magic.'

Tairon's mother was in what the Greeklanders called the *ephemera*. This was the transition from life to death, a short period of time, a day, perhaps two, when she was shifting between this world and the deep valley that descended to the branching caverns of Hades, to the sanctuary of Poseidon where she would be required to undertake the tests of time; to choose which world she entered next, or to be chosen against her will.

The *ephemera* was her time of practise, her time of preparation. The body was dead, but her life, her shade, could transit instantly across the gleam of the eyes, as long as the eyes were open.

Tairon would soon have become aware of this, but he had at least caught that dying flicker of life. I was pleased for him.

Meanwhile, I went to the outer courtyard to find Niiv. The two servant women were sitting there, peeling oranges, and looked up at me with little interest as I approached them. 'Where's the girl?' I asked.

The younger woman frowned. 'She went back to the street. She was curious to see the festival. She said it would be all right.'

The way they smiled at each other – knowing, sneering – compounded my sudden anxiety for the foolish Northlander. Niiv – as all of us, save Tairon – was a stranger in this city close to the Chamber of Discs. To stay together was safe; to separate, to wander alone through the labyrinthine streets, was a stupid risk to take.

20

Dream Hunt

I ran for the street, hauling back the door and stepping out into the fierce sunshine. The older woman had scurried behind me, pushing the door closed again, shutting me out.

Almost at once a crowd surged around the corner, pressing me back against the house.

They were children of all ages, garlanded with flowers, grey-green herbs and leaves, all dressed in pale green or bright yellow tunics, the boys with their faces painted an azure-blue, the girls painted scarlet-red. They flowed past me as a turbulent stream, shrill and insensate. Then there came a cry from behind them and the whole crowd turned as one, with all the sudden speed of a shifting shoal of fish, and began to run back along the street. Then a horn sounded from elsewhere and again they turned as one, retracing their steps, streaming past me once more, a single mind, a single purpose, a stampede of celebration.

And in the middle of them I saw suddenly an unpainted face, but a familiar shock of hair. Niiv was small, and many of the children were taller than she, but her features were as bright and as recognisable as a comet in the heavens. I plunged into the running throng, fought my way through the heave of small bodies as they crushed in their haste, wheeling round into a narrower street, following the horn call.

I managed to grab Niiv by the shoulder. She turned in alarm and fury. Her eyes were intense with ecstasy. She stared at me, not knowing me, caught up in the madness. I held onto her, despite her struggles and screams, and eventually the last of the shoal had passed. The street was silent.

Her eyes focused. The trance lifted. She came gently into my arms and rested her face against my chest.

'That was so strange. Merlin! So strange.'

'What have you done?' I whispered. 'What have you let yourself do this time?'

'Strange! Strange!' she repeated, holding me in a lover's embrace, embracing my gaze with hers. She tried to kiss me. I drew back. Her grip hardened, then her hand reached for my cheek, tugging my face closer. She was feral and panting; cat-breath was strong on her lips and tongue and she shuddered for a moment, finding the kiss she desired, for that moment, that stunning, urgent moment – before I flung her against the wall of the house.

She growled now, slipping down to her haunches, disappointed and angry, watching me with eyes that might have said: *I'll have you*, or might have said, *How dare you!*

Again I rescued her, lifting her gently to her feet. 'Tell me about strange. What was strange?'

Softer, then, she turned into my grasp, head on my breast. 'The woman,' she said. 'The quelling woman.'

The name made me uncomfortable. In the word she used came a feeling I was used to. Her word reminded me of the feeling of the woman who had possessed the cave at Akirotiri, when we had first found harbour on the island, a few days ago.

'It was so strange, Merlin,' Niiv repeated. Was she still in a trance?

I asked her to describe what she had felt and seen, but she became tongue-tied, struggling to put into words an experience that had both shocked and thrilled her.

I decided to take a quick look behind her eyes, a mere touch of her recent memory, nothing involving her future or her deeper feelings – just the encounter with the child-swarm. Her gaze grew canny as I passed it, as if she knew what I was doing, and then I was reeling!

She was running, not in the winding streets of a town but along the winding paths of a forested mountain. She screamed as she ran, one of many, their howls and cries not those of humans but of wild-cats. Wolves and dogs sometimes hunt in packs, but these were feline and furious – and huge; a pride more numerous than any I had ever witnessed before.

They were strange in more ways than this: there was an element of wolverine about them as well – as if two creatures had bred together to form a fast, vicious and monstrous chimera.

Dozens of us (I felt as Niiv had felt) raced in a mass – a pack, a swarm, a single entity – through the nightwoods, up and down the moonlit mountain slope, following the scent of a single creature.

And behind us, calling and singing to us, each call, each melodic vocal switch, causing us to turn, to pick up a new scent, closing, closing on our terrified prey.

It was only as the confusion cleared that I became aware of the wild figure above us on the slopes of the mountain, a woman, ringlet hair flailing as she rode on the back of what appeared to be a gigantic wolf.

Her arms rose and fell, an incomprehensible series of signals that accompanied her ululations and shrill shrieks, a chaos dance, a mad song inducing mad movement in the child-cat hunters.

Ahead of us ran the terrified creature and I touched it briefly, finding an echo of its panic-stricken thoughts as it fled from cave to tree, from narrow defile to the scant shelter of a ruined house, stone-tumbling down the hill.

Part man, part beast, part bronze, this creature *knew* it was destined to die, but some mechanism within its flesh and metal kept it running. It seemed bound by twin instincts – to survive in the flesh, and to protect that which was forged from the hot ores in the shaping caves.

In that brief contact, from within Niiv herself, I was made powerfully aware of the creature's desire to find one of those 'shaping caves' – for there it scented safety, a release from the relentless pursuit.

But it was lost on the mountain-side, and the wild woman and her wild beast could see him clearly; she made the hunting pack dance to her commands and soon they were closing for the kill.

(And yet, for a fleeting moment the woman's wild calls ceased and she sat quite motionless on the wolf, staring down the slope, half illumined by the moon.

Staring at me!

She had seen, or sensed me in the pack, and she was angry.

Then she had ridden on, leaving behind only that sense of curiosity and profound irritation.)

All of this in an instant and then I was back, and Niiv was watching me with hunger and delight.

'You saw it! You saw it! Wasn't it strange?'

'You have drawn attention to us,' I told her. 'And I suspect it's unwelcome attention.'

She pouted at me, as usual, defiance alive in her expression. 'Are you going to tell me *again* that I've gone too far?'

'No point in telling you. You never listen.'

She slumped back against the wall. 'I didn't look *forward*, Merlin. I didn't go to the unborn future.'

'You looked, though, and sometimes that's enough.'

She was gloomy for a moment, before asking, 'Do you have any idea what it means? All that chasing? That strange creature?'

'I'm beginning to get one. But Argo is only opening up slowly.'

'Why is that, do you think?'

'She's a ship. She has a truth to tell. We must let her tell it in ship-time.'

Beside us, the door to Tairon's house opened and the tall Cretan stepped out into the street, blinking at the bright light. There were tears in his eyes and on his cheeks.

'My mother is dead,' he said quietly when he saw me. 'She was already dead when I arrived, but still living in the hinterland and still able to recognise me. And she has told me of events here that make it dangerous for us to stay. We should return to the ship and be on our guard.'

I told him that I couldn't have agreed more, then asked about the 'events' to which his mother had referred.

'There was a war here,' he said, though his expression was vague. 'The land has been transformed by Wild Creature Lady. She has almost won the war and is again the voice of day, moon and season. She is reclaiming everything that had been lost and is hunting down the last survivors of those who had worshipped the Shaper. The Daidalon.'

He hesitated before glancing at me again. 'My mother told me that something wonderful had been happening here, something that had been continuing from long before she was born, something so new it was as if the stars themselves had sent envoys to greet us and tell us of new wonders. But the Daidalon was stolen and the Wild and the Old has returned. Snake Lady, Dove Lady, Earth Lady Who Nourishes; my mother's names for her. I knew of her, of course. I knew of the Shaper. The Daidalon. But I was just a child when I passed through the Shaping Chamber into the labyrinth and was lost. I'd had no idea of the turmoil that was occurring.

'She said that for generations this land had been the source of creations from the imagination of a man just like ourselves, and not of the earth or the mountains or Wild Lady. His shaping was new. The war occurred out of sight of us, by night and in shadows, but it was vicious and brutal and bloody, and was shaping us without our knowing.

'It almost ended when the Daidalon was stolen, but it is still not finished.'

Now he looked at me, his expression that of a man who has suspicions and yet a curiosity that needed satisfying.

'The ship has a secret, Merlin. Argo knows something. Something about all of this.'

He was imagining that I was complicit in that secret knowledge. I was not (at that moment) and was careful to allay his suspicions. Niiv listened intently to our exchange.

He went on, 'Time is all wrong here. We are not in the right time. And it is Argo that has brought us to this place, this wrong place, we seem agreed on that. Either you or Jason must get her to speak to us through that *grotesque* creature from the far north.'

'I'm *not* grotesque!' Niiv objected, stunned by Tairon's reference.

'He means the goddess,' I pointed out. She giggled. 'Oh.'

But it would not be through Mielikki, Lady of the North, that Argo would reveal what she knew.

Tairon's foreboding proved accurate. As we approached the river harbour and its expansive area of quays we became aware of the murmuring silence. Crowds had gathered on each side of the river, peering hard at the ship, our Argo. Rubobostes was at the steering oar, Jason at the prow. They had cut their moorings from the quayside and were holding fast in mid-stream. The hill that rose beyond the town was bright with the white tunics of children, all of them standing on the winding paths, watching like seabirds.

The air was full of whispering. Sometimes the crowd would shuffle restlessly, and a low ripple of conversation would break the stillness.

At the top of Argo's mast, a black and blood-red flag drooped in the heavy air; Jason's signal that all was not well.

'How do we get through this lot?' Niiv asked me in a nervous whisper, clutching my arm. Tairon was looking up at the roofs, searching for a way to take us over the heads of this silent but threatening gathering.

'We're cut off,' he said. Alas, his voice was a little too loud. Heads turned towards us, then in ranks as silent and as menacing as the child-swarm, the gathering by the river started to swing towards us, eyes watching, voices beginning to hum tunelessly – although not so tunelessly that I couldn't recognise the eerie melody that Wild Lady had shrieked from her wolf-back, in the mountain dream, glimpsed so recently through Niiv.

Though no one moved towards us, we were clearly being focused upon, and that could only mean danger.

So I summoned the one creature that would scatter these forlorn yet frightening townsfolk: the bull!

I brought him out of whatever Hades these Cretans had created, and he came – monstrous, red and black, hoof-pounding on the road, driving a path through the crowd. As he passed us, I drew him back using words that I had thought I had long forgotten, but how quickly the simpler of the old charms return when needed! And those vibrant echoes of my younger years brought the bovine giant to a standstill, snorting and heaving as it peered down at me. I flung Niiv onto its back, Tairon scrambled for a purchase on its flank; I jumped for its horns as it dipped its head, braced between them, hanging on hard. The creature turned and pounded towards the river, slowing at the last moment to trot majestically to the water, ploughing through the clay jars and crates on the quayside. The alarmed crowd kept very far back.

It was so easy I could almost have laughed.

As we slipped from the bull's back, Niiv grabbed my arm, pointing into the crowds. 'Look! Tairon's twin!'

I followed her gaze but saw nothing. Tairon was already in the water, and Niiv and I followed quickly.

As we swam for Argo, the bull watched us from the quay, then turned to the north. With its head low it suddenly charged into the distance, into obscurity: back to the realm of dreams.

Jason hauled me aboard, then pulled Niiv from the water, but she scurried away from him as she sprawled onto the deck.

As I wrung water from my hair, the old argonaut pointed to where the bull had disappeared.

'You did that, didn't you?'

'Yes.'

'Easy charm. A quick moment from your talents. What did it cost you? A grey hair? A minute of life? Why don't you help us more often?'

He'd been drinking. He was aggressive.

'I help when I can. I help when necessary. I would help more if absolutely necessary. I don't squander my life.'

'Your life? Your *life*? You can't remember more than a fraction of it ...'

I thought, then, of explaining the danger to me of small use of charm, that simple fact which I had never forgotten: that at any moment I would be precipitated into decay, time catching up with me, the old guardians abandoning me. I should have returned to my birthplace long ago, along with the others who had been sent on the Path – trail-walking, as Artemenesia had known it in her own legends. But I was still here, still young, still very much alive; and on 'borrowed time', an expression the Greeklanders were very fond of using.

Borrowed time. That phrase should last for all eternity.

For more cycles than I could now remember I had clung to Time as a child clings to a favoured grandparent, indulged and loved, never criticised, always soothed – yet always aware that night must fall, and the favoured parent will fade away.

At any moment even the simplest exercise of my talents might break the spell. A wren, summoned to sit on a rafter and spy on a king and his daughter. Something as simple as that, something as easy as that, an act of charm that would only flicker in its effect on me, an unnoticeable moment of rot in my body – or as Niiv liked to say, and as Jason had just repeated: one more grey hair, one less breath – such a simple act might be my downfall.

I was not just cautious in my use of charm. I was often terrified of using it.

'Why are you angry?' I asked the man.

'I'm not angry. Argo is angry.' He frowned, as if he had just grasped something he had previously missed. 'When she's in a mood, so am I.'

'You were always her favourite captain.'

He glowered at me. Tairon had stripped and was painstakingly spreading out his amber-coloured tunic to dry, to the amusement of Rubobostes. The Cretan was immune to such teasing. Niiv sat sullenly on the lowered mast, wringing out her new dress, watching me.

'There's something else,' Jason suddenly said. When I didn't respond, he added, 'The children are missing.'

'Missing? When did they vanish?'

'They didn't vanish. They went with Talienze. Earlier. Urtha has gone looking for them. Talienze said they would be the most adept at discovering one of those "shaping chambers" you've mentioned. A cave of creation. There's one hidden in the hills behind this town. The Cave of Discs. But Urtha felt sudden pain, he felt danger. He's very close to his son. He's gone looking for them.'

What was Talienze up to? It was a niggling thought, a quiet distraction. Talienze was one man in the company of five very agile and aggressive youths. He would be no match for them. But what was he up to?

'And something else again,' Jason said wearily.

'Yes?'

'That figurehead. Old Scowling Woman ...'

'Mielikki! Be careful what you say in her hearing.'

'The wooden witch,' he said with a sour grin. He was very much not in control of his mood.

'What about her?'

'She's been moving. Just for a few moments at a time, but definitely alive. So has that wooden warrior. And the witch is whispering words. All I can make out is the name *Merlin*.'

Argo wanted to talk to me, this time I was sure of it. I was being summoned at last.

The boys or Argo: which should I pursue? With Urtha and his men on their heels, the boys could wait. I would find a way to spy on them later.

'Keep your thoughts to yourself,' I murmured to Jason. He watched me suspiciously as I went to the ladder and descended into the Spirit of the Ship.

PART FOUR

THE DANCING FLOOR OF WAR

21

The Wedding Promise

As I stepped across the threshold into the Spirit of the Ship, I had expected to emerge onto the meadow, close to the woods. I had expected to find dreamy Mielikki, in her summer veils, standing waiting for me, the sharp-eared lynx sprawling at her feet.

Instead I entered a marbled corridor, its floor slippery beneath my feet. Sounds boomed and rang in the passage. Light spilled from high windows on both sides. Voices murmured distantly. There was the sound of scurrying, as of men or women rushing about their business.

A wail, then laughter. A clash of bronze on bronze. Shouts and reprovals. Laughter again. I was in a funnel of sound, and I realised I was in a palace; and understanding this, I began to look more closely at the towering effigies that lined the corridor, the armoured gods and robed goddesses, shaped from stone the colour of vibrant copper or the green of tarnished copper. Their heads all stretched forward, some looking down, some to one side or the other, some trying to glimpse the sky beyond the high ceiling.

At once, I knew where I was.

This was Medea's cedarwood and green marble palace, built for her in Iolkos by Jason during the year after they had returned from the Quest of the Golden Fleece.

'Do you remember me?' a small voice asked from behind me, and I turned quickly, startled. A girl stood there. She had dark eyes, a sly smile, a green cloak wrapped around her body. Raven-black hair, tied into a long, elaborate plait, was pinned to her shoulder, before falling free to her waist. 'Well?'

A shiver of memory, but: 'No. I don't. Should I?'

'You sailed with me, Merlin,' she said with a sly look. 'To *Colchis*.

You must remember me. We sailed to Colchis for the fleece. With Jason and his half-human rogues.'

Again, a shiver of memory. 'You mean half-divine.' Most of Jason's original crew had been summoned from the half-world between earth and the heavens.

The girl laughed. 'I mean half-*human*. The divine half didn't stink. The *divine* half didn't need to wash.' She hesitated. 'But a mercenary is a mercenary whether he's the bastard offspring of a god or not.'

'They were brave men. That was a dangerous and well-completed quest. We captured what we sought.'

She laughed sourly. 'And you eat too many lotuses.'

'Who are *you*?'

She put a finger to her lips. 'You were very quiet, taking your turns at the oar, hunting, watching, listening, gathering. Did you think I didn't know you? Did you think I didn't know who you were ... or rather ... what you *are*?'

'Who are *you*?'

She smiled and reached out to take my hand. 'A clue: a wild hag was there before me, something out of the mountains of an island to the south of Greek Land. A goddess of the wild. It took some doing, I can tell you, to arrange for her *un*doing, to send her back to where she belonged. Jason managed that! Before her? A nymph. Before the nymph? Another screeching guardian, from the mountains in the east. *Baabla*. She was more eagle than woman. Her home was an eyrie on top of a tower that had tried to reach for the stars. Come on, Merlin. You must recognise me now.'

I acknowledged that I did. 'Yes. Athena. Our guardian on Argo.'

She slowly clapped her hands together three times, the mocking sound. 'Well done. Though sometimes it was my mother, Hera, who smiled down at you.'

'But you're just a girl.'

'Just an echo,' she corrected. 'When Athena left the ship, this small shadow remained. There are shadows of all her guardians – save for that wild woman: *she who quells*. What a fright! Some of the shadows are so old they are barely whispers. We all now live in our fading worlds. We sleep and play and dream. But not very much of any of those things. Too old, too far gone. That is all I am. Echo, shadow, whisper; dream. But now Argo wishes me to show you a scene you won't remember. She's called me back. You were elsewhere when these events occurred, practising magic, though you would return in a few seasons to be with Jason again.'

She ran past me, beckoning me to follow. The palace echoed and rang with the noises from its halls and depths. The light on the different shades of marble made the corridor seem alive.

She led me to the festival sanctuary, a wide hall, ceiling high above us, walled with the trunks of massive cedars. The way to the centre was a maze of granite rocks, some of them towering the height of a ship's mast. Medea had created the sanctuary at Colchis, but instead of a fissured cavern enclosing the trees and boulders, this place still gleamed with amber-green marble.

Rising in the very centre of the hall, six times a man's height, was the white stone ram, upright on its hind legs, forelegs stretched before it and holding the wide basin of a copper vessel. Its ruby eyes looked to the sides, its horns were threaded with gold. The ram's mouth gaped. A drizzle of molten bronze poured from the furnace in its head to be collected in the basin.

There was the distant sound of a mechanism, hidden within this vast stone effigy, lifting the cooled bronze back to the furnace, where it would again become the 'spit of the god'.

Medea, though she had embraced some of the Greeklander ways, had never abandoned her inherited status as Priestess of the Ram.

The rattle of tambours and the incoherent wailing of women, a barrage of sad song that ended with a sudden high-pitched harmonious scream, told me that a ceremony had just come to an end. Medea and Jason emerged through the rocks, hand in hand. Medea was clad in the black and green robes of Colchis, her skirts voluminous, a great bell of cloth falling from her waist, her breasts covered with a long, wide leather bib, patterned in black and gold and probably made from hardened ram's hide. The lower part of her face was concealed behind a bead-veil of deep-blue lapis-lazuli; her black hair was woven around a tall, thin cone of cedar wood. Jason, by contrast, was wearing the simple woollen tunic of a farmer, patterned, certainly, but not in any regal way. His legs were bare. He wore a single sandal. An amulet in the form of a small blue crystal ship was slung around his neck on a golden necklace.

But he was trim, his beard shaven to a few lines around his strong features, his hair drawn back in five tight braids, clamped to his skull. He was bright of eye, smiling and content. He was the Jason I had first met: young, brash, greedy and confident.

I followed them out of the Hall of the Ram. Medea at one point turned slightly, as though listening.

Was she aware of me? She would have known that I was a few days' ride away, visiting an oracle. But did she sense this echo from the future?

The shadow of Athena, this sprite of a child, skipped along beside me. 'You seem uncomfortable with me,' she intuited.

'No. Just confused.'

'That I'm a child? All gods were children once. All gods were infants once. All gods were two greater gods humping and heaving once. The advantage of gods is that they can journey back and forwards in their lives. You can *almost* do that. Can't you? You're less of a man than most.'

'I beg your pardon?'

She laughed at her own mistake. 'I meant: you're more of something else, something strange, something of Time.'

'Yes. I am. Where are we going?'

'To watch them ...' she giggled. 'To watch them ... embrace? Is that a nice way to say it?'

I stopped in my tracks. 'That's too private.'

'You don't want to watch it?'

'No.'

'Nonsense! You watch all the time. I know you, you young-old man. You never hesitate to watch if you think you can learn something. I do the same, even when I'm real and not a shadow.' She added with a teasing laugh, 'I hadn't realised you were so coy, Merlin.'

Nor had I.

It wasn't coyness, of course, that had made me hesitate. It was remembered love for Medea. *My* love for Medea. But this echo-Athena tugged at my hand and off we went, along the corridor and towards the private chambers of the Colchis priestess and her hungry Greeklander conquest.

Medea's retinue of experienced women and light-bearded youths flapped and flitted around and performed the usual functions, filling bowls with water, small gold chalices with wine, arranging the musty fabric of the drapes that stretched around the bed: a broken tent, strips of coloured cloth, containing the arena within.

Naked, Medea was beautiful; the sight of her, the memory of her, were hammer-blows inside my head. She was so pale in contrast to Jason's dark and thickly hirsute form. When they embraced, when the first kiss had finished, he turned away from me, settling Medea onto the bed, but Medea's eyes found mine as she watched across his shoulder, and her lips signalled that she knew I was there. She returned my gaze from the depths of the past, and for a moment the look was fond; and then the fierceness of the *wolf* was there again, and she nestled into the sea captain, spreading her body as he sprawled, a strong yet ungainly man, across her.

Why had she brought me to this intimate place and this private moment? What was Athena up to? The girl touched a finger to her lips. 'It's the conversation that follows. Argo wants you to hear it.'

Jason reached for a cup of wine and drained it. A breeze blew through the chamber, cool and welcome. Medea lay against his chest, stroking his thigh, singing softly.

'At the next full moon,' he said, running his hand through her hair, 'I will sail Argo anywhere on the ocean that is necessary to find you the gift of your dreams. A wedding gift. Anywhere at all that lies within a two-week voyage. I couldn't bear to be away from you longer.'

'What did you have in mind?' she asked, slightly teasingly. 'Not another ram's fleece, I hope. One ship's hold full of rams' fleeces will last a long time.'

He laughed. 'We've made good trade of them, all but the temple fleece.' Colchis had been abundant with the skins, packed with the particles of gold sieved from mountain streams. Jason and his Argonauts had gathered fifty before their escape from Colchis, and they had traded them for weeks as they had worked their way back along the rivers, south of Hyperborea, before re-emerging into the Ceraunian Sea at the Stochaides.

'No,' he went on. 'I was thinking of a place in the east, the land of Zorastria. They do strange magic there.'

Medea was adamant. 'No! That doesn't appeal at all. I've had enough of rune-stones and spell-stones. Too heavy to carry.'

'Very well: closer to home, on the shores at Ilium. The Chariot with which fair, fleet Achilles dragged the body of Hektor for seven days and seven nights around the walls of Troy. It can still be seen, manifesting on the plain, driven furiously by the shade of the hero, the corpse still attached by leather. To touch the corpse as it flies past allows access to the underworld for a brief period of time. I will take my crew and wait in the darkness for the furious car and its screaming driver to appear, and snare him.'

'No,' said Medea. 'Leave the ghosts to their routine. It's all they've got left. Besides, which *underworld* will be accessed? There are so many, and that of Achilles is not one which I wish to embrace. Think again.'

'To the east, then. To the Stochaides again. There is a long shore, there, a wild, golden strand, with dense forest and hills behind. I have heard that every so often a manifestation occurs: of a great city of huts and tents, a gathering of peoples from different worlds and times, a chaotic place of noise and ceremony. Each dawn the people of the city come down to the ocean to bathe and make offerings to Poseidon. They use small charm boxes to communicate across great distances with their ancestors; some say with their descendants from many centuries in the future. I will take my crew and Argo and bring back a charm box.'

'Communicating over distances is hard,' Medea acknowledged, 'and costly. It drains deeply. But I have no great desire to communicate with my ancestors. My descendants? They are legion, I imagine. As are yours. What else have you and your loyal band contrived for me?'

'What do you mean?'

She laughed provocatively, kissing his chin. 'These aren't your ideas, Jason. You have no ideas of your own. Greed alone leads you to adventure. Someone among your crew is a little more thoughtful, and you've been picking his imagination as a crow picks at a carcase.'

Jason smiled, acknowledging defeat. 'Tisaminas. He seems to know everything about the world. And Merlin too. He came up with several ideas. He's a well-travelled man.'

Medea was intrigued by this. 'Tell me something that Merlin suggested.'

'He talks of mountains in the west, hard to access because of the forest that encloses them. Deep valleys run through the hills, and serpentine caves reach into the depths of the earth from those valleys. He told me of paintings within those long earth chambers. They exist in darkness, but come alive when light is taken into their sanctuaries. To possess the paintings, and the animals they portray, is to possess the spirit of the animal itself. They run through time. A strong spirit links them, from the earliest of the beasts to the last of the beast: horse, bison, wolf, ursine, feline. The last of the beast is in the unknowable future. I will gladly cut out one of those paintings from the rock for you.'

'Leave them where they are,' Medea said. She had gone pale, quite alarmed, features creased into a frown of discomfiture. She sat away from Jason, remembering: a dream, silently surfacing, teasing at the very edge of her recollection.

'Leave them alone,' she whispered again. 'They do not belong in any time but their own time.'

'You know them, then,' Jason stated, curious.

'Of them. Of them. I know *of* them, and they must not be moved.'

Before he could speak further, Medea's mood had become light. 'I don't need a wedding gift, Jason. It's gift enough that you rescued me from Colchis and brought me here. I don't need anything else.'

'I insist. There must be something I can fetch for you that will mark the moment of love between us.'

'Then I know what it is.' She leaned forward and ran a finger round his chin. 'Bring me a cup of sand from your favourite shore, a shore where you beached and found happiness and adventure. A place to which you would want to return, this time with me. Bring me that cup of sand. It's all I need.'

'Far too easy,' Jason said dismissively. 'I could do that in a day. Something else.'

Exasperated, Medea took his face in her hands and kissed him. 'Very well, then. Bring me a cup of ice-cold water from a lake where you have watched the reflection of the full moon as you drank. That will do for me. I will drink it and think of all the moons we will watch together in the years to come.'

'Far too easy,' Jason insisted. 'I have watched the moon in a hundred lakes. The nearest is only a half day's walk into the hills. There must be *something* you want that will test me in getting it.' He was becoming angry.

So was she.

'Very well, then,' she said sharply. 'Sail to the long island in the south, the land of mazes and honey. There is a man there who is treated as a god, a "shaping" god. He creates mechanisms, and labyrinths with mechanisms, and works with fire in ways the Greeklanders have not discovered. I heard that Zeus himself returns to the land to ask this man for advice. His fame had even reached Colchis, but time and distance had warped the truth of his skills. All but the fact that he's dangerous. I have a map of where he hides. I've always been intrigued by him, but never sure about him. But if he exists, I know *where* he exists, three days' sail to the south. I'll have him for my own purposes, to keep here, someone to unravel and learn from while you are away plundering. Does *that* suit you as a wedding gift to me ...?' She leaned forward and kissed him, almost mocking him.

Jason's eyes were alive with excitement at the prospect. 'I'll fetch this man, this *shaper*.'

Medea laughed, shaking her head. She put a finger to his lips. 'You'll never find him, Jason. I'm teasing you! I wouldn't have you put your life at risk, just for a wedding present.'

'Tease me all you will. I'll bring him to you, and you can create your own maze to contain him.'

Suddenly Medea was startled. She grasped his face in her hands, tried to engage his restless look. The blood-hunt was on him. The sea-hunt. 'No! I was teasing! I meant what I said. Just bring me sand and moonlit water. I don't need more than that.'

The man eased her fingers away from his cheeks, stood and smiled. 'I'll bring that too.'

When Medea had fled from Colchis she had had time enough to take a few of her treasures.

With two of her servants she ransacked her private sanctuary, gathering a handful here, a handful there of the trinkets and amulets, the prizes and secrets of her long life. All of these shards of her profession had been stuffed into three sacks and carried to Argo. One of the sacks had been caught in the rocks as the three women scampered towards the ship and the sweating, naked men who were pushing the vessel back into the sea.

The servants were all shot down by arrows as men gathered on the cliff top, required by Medea's adoptive father to stop the departure at all costs. He had no idea who she truly was, or where she had come from. But he had come to depend on her prophecies.

Another sack was lost.

The third sack was flung aboard by an Argonaut, just as Argo was taken by the tide, swinging free of the shore.

Even then, halfway across the ocean, as Medea went about the brutal killing and dismembering of her 'brother', casting his pieces into the water to delay the pursuing ships – the boy's father – as he gathered the carcase for its proper burial, so the third sack had slipped overboard. Only Tisaminas, with his quick wit and powerful lungs, had thought to rescue it, and though most of its contents had been spilled into the black depths, he brought back a small child's weight of figures, shapes and shards, in gold and bronze and stone, and Medea had grasped them gratefully.

Not knowing what small treasure she had rescued, she guarded it fiercely. It would be a long journey later before she could install them in her new sanctuary, her temple, her Ram's Chamber in Iolkos.

And the small, gold map of Crete was among those twenty-seven surviving dreams.

Now she showed it to Jason. He strained to see the detail. The carving was minute, intricate. 'It's all there. All you need to know. Don't ask me how I came upon this map. I dreamed of it, I summoned it, and it was brought to me. I was told that there are only three in the world. One is owned by the "shaping man" himself. And one was owned by each of his sons. His sons died. The story goes that Icarus fell from the sky when his false wings failed him. He struck the land near Cyzicus, close to the Symplegades, the "clashing rocks". His brother, Raptor, ascended so high that he disappeared beyond the moon itself.'

'This man's sons had wings?'

'Their father shaped them. He sent them to search for a realm beyond the earth. They were to be his eyes and ears to the life beyond the canopy of stars. So the story goes. And this map is that of the fallen son. And it shows where the entrances to the labyrinth can be found. And where the Cave of the Discs can be found. And when you find the Cave of the Discs, you are sure to find the "shaping man". He will have chambers there, workshops. So there you are.'

Medea took Jason's chin in her fingers and twisted his head this way and that, staring at him hard. 'But Jason – I will still settle for sand and water,' she said softly. 'A touch of your heart, a touch of an older life you've known.' She kissed him. The kiss was passionate. She drew back suddenly. Jason's kiss had been cold. 'Don't leave so soon,' she begged. 'Wait a while. There's no hurry.' But she knew at once that her words were lost.

Jason stroked the small plate of gold with his thumbs. His eyes shone. He was eager now. He could smell adventure.

'I'll have this copied onto a skin, a large skin,' he said. 'The hide of an ox, so that I can read it without my head aching. You shall have your shaping man. With Argo, and my crew – even without reckless Herakles – I can bring this monster to your sanctuary. You shall have your wedding gift. I promise you.'

Medea's smile (I thought as I watched, a ghost-presence in this chamber) was enigmatic.

Athena drew a discreet veil over the bedchamber then, and with a flourish of her hand and a mischievous laugh said goodbye to me. She led the way at a scamper down the corridor. I followed the flowing green cloak. She turned the corner to the tall, narrow doors that separated the marble palace from the scorching heat of the courtyard, but when I burst out into the light she had gone. The shadow had gone.

Just a shadow whisper remained.

'You are still in Argo's heart, Merlin. Now see how it was after the wedding promise was made. You don't need me any more. But Argo will guide you through the next few weeks ...'

Storm-lashed, but with her sail billowing before the following wind, Argo surged towards the dark mountains of Crete. Zeus himself seemed to be waiting to greet her, the sky black and rolling, rain sleeting, the jagged shape of the land visible only because of a golden glow, a break in the clouds.

Jason and Tisaminas scoured the cliffs for a haven, and finally saw it.

Down sail, down mast, and the oars were run out to slow the perilous approach as the ship heaved through the furious waves towards the cove, where the vaguest hint of colour suggested a strand against which they might beach.

All eyes attentive to what lay below the spume-shrouded sea, Argo struck by rock and reef, the guardian goddess guided her nevertheless to the safety of the shore, and she was flung like sea-wrack against the strand, listing and throwing several of the Argonauts onto the shingle. By the now the oars had been run in, and with a second surging wave the vessel was set more firmly on the land.

Ropes were slung about the hull and the memory of lost, ever-adventuring Herakles invoked as twenty men hauled Argo above the tide line, then pinned her down, a leviathan cast from the depths, made sound and stable against the wind. Lashings were stretched from her mast, canvas slung over them to make a shelter against the storm. Jason gathered four large stones to make an altar, filled it with fire. Youthful Meleager, still burning for adventure, had forced his way inland against the gale and found a flock of goats, bringing down a kid with a weighted rope. Jason sacrificed the animal in thanks to Poseidon for the safe crossing. The meat was then stripped and spitted over a wood fire.

Poseidon accepted the offering. By dawn the storm had abated. The clouds hurried to the east and the sun warmed the beach, and dried the sodden and ragged crew.

With Argo propped up on banks of sand, Jason went back on board. Keen-eyed Lynceus had taken possession of the maps of Crete, drawn from the star-bronze, and unfurled one now. He scanned the hide as if he were a hawk, soaring over the hills and valleys.

'Where have we beached?' Jason asked.

'Somewhere here,' said Lynceus, indicating a long length of the northern coast.

'Could you be more precise?'

Lynceaus drew out a thin slate marker, scored off in units. He laid it this way and that upon the map and counted off numbers in his head. He did this for a long time.

'Somewhere here,' he repeated, stabbing the map, indicating exactly the same long stretch of coast.

Acastus chipped in. 'There are three valleys leading to the interior, and they all meet at the same place, a city crushed between hills, with caves all around. One of them must be the Cave of Discs.'

Jason nodded. 'The Dyctean cave is close as well, and we should avoid that. It will be well-guarded, even if Old Man Thunder isn't in residence.' He smiled to himself.

Meleager said, stabbing at the hide, 'Look ... if those marks mean what I think they mean, there are shaping caves in every valley. There are shaping caves *everywhere* on this blighted island. He could be hiding in any one of them. Which one should we look for?'

'He will be somewhere close to that city,' Jason stated bluntly. 'Unless Medea's auguries are wrong, we will find him there. She told me he's old now, and rarely uses the caverns. And if he *does* flee into the hills, we can easily find the route by which he has escaped.'

'How do you know this?' Idas asked irritably.

'Medea told me.'

'Medea told you. Medea told you.' Idas was in sneering mood. 'How in the name of Thunder does *she* know?'

'I trust her. She knows more than I know, and I don't argue with dangerous women. I suggest you don't argue with dangerous men.'

Meleager piped up again, 'The caves are all linked. According to Aeoleron, this shaping man can move from one end of the island to the other in a single step. Are you that fleet of foot, Jason?'

Jason slammed his fist against the map, irritated and frustrated with this argument. He took a deep breath. 'We're here for piracy,' he said quietly. 'Let's get on with piracy. That's what we're here for. Let us do it. Don't listen to the gossip of magicians, not even a good one like Aeoleron. And take no notice of how this island has spun its tales. Old Man Thunder – Zeus – was born here?' He looked mockingly wide-eyed at Meleager. 'Truly? Do you believe that? When we sailed into the estuary of the Daan, with the Fleece, after our escape from Colchis, after we had rowed like fury across that great sea, we met the Istragians. Remember? They claimed that Zeus was born from black rock that had fallen from the heavens and had been kept in a copper vessel for twenty generations. It burst open and released the young god only after a peasant woman had been stretched across its rounded surface and raped by her brothers. How likely is that? How likely is anything when it comes to Old Man Thunder?' Jason was enjoying this mortal challenge to the god, staring at the new dawn, eyes gleaming, waiting for the gathering of dark clouds, for the moment of the angry strike.

The clouds stayed away. Jason mocked the skies, then turned back to his crew. 'No. This man, this Daidalos, likes his bronze and is proud of his discs. We'll find him where the mystery is most profound.'

'What exactly *are* the discs?' Meleager asked. 'Are they dangerous?'

'Don't know. Don't care.' Jason peered hard at Meleager.

'Dangerous? Since when did danger make you tremble?' He ignored Meleager's protests, continuing, 'The discs might be the cogs that spin the stars, for all that it matters to me. They can contain the knowledge of twenty thousand generations! For all that it matters to me. They can hold the details of our future lives, and the time and manner of our deaths ... for all that it matters to me.' He patted the youth on the cheek. 'I don't understand discs. I leave it to others to understand *discs*. But Medea wants the mind that conceived them, and she needs the flesh that holds that mind. To play with in her own way. To cut up that mind like a child cuts up a bird to see the creature's beating heart. In her own way! And that's what she'll get. As a wedding gift. A disc-maker. A beating heart. And beyond that, apart from spoil and salvage ...'

There was a low cheer at the offer of spoil and salvage.

Jason grinned. 'That's all that matters to me.'

Leaving five of his crew to guard Argo and the beach, Jason led the way inland, following a watercourse, looking for features in the surrounding hills that might indicate which part of the map they were following.

They soon found it: a blood-drenched grove, the dismembered parts of animals scattered around, crow-scavenged but still raw enough to suggest a recent ceremonial. The tall stone effigy of Snake Lady rose from the central tangle of olive trunks. Her eyes were empty but all-seeing. Living snakes were coiled on her exposed granite breasts, lazy in the sun. The stone snakes in her hands were painted a vivid red and green and could have almost as easily been alive.

This shrine was marked on Medea's dream-wrought map. The Argonauts could now see the valley approaches that would lead them to the Cave of Discs.

A day later they were standing on the ridge of a low hill, staring across the sprawl of a city, through which a bright river flowed. Hills rose beyond. The whole urban area was crowded and confusing. Tall, stepped buildings, faced in black stone, suggested temples. Otherwise, the city was a blaze of colour. There was a labyrinthine feel to the place, and below their feet, the earth grumbled in a rhythmic way that suggested the movement of mechanisms beyond their comprehension. If the Argonauts were unnerved by this they didn't show it. Hard eyes surveyed the scene.

'A river. And navigable,' Idas pointed out grimly. 'We could have saved ourselves the walk. My feet are blistered on those blasted rocks.' He held up his ruined sandals.

'The river isn't marked,' Jason said. 'There must be a reason for it. This place is not meant for visitors.'

'Maybe so. But send for Argo. I don't want to walk all the way back.'

Jason suddenly held up his hand. 'Do you sense it?'

'Sense what?' asked Tisaminas.

'We're being watched.'

'From where?'

'From somewhere – up there, on the mountainside. Well, well. Closer than we'd realised.'

22
Shaper

There was often movement on the tracks that wound around the base of his mountain, cutting though the woods and leading along the river, so the file of men moving purposefully below him did not alarm him.

They were almost certainly hunters, though their tunics – dark red on black – were not the familiar colour of the hunting parties that scoured these hills and forests for the rich and complex game that could be stalked there. And something else about them was odd, yet he couldn't see it. They carried spears and bows; and they were not looking up towards the false cave that hid the deeper cavern. They were minding their own business.

To be on the safe side, though, he sent the high call to two of his guardian dogs. Their long, lean wooden backs rose above the undergrowth as they untwined themselves from their sleeping curl. Bronze muzzles turned briefly towards the cave, then lowered again as the two beasts began to slink towards the track, one ahead of the band, one to its rear. They would not attack unless the men left the path.

Satisfied with this, Shaper turned his attention back to the task ahead.

At the first streak of dawn he had seen fire fall from the sky. It had descended to the west, flaming through the darkness, so straight for most of its fall that he had decided it was, indeed, only a shooting star. But then it had curved towards him, seemed to shake in the gloom as it approached the early morning light, before vanishing into the dawn shadow of the land.

Raptor's accuracy, casting these discs from wherever in the Middle Realm he had landed, was getting more accurate, but more risky. Whatever was happening up there, beyond vision, beyond comprehension, there was clearly a sense of urgency about these later falls.

All around the island the seabed was scattered with Raptor's earliest attempts. The mountains in the far west still contained hundreds of the discs that Shaper had never been able to find. That was the country where Queller held power, though, and it was always hard to enter her brute-howling heartlands to recover the bronze plates.

Now Shaper walked back through the mountain, through the winding passage that skirted the central cavern and emerged facing exactly towards the midwinter setting sun.

He pulled his pack across his shoulders, selected a strong staff to support his descent, and a small cage of bees. Alerted to the task ahead, the small creatures began to stretch their wings. The cage rattled with the impact of their small bronze faces and their crystal-faceted eyes. Then they settled.

When he reached the bottom of the mountain, Shaper released his scouts, and the bees buzzed away in a flicker of light and colour.

He continued to walk due west.

After a while, one of the bees returned, flew twice around his head before settling on the ground and beginning its curious, looping dance. After ten turns of the intricate pattern, Shaper knew where the disc had fallen. He changed his direction, and a while later could smell the burning of wood.

He found the disc embedded in the trunk of an aspen. Blackened from its descent from the heavens, a brisk polish with a cloth soon began to reveal the spiral of images on each side of the thin plate.

Shaper studied the figures and shapes for a long time. He recognised many of the forms, but there were new ones too, and that meant more interpretation. More interpretation, yes, but therefore more knowledge of the Middle Realm.

And perhaps this time he might find the one message he had been longing for, the few images that he might interpret as his own name, and a cartouche of shapes in which he might find a message more personal to him from the boy he had trained to fly, and had lost in the final, brilliant flight.

He packed the disc carefully and turned back towards his mountain. One by one the bees found him and flew into their cage, settling quietly on the floor.

It was now well after noon, the sky darkening with clouds scudding in from the north and west. The forest was restless. His mountain loomed ahead of him, apparently no more than a wooded, rocky façade, though his trained eyes could see the shadow pattern where the small entrances and exits to the cavernous complex inside breathed in the fresh air, breathed out the damp of the rocks within. Like gills on a fish, these narrow crevices could close to the passer-by, or open when wishing to attract and consume an unwary animal.

Animals!

The skin on his nape began to prickle, and the hundreds of tiny bronze hairs he had inserted on his back sent warning signals through his body, the rippling pattern of the sensation alerting him to the south and east.

Queller!

He had allowed his guard to fall. He had ventured west alone and unprotected. But she had not dispatched her monsters as far to the east as this for a generation or more. He could just hear the rasping movement of snakes, her favourite form of terror. But others of her fury-fashioned creations were moving stealthily through the trees.

He began to run. As he ran he released the bees, all but one being sent to harass the approaching coils, jaws and claws.

That single bee he sent to alert the hounds, and at the same time he began the high call, the silent whistle of summoning, though he suspected he was too far away from his fortress.

Running, then, he found new speed with the enhanced tendons and ligaments of his legs. He opened his heart and strengthened his spine. He closed off all unnecessary senses. The forest, streams, rocks, low cliffs and tangles of thorns became smaller to him, and he wove his way through and over, heart pumping, sure-footed, head singing with the songs of distraction, a wailing mind-music that he laid behind him like a stunning, snaring trail: to confound and strike apprehension into Queller's beasts.

He began to feel his great age.

Slumping down at a pool, he sucked in water to refresh and revive himself. As the surface calmed he stared down at the sodden and lank grey hair that fell around his hollow, haunted face. His gaze was returned through eyes that were as bright as a child's, but nothing other suggested anything else than time's ruin. And then his face transformed into something simian, something blue, something out of nightmare: a fear-forged monstrosity, a nature's child born from a twisted womb.

A Queller thing.

He was up at once and running again, but found himself scrambling up a steep incline, towards a ridge of granite. Too high! Too impenetrable!

He need not have worried.

Seven dark forms flew out across that ridge, the fading light catching on bronze and wood and the wet foam that streamed from their gaping mouths. His hounds had heard the call, heeded it, and now bounded into the tangle of cover, to howl and bay as they hunted and pursued the creatures that Queller had sent on this skirmish.

Shaper caught his breath, then slumped down against a hard rock, fingering the new disc through its pouch, glancing up at the first star, low on the horizon, the evening star, already bright.

The killing seemed to take an eternity, but soon five of his beasts came bounding back to him, torn, incised, scratched, covered in clinging ivy and snagging briar. They lay panting at his feet, staring at him hungrily for a while before busying themselves with tearing the thorns from their flesh, teasing the creeper from their bodies, jaw-working furiously to rid themselves of these natural pests.

'Well done,' Shaper whispered to each of them. 'You got rid of her hideous inventions. Well done. Hers are too old. My new ones are stronger. Well done, my beasts. My star-fashioned beasts.'

Each in turn glanced at him affectionately before returning to its grooming.

Later, Shaper returned to the cave, his guardians snuffling and snarling their way behind him, scavenging for a little wild food – a *memory* of the wild, a mere illusion of wildness in their wood and metal bodies – before they returned to their stations. Shaper had made them well. In their quiet moments, away from their duties, they dreamed of the life in whose image they had been constructed.

Shaper returned to his chamber, his small shaping chamber close to the main cavern, and placed the disc on the polished stone surface where he worked. The phosphorescent light from the walls made the surface shine. The carved symbols in the walls of the chamber were reflected in shades of pink and green from the stone. The dark disc and its latest news drew him steadily downwards, downwards into its mysteries.

It was then that he heard the soft echo of footsteps, deeper in the mountain, and at once realised that his cavern had been entered and was being searched.

How could anyone have passed his guardians to get so close? What was happening? He had been taken by surprise for the second time in a day!

He ran softly to the entrance to the cavern. Five men were prowling through the mechanisms, swords bared, shields lowered, their hard faces etched with curiosity as they studied the strange forms around them. One, the tallest and most authoritative, was spinning the rack of discs and laughing as they made their low sounds.

These were five of the seven he had seen that morning. Not hunters at all. Adventurers. And now he realised what it was about them that distinguished them from the local people.

From the curious way they braided their hair, from the swords and round patterned shields they carried, they were Greeklanders.

They had patrolled the base of the mountain for the better part of the day, adopting the movements and postures of hunters, each in turn taking the opportunity to glance up at the cave, to assess the approach and the dangers that had been laid for them.

The path to the cave mouth was complex; Jason would have expected nothing more from the shaper of mazes. Lynceus with his sharper eyes constructed a mental map of the convoluted approach. The measure of the dangers awaiting them became obvious soon enough, when two bronze and cedar-wood hounds, snarling and fierce, pounded into the group, intent on savaging the intruders.

Flame-hardened Iophestos knew about metals. He had been apprenticed in the forges of Haephestus before following a dream-call to join the Argonauts on the Quest of the Fleece. Whilst working at the forges, Haephestus's favourite apprentice had collapsed in the heat and spilled molten bronze onto his stomach. Iophestos had scooped the deadly metal from the boy, flung it into the flames, before opening one of the water sluices, cooling the wounds on the boy and on his own hands.

As thanks, Haephestus had made Iophestos's hands capable of melting bronze by touch alone. The leather-skinned man now flung himself at each beast in turn and fused the gaping muzzles.

After that it was easy to twist a sword through the wooden skin of each hound to the sapwood heart.

Other terrors awaited the Argonauts as they ascended the

mountain, but these men had vanquished the so-called *harpies*, those stinking reptilian flying creatures that had tormented poor, blind Phineus, thus earning the Argonauts the final directions in their Quest for the Fleece; they had defeated the army of the Dead that had sprung from King Aeetes' 'dragon's teeth', as they had fled from Colchis, Medea and the fleece in their possession; they had out-sung the singing heads in the groves of the Hercynians, cut down the Teutonean *Ig'Drasalith* before those monsters could uproot, in the forests at the source of the river Daan; to these men, then, the devices of the 'shaping man' seemed simple and crude, though not without a certain charm.

Imagination had gone into their making. But they were no match for Jason and his half-human retinue, though they had delivered mortal wounds to Acastus and Meleager.

'Just like old times,' Jason had breathed, with a smile, as he and his crew reached the rim of the cave.

Now they prowled the Shaper's realm, bemused and amused by the towering figures and strange mechanisms that filled the cavern. Some of these forms were designed for flying, some for walking. Shaped wood and hammered bronze abounded, but there were eyes made of many facets of crystal, in faces that had more in common with dragonflies than hounds. And half limbs, and whole limbs, and the heat from fires contained within bulbous cauldrons, narrowed at the top.

The discs fascinated Jason. As he spun them around, they made a sound, deep and mellow, like a voice heard in a distant dream. There were racks of them. They were suspended in such a way that to spin one spun them all, and an eerie and unharmonious sound emerged for a few moments until they were still again. But in those few moments, when the cavern filled with the vibrant moaning, the mechanisms that surrounded them seemed to shudder, as if struggling for life.

'Haephestus's hammer! What *are* these things?' Tisaminas breathed nervously.

Jason was thoughtful, examining several of the bronze plates in turn. 'I don't know. There are figures marked on them; some I recognise: men, a man walking, helmets, crests, ships, towers, constellations of stars. Others make my vision spin. I've never seen anything like them.'

'They are voices from a world beyond dreams.'

Jason turned, startled, as the words were whispered in his ear. Tisaminas and the others too had swung round, blades singing from sheaths, shields held before them defensively.

'Who's there?' Jason demanded. There was a long silence. Then the same quiet voice, speaking in clipped syllables: 'The collector of those voices. You have had a rare privilege, whoever you are. You have listened to the song of a world that exists, unseen and unknown, between the earth and the heavens.'

'Where are you?' Jason asked. 'Let me see you.' His words echoed in the cavern. The Argonauts had formed a defensive circle now, eyes lifted to the vaults, scanning every dark cranny in the rock. Again, that long, uncomfortable silence.

'Who are *you*?' the voice came at last, harder now. '*What* are you? What are you doing here? What have you done with my creatures?'

'What creatures?'

'My guardians. My dogs. My hawks.'

'They attacked us. We slaughtered them. They gave us no chance.'

'Liar! They gave you every chance! They took a great deal of time to shape. They would have stalked you but left you alone, if you had stayed on the marked paths, on the tracks, hunting wild game. But you are not here to hunt.'

Oh yes we are! Jason thought grimly.

'We have company,' said Idas, pointing into the mountain, and with a rattle of arms the Argonauts turned to face the apparition.

He was tall and lean, long-haired and hollow-cheeked. His long tunic was a vibrant mix of those colours that were always associated with this island: sea-blues, in vibrant hues, and the green of emerald, the reds of blood and sunrise. His eyes, though, were grey and hard, his brow furrowed as he scoured the features of the men opposed to him. Thin-lipped, exuding confidence and barely restrained anger, he stepped closer.

'There is a creature on this island,' he enunciated carefully, 'shaped like a woman. Dreadful. A dreadful creature. Born from the mire of the forest, mistress of all that is wild, and old, and dedicated to the dead clay below our feet. She can summon snakes and doves with a single breath. It's one of her confusing tricks. She does what she can to destroy everything that I shape. She fails. She regards me as an abomination on the land. For my part, I try to winkle her from her stench-ridden womb in the earth. I fail in turn. We are doomed to fail, she and I. Against each other. But where she has failed, you have succeeded. You have undone whole years of work. Those hounds were precious to me. They served me. There was no need – no need at all – to have killed them. Do you even know what I'm talking about? I doubt it. Who are you? What do you want? Answer me quickly. I have hounds to shape again.'

'My name is Jason. Son of Aeson. Servant of Athena. From Greek Land. These are some of my crew, my small army of comrades.'

Shaper stepped closer, peering hard at the man before him. 'I recognised you as Greeklanders. I didn't recognise you as Jason. I've heard of you. The reasons escape me.'

'And I've heard of you. Daidalos. That *is* your name, isn't it?'

'Yes. I don't recognise the way you pronounce it, but yes.'

There was something about Shaper's manner, his expression. He seemed both excited and concerned, his hard stare drawing Jason closer.

'Why have you come here? Why have you been so determined to find me?'

'To invite you back to Greek Land. To meet someone who has heard of you and admires you. She wishes to discuss enchantment and invention with you, matters that are beyond this simple man's comprehension.'

Shaper searched for the truth. 'An invitation from armed men,' he said sourly.

'Just as well we were armed,' Jason reminded him. He sheathed his sword and placed his shield on the floor. The other Argonauts did likewise.

'Why do I know you? Why do I know you?' the gaunt figure repeated. It had become apparent to Jason that the image of Daidalos was confined within a mirror, though from where the reflection came was impossible to tell.

'He led us on the quest for the fleece of the Ram, the golden skin,' Idas announced proudly. 'The story is already dispersing on the four winds, sung by poets, even echoed by gods.'

Idas's words were still echoing in the high chamber when the discs began to turn, some fast, some more slowly. The cavern was filled with mournful sound, which began to rise in volume until it was unbearable.

The image of Shaper had gone. The man had seemed to frown, then step back into the shadows.

Three of the Argonauts picked up their shields and withdrew quickly, running back to the entrance to this cave system. But Jason and Tisaminas stood their ground, armed again, nervously watching the mechanisms that towered over them. When Tisaminas suggested a rapid withdrawal, Jason shook his head. 'Stay with me. There has to be a way into this mountain.'

Once again Argo shifted the scene as she dreamed, as she remembered, as she spoke to me through those dreams, showing me events that were causing her pain. How had she seen Jason and his men approaching the Shaping Chamber on the mountainside? Perhaps she had fed off Jason's own sleepy memories as they had returned from Crete to Iolkus, the hold of the ship filled with goats, wine, booty and a screaming, angry man.

That man – that Shaper – had moved through the tangle of passages and shafts that he had created, and now watched Argo on the beach. To the north lay Greek Land. Behind him, the shuffling movement of a man whose determination seemed to have helped him avoid all the traps that were set in the labyrinth.

Shaper was afraid of Jason. But now that he could see the ship on the shore, he began to relax his guard. He knew this ship. This ship was an ally and an old friend. Now he remembered more of the story he had heard, of that quest for the golden skin of the sacred ram. Jason had sailed on a ship he had rebuilt using oak from the sanctuary to Zeus at Dodona. The goddess Athena had lent her voice and eyes to the old ship.

But to Shaper, the earlier vessel was as clear to his eyes as was the memory of his own possession of her, those few years when he himself had been her captain, and she had taken him on voyages through the night and through the underworld that he would never forget; and which had drawn his talents out to the full.

He had known of her as *Endaiae*, which in the coarse tongue of this island meant, *the fearless guide*. He had stripped the screeching hag from her figurehead, after Queller had possessed her when she'd been wrecked on Queller's shores. He had put in place a gentler guide. He had entered her spirit and built things within her that gave her greater strength, greater fore-knowledge, and something she had longed for:

He had opened her wooden memory to the earliest of times. He had turned her vague dreams into palpable memory. He had resurrected the ship after the millennia in which she had wandered the oceans and rivers, always at the whim of her captains, not all of whom had proved as worthy as she had needed.

Their time together had been short, but it had been a turning-point in his life. He had been able to tap sources of knowledge long forgotten. He had found a freedom from the oppression of the labyrinth. He had had a brief taste of those wonders that only his sons were destined to experience, the one more than the other (poor Icarus – lost, with all the possessions his father had given him); that other – Raptor – even now experiencing worlds beyond all knowing.

He drew back from the shore now and found his way to the Shaping Chamber at Dictaea. He used the discs there to send a sound of summoning to his pursuers, and in due course Jason edged cautiously into the arena, his sharp-eyed, canny colleague behind him, both men ready for the fight.

'Armed again? Always armed!'

'I smell the ocean,' Jason said. 'We've chased you for no more time than it takes to chase a horse into the hurdle. These tunnels are twisted.'

'They are. Twisted is the very word for it. And you're right. The ocean is here, and so is your ship. I know your ship, now. I called her Endaiae. I've forgotten how you named her. Athena?'

'Argo.'

'Yes. Of course. Of course. Argo: for the master shipwright – Argos was it? – who carved and hammered Dodonian oak into her keel. He stripped out half her past and replaced it with the most powerful of Greek Land magic. She is an oracle herself now. Yes. Of course.'

Jason was curious. He had sheathed his sword. The man with Jason – Tisaminas, was it? He had heard the name as Jason had approached – was also unarmed, eyeing the shaping chamber with great intensity. The old signs and time-maps were of most interest to him, but this might have been because they drew him, wolf to the light, much as Shaper himself had been drawn when first he had found them. This other man asked carefully, 'You knew Argo? You sailed her?'

'I rescued her,' Shaper said quietly. 'She was not so magnificent then, she was sea-wrecked, sea-shattered, her paint dulled, her eyes dimmed, her sail tattered. Her decks were rotten, she was a rotting ship, her dreams now a desperate memory, her spirit bored through, like her hull, with neglect and weather. There was old wood in her, strong wood – someone had once built her with love – but the new was patchy. Careless. She had been trapped in the west of this land, possessed by *Queller* – the dreadful female entity – and used by her, because of something she contains.'

'That space through time. That threshold to other worlds.'

'Ah. You know about it.'

'The Spirit of the Ship.'

'The Spirit of the Ship,' Shaper echoed. 'Like any threshold that has been neglected, I helped clean it up. I threw down everything that was foul, all the dark guardians that had been placed across the Spirit. Queller's monstrous creations. I made the ship clean again. I brought back the wildwood. I brought back an older beauty. I even glimpsed her birth.'

'Her birth?' Tisaminas queried. 'A ship can be born?'

'A ship can be built.'

'Yes, of course.'

'A boy built the ship. Your Argo is that ship, grown older, made older, made more profound by many captains, many creators, many carpenters. Argo is old now, and no doubt will always get older. But how fresh is her heart, I wonder?'

'Fresh enough,' Jason said. 'I had no idea that she'd had such a history. I'd welcome you aboard, Daidalos. Come aboard as a friend and as a guest. Go aboard alone, if you wish. Renew the acquaintance.'

Shaper stepped back a little. Everything in this Greeklander's face, in his eyes, was sincere. Still his companion looked around him, enthralled and overtly curious.

Jason's hands were bare, the fingers spread. He was talking about how much the old ship would love to see the old man again.

'Her mast will burst with roses when she sees you.'

How much he wanted to step back into her spirit. He had planted something there, hidden a device that he knew would bring her long sea life, and would take her to seas unknown. But the device had been crude, fashioned quickly, fashioned with passion and raw power; it had not been tested. Was it still in her heart?

He longed to find out.

But this Jason …

His face, his eyes, belied the hunter in his chest. The wolf in his belly. The cat in his legs. The hawk in his cold, calculating psyche.

This was not a man to be trusted.

Then Jason reached to a pouch at his belt and drew out a small metal shape, a piece of bronze, bloomed with the green patina of decaying copper. Without taking his gaze from Shaper's he said, 'I've brought you a gift. It's a very small thing. It may be worthless. But it's yours if you would like it. I can see that it's a map, and a map of this island, but the symbols mean nothing to me.'

Shaper took the bronze. His heart pumped fast, his head felt as light as a feather. As he stared at the metal, he remembered Raptor, his lovely son Raptor. The boy had stood on the edge of a cliff, testing the new wings, using his arms to haul the struts and wires, making the great device, sewn into his body, flex and bend, catching the wind, holding the wind, stretching with the power of the breeze, then drooping and releasing the wind to its normal travel, relaxing the boy.

In his hands he held the map his father had given him, thumbs stroking the metal, reminding himself as a blind man reads the marks in clay, how to return to earth if the fire in the Middle Realm should blight his vision.

'Where did you find this?' Shaper asked quietly.

'It fell to earth,' Jason said, 'near Colchis, beyond the Symplegades. It was one of many objects gathered and brought to my home city of Iolkos. In Greek Land.'

'Do you know what it is?'

'I recognise it as a map, of this country. And that it's made of bronze. That apart, I only know that the friend who wishes to meet you thought it might be of interest to you.'

Shaper clutched the map. He used the waxed cloth he always carried to cut through the patina of corrosion, enough to see his original markings. Yes, this was Raptor's guide. No question about it.

He had them both now, both of his parting gifts to his sons, the two maps, forged as one and cut down the middle.

'Thank you.'

Jason seemed pleased that his gift had been appreciated. 'I hope you'll come to Greek Land with us. I promise to bring you back when you and my friend there are tired of discussing the unworldly.'

'No,' Shaper said, 'not to Greek Land. Not again. Bring your friend here, if you wish. But I stay here.'

'She'll be disappointed.'

She?

Of course! The sorceress from Colchis. More of the story he had heard of Jason came back to him. The priestess. She was a worshipper of the Ram. She had inherited a tradition as old as Shaper's. It would be fascinating – and dangerous! – to meet her.

When he said this to Jason, the Greeklander was disappointed, and said as much. But then he smiled and turned for the entrance to the cave.

'I have to wait for three of my men to return – your cedar-wood beasts killed the other two! I have no ill feelings about that. They knew we were entering dangerous terrain. But while I wait for them, if you wish to visit Argo, as I said before: you are my guest. And hers. When I have my crew together, we'll leave. With you or without you, if you can't be persuaded.'

Jason and Tisaminas began the long walk down the mountainside, to the track that ran by the river; to the river that opened to the sea, where the ship was beached.

Shaper watched them go. Then he made his way ahead of them, by the maze, to where the sea was breaking hard, in hard wind, against the rough shore, and Argo, below her tethers and canvas covers, was shuddering with the coming storm.

She was aware of him at once. He felt her call.

23

The Wedding Gift

She was aware of him at once. He felt her call. The sea was wild by the time he reached her. The Argonauts were huddled in a wide circle around a glowing fire, below one of the canopies. For a moment Shaper entertained the idea of joining them, but they were in their cups and argumentative, miserable with the conditions that prevailed. He climbed the rope ladder as quietly as he could, dropped into the hold among the bales and barrels and the spare oars and sailcloth. He knew just where to go, and he approached the threshold cautiously.

To his surprise there was no one waiting for him. There should have been a guide. Athena, or her mother, Hera. A small part of the Greeklanders' goddess should have been hovering at the edge of the Spirit of the Ship. Instead, he faced a sun-baked, stony landscape, a hot wind driving dust into his eyes. Scrubby trees and parched vegetation were scattered among the stones. There was the fragrant smell of strange herbs on the air, and the distant tinkle of bells, probably attached to the necks of animals. Horns were sounding, their droning low and sustained and seemingly without pattern. Shaper was unnerved by this. He enjoyed pattern. He was fearful of the random structure of nature and the chaos that was created by men who tried to imitate the natural world.

He called now to the ship, summoning the spirit by the name he had given her when he himself had been her captain. She didn't reply. He called again, this time to Argo. And after a while she came to him through the dazzling heat, a blurred image at first, then sharper as the haze flowed away from her body.

She came as a small, nervous child, dressed in archaic clothing, face smudged with the desert, hair crudely tied into flails of dust-lightened auburn. Her eyes were green and fierce, her hands very small. She held a water flask and a straight bone knife. But she was apprehensive. He thought she seemed sad.

She sensed that he was confused.

'Who did you expect to see?' she asked.

'I don't know. The Greeklander goddess, perhaps. Or my kolossoi.'

'Your kolossoi is there. Behind you. You didn't make her to last.'

Shaper turned. The small and exquisite bronze and wood statue sat upon a chair of rock, leaning slightly, hands folded between her knees, head lowered as if she were in a brief slumber, or slumped in despair. The bright bronze, interweaving with the hard polished wood, was as vibrant as when she had stepped into the vessel. But Shaper knew at once that she was dead. She had never truly been alive. She was simply a device, a mechanism whose discs – she was replete with discs, all of them tiny, all of them designed to spin within and against each other – would have kept a record of the life of the ship. As they spun and spoke to each other, so he had conceived that the symbols would re-arrange themselves, to become meaningful, to become a history.

He had been too ambitious, clearly. He had not read the sky discs from his son Raptor well enough. He had not understood the nature of the code.

'I tried,' he said.

'She was wonderful,' said the fierce-eyed girl, 'while she lasted.'

'While she lasted? Were you here when *she* was here?'

'I'm always here,' the girl said quietly. Again, that flash of desperation and sadness in her eyes. 'I love my captains. All of them. What am I without them? I've loved them all. I was never anything other than a *barque* without them.'

'Like lovers,' Shaper said. 'But you're too young to have had lovers.'

She laughed. 'Not that young at all. When the boy made me, the boy who couldn't tie his laces, when he spun in the river, nearly drowning, when that first boy made me, I was already old. It was just that I had never had the wood and leather of the *hull* to occupy.'

From where was I watching? Who was showing this to me? The thought was a fleeting flight of panic before I recognised the fierce-eyed girl to whom Daidalos was talking. This was my own childhood love! This was the child who had haunted me, and taunted me. This was Medea in her earliest form. My first small ship, that 'Voyager', had drawn for her first guardian on the very spirit of the tantalising child who had been both my nemesis and my delight, my first love and my first enemy.

In a time before gods, who else to be guardian of a ship than someone close to the captain's heart?

Now! Now I began to understand! And I watched as Daidalos, this poor, forlorn Shaping Man, stepped into the trap that Jason had set for him.

'Have you missed me?' Argo asked through this first guardian.

'Yes I have,' Shaper replied. 'I've missed you very much indeed. I was so curious about you. You are one of the several wonders of my life. My sons ...' he paused, staring at the girl. For a moment it seemed strange to be talking to this ancient echo, this young-old form, this ghost, this child, this memory ... but he was rational. He knew that he was in the presence of a creature, a spirit if you like, that was as real here as was the sun-scorched rock around him. What, after all, was Time? Merely a moment of existence in *any* state of being. Time flowed, flowed here and there, and could break into the present, from past or future, at any moment. What controlled that seepage, that sudden intrusion, was one of the many mysteries he had been attempting to decipher from the star-cast discs that arrived from the Middle Realm, where his own voyager, his son, his hawk, his *Raptor*, had finally landed.

Argo, as ancient and childlike as she seemed, was still a *ship*! And the ship carried Time. And the ship carried memory. And she was a part of Shaper's memory, and he a part of hers.

'My sons were wonders to me,' he went on, finishing the thought, thinking of their birth. 'Twins. But birds from two different flocks. I knew it the moment I saw them.'

'I know.'

'Their mother did not survive the birth.'

'I know.'

'Yes. I've told you all of this before.'

'To you, though, I was just a curiosity.'

'More than that,' Shaper insisted, uncomfortable with the sudden frown, the sudden change of mood.

'Just a curiosity,' Argo whispered. There was a moment's anger in her eyes, then that uncertainty again. 'I was made in such a way that I loved my captains. They each became a part of me. I was loyal to them all. Even when they sailed me into the extremes of nature, or to the underworld, I always trusted them, I always obeyed them. It's how the boy made me: to be loyal. To love.' Her eyes were misting.

Shaper was silent. Something was very wrong.

The girl turned and ran away, calling through her tears, 'You shouldn't have come. Your time with me is in the past. I'm loyal to Jason now. You shouldn't have come!'

The land around him dissolved into darkness. He felt cold wind on his face, the icy touch of sea-spray.

Turning back to the threshold, he fell heavily on to his side. His hands were bound behind him; his feet were bound. His body rocked – the ship was at sea, in a storm. He could see the heavy night sky above him, thick clouds edged with moonlight.

Two men stood over him, peering down. In the hold, others sat huddled, miserable. The sail billowed, catching wind and rain as the vessel ploughed through violent waves.

He tried to speak, but no words emerged. His tongue was thick, his sight beginning to blur.

'Make sure he's kept warm,' said Jason to his close companion, the man called Tisaminas.

'How long to Iolkos?'

'Another two days at most, even with this weather.'

'We should feed him. He's been trussed like this for two days.'

'He'll survive. Medea's drug will keep him calm now. Keep him trussed. I don't trust his hands. There's metal in them.'

The drug took its effect on Shaper. He drew inwards and downwards, feeling the bitter poison as it coursed through the channels in his body. Numbness and then a dreamless sleep ensued. His last thoughts were:

Two days. She kept me talking for two days, even though it seemed like moments. Long enough for Jason to get back to the beach and capture me.

She has betrayed me. Argo! My Argo! That explains her anguish. She betrayed me using the very mechanism that I had installed inside her. Betrayed me. For her new captain. She has killed me ...

And the last words he heard were the words of the sea pirates.

First, Tisaminas. 'If we can't trust his hands we should cut them off.'

Then Jason. He hesitated, before grunting his agreement. 'Very well. Cut off the hands. But carefully. Keep them fresh so Medea can sew them back on. Medea wants all of him for her gift. She'll need all of him if she's to have her fun with him.'

24

The Memory of Wood

It was snowing hard, yet the land was not quite a featureless white. I could see the shadowed edges of the silent woods nearby. The only sound in this winterscape was a woman's laughter. Clad in white fur, throwing snowballs at her prancing familiar, the lynx, Mielikki was almost invisible.

When she saw me she made her way towards me, stepping through the deep drifts, her breath frosting. I was still in the hinterland, on Argo's side of the threshold.

Mielikki was in her pale, beautiful form, the enchanting woman of middle years.

'Did you get your answer?' she asked me.

'Some of it. Some of the answer. Argo betrayed one of her captains, the man we know as Daidalos. That betrayal is haunting her.'

The goddess was thoughtful. 'Yes. She loves her captains.'

'I knew that. I've always known that. That was the way I made her, when I was a child, when I first shaped the vessel. She reminded me of the fact.'

'And so: what else is there to find?'

What else indeed?

I shrugged, beginning to feel the bite of the chill beneath my clothing. 'I need to know what happened next. How did Daidalos end up in the Otherworld of Alba? Alba is a long way from Shaper's home.'

'You could take a look ...' Mielikki teased me. 'Use a little of that hidden charm.'

I was surprised by this uncharacteristic playfulness. Had she been colluding with Niiv? Both women were from the same frozen, northern homeland. Niiv, however, could not gain entry to the

Spirit of the Ship. She was protected by the Lady of the Forest, but not intimate with her. It was more likely that the goddess, like all guardians of the ship, had become aware of the play, the passion and the dissension between the various members of Argo's crew. And I couldn't deny that she was entitled to a little fun herself.

Take a look into the past? Use a little of my charm? Why? Argo, step by step, was educating me.

But I replied to her taunt, 'I'll probably have to. But I'm too cold here ... I have to go. This snow – it's a surprise.'

'Not welcome?'

'Not welcome.'

'I was homesick,' she explained with a pale smile, holding out her hand to catch the falling flakes. Snow sparked in her features. 'I miss the North. I miss the ice.'

'Yes. I know you do. And I'll make sure you return there as soon as we can. But for the moment, I'm hungry. And I miss the sun. I miss warmth. I miss being drowsy.'

Again she acknowledged my words with an understanding and gentle look in her eyes. 'Off you go, then.'

Even a goddess could be shaped by events, by circumstances. Foul or playful: her decision. Why should she need to be predictable?

I crossed the threshold, back into the ship's more earthly embrace, there to find Jason crouched before me, watching me closely as I emerged from the trance. He seemed startled.

'I'll never get used to that,' he said.

'To what?'

'To the way you transform from flat wood to fat flesh. But never mind that. Two of the boys have come back alone, following the river. No sign of Talienze and the others. No sign of Urtha. Come and see.'

I hadn't remembered their names. No doubt I'd heard them at some time since our departure from Alba, but they were just two of the group of youths who had eagerly put their backs into the rowing, and otherwise sat quietly, part of the *kryptoii* that Kymon and Colcu had formed.

Bollullos had drawn back the sacking covers. The water-bloated features were as smooth as masks. Flesh pale, hair sodden, their eyes watched blindly from behind swollen lids.

'They've been attacked by animals,' Bollullos said. 'Gut-clawed.

Gnawed. But that was after they died. They died from snake-bite. Look …'

He turned one of the corpses over. The boy's shirt was torn open. Two black fang-marks were clearly revealed, enclosed within a pattern of cuts made with a knife. At first glance the cuts seemed random, but only because death and water had distorted them. In fact, they were revealed as a crude representation of wolves on their hind legs, facing each other, fore-legs reaching above the area of the reptile's strike.

The fang-marks were a hand's span apart. A big snake.

When I pointed out the rough design, Niiv grasped the significance at once.

'These are similar shapes to the entrances to the hostels, back in Alba, at the edge of Ghostland.'

'Well remembered.'

'This is curious,' Bollullos mused, scratching his beard and tracing the knife cuts with a brawny finger. 'Very curious.'

'Curious or not,' Jason said gruffly, 'that man Talienze has taken them, and he has put them in danger. Merlin? Time to act.'

His look meant business. He was sober now and still very much in the mood to argue. I didn't want to argue.

There was something of *death* about Talienze, I had thought it from the moment I'd met him.

I could either pursue him as *Morndun*, the ghost in the land, or as *Skogen:* the shadow of unseen forests. All forests were permanent, though their limbs died, rotted and fell. All forests cast a shadow through the generations and Talienze, if he *were* associated with death, would have left his shadow among them.

Indeed, the more I thought about it the more obvious it became: Talienze was not like me, not like Medea, not of the oldest of the world: but he was a servant of that world. He was constantly refashioned, given fresh life; a carving given a trim and a polish whenever its wood became soft and corrupt on the outside. The question, then, if I was right: was he a creature of Shaper? Or of Queller? He might have been either.

I would travel as Skogen, I decided. The shadow of unseen forests. The memory of wood.

I summoned the mask, unable to stifle a cry, startled by the unexpected pain as the wood flowed into my face – that was something new! Then I summoned the form. And when I was shrouded in forest, I summoned the oak image of Segomas from Argo. The lost warrior crept quietly into one of my groves, found a place of security and bound himself to the trunk of a tree. I could feel the pulse of his heart, the brew of his thoughts, the hope and fear at what he might find.

A dead man (whose name meant 'victorious') in tow, I began my journey across this secretive island.

I flowed over the hills, following the course of rivers, touching the caves and walled enclosures that appeared, suddenly and mysteriously, in some of the remotest of areas. Segomas had taken on a more human form now, searching for his remains. He was lithe as he clambered over walls and ducked into the dark mouths of caverns.

When we engaged with another forest, we felt empowered, as if the living woods were giving succour to this ghostly echo briefly co-existing alongside it, moving steadily onwards.

We paused for a long while at the Dyctean cave. The scent of Queller was strong here, and there were echoes of younger creatures. Ahead, to the setting sun, stretched low hills, then grim mountains. But the youths could surely not have travelled so far in this short time.

Skogen turned to the south and we began to search these closer hills.

Everywhere, fallen among the trees, slumped in forges, were the green, ruined giants, Shaper's talosoi, the island's guardians, from the time when he was strong. Their sad features were homes for birds and bats. Their outstretched hands were almost indistinguishable from the thick mossy roots of trees. Had they all fallen together, I wondered, or had they fallen over time, each seeking out a place to die before collapsing with the groaning of forge-cast metal into their eternal slumber.

Home to birds and bats. It was Segomos who sensed in one these leviathans a different form of life.

Small, terrified life, hiding in the metal skull.

I would have shed Skogen at that point, but Segomos asked me not to. I wrapped the forest around the broken giant and Segomos descended into one of the eyes, acting with a lack of caution that no Argonaut would have dared.

He emerged with one of the kryptoii, a boy called Maelfor, we found out. He was bleeding from the face and mouth, his clothes ragged, his hands filthy with earth and mould.

I manifested my form in the small grove. He seemed anxious for a few moments, then, peering more closely, recognised me and relaxed. Relief, indeed, made him sink suddenly to a sitting position, his battered head cradled in his arms, tears flowing quite freely.

When he had recovered a little, Segomos knelt down beside him. He'd found water, which he offered the lad in a piece of bowl-shaped bark; and grapes from the vineyard into which we had flowed. Ghostly though Skogen appeared, we could feed off the land through which we passed as shadow.

'Tell us what you know,' the Coritanian asked. 'Where are the others? What happened? Tell us whatever you can.'

'I don't know what to tell. Talienze had told us that we should scout the land for clues to the disaster on Alba. That our eyes and minds were sharp because freshly honed. That things hidden would be revealed. That we were to bring them back to Alba.

'We followed an old track for a day and half the night. It's a bright moon at the moment. And our eyes soon got used to the dark. But soon after we'd settled for the night the woman creature rode into our small camp. She was terrifying, wilder than any mourning woman in my land. She was straddling a wolf, or some creature like a wolf, the size of a horse. It ran at Talienze. He flung his cloak across its face and shouted to us to run. I don't know what sorcery he used, then, but he kept the woman at bay with astonishing fury. Fire and ice seemed to flare and freeze between them. He howled words that were meaningless. The woman was screeching, but her gaze, a terrible look, was on the group of us who were running.

'Talienze saved us. His last words were a scream of "Find discs! Find Merlin!"

'His abilities were limited. He seemed to droop and the wolf leapt at him and took him in its jaws, grabbed him by the throat and bounded away. He was very limp. The woman's hair was long, like a cloak of flails, tipped with bone. She shook her head violently as she rode off, and the flails whirled about her.

'Then other creatures came, strange animals, neither wild cat nor hound. Kymon, Colcu and I were making a better run of it, but Dunror and Elecu fell beneath the claws and were dragged away screaming.'

'What happened to Kymon and Colcu?' I asked.

'Lost on the hillside. We were hunted until the moon went down below the mountain. Then for a while we just ran. And the next night I slipped and tumbled into the ravine; I landed on the face of a giant metal man. I was able to hide there. He's not hollow but he has hollow parts to him. The creatures that pursued me prowled about the ravine until dawn. I suppose they hadn't got my scent. I was too frightened to come out. There was a lot of movement in the metal man, from further down. I didn't care to find out what it was. That's all I know until you found me.'

Queller had taken Talienze, and by the sounds of it, killed him in the taking, and she had left it to her pack to hunt down the boys. There was a chance that Colcu and Kymon were alive, but now the matter was urgent. I had dismissed that urgency before, too anxious to hear what Argo would have to say, to try to understand the significance of events in her life. That had been a mistake.

But those boys would be somewhere nearby, somewhere in these gouged hills and forests, perhaps close to a river, perhaps hiding like Maelfor.

Maelfor had imagined that the hunting animals had failed to get his scent, but perhaps there was another reason why they hadn't leapt in through the gaping eye of the giant and torn him to pieces.

The talosoi was a Shaper creation. It had been a king's guardian on the coast of this island. It had been hated by Lady of Wild Creatures.

And Segomos also was a Shaper invention, woodwork and bloodwork, fused and fashioned from the visionary mind of a man who had taken ideas flung at him from the heavens. He had constructed such virile figures of oak for the amusement of warlords, in Greek Land, when it was still known by its more ancient name. And he had constructed them again, centuries later, in Alba, from his prison in the Otherworld.

It seemed that Queller was still afraid of Daidalos's constructions, even when they lay dead and broken. Even in the breaking, then, perhaps they kept a certain power.

And this is why Argo had brought along Segomos, with his faint flicker of a broken life; to be a shield for us. Perhaps.

This is why Snake Lady had so swiftly savaged Talienze, a weaker creation.

Perhaps.

But first: to find a son and a nephew of two kings. One of those kings was also at large in these hills. Urtha and his *uthiin* would be a poor match for what Queller could throw at them, I imagined.

They had run like beasts, tripping and stumbling, pausing to gasp for breath and ease the pain in their lungs, then finding new strength in their limbs to carry them further from the howling and screeching of the pack.

Descending hillsides, crossing waist-deep through the crystal waters that flowed between the slopes, clambering through sparse woods, finding brief shelter in the crush of and hollows of rocks, they became lost in the land, disorientated and confused. There were times of quiet. These were the times when they heard the rumbling of their stomachs, the drumbeat of strong hearts pushed to their limits.

Then, always, the pack.

It was quiet during the day, and they made slower progress, even managing to scoop a large fish from a shallow area of a river. They cut it up and ate it raw.

There was never any shortage of water.

Then night, and the land began to bay. The cry of a woman was sudden and distant, shrill and songlike. It came and went on the breeze, but even the wind seemed to shift with each ululation. The clouds shuddered as if being commanded. The land rumbled deeply, as if shifting its hidden channels.

The pack came closer.

During that second night, as they scrambled in the darkness along a ridge, illuminated by the moon, vulnerable and terrified, Maelfor suddenly cried out. He had slipped and was rolling and tumbling into the darkness. His cry lasted a long time before he was suddenly silent.

Kymon could hardly move from the shock of it. Colcu grabbed his shoulder. 'He's gone. We have to move fast.'

'I know.'

Kymon knelt down on one knee and stared into the ravine. 'Make your way home as best you can. That was a good run, cousin.'

'I didn't know he was your cousin.'

'Would it have made any difference? Let's get off this ridge.'

On the third day, in a valley, in woodland, Colcu spotted a young boar, and the two boys hunted it, Kymon stalking it from the side,

Colcu from the front, both wary for bigger members of the family. When the squealing animal broke cover, they chased it hard, leaping fallen trees, somersaulting over rocks, jumping up to branches to get a longer view, signalling with whistles and hand signs which way the black, sleek creature was moving. This was the best run of all. They had been born for this particular chase!

The pig was fast and well knew the shortcuts through the wood. It was up against experienced hunters, however, and no matter which way it turned, one of those hunters came racing up to it and flung his sword, narrowly missing, narrowly missing again, but the pig's day was coming to an end.

It turned, cornered against a tall face of grey rock. Squealed. Made a stranger sound. Summoned its guardians, begged its guardians to hear its call. Then squealed again as Colcu's knife plunged down into its neck, sending the thrashing beast to the ground, its small tusks inflicting small wounds on the Coritanian's left arm.

'Well chased!' Kymon complimented the older boy.

'Well chased yourself,' Colcu replied with a grin. 'And well run, young pig,' he said to the dead animal. 'You'd have been fit for the forests of Alba.'

They had no means of making a fire, so they gutted the boar and shared the warm liver. Then they cut the softer meat into strips and chewed quietly for a while.

Colcu removed the tusks, and the strip of bristles from its neck.

'The pack will soon get the scent of this,' Kymon said, and Colcu agreed. He looked around nervously, wiping blood from his mouth.

'We should wrap the carcase in moss and leaves and bury it.'

Kymon had stood up to search around the area where the hunt had finished. He realised, looking up, that this was no ordinary face of rock, but a fashioned stone of enormous size. There were markings on it, so obscured by wind and rain that they could not be clearly seen. As he walked along its base he found a narrow passage, a mere slit between two faces of the stone. He edged inside. The passage was maze-like, but he persevered until he could see to its distant end, where daylight illuminated an open space, and something gleamed there, bright, then dull, as clouds shifted across the sun.

Edging back and calling for Colcu, he returned and completed the squeeze through the rocks, emerging into a small arena where the grass was dry and high, growing around a dozen or more stone, sleeping human figures. Five low openings in the curving farther wall suggested chambers or passages leading away from this sunlit space.

The shining object in the centre, perched on a stone platform, was a crystal or glass amphora, with a curled human figure inside.

Kymon waited for Colcu to arrive. He eased from the passage, grunting with the effort of hauling the boar's carcase by its back legs. 'That's a girl,' he said in surprise as he saw the glass pithoi. 'She looks dead.'

He dropped the beast. Together they made their way through the grass and thistles to where the sweet face, eyes open, stared towards the entrance to the arena. The child was small, hands folded across her chest, legs tucked neatly below her, white tunic caught as if shifting in a sudden breeze. She was suspended in a pale yellow liquid, and Kymon intuited at once that it was the product of the bee.

Colcu walked around the pithoi. 'She has wings.'

'Wings?'

'Look at this.'

Kymon stood by his friend and marvelled at the folded wings, black and white feathered, stitched and tied to the girl's shoulders, neck and waist by tethers and tendons of various hues and varying girths.

The significance was not lost on either youth. They had both listened to Tairon's tale of Icarus and Raptor.

Colcu broke away, looking around him anxiously. 'What *is* this place?'

Kymon, though, had begun to study the pictograms on the edge of the round stone base. 'That image again,' he said to the curious Colcu. 'You didn't see it, but I did. The same image as the shape of the entrances to the hostels at the edge of Shadow Hero Land. Look here ...'

He showed Colcu the repeated pattern of two animals facing each other, on their hind legs, separated by a strangely featured woman, whose hands rested on their heads. There were ten such triplets of woman and beast. She held a pair of wolves, stags, tusked boars, bulls, hounds, cats, cranes, eagles, hares, and rearing snakes.

'What do they mean?' Colcu said aloud, thinking out loud.

'She's quelling them, subduing them. These are images of that flailing woman who's pursuing us. Lady of Wild Creatures. This plinth is hers.' Kymon stood, scratching at his chin cut, searching the openings in the wall. 'But I don't think this was always her place.'

'Because of the wings.'

'The wings puzzle me.'

'He had started to apply his invention to his daughters ...'

'I wish Merlin was here. He'd have a better understanding.'

'But he's not here,' said Colcu firmly. He tapped the blade of his sword gently against the glass pithoi. 'If that *is* one of the Shaper's daughters, and this,' he tapped the stone plinth, 'was put here by the Wild Woman, then—?'

'Then this was his place, his arena, and she has possessed it in her own way. Made it hers. Sacrificed his daughter in honey.'

'A honey child.'

'Well put,' said Kymon.

'This is the forecourt of a Shaping Chamber,' Colcu whispered. He looked round at the entrances to deeper caverns. 'And those are the ways in.'

'We've found what Talienze asked us to find, I think.'

'Talienze is dead. Probably.'

'And we don't know what it was he wanted us to bring back from the chamber.'

They were silent for a while, trying to see into the darkness of each of the doors in the wall. It was Kymon who articulated the thought that was in each of their minds: that it was into such an opening that Tairon, a labyrinth-runner, had entered as a youth and had not returned. They had heard his story, told on Argo. In the hills of Crete there were mazes beyond comprehension. And all or none of these five gaping invitations to mystery might have been the beginning of such a consuming, eternal journey.

Colcu suddenly started to pluck long grass, whole handfuls. He knotted the dry ends with the moist roots and, strand by strand, he produced a thin and fragile thread. 'There's a story about this,' he said as he worked. 'Can't remember much about it. Traveller's tale. It probably happened here on this island, though. It was all about mazes. Don't hold too hard or tug too hard at either end, but this will be a guide back to the light.'

'Which of us is going in?'

'To be decided. Can you knot? We'll need a long thread of grass.'

*

It was getting dark. I moved swiftly towards where the *kryptoii* were echoing Ariadne in their exploration of this Shaping Chamber. The dream was hazy, but the vibrancy of their words, the energy in their actions, the pure youthful sense of their own supposed immortality, had struck a profound chord in my mind's eye as I absorbed their actions through the face of the Moon.

I had forgotten how slow Moondream was in the pursuit. Cunhaval the hound would by now be wrestling with them; affectionately, of course.

I had begun to realise, also, that I was behind in the chase. The screeching woman was ahead of me, song-singing her flock of predators, spreading them out across the hills as she scoured for these stranger-intrusions into her newly conquered land. Queller was determined to eliminate all that she did not comprehend.

She was very close to them now.

Again, I entered the dreamhunt, absorbing the experience that was Kymon's as he explored the first of the chambers.

This was a place that Shaper had used to draw on the past. It was a place I knew well, at least in its design: a gallery of painted images, some familiar, some obscure. Animals roamed and leapt and curled in upon themselves, as if asleep, or killed; in other parts of the chamber, lines of strange characters, squares and circles, densely painted signs and symbols: all suggesting an attempt at expressing a forbidden knowledge. I knew better.

Kymon was astonished at the beauty of the animals, especially the horses. They seemed almost to move across the wall, some of their heads raised, others lowered, a motionless stampede of movement, vibrant reds and browns in the shaft of light from the entrance. He could hear the sound of their wild ride in his head; no doubt the ground below him shook with the gallop as his eyes engaged with this gorgeous panorama.

The symbols, the circles and the lines of strange marks almost made his head swim. They seemed to draw him in, freeze him in his tracks. He was strong enough to pull away from this embracing charm.

Deeper in the chamber, there was no light, just the moan of a distant wind, and he didn't venture there.

What Colcu had discovered I couldn't tell. I was dreaming Kymon.

In the fading light he had explored a chamber where, as in Jason's memory, there was a workshop of moving parts, subtly moulded from metals, carved crisply from the hardest woods, cedar mostly, and whole sheets and cylinders of crystal. They were scattered everywhere. The walls where once designs had been depicted were savaged, scratched through. Only one thing remained intact, beyond ruin, to the boy's hungry eyes. To look up, to look to the roof, was to see the night sky. It was still day outside, but here he could see the stars; and even as he watched, so a star shot across the night. There was a milky veil up there, a stretch of floating gossamer that drew him towards it as much as the older signs in the first chamber.

He picked up discs of bronze, and thin lengths of silver, gathering them into his arms, adding several shards of crystal that appeared to be engraved, heaping up the ruins until his arms could hold no more weight. Then he followed the grass thread back from the deepest gloom he could manage to have entered, back to the dying day, and Colcu.

'That's a good haul,' Colcu said with a half-smile.

Kymon let it all drop to the ground. 'A good haul of nonsense. Talienze had something in mind for us to fetch. He should have told us what it was.'

'Perhaps he didn't know what it was,' Colcu observed quietly.

Kymon sifted the spoils, picking up a small disc, no wider than his hand, turning it in the light, peering at the spiral of drawings on each face. 'This means nothing to me.'

'Why should it?'

In frustration Kymon hurled the disc across the grass and sleeping statues of the arena. Flung from the wrist, the disc curved through the air and clattered from the rock wall, close to the entrance. 'A good weapon, perhaps,' the boy observed.

Colcu was amused. 'I don't think that was his intention. But if you and I have to fight in single combat again, I'll be sure to have three or four of them in my belt.'

He stood and walked through the grass, picking up the battered disc of bronze. Something caught his eye. 'We've forgotten to cover the pig,' he called. 'There are flies everywhere. Can we still eat it, I wonder?'

'There's a lot of that pig that the flies won't have reached,' Kymon called back, still searching through the artefacts.

He became aware of Colcu's silence. The taller boy was standing over the dead animal, staring down. 'What *is* this?' Kymon heard him say aloud.

Suddenly alarmed, Kymon swept an angry hand through the trinkets from the chamber and walked over to where the carcase lay stretched out.

Open-bellied, its hind-quarters hacked to supply the earlier feeding, the young boar was a gruesome sight, stiffening and distorting as heat and time tugged at its dignity. Colcu had thrown it down so that its head was against the rock, as if slouched against the wall.

A child's face, etched in white, watched them now from the tusk-drawn skull. A child!

'Urskumug,' Kymon breathed. He started to shake. The pallid features of the human face seemed to leer at him. 'Urskumug.'

Colcu just stared at him, understanding nothing except that Kymon was in a rage of intuition, and was frightened.

'We're in danger,' Kymon said. Colcu stayed silent. And it was through that silence that the singing of the Wild Woman and the baying of her hybrid pack reached their hearing. It was still very distant. 'We should leave this place and take our chances in the woods. It'll be dark soon. We're not safe here.'

'I'm not sure I agree,' was Colcu's retort, but he ran with Kymon to where the artefacts lay scattered. They gathered as many as they could carry in one crooked arm, then ran back to the cleft.

Too late. The howling and wailing song were much closer.

'We're going to need a god's help now,' said Colcu.

'Not a god,' Kymon whispered, his eyes suddenly bright. 'We need to make a sanctuary to Urskumug.'

'Urskumug again. You say the name like a boy in a fever.'

'We have to make his sanctuary! It's just a chance.' He listened nervously to the first sounds of approach through the rock.

'You have the stink of madness about you,' whispered Colcu.

'Then you have a keen nose. This *is* madness. But what have we to lose? Give me the tusks. The boar's tusks. And those spines from its neck!'

Reluctantly Colcu unwound them from his belt. Kymon grabbed the trophies and ran to the honey child, dropping to his knees and fingering one of the faces of the stone plinth on which she stood. 'No. Not here,' he said urgently. 'This is Queller's stone.'

As if responding to the sound of the mistress's name, Queller's cat-hounds came pouring through the gap in the rock, howling, fangs bared, large eyes luminous with blood-lust. At the same time a torch was flung into the arena, and the grass began to burn fiercely.

Colcu and Kymon reacted as if in combat, instinctively and furiously. They ran at their attackers, drawing their swords as they did so. Colcu seemed almost to fly as he somersaulted over two of the creatures, sword-blade flashing in the moonlight and firelight as he struck one down. He leaped back up at once and turned in the air, blade extended, doing fierce damage.

Kymon was also adept at the feat of the five leaps. The earth might have been a blanket, throwing him up into the air. He was sprayed with blood twice, dropping to a crouch after the fifth leap, waiting for the pack to pounce.

They had circled him, feral and furious. The stench in the arena was foul.

Four of them attacked him all at once, and two cat-like heads flew through the air. Then Colcu appeared out of nowhere, and Kymon found himself below two pumping, foul-smelling carcases.

The fires were fanned by a wind. The two youths stood back to back, breathing hard, preparing for the next assault.

It didn't come. Kymon looked round, looked up. Rising there against the night sky, on top of the rock wall, came the sinister figure of Wild Creature Lady herself. Peering down, pale and silver, hard-eyed and dispassionate, Queller sat on her mount, arms outstretched, fingers spread. The strange, subduing tune ceased. Her gaze never left Kymon's.

Then she sang briefly.

Her hunting creatures spread out widely, a steady encirclement, some sidling through the smouldering grass where the torch still burned.

The moon emerged from behind a cloud, and the arena was alive with the gloss and glow of watching, waiting eyes.

Kymon took his chance. He darted forward and grasped the burning torch where it lay. He smoothed the flames from the handle, then raced to the first cave, calling to Colcu, who needed no second urging.

They made the entrance as the pack clawed at their heels, plunged into the darkness, waited for the assault. But the glowing eyes stayed outside. This place still had Shaper's power within it.

It was the chamber of paintings. The images seemed to writhe, shadow movements from the dying flame of the torch.

'Thank you for that leap,' Colcu said. 'I owe you one leap.'

'I'll be claiming it, be sure of that,' the younger boy said breathlessly, and with a smile. Colcu looked back into the depths of the chamber.

'I'm not going down there. Life is too short to risk an eternal walk. A Tairon walk.'

'I agree,' said Kymon as he started to search the chamber's walls.

When he had been here before he had seen the way each of the niches had been dedicated to a different animal. He was certain he had seen drawings of a boar.

'Be quick,' Colcu said. 'Whatever you have in mind, do it quickly. Our friendly fire is guttering its last.'

Kymon held the torch very still. It was a crude affair, and the flame was small, the light a tiny relief from the blackness. He moved around the chamber with caution, gaze intent on the images. Bulls, horses, cats, hounds ... at last he found the boar, three of them, overlapping and ferocious in their illustration.

He fumbled at his belt and produced the souvenirs cut from their last meal, tusks and spine, and placed them in the niche.

'Do you know what you're doing?' Colcu asked.

'Of course not. But what makes a sanctuary? Something dedicated by priests with ritual and secret knowledge? Or something needed by the heart? Urskumug told me I could summon him if needed.'

'We need *something*.'

Kymon called for Urskumug. He knelt before the three boars and reminded Urskumug of his promise, during the Moon Hunt. At the entrance to the chamber the pack howled. A few feral faces started to peer inside, cautious, nervous, testing the threshold. They became bolder.

'Urskumug!' Kymon finally cried in desperation and anger. The torch was flickering. Even as Kymon's anguished shout died away into the silence of the tomb, the fire flared briefly and died.

But at that moment, the chamber shook. There was the sound of laboured breathing from the deep recesses. A snorting sound, a grunt: a boar-sound.

As the beast emerged from the tunnel, its flanks threw Colcu against one wall and Kymon against the other. Its spiny hide was as sharp as a sword blade, and both youths were grazed badly. The massive animal stalked past them on all fours, ignoring them, head lowered.

The pack fled before it. It rose on to its hind legs as it reached the arena and stared hard at Queller. Beast and Beast Woman exchanged a long, impassive gaze. Then, astonishingly, Lady of Wild Creatures backed away across the rock, eyes alive with anger and frustration. With a flailing shake of her head, she had suddenly gone, and her creatures slunk back through the passage, to the land beyond.

As Kymon emerged cautiously from the cave, Urskumug turned briefly to glance down at him. The human face, chalk-white and angry, gave no sign of recognising the young Cornovidian.

'Thank you,' Kymon said. 'I'm astonished you heard my call. But thank you.'

Still no response. Urskumug looked away, stared at the small, dead boar by the entrance. Kymon felt his heart race, uncertain about Urskumug's response to its slaughtered kin. But the great beast dropped back to all fours and bounded across the smouldering grass to leap up the rock wall, landing with a single jump on the very spot where Queller had watched proceedings. It turned its snout up and sniffed the air, then looked into the distance.

A last, lingering glance at Kymon and it was gone, out onto the mountain.

Where Colcu and Kymon stood, stunned by the speed of arrival and departure of this ancient apparition, the crystal container lay smashed. Urskumug had kicked it over when it had run for the wall. The honey child lay in the shattered glass, a crumpled figure, coated with the sweet sticky product of the bee.

'It did that deliberately,' Colcu said quietly. 'I saw it.'

'Why? Why break the tomb?'

Before Colcu could reply, a voice spoke to them from the channel in the rock. 'I think it means we should take her with us.'

The youths were startled for a moment as they stared at the apparition that stood there, face like the moon, body clothed in dark material, but clothed in a familiar way.

'Merlin?' Kymon asked cautiously. And then with a great sigh of relief: 'Merlin!'

I had found them. And they were alive. And Kymon was proud of his makeshift sanctuary, and I would not let him know that, when

I had realised what he was doing, I had given a good shout to the Oldest Animal myself. That had hurt! Deep in the bones.

I let Moondream slip away.

Kymon grinned as he saw my true face. 'How far are we from the ship?' he asked.

'A long walk. Wrap the girl in my cloak.'

'The girl? This girl? She'll start to stink.

'Not for days. She's well covered. But flies will be a problem, feeding on the honey. Quickly. We have someone else to find before we can go back to the harbour.'

25

Cloak of Forests

Segomas and the boy were not where I had left them, in a grove cloaked by silent forest, a still wood, sleeping quietly in the temporary absence of the mask-wearer who had summoned it.

Kymon noticed my sudden alarm. We stood on scrubby hillside, looking into the valley, to the pale, mist-shrouded east.

'I left them here ...'

'Who?'

'Segomas. The oak man. And your young friend Maelfor.'

'Maelfor is alive?' Kymon asked. His eyes had brightened. 'He fell a long way.'

'He fell into safety.'

What had happened to Skogen? I turned a full circle where I stood, drawing in the land. But younger, sharper eyes than mine found it. Colcu's! He was laughing and pointing down the side of the hill, where the woodland, I could now see, shimmered in an unnatural way. At the edge of the wood stood a boy and a man, and the boy was beckoning to us.

The survivors of the *kryptoii* skidded and slid through the tangle of tight undergrowth, down the slope to greet their old friend. I followed in a more dignified, but less hasty manner.

Skogen had simply 'slipped' down the hill, finding a more natural and easier resting place. I should have remembered this about the masks. Leave them, without sending them back, and they find their own place of safety: Morndun slipping deeper into the underworld; Sinisalo seeking out the company of children; Moondream finding night and the mysterious pull of Luna herself. And so on: the hound to the moon-gazing pack; the fish to the waters where it spawned;

the eagle to the eyrie where it could survey the circle of the world through its twice-sharp eyes.

Segomas drew back into the shadows; the boys huddled.

And a second surprise was waiting for us. Urtha and Morvodumnos stepped out of the gloom. They were both ragged and thorn-cut. There was so much leaf-matter in their hair they might have been participating at one of the Speakers' evergrove rituals. Kymon hardly recognised his father for a moment, then flung himself into the man's embrace.

Urtha was on his knees, brawny arms round the chattering boy. Kymon was both relieved to see his father and anxious to tell of his own strange experience, the words tumbling from his lips, incoherent and childish, bright with passion if confusing in the detail.

Urtha, I was able to glean from Segomas, had found a haven from pursuit – the pursuit, no doubt, of Queller's night creatures – in a small cavern, just beside the brook that flowed through the valley. We had all been drawn to this region, a part of the island that was certainly patrolled by Queller, but which retained a memory of the Shaping Man. We had all encountered the quelling force; we had been lucky to survive. The loss of the boys was a tragedy, that of Talienze a puzzle that would probably never be resolved. They had been unlucky in the chase.

Segomas was forlorn. He stood now in the brightness of the woodland edge, his back to the bare land. I went up to him and saw sap glistening in his eyes.

Though there was a tawny tinge to his skin, he seemed almost human. There was even the suggestion of a beard on his face, an echo of the man growing back through the bark as the hard oak was softened by Skogen.

'I have to leave you,' he said. 'I have to find what remains of me.'

He was trembling. Behind me, Urtha was laughing and the youths talking excitedly. They might have been sitting in the king's enclosure in Taurovinda, at the end of a day's hunting, for all their relaxation.

'Segomas,' I said to the Coritanian gently, 'You died, or were executed, in Greek Land. This is *not* Greek Land. And you died, or were executed, at a time that has not yet come into existence. Do you understand? Argo and this island have played a fine set of tricks with us. When we leave this place, we will soon go back to where we belong, but that place is unborn as yet. Your death is still to come. You can't find your remains here. They *aren't* here. It would be a senseless quest.'

'I'm here,' he insisted. 'I had a dream while you were away. I heard the battle that raged in Delphi that time. I saw my fate. You were right. I was reduced to a cloak of skin and a cruel skull-mask. It hangs in a shrine here, with fifteen of my friends. They brought us here as tribute, in exchange for something. The dream was very clear. If I have to wait a few years, I'll wait. But this is where I was brought, and it's from here that I can return home to my proper grave.'

He was insistent and strong. The sap glistened on his mouth as well, and on his brow.

It occurred to me then how many aspects of the masks I didn't fully understand. Not just that they would find a place of comfort, if abandoned, but that they had qualities and abilities beyond that which could be summoned by the user at the time: in this case me.

Skogen is a forest that casts a shadow through time, and not just to the past but to the future too. The 'cloak of forests' had detected Segomas in the future of this land, somewhere in a cleft in the hills, a gap in the rock, a painted room, a stone building filled with burning herbs and flesh, some future sanctuary.

So Segomas would stay and Segomas would wait.

Like his name, I suspected, he would eventually be 'victorious' in his small, sad quest.

26

A creature Caught in Amber

The island was behind us, a memory as dark and obscure as had been the westernmost mountains, the last sight of the land, all colour draining from their slopes, just shadow marking their rise above the sea. Crete, the island of old lore and invention at war, vanished as fast as the setting sun, as wind and ocean favoured Argo and impelled us north and west.

There was a moment – Tairon felt it, as did I – when the strange forces that had governed our expedition to Shaper's Land left us. Time was re-established. The future had been clawed back. The Echonian world that Queller had created, and which Argo had used to show us certain events, was consumed by the very ordinariness of sea-surge and the hard breeze that was to mark our long journey home. To Alba.

We were a quiet crew, a much diminished crew, glad of kind winds and a lack of storms, so that we were able to make the Pillars of Herakles. Here we rigged sail and caught the northerlies, taking us along the dangerous coast of Iberia. And it was here that for the first time we formed a council to press Jason on events he had claimed not to remember.

It was clear, to me at least, that Argo had removed the barrier of obscurity from part of the events in Jason's past with her. From the moment we had passed the Stochaides, off the coast of Gaul, Jason's demeanour had changed. He had become troubled and thoughtful. He had taken more time at the steering oar than was necessary, and his gaze – whilst attentive to the sea – had been distant and personal.

Argo herself had remained aloof; the goddess, hag-like, scowling, would not respond to requests for conversation.

*

I had tried, without success, to explain the twists of Time that Queller and Argo had settled upon us during our stay on Crete. Tairon understood to an extent – a labyrinth-runner and a man used to mazes, it was natural that he should have at least a feel for the maze that we had just left. But it was beyond Urtha's capacity to comprehend how Segomas, for example, would now live through hundreds of years until, distantly, he would be born; and grown; and dispatched to a foreign fight; and despatched cruelly; and slung, still alive, in a Cretan grove, to be flayed and his organs eaten, the skin dried and made into a cloak, one of many layers, the others being his companions-in-arms, also captured; and how he would be discovered by the oak-image of his carcase that had been made by an estranged and exiled spirit from the very beginnings of the island where he, Segomas, would finally find his otherworldly peace.

Truthfully, I too found the whole thought a little confusing, so how these other men could comprehend the play-of-centuries was never a question that needed to be asked: they simply couldn't. And as for Queller's conjuring with the multiple echoes of land and events that co-exist in any one place ... well, it was best we left the concept unquestioned and not discussed.

Argo had led us towards an understanding of why Urtha's land had been subsumed by Ghostland.

The question now? How had Shaper come to be in Ghostland itself, a Shade Place, yes, but of haunted shores, hunt-howling forests, iron-bloodied plains and rafter-ringing hostels in which he did not belong?

Jason watched me from the huddle of men who surrounded him. The weather was poor, a steady rain falling into Argo, running off our sheepskin covers. We were not watertight. We were miserable as Argo found passage north. Bollullos at the oar scowled as he kept the ship steady. Rubobostes waited his turn. Kymon crouched with his father below a canopy slung between the rails, each of them thinking of Munda: the one with hopes for a fatherly reunion; the other, from the scowl on his face, with thoughts of subjugation.

'What did you do with the Shaping Man?' I asked Jason.

He looked up at me, the greying hair plastered to his face, the grizzle in his beard saturated and dripping water. But that intensity of gaze! It had never deserted him. And it was a gaze that was now inflamed by memory, the memory of a second great adventure.

'It's not what Jason did,' he said, oddly referring to himself in the third person. 'It was the witch. She had scoured him, scourged him, broken him, drawn the essence of his bone. She had consumed him as a dragonfly consumes a smaller member of its kind, eating him from the head downwards. And the more she ate, the more she hated. The more she consumed, the more fury consumed her. And why?'

'Why?' Urtha asked when a long silence had passed from Jason's last, enigmatic statement.

Jason stared at the king for a long time, thinking hard. A sour smile touched his lips. Then he glanced at me.

'Because that man knew how to hide his talent. And Medea ate nothing of his heart. She learned nothing. All he would say to her was: "Brightness falls from the air". She knew he referred to the bronze discs that were flung from somewhere nearer than the stars, but he would never explain what they were or from where they had come. She became frantic. She clawed her own breast with impatience. She was betrayed by impatience. She destroyed the wedding gift because that man, or whatever nature of being he was, dispatched himself – in terms of his abilities, at least – before my good, dread wife could find a hole in his defences and tug out the tough tendon of his invention.

'She spat him out, cast him out, rejected him. His guts, chewed and undigested, she spat on the floor. The bones, after she had cracked them between her jaws, she then pounded into flour and cast them to the wind. I don't speak literally, of course ...'

'Of course.'

'But I remember how she kissed his eyes before she plunged her nails into them. And I remember how he laughed.'

'She learned nothing from him?'

'Nothing of consequence.'

'And so she killed him.'

'No,' Jason said quickly. 'Not at all. She gave him back to me.' He frowned at the memory, shaking his head. Then he laughed quietly. 'Yes. She gave back the gift. I didn't realise it at the time, but that was the end of us, the end of the union. Love had long since fled. She abandoned me as quickly as she abandoned Shaper. I didn't see it at the time. He had been her plaything. I was still entranced by her, and welcomed inside her. I hadn't noticed how her taste had turned sour. Or if I did, I put it down to Moon-change, or some such transience. It was only later when, abandoned by her, I'd found a brief happiness with Glauce, that she turned the dagger on the table, to point to me, to insinuate that I was the wrong-doer. And went on to kill everything I loved, my sons, my beautiful sons. I was her plaything too. But by then, she was tiring of the game.'

We trussed him up in canvas (*Jason continued*), this broken man, Daidalos, half metal, half flesh, star-crazed, dreaming-strange, the discarded flesh of enchantment, the discarded gift of love, crying in strange tongues, des*cry*ing misfortune for the wolf-hearted sailors who were now taking him away from Iolkos for trade. We had heard of strange countries, unusual wealth, far to the north, where five rivers rose, two flowing east and west, two north and south, and one that beguiled.

This was the second great adventure with Argo.

But Shaper foretold disaster for us, summoning the vision of his magic. He didn't reckon with the callousness of men. We found him amusing. We hoped others, strangers, would be more beguiled.

One of us was dedicated to making sure he wasn't ill, or his limbs dying with the tightness of the bonds. We put a blindfold round his eyes, just in case: even blinded eyes can do more than see; and plugged his ears. That is how much we were afraid of him. We fed him and watered him. We had taken hellebore to help with any pain he suffered. We paid attention to his need to piss, and the rest. We turned him regularly to avoid the black blood that can kill a prisoner like this. We fed him and kept him comforted with water and rough wine.

And we rowed on our adventure. He was tradable, if we could find the right kingdom with the right goods to exchange and the right degree of simple-mindedness that we could leave this Shaper to work what we regarded as his feeble magic.

And we found such a place, and such a man. I forget his name. He was a king of the land, an arrogant man, obsessed with wealth and wine, horses and wives. His priests were a cruel bunch, scarred and silver-haired, secretive and given to brutal sacrifice.

They greeted the offer of Shaper with a scavenger's greed and ferocity. So we traded him, up there, close to the river I now know is called the Rein. They took him to their enclosure and that was the last we saw of him. In exchange? Amber! Some of the strangest amber we had ever seen. That was the reason for our voyage up the rivers and over the land. Creatures imprisoned in the soft jewel of amber. We knew we could trade such pieces for a greater wealth to the sanctuaries of the islands of our own homeland.

Jason shrugged, raised his hands. That was that. What happened to our inventor afterwards? I suppose he died. I forgot about him quickly. A season later, back in my palace, Medea tried to kill me. I tried to kill her. Arms were no match for sorcery, and I withdrew from her compound, leaving her there to rot. I hadn't realised how easily she could reach my sons, to sacrifice them. And the rest you know. At least: Merlin knows.

He said no more and I asked him no more. We had the most difficult part of the voyage home ahead of us, and we bent our backs and our skills to the task.

27
Wraiths

'We've got company.'

Niiv's whisper awoke me. She had her hands on my face, watching me in earnest. I had been sleeping below several skins, exhausted from a long stint at the oars. There was the smell of fresh, moist dawn about Argo, and I could see, by the slow movement of branches above me, that she was being taken slowly into the region where Nantosuelta narrowed before entering the main land of the Coritonian king, Vortingoros.

'Company?'

'Riders. Mist riders. Urtha is anxious.'

Not so much mist riders as riders in this misty early morning. The river was still wide here, and lined by willows and alders, all of them green despite this autumnal season. They shimmered with moisture. Where there were gaps in their dense growth, the fog-shrouded landscape was clearly being tracked by bands of riders, keeping a slow pace with us. They were moving on both sides of the river. The occasional flash of light on helmet and spear-point was startling and threatening.

All the men were at the oars, save for myself. Niiv and the youths had also been sleeping, after crossing the sea. Bollullos and Rubobostes, next to each other, were stripped to the waist and putting a massive heave into their strokes, four brawny arms keeping Argo moving at her sluggish pace. Now we all moved to our benches and added speed to her progress.

The riders in the mist increased their pace to keep alongside us. Their horses snorted loudly. Harnessing jangled.

'What do you make of them, Merlin?' Urtha asked as he strained at his oar.

Insubstantial, nebulous, I suspected those on the southern bank were from the Shadow Hero Realm. Those on the north were strangers. They felt wrong.

Even as I gently probed our silent escort, they seemed to sense my presence. Those to the north galloped swiftly ahead, soon lost to filmy sight and awareness. Almost at once the southern riders also turned away from the river, melting into the haze.

The sun began to rise above the horizon behind us, burning off the damp fog.

We rowed and rested, hoisted the sail whenever there was even a breath of wind from the east. The boys hunted for small game; Niiv swam in the river and fished in the fashion of her own people. But progress upriver was slow, and we were a weary crew.

When at last we came to the moorings, close to the Coritonian fortress, we sent Colcu to his uncle. The lad returned with three men and three more youths of his own age to help us row, but Vortingoros had closed his gates and was lurking in shame and insecurity behind his walls. With the three men he had sent five shields, five spears, five swords, all of them showing signs of past use.

Colcu was furious. He was silent and pale, hardly able to look the older crew of Argo in the eye. Urtha himself was not as angry as I'd expected him to be. 'He might at least have loaned us horses,' he muttered.

Jason laughed. 'We could take them. Rubobostes and I are good horse-thieves in our own ways.'

'Vortingoros did enough for us in the past. That's my judgement,' the king said dryly, staring into the distance, to the hill now defended even against its friends. He was a king in difficulty who understood the difficulties of a king. 'Let's leave him to his misery. Just knowing that we're back may be his best counsel. And besides – whether he likes it or not, there will be more mutual help needed before our lives – all of our lives – are done with.'

'There are horses to the south of the fortress,' Colcu whispered suddenly and eagerly. 'I saw them. Forty or so. Wild-breed, nervous. And twenty cattle. He's been raiding to the north, my uncle: I know his style. I'll fetch them for you with pleasure. Horses *and* cattle. I can get them. Riding them down to obedience ready for harnessing can be done easily. We're experts! You'll need Rubobostes' arms for the rowing. We're ready for raiding.'

'You'd steal from the man who has become your father?' Urtha stared hard at the tall lad. But Colcu was not intimidated.

'Think of it as borrowing. And as you have just said, Warlord Urtha, in the end we will be two kingdoms fighting for the same life.'

It didn't take long: Urtha agreed. He wouldn't allow Kymon to go on the raid, however, despite his son's protestations. Kymon was keen to stay with his own *uthiin*, still keen to contest leadership with his friend. And he pointed out to his father that with a horse beneath him, he could leap the river, crash through the hostels, and ride to Taurovinda faster than he could run, or row.

'This is about your sister,' his father reprimanded him. 'You are thinking only of how to throw your sister from the walls.'

Kymon bristled at that, challenging his father's gaze.

'I would have thought you were thinking of my stepmother.'

'Ullanna? I dream of her every night. I think about her every moment of the day. We are all a family, and we all, in our own ways, rule at the Hill of the Bull. A great man lies in its depths. A great dynasty has followed him. That is my view at least. And my daughter is part of the line of kings that began with a broken king, but went on to become a great land. You and Munda must be reconciled.'

Kymon laughed sourly. 'From the moment she entered the Hostel of The Red Shield Riders, she changed. I can see it. You cannot. I don't want to see *you* a broken king. I will not inherit a broken kingdom.'

'Then trust me to know better than you. You will not skirmish with Colcu.'

Kymon finally accepted his father's decision.

Colcu and his three young recruits spoke with the three older men from the fortress, not wishing to compromise these new volunteers. They too agreed that Vortingoros could spare his own plunder. They too were disillusioned with the Coritanian warlord.

It was as well these three men stayed on Argo.

Another mist-shrouded dawn. The river was alive with fish and the overhanging trees nervous with the movement of deer that had everyone at the oars watching for the opportunity to hurl a javelin and win a good supper. Above us, cranes flew in circles, twenty or so, disturbed from their high perches. Crows, invisible to us, were raucous.

The nets came up from the water so suddenly that for a moment we all imagined we were dreaming. Argo was snagged; she lurched; we fell across her bowels, oars in chaos. And then the wild shouts!

We were in the shallows, and the horsemen emerged from the northern screen of willow, plunging their dark-maned beasts into the water to fore and aft of us. Heavily cloaked, dark-masked, short spears and arrows bristling from quivers on their backs, they came around us like wolves. Two of the riders flung themselves onto the ship. Jason hacked down the first, and Bollullos drove the second back into the river with a powerful lunge of his body, but sustained a deep and crippling blow to his shoulder in the process.

Arrows hissed past. Argo whistled with their flights. A short spear seemed to curve in towards Kymon, who leaned with the *lithe* of youth to the left and snatched the shaft, sending it singing back to the man who had hurled it, finding only a shield.

The screaming of the horses was no louder than the wailing war cry of these attackers. Above all, the river churned noisily as they circled us and tried to board us. They were murderous and fast. One of Vortingoros's men fell below a blade as the man who attacked him leapt from horse to ship, then back to horse.

Niiv cowered below skins.

Tairon produced a sling from his belt, stone-shot from his pack, and calmly swung at the attackers. Then an arrow caught him in the chest and he was flung backwards, jerking and scrabbling at the entry wound, his lips blood-foamed. I saw Kymon haul him below the growling figurehead of Mielikki, and Niiv rushing to tend the wound.

'Who are these bastards?' Jason cried above the confusion. He and Rubobostes were crouched, Greek-style, jabbing and slashing, an organised two-man army against the chaos of these masked horsemen.

'*Dhiiv arrigi*!' Urtha called back. 'Vengeful Outcasts!'

'Then you've made a lot of enemies,' Jason roared. There was laughter in his voice, tempered by the grunting of his blows. He was a man born for this sort of fight.

They had been waiting for us, these 'vengeful outcasts'. But how had they known we were coming? This was opportunism of the crudest sort, an attack on Urtha governed by no more than the basic instinct to which these once-friends, once-champions, these men who had betrayed the king and were made to live wild, had been reduced: a moment to claim back their pride by assassinating the man who had cast them out.

They were savage, but they were nothing of importance, though their weapons were inflicting severe damage on us.

I suddenly realised that Jason was yelling my name. As Argo was hauled by the net, listing dangerously, my old friend was asking for my intervention. Niiv too seemed to be screaming at me. Her face was a distressed mask of tears and anger. But Tairon, embraced in her arms, was waving a hand towards me: *no*, he seemed to be saying. *Do nothing*.

Had he seen or sensed what I had failed to see or sense?

Suddenly, out of the trees, out of the haze, other riders came, ethereal men on big horses, man and beast spectacularly armoured. If this band had been ready to assault us, no one among us would have survived the river encounter. But the Unborn were here as guardians. It was they who had shadowed us from the south of the river, perhaps keeping a wary eye on the band to the north. They powered into the river, engaging in brutal combat.

Again I heard my name cried, from one of these new arrivals. And I glimpsed, through the metal faceplate of his helmet, the grinning features of Pendragon. He and twenty others routed the *dhiiv arrigi*, hacking them down, grabbing their steeds and hauling the screaming animals towards the shore. The river ran red for a while, but not for long.

As Kymon and his father cut through the snagging net at Argo's prow, releasing the ship, which lurched violently in the water, Pendragon and his wraith-riders splashed noisily from the river, pushing through the draping willows, hooves seeking a firm grip on the muddy bank. The horses of the Outcasts struggled after them, caught by tethers, and this rescuing band were gone as abruptly as they had appeared.

Then Pendragon's voice could be heard: 'We'll wait for you where you camped when the river swamped you.'

And that was that.

Later, Argo abruptly turned in the river, a move so sudden that we were caught by surprise as our oars snagged the water. Half-thrown from our benches, we quickly hauled and stowed the oars and Argo nosed into the gentle slope of the bank, a place where cattle clearly came down to water.

This was her way of saying goodbye for the moment, and we quickly offloaded our stowage, taking care with the honey child in her many-layered shroud. Bollullos, his arm bandaged and in a sling, was the first onto the land, and he ran quickly to where he could survey the scene beyond the river, a natural gesture of protection for his king. When he signalled that everything was quiet, Urtha and Rubobostes jumped down into the shallows and received the limp but living body of Tairon. Niiv had performed wonders on him, but his breathing was strained and shallow and he had turned paler than the corpse he had almost become. No one believed he could live much longer. 'My night will be sooner than yours,' he had whispered to Niiv, but Niiv had put a finger to his lips.

'Not if I can find what I need to find. If I could only get you North! But I'll sniff out the root I'm interested in, and you'll eat it, and be ready again to die another day.'

By evening we had marched through the forest and come to a wide grove where five rose-briar-covered stones stood, all of them in a line, all patterned in different ways, the different emblems of an older age. They each rose from a shallow mound. This was the Sanctuary of the Five Sisters, and was one of those places sacred to the priests that was used at certain times of the year. It was also one of the markers that divided Urtha's territory from that of Vortingoros.

In other words, we were close to the new river, the silver arm of the Winding One that had cut Urtha's heart from his fortress.

We rested in this place, exhausted from the walk. The moon rose over us, more than half-full. The stones on the mounds of the dead began to sing; to me, at least. The moonshadow that grazed the inscribed circles and spirals set up a song, inaudible to Urtha and Jason, but as clear to me as some sounds are to hounds. I watched as the shadows of the spirals deepened with the movement of the bright half-disc. I listened as the melody deepened, became extended, rose in pitch then became a long moan, fading as shadow consumed all.

Niiv, I believe, also heard something of this ancient song. She huddled by me, one foot resting on mine, a tentative touch of companionship, a signal of love.

Her eyes, though, were on the monuments, and her frown suggested curiosity.

'Can you hear the music?' I asked her.

'I hear something. Something strange. These stones have strange ways.'

We sat in contemplative silence for a few moments, and she asked, 'Are they prisons? Or palaces?'

'Places of the dead. Gateways. Entrances.'

'But prisons or palaces?'

'The dead come back here.'

'Prisons or palaces?'

'I don't know. What do you feel, Niiv? Prisons or palaces?'

She hunched over her knees, her gaze catching mine. 'I'm not sure there's a difference. No matter how grand, no matter how sprawling, there are always walls to turn you back. From what I've learned of Jason, of Medea, of that whole, hot southern world, with its marbled rooms and circular corridors, no, I'm not sure there's a difference. Now where I come from: the land itself is a palace. I could walk the snow and the forests for a year and never find a wall.' She tapped her foot on mine again. 'And you know this: by the Lady of Snow herself, your world is larger than imagining. Your palace is the world itself. No walls, just a return to the starting point. Where *did* you start from, Merlin? I never asked you ...'

'A deep gorge, wooded, full of caves, full of images, a place where several rivers came together; a place where valleys stretched away in different directions. A place where men had visited and stayed. I'm old. But where I come from, the people who raised me were not as old as the first people of the valleys, where songs and visions were learned.'

Niiv stared at me, a half-smile on her lips, the stars alive in her pale eyes. 'Will you go back there? At the end?'

'Of course.'

'So that place is your tomb.'

'My palace. My prison. Yes. I'll go back there. Not yet, though.'

'I'll find you there,' she said quietly, mischievously. 'I know I'm just a passing fancy in your life.'

'More than that ...'

She dismissed the comment with a laugh. 'No, no. I know you too well. I know too much about you. A passing fancy. But I'll find you there, when you finally cast aside the packhorse, the back pack, the walking staff, the illusion of virility. The Path itself. When you go home to paint your animal memory on the wall of the cave: look for me. I'll make an arrangement with Mielikki. A thousand years from now? I'll surprise you with a kiss! We'll step into the mountainside together.'

I drew Niiv close to me. She huddled into my embrace and we fidgeted with clothing, so that we could touch and warm each other, not that we needed warming on this humid autumnal night.

She was in a strange mood. I tried to divine it with ordinary feelings. I didn't want to probe. She was sad. She was wistful. There was something ... how can I put it? I try to remember that moment, now, after so many years have passed ... she was: lonely.

We slept, then.

I woke to the sound of grunting, the heaving strength of Rubobostes hauling up a stone that had been buried in one of the shallow mounds. He had freed it from the slipping earth, and let it fall back to the ground.

A shadowy figure appeared behind him, peered at the exposed entrance and nodded.

The man dropped to a crawl and entered the mound. Rubobostes then heaved the huge stone upright, pushed it back into place, then stepped away, ran forward and gave it a mighty kick, wedging it firmly in the slope. He patted back some of the rough turf that had covered it, then made an odd sign to the monolith that towered above him.

Before I could ask him what he was doing he came over to me, nodding to Niiv, the girl visible only as a pale face swathed in my cloak, and dropped to a crouch.

'He said to say goodbye.'

'Tairon?'

'Yes. He's dying; he knows it. He said to thank you for looking for the root that might have stemmed the bleeding.' This was addressed to Niiv.

'I couldn't find it,' Niiv whispered sadly.

'He told me to say that he's going home. He was home for a brief while and he left home again, to help us all get here on Argo. But now he'll find his way back through the maze.'

'What maze?' Niiv asked.

Rubobostes glanced round at the tomb. 'That's exactly what I asked him. He said he's sure this particular sister is the entrance to a part of the labyrinth. If it is, he can work his way back to the island.'

'And if it isn't?'

Rubobostes looked confused. 'I didn't think to ask him that.'

The Dacian took his leave, to grab what sleep he could manage before dawn. Niiv sighed and settled back into me. Her last words that night were words of sympathy for our Cretan friend.

Tairon will take no further part in this narrative. But I remembered Niiv's observation as we had scurried back to Argo after the encounter with Tairon's mother, and all the events of dream and the wild hunt associated with Queller: that she had seen, or thought she'd seen, Tairon standing in the crowds by the harbour.

The maze-runner had made it home, I was certain. His story after that is his to tell and his alone.

Towards the end of the following day we began to feel a rhythm in the ground below us, waxing and waning, a peculiar sensation. The forest around us seemed to react as well. It was silent and tense, except that birds flew suddenly in wheeling curves before suddenly settling.

'It's coming from behind us,' Jason said.

'No. From ahead.' Urtha was staring anxiously towards the setting sun.

'No. There!' cried the Greeklander, and as we turned so four small figures on breathless ponies came screaming towards us, legs kicking, hair streaming, each leading a handful of horses that bucked and bayed but followed in the race.

Colcu and Maelfor slid triumphantly from the blankets that covered their own steeds' backs. Sweating and grinning they greeted us. 'Only eighteen,' Maelfor said to the men, 'but we were lucky to gain even these. Colcu saw the horses—'

'But I didn't see the guard,' Colcu confessed, though he too was amused, glancing at Kymon. 'They ran us a good chase.'

'Fortunately they were drunk,' Maelfor concluded. 'Else this might have been worse.' He turned his neck to show the long red streak of a spear-thrust that had grazed his flesh rather than stuck into his spine.

The riders and their animals were settled. They needed water more than anything, and there was a small stream close by.

Then Bollullos said, 'I can still feel the earth thumping.'

It was a rhythm – or rather, an overlapping series of rhythms – such as could be heard on a ship, the drum-beat signalling the stroke rate for the oarsmen. Some of the beats were faster than others. The whole sensation was of mechanisms in the earth, earth-sound, the heartbeat of invention.

Jason and I exchanged a quick glance. 'Shaper,' he said quietly.

'Shaping Chambers,' I added.

He nodded. 'We're nearly there.'

PART FIVE

THE BEAUTIFUL DEATH

28

Dreams of Kings

The forest was crowded with spirits. This is how Niiv described them, but they were very earthly, fleshy ghosts, a legion of the Unborn from different times camped in groups along the ridge. On this side of the divide they were alive, and in need of food and warmth, and their fires burned and their meats roasted as dusk settled. There were fires as far as I could see.

Sprawling along the eastern hill, they looked out over the wide, deceptively quiet flow of new Nantosuelta at the edge of the new Realm of the Shadows of Heroes. The sky to the west was a blazing streak of glowing ruby. The hostel we could see from here was dark, shadowed, already embraced by the drooping, thickening boughs of trees. Legion watched a land that belonged to them, in which they should have been waiting. But it was apparent, from the numbers we saw as we rode among them on our nervous, half-broken horses, that they too had felt the need to flee from the advance of the Realm.

I tried to recognise which hostel was which as we rose through the opposite woods, but they had grown grotesque and deformed with time, extensions of both hill and forest, their once-clear carvings now twisted into cracked grimaces, splintered faces and malformed limbs. That said, light gleamed in their recesses.

And under all, that dull set of booming beats, some fast, some slow. We felt it in our feet and in our heads; and Nantosuelta signalled it in the subtle waves and disturbances on her surface, fracturing the light of torches and of the twilight into a display of colour that danced across her width. By the time the sun had gone, we had passed two more hostels.

I searched for Pendragon. Kymon and Colcu cantered ahead, also calling. Eventually I heard my name shouted and rode up to the tall, dark-haired man who stood before a circular tent. I recognised him, but failed to remember his name.

'Bedavor,' he obliged. 'I am Pendragon's shield-carrier and sword-healer.'

'Ah, yes. I remember you.'

'Then remember me well,' the dark-bearded man said with a smile. 'We've taken so many blows in this world, away from our own realm, that we're likely to be born so scarred as to be unrecognisable.'

I understood what he meant. The curse of the Unborn, exploring the world that would be theirs one day, was to carry into their true life all scars and breakages of bone that occurred during these premature voyages.

I slipped from the uncomfortable position on my small horse and ducked into the tent. Urtha started to come after me, but Pendragon's shield-carrier put out a gentle hand to stop him. I glanced back at the encounter.

'He means no disrespect to you,' Bedavor said to the king, 'but it would be best if you said nothing and asked nothing. This is a dangerous time for some of us.'

Urtha agreed, though he seemed perplexed. Kymon made to follow his father, but he was held back, as was Bollullos, who glared so hard at Bedavor that I felt their stares would shatter like heated rock. But Urtha's man stepped back. It was Jason who stooped to enter the spartan interior of the tent, tugging at his grizzled beard as his sharp eyes scoured the interior.

Pendragon was seated on skins, at the head of a small circle of his companions. Their shields and arms were a clutter at the centre of their conference, and each had a plate of meats and a clay cup beside him. Those with their backs to me were looking round curiously, hard-faced and unwelcoming. There were two spaces in this circle, and I took the one opposite the war chief himself. Jason hunkered down uncomfortably to my right, setting his own sword, still sheathed, on the pile. He nodded in a perfunctory way to Pendragon, a Greeklander as far from his birth in the past as was his host from his birth in the future. Urtha crouched on his haunches by the entrance, drawing his ragged cloak around his shoulders as if to conceal himself, aware, I was sure, that he was in the presence of an unborn king of his own line.

The companions were cut raw, blood-scabbed and dishevelled. They were not a contented band. The man whom I remembered as Boros was missing two fingers on his sword hand, and he fidgeted with the bloody, knot-tied stubs as he stared at me, much as a child fusses distractedly with a broken toy. I wondered if he was already aware of the broken childhood that he would now face in generations to come, after his wailing eruption into the world.

I was surprised to learn that these wounds had been taken in defence of Argo against the *dhiiv arrigi*. Pendragon's horsemen had seemed to rout the Outcasts with ease. In fact, that skirmish had been the last of several. In Urtha's absence, when more than two hundred of the ragged mercenaries had gathered and begun to pillage the villages of the Coritani, Pendragon had decided to take a hand. Vortingoros had barricaded himself in his enclosure.

'I know what debt you owe to the High King,' Pendragon addressed Urtha through the circle, 'so I thought I would help with the repayment.'

'Thank you,' Urtha said quietly.

'How they knew you were returning, I don't know. But they did, and they waited for you at various points along the river. Bit by bit we cut down their numbers. But,' and he looked at me rather mournfully, 'we've lost too many of our own. I have had several dreams of my time as king, and the good companions, my horse knights, who will ride with me. In each dream that retinue is smaller. Too many will be stillborn. It brings home to us that we've been reckless. That to experience life before birth was folly.'

I knew what he was saying. He and the surviving members of his companions – Bedavor, Boros, Gaiwan, a few others – would have to ride back through the Hostel of the Overwhelming Gift, if they could, and remain for the rest of their waiting time where no harm could be done to them. I could be certain of one thing: that this man, when he was finally born and grown, would not be reckless in his actions. Though he would carry many scars from his actions in Urtha's time, folly would not be among them. He would be a circumspect king. No doubt he would be reckless in his dealings with women – there is no charm known that can cure a man of that – but he had positioned himself in Time to be a strong and powerful leader.

I quite looked forward to encountering him again.

'There's a different sort of danger waiting for us back in the Realm,'

Pendragon agreed. 'Imprisonment. Abandonment. Desolation. If rumour is right, then for each of us there will be a ship that comes to fetch us to our new lives.' His gaze darkened, his eyes fixed on mine in their focus. 'There's something I need to show you. But later, if you wouldn't mind.'

'Not at all,' I replied.

'To practicalities: we all, here, have to return. But once there, we will fight to return the Shadow Realm to its proper boundaries. When my small retinue rides like fury back across Nantosuelta, we can take others with us, not many, but if you, Merlin, can spare a shade of charm to disguise them, then we can smuggle several of the king's men into his own land.'

He stared at me again. 'Are you game for that?'

'I can manage it,' I said, trying to think how I would do it.

'Good. On another matter: Boros, Gaiwan and I ventured back while you were away. You've been away a long time, I don't know if you realise that. The Realm is half asleep. It's a strange land beyond the hostels, but at the centre, your fortress—' he glanced across the tent at Urtha, 'it's a prison. A place of isolation. It's like an island. There is a man there called Cathabach, who knows you—'

'Cathabach is alive still?' Urtha shifted into a half-crouch.

'He was when we met him. And so are your wife and daughter. They are hiding below the hill. He has a message for you: that Munda's dream was from the Gate of Ivory. A false dream, I believe he meant. He said that and gave me three other messages; for you to "hear, ponder, understand and respond to". Cathabach's words, not mine.

'This is what he said:

'A crooked dream has raised the Dead.

'Vengeance and a longing for life drive their actions.

'The son of a broken king is responsible for the crooked dream.'

There was silence for a while, then Pendragon murmured something to the man on his right and his companions all stood and left the tent. As they left, so one of them touched me lightly on the shoulder, another signalling to Jason in the same way. We left the tent. Urtha remained behind.

When he emerged he was quite pale, concerned but not distressed. 'That was a strange encounter,' is all he said. 'Pendragon promises to remember me through stories. And through his choice of name. It seems he dreams of his time to come.'

'I know. I heard him say so.'

'You did. Meanwhile, I have to return to my fortress. Will you cloak me with charm, Merlin? Can you do that?'

'You know I can.'

'Good. And what do you make of Cathabach's rhyme?'

We walked a short way from the tent, to a place where, through the woods, we could glimpse the far side of the river.

I wanted to tell Urtha that the form of the words were suspiciously like those of a dead man, speaking from after the moment of his death. They were not in a style of speaking that I would have associated with Cathabach. But they had the ring of truth to them.

'It's about Durandond,' I said. 'Durandond holds the key to this.'

'Durandond? He's been dead for generations.'

'He's now in the Otherworld. He's in the Realm of the Shadows of Heroes. He was never there before. It hadn't occurred to me until now, but when we went into Ghostland a few years ago, he wasn't there. He was not among the Dead. He has always been below the hill, in the deep of Taurovinda.'

'The founding king holds the answers? Answers to what has happened?'

'I'm sure of it.'

We stared in silence at the crumbling façade of the hostel across the Winding One. It seemed to moan at us, almost beckoning us to risk, recklessly, a visit to its engorging depths.

'What do we do?' Urtha asked quietly. 'I'm at a loss for a strategic plan of campaign.'

'You go back with Kymon and Pendragon. And as many of your *uthiin* as your descendant thinks is safe.'

'And you?'

'I'll find Argo again. She hasn't left us, not yet. She knows ways into the hill. Durandond will be there. And then we can find a way to take on Shaper. Or whatever it is that Shaper has created within your boundaries.'

Urtha shivered, shaking his head. He didn't meet my eye. 'You intend to raise Durandond from the dead then.'

'I have no choice.'

'We call him the sleeping king.'

'I know. I've lived in Taurovinda for a long time. I know how you think of Durandond.'

‘To disturb him has always been thought of as unwise. There are prophecies about it. The bards have poems about it. They hardly ever speak them.’

‘It seems to me,’ I pointed out, ‘that your sleeping king has already been rudely awakened.’ I put my hand on his arm and the frowning king paused in his slow walk through the camp. I said, ‘I never told you this, but I met Durandond when he was a reckless youth.’

Surprised, Urtha simply raised his eyebrows, waiting for explanation. ‘Yes. He came to me for an insight into his future. I didn’t give it to him. Well, no more than that he would find a hill and make the hill his citadel. Which he did.’

Urtha smiled. ‘Taurovinda! But he came from a land of exiles. He came with a thousand champions, a thousand women, a thousand children, and a thousand wagons, piled high with the ancestors of his land. That’s what we learn. That’s all we know. Shafts were dug into the hill, and the ancestors and then Durandond himself were buried there. Cathabach’s sanctuary, the orchard, hides the entrances. Nothing must disturb them, or Taurovinda’s walls will slide out onto the plain, and the bones of the hill will be exposed. That’s what we learn. That’s what we know.’

Behind us, Bedavor called my name. He was standing by the tent, beckoning to me. Pendragon was leading his horse away from the river.

My last words to Urtha were, ‘You’ll soon know more.’

Bedavor had a horse for me as well and I rode through the forest with Pendragon, his ‘sword-healer’ and four of his companions riding behind us, until we came to the edge of a shallow, reed-fringed lake. At its centre, a tall heron perched on the prow of a small, sunken boat. The wood looked rotten. The proud bird, suddenly aware of us, launched itself into a slow and sinuous flight, circling the mere before gliding into the clutches of the woods.

Pendragon was searching around on the ground. He picked up four small stones, passing two of them to me. There was the hint of a smile on his face. ‘Can you hit that wreck, to you think? Without using trickery, I mean.’

‘I resent the implication that I would cheat.’

He laughed. ‘You’ll be no damned good to a king in the future unless you’re prepared to cheat, my friend. Watch this!’

He flung a stone. It caught the sunken boat on the prow. A second bird appeared from nowhere, flapping away in dismay. It must have been nesting out of sight. I flung one of the stones he'd given me. It curved to the left and missed by a man's length.

'This way is interesting,' he said, and skipped the stone over the surface of the water. Five skips and it fell short.

I skipped my own stone. It struck the water seven times, then hit the boat just above the surface of the pool.

'Our lives in two throws of a stone.'

'I don't understand,' I said as Pendragon grinned at me, searching my face, looking me up and down.

'Of course you do. I've had my dalliance with the land that will one day be mine. Now I shall go to sleep until called back through birth. A single throw. You will skip across the years, touching here, touching there, until one day you find me.'

'You seem very confident that we're destined to meet in the future.'

He tapped his head. 'Dreams. Have them all time. Seen you many times. That's why I sought you out, several years ago, when you first came to Alba on that lovely ship.'

He looked gloomy for a moment, his gaze across the mere. The surface rippled with a breeze and behind us the horses snorted restlessly. 'One dream was more like a waking dream. Right here, right where we're standing. It was misty and cold. We were moving east to wait for you. There was a band of mercenaries who had the same idea and we were keeping a close eye on them. Bedavor and the others were sleeping. It was towards dusk. Out of nowhere a small boat came suddenly gliding across the pool, turning away from me. Two women in the strangest dress I've ever seen, brightly coloured, flashing with blue stones and the gold of metal, were rowing steadily, their eyes on me. A third sat with her back to me. Her cloak was green and fringed with red. Her hair below the green cowl was the colour of bright, red copper. She was singing: an eerie voice, but quite beautiful; and the song, though I didn't understand the words, was haunting and thrilling at the same time. It set my skin crawling. As they vanished into the mist she glanced over her shoulder, and then I noticed a man's arm draped over the side of the craft, his fingers just touching the water. And they were gone.'

'You think this was a dream of your death,' I suggested.

'I'm certain of it.'

'Perhaps it was a dream of your transport from Ghostland to new life.'

'I hadn't thought of that,' he murmured with a frown. 'But such strange women. Where did they come from? Everything about them was wrong.' He glanced and me and smiled in a resigned sort of way. 'Not the time nor the place to ask such questions, I suppose.'

'Wise thinking.'

'Back to skipping stones,' Pendragon went on as we walked back to Bedavor. 'You've skipped across the centuries, leaving ripples. But you haven't hit the mark yet. You'll make your mark with me. I know in my heart and in my deepest dreams that you and I will be busy, one day, minding each other's business. So ...' he gripped my arm strongly. 'Keep a lot of what you call charm in reserve for me. You have a reputation for not squandering your abilities. In years to come, I don't want you old and frail and easy prey to rogues and the wiles of women such as your delightful Niiv.'

'Too late for that,' I muttered under my breath.

If he heard me he didn't show it. As we swung ourselves into the saddle, turning for the ridge, the legion and Nantosuelta, he said, 'I can take Urtha, Kymon, one, perhaps two of his companions. The rest will have to take their chances with other returning bands. It's not passing through the hostel that will be difficult; it will be protecting them on the other side.'

'Kymon comes with me,' I responded. I already had plans for Kymon. 'Take Colcu?'

'Agreed. And Jason? What about Jason? While you've been away, a young man has been asking about him.' We broke into a hard canter, sensing the swift coming of night.

'How young a man?' I called. Pendragon's cloak streamed behind him. His voice was harsh. Other thoughts were occupying him now.

'Travel-weary. Skirmish-marked. *Killer of kings*, I think he said his name was. Or King of Killers. A Greeklander. An arrogant bastard. Could hardly understand a word he said.'

'Orgetorix?'

'Something that sounded like that. Yes,' he shouted back. 'He's come to kill Jason. Better warn Jason.'

Pendragon and his sword-healer were far ahead of me, and the sky was lowering.

And in the confusion that was the edge of Ghostland, Jason's surviving son was prowling.

During the night, bands of Unborn returned to the Shadow Realm, noisily crossing the river and riding quickly through the open doors of the Hostels. The legion was ripped in two. But fires remained on the ridge, a determined army of men, women and children who were prepared to risk their future lives to stop the expansion of the Shadow Realm into land that had been shaped by their ancestors, and was theirs to shape in generations to come.

At some point in that night, Pendragon and his retinue crossed as well. Urtha and Bollullos, Colcu and Morvodumnos rode among them. I had masked them with a simple charm drawn from Cunhaval, the spirit of the hound in the world. It was the best I could think of. To any watching eyes it would have seemed as if Pendragon rode with his men and dogs. The illusion would have been easily penetrated, but these future champions rode with vital urgency.

Caiwain and Vortingoros's men would come with me.

With Niiv clinging onto my arm (she was nervous, upset that I'd disappeared from the camp for so long), I went in search of Jason. The ridge was a confusion of bright fire, illumination from across the river, and total darkness. The surface of Nantosuelta gleamed like rippling gold.

Kymon followed us, silent and surly. I could tell he was eager to the point of frustration to return to his land, to find his sister. I had persuaded him that to journey on Argo would bring him closer to the girl and his stepmother. I hoped I was right.

I found Jason at the river's edge, wrapped in a dark cloak, a pack of supplies slung over his shoulder. Rubobostes was crouching on the bank, holding a small, shallow craft by a rope tether. A simple rowing boat, very primitive, its sides were painted with luminescent green and blue, fishes and trees caught in an intimate embrace, a narrow band of decoration that I instantly recognised as the sight of it opened memory.

This was Medea's craft; the pattern – using powdered, night-glowing rocks she had found in the valley where we had grown up – was how she had decorated her own first boat, while all I had done with mine was to use chalk to scratch lines and spirals. Fierce Eyes had been disparagingly amused by my small talent in art.

Did Jason sense the source of this frail vessel? As I approached him, he turned to look at me, and confirmed that he did.

She had been standing among the trees, watching him. She had been wearing the robes of the Priestess of the Ram, but the head-veil was lowered now, exposing her face. She was holding two small, identical boats by tethers, restraining them against the tug of the river; but shortly after Jason had arrived at the far bank, she let one of them go. It slipped away, turning on the water, soon lost in the night save for that glimmer of phosphorescence. The other vessel, when she released it, came straight across to Jason and Rubobostes, as if charmed: which of course, it was.

Rubobostes had caught it by the trailing tether.

'She's still watching me. I can feel it,' Jason said. His mood was bleak and uncertain. 'What does she want? This is a lure and I'm her prey. I'm sure of it.'

I said nothing. If I had expressed a view it would have been that from personal experience nothing was ever predictable with Medea. The truth might have been the very opposite of his fear. And I remembered my last conversation with her, when she had seemed so mellow.

'And the other boat,' he went on, staring along the river. 'Why two boats? Who's crossing in the second? What's she up to?'

'There's one way to find out, and that's to cross. Your safest course is to stay here and defend against whatever might come through those Hostel gates in time to come.'

Rubobostes growled at my suggestion, standing up, still holding the rope. 'Don't listen to him, Jason. The second boat was meant for me, but it slipped away. I'm the one who must stay here. Are you taking Argo further up the river?'

I realised the question was addressed to me. 'Yes. She can take us below the fortress.'

'Then eventually she'll need her captain,' the Dacian responded, turning to look over his shoulder at the Greeklander. 'The boat won't take two of us. I'll wait here for you. Pick me up on the way out. And if you find my horse? I'll be in your service for the rest of my life should you find my Ruvio, my good horse. I miss the beast.'

Jason glanced at me as he shrugged his pack off his shoulders and tossed it down to the Dacian, to sling into the boat.

'What's she up to?' he whispered again.

Should I tell him about his son? I only had Pendragon's account of Orgetorix being in the land, looking for his father. If boy and man were to meet, then it should be under circumstances that were not controlled by me, or any other person, though Medea, I was sure, was taking a guiding hand.

Even now I cannot understand why I took the decision not to tell Jason about the presence, close to him, of his eldest son, a once-favoured boy now grown to a man, who had dealt brutally with his father in the recent past, unaware of the true circumstances of his existence in this modern age. It seemed that vengeance was still strong in the younger man's mind. He had pursued Jason across half a world, half a world from the oracle at Dodona, in Greek Land, where they had last faced each other.

Then again: perhaps he was pursuing his mother.

This was an outcome I would leave to whatever 'fates' were miming the story of Jason and his bull-leaping son.

'Rubobostes is right,' is all I said, and with a shrug Jason clambered into Medea's boat. The Dacian heaved and sent the craft across the river. Jason used a small oar to keep it moving even as Nantosuelta swept him out of sight downstream, taking him to darkness and the Otherworld.

As soon as he had gone I found a piece of wood, stripped off the bark and sat down, leaning against a tree, to carve a charm pattern. I hadn't done this for ages, and it was cathartic and engrossing. I suppose I drifted into some form of reverie, half aware of what I was doing, half drifting through memory.

At some point in this detached state I heard Kymon, who had been scavenging, slip down the hill and sit down next to Niiv. The woman had been keeping a distance from me, watching me, but absorbed in thoughts of her own.

'What's he doing?' I heard the king's son ask. 'What's he doing down there, Niiv?'

'Carving on a piece of wood.'

'Why?'

'I get the feeling,' Niiv replied after a moment, 'that when he's finished carving ... we'll all be going west.'

There was silence for a while. Then Kymon said, 'Good. I will go in no other direction. And when I get there ...'

He brooded. Sullen.

'When you get there?' the Northlander persisted.

'It doesn't matter what I find in that world when I get there. I'm taking that world back.'

'Will that world be surprised to see you?' the girl teased.

'It knows I'm coming.'

Later, he walked down the slope to the river's edge, his

moonshadow falling across me. I looked up at him and met his steady gaze. His face had hardened, or was that just a trick of the light?

'Are you awake? Or drifting in some dream?'

'I'm awake.'

His gaze never wavered. 'My father once told me that I could never be a king as a man unless I accepted being broken as a child. Now I know what he meant. Ambition tempered with anger, petulance and the jealous play of childhood leads to strong kings and weak kingdoms. Ambition must always be tempered with wise council. An understanding that can only come with age.'

'So you've found out you'll not be a great king, just for the moment.'

'Just a man in the shadow of great kings. Among great men. More than that is not for me to judge.'

'You've been dreaming? This is a vision?'

'I've been thinking. No more than that. I'll trust visions to you. To men like you. But don't give me visions of my own life ahead, nor of Munda's.'

'I'm not a *fate* ... to "mime" your life, to act out what you must do. I thought you knew that.'

He shook his head. 'I don't understand what you mean. You talk in riddles, Merlin. That's what I expect of minds that play with Time. My father's words also. Good luck to you. But none of that matters now. My father and I have chosen to cross the river separately. That much is broken. But Colcu, my great friend, has also chosen to ride separately from me. To help me in my own country. So that much is *forged*. Most importantly of all, my grandmother and my mother still lie in that land. Did you know that an owl circles my grandmother's grave?'

'Yes I did.'

'And that a bull rises from the earth to protect my mother's?'

'Yes I did.'

'Wisdom and strength. Even though they're dead, they will be a force to be reckoned with.'

'Mothers always are.'

'You're laughing at me.'

'No. Not at all.'

'I'm talking like a child. Obvious things.'

'Not always obvious, I assure you, even to dying men. Did your father also tell you to think clearly, to listen with attention, and never to act in haste?'

'Probably. I don't remember. Except for the bit about haste. What he said was: there is always a time to act with anger; but that time is never when you are angry.'

I tossed the charm-stick into the river and watched it float away into the night. 'I know those words. Another man, a king, once said them to his own son. Your father couldn't have known him, though.'

'Who was he?'

'He was called *Odysseus*. A Greeklander, from Jason's time. Have you heard of him?'

Kymon thought for a moment, then answered in the affirmative. 'He fought the sea after fighting the Trojans. I remember now. An inventive man. His great war-horse was made of wood. He rode against the city walls and broke them down. And he claimed men were the equal of gods. He was punished for arrogance. The sea abducted him to be a sea-slave for a lifetime. There was an angry god in the sea. But eventually, out of pity, he granted Odysseus a single cycle of the Moon to be with his wife, before he was taken back to the sea. That's the story Cathabach told me.'

What should I add of that old story for this proud boy? Should I inspire him with an account of how Odysseus had claimed back his home during that brief gift of time? Of his coldly calculated slaughter of the lesser men who had arrived in his absence, bees to a flower, to seduce Penelope, his ever-mourning wife? One moon-cycle granted with his wife after a lifetime lost.

And she hadn't known that he was already dead when Poseidon – the abducting god – gave him that brief release. Love transcended death. The wife herself was already dying when they met for that moon. I expect they met again later in Hades.

But during this time in his land he cleared that land of the imposters, encouraged his son to be a great king, and brought a blush back to the pale cheeks of a woman who had thought herself abandoned. So much achieved in so few days.

How much of the story could truly influence a growing mind, an ambition being tempered with caution, eyes wide open, heart racing, words ringing in ears that were now, like the man he was becoming, prepared to hear? A young man with an eagle's mind, prepared to embrace the notion of restraint.

I do not know what had happened to Kymon since we had left Crete. But his thoughts of Munda were changing. For a second time that night I chose to hold back a comment for the simple reason that I did not think it was my role to play.

Kymon withdrew and Niiv slid down to be with me, squirming to get inside my cloak, breathing gently as we waited. The hand that engaged with mine was cold. She was shivering. I suppose we slept.

We awoke at first light, saturated with dew, the river obscured by heavy mist. Argo's hull was rising from the water close by, her keel furrowing into the mud as if she were approaching at full stroke. But she came gently, cutting the earth, nosing up beside us in silence, propelled by unseen hands, vast and draped with weeds, planks creaking, the sly eye on her keel, azure-blue, framed in scarlet, watching us as she crept closer to nudge us from our sleep. She leaned and sighed, towering over us, shedding her cold tears; the water refreshed us. Kymon came slipping and sliding down the ridge.

Get aboard and hurry!

I invent the words, though I am sure they were whispered to me. Everything about Argo suggested the haste of this invitation. I called for Caiwain.

Again, the ship seemed to whisper to me: *Leave them.*

Kymon had run down the slope and somersaulted into the hull, then leaned over to help Niiv walk up the planks before drawing her over in an ungainly way. I heard their laughter as they tumbled out of sight onto the benches.

Then two heads popped over the rails, one dark, one fair, both bright with youth.

'Come on Merlin.' The boy's voice.

Hands reached for me and hauled me in. Bones grated in my lower back. Mielikki scowled from the stern. Or perhaps it was suppressed laughter. Argo slipped back into the Winding One and the fog closed over us.

'Do we row now?' Kymon asked as we huddled among the scattered cargo.

'I think we wait,' was all I could think to say.

'I'm hungry,' Niiv announced.

Kymon flung back the outer covering of the honey child. The body was beginning to make itself known, despite our best efforts to keep it cold. 'Have some honey,' he said with a laugh.

Niiv scowled at him. 'Wait until *your* belly starts to rumble.'

By evening, we were in Urtha's land. And Urtha was there too, and Jason, but we were at a distance from each other. It was Niiv who said it, as we peered from the river at the movements and mysteries of the new Otherworld:

'This feels like a swan dance. Where you all circle the winter field as the music plays, and you have to guess who your partner is. It's a tradition in the North. Everybody wears a bird mask, and covers their hands with feathers. Hands are too revealing, even with only the light of torches. Every so often you pick someone and meet them in the middle. And you twirl and dance in the snow and then you find if you've got the right person. If you have, you stay at the centre. If you haven't, you go back to the edge. And keep on circling. And it's like a swan dance here. Isn't it? It's a dancing floor. But a dancing floor of war. Everything is at the edge at the moment. Now we must find the centre.'

29

Passing Shadows

'There is something wrong here. I can smell it.' Niiv was looking alarmed.

'You can smell it? How do you smell wrongness?'

She looked at me sourly. 'Rightness has a different fragrance.'

I couldn't help laughing at that. But she was right.

Though the realm of the shadows of heroes had advanced across Nantosuelta, flowing into Urtha's territory, consuming forest and plain, village, pasture and fortress, the Otherworld had not fully possessed the place. It was an uneasy conquest, a defiant appearance, a raging presence. But the land had not been subsumed. It had merely been subdued. Along this stretch of Nantosuelta I had seen the growth of Hostels, but they were still unformed, gathering their shape, bulging from the earth, but still struggling to rise and defend Ghostland.

'Shall we go ashore?' Niiv asked.

As if in answer, Argo pulled away from the shallows and continued upriver. Kymon now seemed to intuit what was happening. As we came to the bend in the river that marked the beginning of the evergroves, so he became more excited. 'There! Look there. Our landing place!'

The evergroves! A sprawling place of mounds and magic, a wooded area that stretched along the river for as far as it was possible to walk in a day, and spread towards the fortress of Taurovinda, across the Plain of the Battle Crow. A thousand or more tombs, more pronounced than the Five Sisters, lay concealed within it, some so large and so old that they were covered by the woods themselves; others nestled in the groves, low stone entrances whispering with dawn and sighing with dusk.

Here resided the physical remains of those who rode wildly in Ghostland. Most of the tombs were mortuary houses; a few were 'ways under'. I had always been most intrigued by those.

Now, though, it was the fleeting glimpse of a tall, ageing man walking one of the many track-ways through the evergroves that caught my attention. He kept pace with Argo's sluggish drift on the water. He was dappled with light and shade. He was neither here nor there. He was a dead man. And Kymon, delighted at first with the recognition of our friendly stalker, suddenly became gloomy.

'It's Cathabach. But he never walked like that in life.'

At length, where a small, shallow creek cut into the groves, Argo nosed through the trees and came quietly onto the mud. A small tumulus rose on each side of us. The shattered bones of the figures that had been erected to guard this place leaned down towards us, their clothing ragged, their skulls greened with moss, their postures that of drooping men; and yet they would have power, small power, to turn away intruders.

Cathabach stepped up onto one of the mounds, looking down at us. His sallow features suddenly flushed with crimson; his hollow eyes glinted. His flesh strengthened. I had not done this, but when I looked quickly at Niiv she turned her head away.

For once in my acquaintance with her I did not criticise her rash use of her small charm.

Kymon leapt from Argo and walked briskly to the old man, to Speaker for Kings; and without thought for what he knew was the case, that Cathabach was dead, he put his arms around the druid's body, hugged him, then took his hand, knelt, kissed the cold fingers.

'I'm glad to see you.'

'This is a passing moment, Kymon. Very little time.'

'I know. On the island we've just sailed from they call it "the ephemera". Who killed you?'

'It doesn't matter. There are more important things.'

'We'll deal with those,' the young man said, standing up. 'We'll deal with them first. But I need you to tell me who killed you. Because later I will need to deal with that.'

'And later I will tell you.'

'The moment may have passed by then.'

'You'll find out who did this to me. I assure you of that. I need to speak to your father.'

'Ah.'

Cathabach looked at me. 'Urtha dead?'

'Far from it. But he's crossed separately from us. He came in through one of the hostels.'

Cathabach considered this information, looked resigned. 'He'll be taking his chances then. All I would have told him is that his fortress is now possessed. Perhaps you can understand this, Merlin.'

Kymon withdrew as Cathabach walked down to stand in front of me. He acknowledged Niiv. The woman was pale and tense, her eyes moving in that way that suggests trance. There were lines on her face, and a strange smell coming from her skin. She was helping Cathabach stay as he was, but it was costing her. I quickly put my arm on her arm, took possession of the charm and applied it to the Speaker for Kings. Cathabach was unaware of this transfer of power, but Niiv gasped, bent double, choked for a moment, then subsided to a sitting position, her head down, hair shrouding her features, breathing laboured; she might have been someone recovering from too much strong drink.

'Urtha has crossed in disguise. He and several others are making their way here with an Unborn king.'

'Pendragon?'

'Yes.'

'Then he'll be safe. But when you meet him, warn him that he should not enter Taurovinda itself.'

'If I know Urtha, and I do know Urtha, he has every intention of taking back his hill.'

'As do I,' said a small voice from among the bushes. Kymon gave me a look that said it all: you tend to your business, my father and I will tend to ours. I hadn't realised he could hear this whispered conversation.

There was a half-smile on his face, though, and a steady gaze in his look that testified to his blossoming strength.

This would be tricky. Kymon wouldn't be speaking as he did unless he meant it. Cathabach would not be struggling to stay in the present unless he knew something.

From where we stood, deep in the evergroves, Taurovinda was a distant hill, high-walled, high-turreted, a dark shadow against the sky. It seemed lifeless, but that was just illusion.

Cathabach said, 'The town looks no different. But below the town on its surface, the hill is transformed. There are chambers down there that seem safer than others. The river is raging through the passages. The well has overflowed and is dangerous. But there are descents inside the orchard. They're not very obvious, but all you need do is listen for the sound of the earth breathing. Two descents; one leads to the founding father.'

'Durandond?' Kymon asked.

'Yes,' said Cathabach. 'Another – the old descent – leads to the overwhelming force that is transforming the land.' He glanced at me as he said this, then returned his watery gaze to the boy. 'But first, you should find Munda. She's in hiding and starving. She's very scared.'

Kymon frowned at that. 'It's because of my sister that the Dead overwhelmed the hill. It's because of my sister that they breached the hostels. She encouraged them. She welcomed them.'

'She was wrong,' Cathabach said quietly. 'She found out soon enough how wrong she'd been. She was unaware of the force that was driving the invasion. But now she's your only chance of taking back the hill. Be very careful how you judge her.'

Cathabach looked at me again and for the last time. 'You'll find me somewhere here, when the time is ready. I'd expected to cross the river, but the river has saved me the trouble.'

'I'll miss you.'

'I believe you will. If I'd had a few more simple skills I'd have stayed around to help. Help is on it way, though. Watch for the flash of light.' He frowned, then. 'It's very strange. When we spoke before, a long time ago, when you hinted at a mind behind the invasion that was building, I got the impression that you were referring to a man. But it's not a man. Very strange. Whatever it is, it's in the hill – transforming the hill. Be careful.'

He stepped past me, mournful of face, cold of flesh, the last glimmer of the 'ephemera' fading from him as he went to seek a place in which to wait for his body to be discovered. He would curl up against a tree, I imagined, or in the overhang of one of the great, grey stones that towered over the mossy ground.

Whatever it is, it's in the hill – transforming the hill.

So now we knew where Shaper had established himself.

A small, cool hand took mine. 'Don't be sad,' Niiv said.

'Do I seem sad?'

'You can cross and see him at any time you like. He will never be far away from you. You can travel.'

'Yes. But Urtha can't. Did you know that Cathabach was his brother? If I'm sad, it's for the king.'

'No. I didn't know.'

As one, we looked to where Kymon was standing. He was framed between two trees, a small, bold shape against the startling light that had suddenly flooded the Plain, a glimpse of sun through the raging skies. He was staring at his home, arms folded, very calm. As Niiv and I approached him, he glanced back briefly before returning his gaze to the feasting place of crows.

'Is it my eyes, Merlin? Are they failing? Or was Niiv right? There is something wrong. I seem to see two lands out there. One is the plain. MaegCatha. The other is very like the island we've just visited. I can smell autumn on the plain, and see the smoke from villages, and there are cattle grazing, and horses running. But it's summer in the other place. And I see those grey-leaved trees. Olives. And stunted oaks. And fingers of granite, like broken teeth; stone everywhere. And what do you call those fragrant herbs? Rosemary, was it?'

'And thyme. Lavender. Sage.'

'Their scent is everywhere. I'm looking at Tairon's land.'

'I told you I could *smell* something wrong,' Niiv whispered.

Taurovinda rose in the distance, a black mountain, its high walls and towers appearing as an uneven ridge, stark against the sky.

On the plain between us, the forest was growing back. Herds of creatures roamed and grazed; horses stampeded. Occasionally, the flash of silver told of a hunter in full pursuit of his prey.

All of that, a ghostly presence inside the scrubby, fragrant hills of Crete.

Getting through this new Ghostland would be difficult.

Then, just as Kymon was growing impatient with my hesitation (eager to get within hailing range of his fortress), a flash of gold appeared in the distance. Then a second. A spark chasing a spark across one of the overlapping lands. The sparks disappeared below a hill, then came dancing over the ridge, veering this way and that. They vanished again, this time behind woodland. When they emerged it was from the broad face of the forest, and one spark came directly towards us, the other weaving in its wake.

Soon, we began to distinguish the shapes of chariots. Soon after that, the high-pitched hailing cries of the charioteers.

A valley consumed them for a moment, and when they reappeared it was so close to us that it startled us. Conan was in the lead, Gwyrion furiously whipping the two white steeds that drew his own car, trying to catch his brother.

When Conan at last reined in his horses, making the chariot slide noisily and dangerously to the left, he was breathing hard, but smiling broadly. As ever.

Gwyrion was cursing as he came in a close second. He flicked the reins and his two whites leapt over Conan's chariot, making the young man fling himself to the floor. The animals fled a way into the evergroves before slowing.

Gwyrion's golden chariot overturned and smashed against a tree, though its driver had also leapt at the last minute, following his steeds in an acrobatic jump over Conan's head.

"My brother won the race, but I have more style,' he announced cheerily. Then he frowned, looking around. 'Where are the others?'

'Others?'

'We were sent to fetch ten or more of you. Jason? Urtha? His *uthiin*?'

'Travelling separately, though I imagine they could do with help. Who asked you to intervene in this?'

As I'd suspected, the answer was 'Cathabach'.

'He called to us from the groves,' Gwyrion added. 'We weren't far away by then. I don't know what charm he used, but we found him. Unfortunately, he sent us to the east, to the new river. We've been scouring the edges there for days.'

'Until it occurred to me,' Conan interrupted, 'that Argo would be slipping back towards the fortress itself.'

'You claim that insight?' Gwyrion challenged darkly.

'I do,' said Conan with a smile.

'It came up in conversation, as you well know.'

'Yes. But I initiated the conversation!'

They argued for a while.

Kymon was inspecting the chariots. He was very impressed by them, tracing out the symbols and faces on their flanks with his fingers. 'Two?' he said after a while, a smile on his face as he glanced at Conan. 'You've stolen *two* chariots? Your father must be in a fury. He'll have your heads, then start a new family. You're dead men, and no mistake.'

'Not at all,' Conan said. He and his brother held up their hands.

No further fingers had been taken and replaced with wood by their censorious father. 'Llew, our radiant parent, has lent the chariot from his own garages. He is angry at what has happened to his peaceful Otherworld.'

'As is our uncle, Nodens. This is his own contribution.' Gwyrion hauled the car upright and inspected the axles and the wheels for damage. 'It's heavier to drive than our father's, which is why Conan had the advantage in the race.'

'Nonsense. I gave you a good head start to adjust for exactly that.'

Again, they challenged each other for a moment or two. Niiv had walked stealthily back into the evergroves and now led Gwyrion's sweating horses back to their chariot, soothing them softly. It was decided that Gwyrion would go east in search of Jason and Urtha's entourage, riding with Pendragon. Conan would transport us in style right into the bosom of the hill.

He belonged in this other world and could come and go without suspicion. Even in a chariot of gold!

30
Foresight and False Dream

Munda woke up so suddenly, and with such a startled cry, that Ullanna, curled up next to her on the narrow pallet, screamed with shock. The older woman slipped from the furs and tumbled onto Rianata, who also awoke with a start. Munda was sitting upright on the bed.

They were in Cathabach's house, inside the orchard. Six other women slept there too. The house was low-roofed, but cosy. Eight thin windows opened to the night air. A touch of moonlight illuminated the tools of the Speaker's art; the masks and gangling figures, woven from various woods, were eerie. But the women had become used to them. The place was fragrant with forest herbs.

'What is it, girl?' Ullanna asked as she crawled back to the hard bed. Then she saw the look in Munda's eyes.

She took the girl's face in her hands. 'What *is* it?'

'The bird is here. The swan is here.'

She was experiencing *imbas forasnai*; the foresight!

Ullanna backed away, igniting a small wax candle, watching the girl by its light, noticing the arching of the back, the widening of the eyes, the half-smile, the inner searching.

'Tell me more,' whispered Rianata. 'Take your time. Breathe deeply.'

The High Woman came round to the girl and used her night robe to wipe the running perspiration from Munda's face.

Munda declaimed:

'The bird is here. The swan is here.

'I see the quelling force.

'It sleeps. It will wake.

'It comes with a brother who is full of rage.'

She swung from the pallet, stood up and ran to one of the small windows, staring through at the orchard. Two enormous eyes opened to stare at her and the metal hound growled deeply in its throat, rising from its guarding position and stepping menacingly towards the lodge. Munda stood her ground, small eyes meeting gleaming gaze. The girl was in a trance. After a moment, the hound turned away and went back to where it had been curled up.

'A ship of shadows!' Munda whispered.

'A man who wears a cloak of forests!

'Two fathers seeking, both afraid.'

Then, breaking from the overwhelming vision, she turned and fell into Ullanna's arms; a girl delighted by what she had understood.

'Merlin! He's coming. He feels so close, he could almost be here now, in this old man's house.'

Ullanna looked around at the skins and leathers, and the thin wooden shields and masks that were slung through the lodge, creating hidden areas, making a maze of the Speaker's sanctuary.

Munda touched a gentle finger to Ullanna's chin, as if aware of the woman's nervousness; made a sound of quietening.

'Here's here. He's close. We should try to go out, try to meet him.'

'Go out?' Ullanna longed to return to the outside world. The gate was close by, but they had seemed so safe here. Thank the forest goddess Nemetona for bringing Cathabach to their aid, just when it seemed they were lost. He had dragged them into the orchard, almost pushed them into the lodge. He had returned with food and water, and others from the women's lodge. He had sealed the door. Then he had gone, suffering who knew what fate after that.

And *after* that? The hounds had come, two of them, and the orchard had become a prison.

And yet it had all begun with such a surge of beautiful transformation.

Munda still dreamed of the flow of Ghostland. It had come in the evening, the twilight time. Shouts from the western wall had brought her running. Rianata, her guardian, had gone running with her, confused and anxious for the sprightly, uncaring child.

Every animal in Taurovinda was disturbed. The howling of dogs was deafening. All the young children were screaming. The sky above the fortress was spiralling, cloud formations that moved faster than she had ever seen, and which suggested a whirlpool. The land was shaking. The fires in the forges began to draw and become fierce as if the bellows were being pumped by magic.

To the west, hills rose above the horizon. They shone with unnatural light. The forests flowed. The land became silver as if water was flowing, spreading in a flood. An ocean seemed to swell and surge towards the fortress.

Munda clapped her hands and laughed with joy. Nothing in the apparition frightened her. Ghostland came to Taurovinda, and with it, the memories and mysteries of the ancient world.

She almost flew around the walls, to north and south, a terrified Rianata running behind her, anxious for the girl, consumed by fear at what was happening.

'Look there! Look there! Such a pretty island.'

Munda clung to the parapet wall, watching as islands drifted serenely across the drowned plain, much as a log-jam might flow on Nantosuelta after a storm. But these were vast expanses of forested land, with pastures and hunting trails, and even as they passed Taurovinda, so she could see riders galloping headlong to the east across their open meadows. Bright riders, cloaks flowing; the denizens of past and future eager to see the new edge of their world.

She didn't know where that edge might be, just that it was somewhere towards where the sun was still rising, and she shaded her eyes against the glare to try and imagine where the new boundary would be.

The passage of islands continued for some time. She was thrilled to recognise them: there, the Isle of Youth; there the Isle of Stone; and there, she was sure, the Isle of the Stalking Birds. Later came the Isle of Dancing, and the Isle of the Silent Cliffs, behind whose summits the greatest of adventures lay.

She identified them all, even though she had only heard of them in stories.

Rianata stood beside her, trembling, agreeing with everything her young charge whispered, cooed and shouted.

The ocean receded into the east. The land dried out. It became barren, bleak, lifeless; but not for long.

Now the forest came, a great swathe of wildwood that surrounded the fortress. It grew and shrank before the eyes of the startled girl; gigantic trees stretched above the sea of canopy, then fell majestically, to be swallowed by the green. Towers and turrets sometimes probed above the woods, crumbling as quickly as they had risen.

The forest flowed away.

Then came fire. The land blazed. It gave off smoke and flame, but strangely, no heat.

The fire died and the snows came. And when the snows themselves receded east, the land began to swell and roll, changing in colour, becoming fragrant and hot. This heat embraced Taurovinda, warmth like no summer Munda had ever experienced; smells of herbs that she vaguely recognised from Cathabach's lodge, lavender among them, the heady, warming perfume of lavender.

With the fall of dusk came the men and beasts of bronze, striding from the west, passing across the land, hounds baying, the strange warriors making liquid cries in the night. There was the sound of wings. The stars were blocked by creatures that flew, circling low over the fortress before striking in the direction of the land of the Coritani.

Now Munda felt impelled to follow. Rianata tried to stop her, but the girl shrieked and shook off the older woman's grasp.

'Don't be afraid,' she urged the High Woman. 'There is nothing to be afraid of.'

She found her pony and whipped it to the eastern gate. Ullanna saw her, shouted out, realised that her words were lost on the girl and raced for her own horse, summoning her retinue. Munda rode like a night wind, like a storm surge, and the Scythian, despite her skills in horsemanship, was hard-pressed to keep up with her.

She had expected to arrive at lines of encampment, an army that she had felt moving through the land as she had watched from the high walls of her father's stronghold. Instead, with Ullanna now riding beside her, she came to the snow, then the fire, then the forest, then a river that she seemed to recognise, even though no river had existed here before.

She passed through the corridors and halls of a hostel. The place rang with life and laughter. A hound stalked ahead of her, glancing back, metal muzzle grim, eyes searching, but a beast that was leading her to a place it wished her to go.

She stood, at length, in the entrance to the hostel, and stared across the river at the flare of torches on the other side, and at the wan faces of the men and women who crouched there, returning her gaze.

Prominent among them was her father, and as she stepped through the door of the hostel her heart surged with pleasure. She raised a hand to wave at him, then realised something was not right.

Why did he look so sad? Why in such despair? The river would not have stopped him crossing back.

Again she waved to him. Then she shouted, 'Your land has become wonderful. Don't be afraid! Come back to us.'

Perhaps it was the full flood of the river that frightened him. Nantosuelta had certainly swelled. But she would calm down.

And then her father had risen to his feet, head bowed, forlorn. Why so forlorn? Merlin was close behind him, watching. Surely Merlin would understand what was happening; how safe it was; how beautiful the transformation.

And then they had moved away. She felt such sadness. Behind her, the sounds of celebration were loud, raucous. It was not the din of triumph, but the dancing-cry of marriage. The marriage of lands, of kingdoms.

Across the river, in those bleak, dark woods, there seemed to be only chaos. Horses and men struggled away from the Winding One. She soon lost sight of her father and that great bull of a man, his shield-guardian and sword-healer, Bollullos. The brute. She had seen him point his sword at the hostel. Then, later, he had almost seemed to carry his king north.

'Why has he abandoned me?' she asked sadly. The woman who stood behind her rested an easy hand on her shoulder. She was comforted by that touch.

'He'll come back. And when he does, we shall be waiting for him. We'll be ready for him.'

'A feast of a welcome home,' the girl said happily.

'A feast of a welcome home,' Ullanna agreed.

The hound pressed against the window, baleful eye staring into the silent lodge. The women backed away, drew furs to cover themselves. A moment later the door was pushed open and a second hound pushed through the narrow opening. The sound of its breath was the sound of bellows, blowing the fires of a furnace. It stepped cautiously into the lodge, as if expecting a trap. It sniffed the air, then squeezed its metal body into the rough space, and nosed up to Rianata, who sat her ground as the bronze maw drank in her fear and sweat.

There was a brute intelligence behind the eyes. It found Munda and approached her, one careful step at a time, in the manner of a hunting dog, a dog stalking a quiet prey.

It had hardly reached her before it took a backwards step, leaving the house, a last glance around, then back into the night. Rianata ran to close the door.

This was their seventh night of incarceration. None of the women, not even Munda with her insight, could understand what had happened to have made the hill – until seven days ago a place of welcome – into this prison.

Munda turned suddenly, staring towards the back of the lodge, where a breeze ruffled the skins and hangings, and the light, wooden masks clattered gently together. 'My brother is here,' she whispered, and Rianata walked boldly forward and peered into the dark corner.

'And Merlin too,' the girl said, her face brightening. 'They're here. They're in the house.'

'I can't see them,' the High Woman said, but Ullanna laughed, tugging her hair into a high tail and knotting it. 'Don't argue with the girl,' she said. 'If she's says the boys are here, then the boys are here. Show yourselves!'

I stepped out of the shadows. The shock nearly caused Rianata to collapse. She clutched her chest, stepped back, uncertain and confused. Ghosts don't usually appear with such alacrity.

I pushed Kymon forward. He stared at his sister, and Munda returned the gaze from her brief time of anger.

'How long have you been watching?' she asked.

'Not long.'

Then, to my surprise, the young man dropped to one knee and bowed his head. Munda knelt before him and embraced him, puzzled and slightly tearful.

'Why? Why are you kneeling?'

'Because I was wrong.'

'You weren't wrong! I was the one who was wrong.'

'You don't understand,' Kymon said. Together they stood, smiled, reached for each other's hands. 'I doubted you, yes. But I abandoned you. I should not have abandoned you. We were and *are* in this together.'

'I was wrong,' the girl said in a voice that was close to a growl of self-anger. 'I was blinded.'

'All our eyes are open now.'

'I had the foresight. My foresight was mistaken.'

'Merlin told me about your foresight. The foresight was as clear as a winter pool. You interpreted it wrongly, that's all. Value the talent you have. I'll be here from now on to help with the interpretation!'

She mocked him with a laugh, squeezing his nose between thumb and forefinger. 'Yes. And I'll be here to help with your arrogance!'

Then she frowned, looking at his chest. 'Was your amulet stolen too?'

'No. It tore from my neck as I clambered aboard Argo, the last time; as we were preparing to sail back here. It fell in the river. I dread to think what my father will say. Yours was stolen?'

Munda's look was dark. 'One of the hounds. It pinned me down and took it in its jaws. I thought it was going to kill me, but it let me live. It ripped the amulet from the cord, though.'

'I wonder why?' He folded his arms. 'Do you have a solution?'

'No. Do you?'

'No. But Merlin does. I expect.'

They looked at me as one. I was amused and impressed by them. Ullanna was watching me too, her eyes hooded with a deeper wisdom, a greater understanding of the task ahead. Her steady gaze was as clear a question as any she could have voiced. *Do* you have a solution?

I said to them, 'There is a way down into this hill, down to where Durandond has his chamber. Does anyone here know its entrance?'

'It opens in the centre of the orchard,' Rianata said in a quiet voice. 'I know the pattern of the paths that will lead you to it. Cathabach taught them to me. But what does a dead man have to do with anything?'

I almost laughed. A dead man had everything to do with everything! 'Durandond may hold the final answers to a question that's puzzled me. If I can find a way to talk to him ...'

'We all know you can find a way to talk to the dead,' Ullanna murmured.

'I'm sure I can.'

'Those metal hounds won't let us pass,' Rianata said, glancing to where a huge, baleful eye watched us through the narrow window.

'The hounds are subdued. It doesn't take much to subdue mechanisms like that.'

Niiv slipped a teasing arm through mine. 'Merlin's been working very hard for us. Haven't you, Merlin? Such a strain on him. He'll soon need a stick to walk with.'

I gently disengaged myself from the girl, then reached for Rianata's hand. We left the lodge, watched by the growling and uneasy guardians, and slipped into the heart of the orchard. Rianata led me in a winding pattern along paths that she had memorised. They were now overgrown and difficult to walk. One of the hounds followed behind us, curious, but keeping a cautious distance. And quite shortly we came to a huge grey stone, lying flat, split vertically, the gap wider at the base. The cleft was narrow and signified nothing of the passage below. 'It's a tight squeeze to begin with,' the High Woman said unnecessarily. 'I've never done it, but Cathabach has entered as far as the first chamber. I have no idea why he spent so long here, listening to the breeze from below. Part of the mystery of the man, I suppose. Communing with the old king.'

'I imagine he was. Or at least thinking about the old kings, and reminding himself of how to speak of them. This was probably a very special place to all Speakers for Kings.'

In the short time that I had been in Rianata's presence, she had shown no sign of grief. She and Cathabach had been both guardians and lovers. The relationship had been strong. Speaker for Kings and the High Woman were the surrogate parents of the royal children, and though they had kept their presence as discreet and under-influencing as was necessary, they had been constant protectors of Urtha's brood. They had not been able to save his youngest son, Urien; but that terrible time had occurred during the abandonment of the fortress.

No grief, no tears. I wondered if she knew that the man was dead. How to ask her?

We were crouching by the narrow cleft, listening to the whisper from below. I put my hand on hers. 'Cathabach ...'

She smiled and met my gaze, turning her hand in mine to grasp my fingers. 'Is dead. Yes. I know. And there will be an appropriate time to think of that, and to find him, and lay him quietly down.'

'Kymon met him in the evergroves, and will be asking questions: who killed him; how; why. He is determined to avenge his father's brother's death.'

Rianata sighed. 'There is nothing to avenge. Cathabach was using what skills he possessed to hold back those creatures. He held them long enough for us to slip into the orchard, and into the lodge. He was convinced that we would be safe in the lodge. He had put up some sort of barrier, he said. Once inside we'd be prisoners, but safe from Shaper.'

He had used all his strength, all his small talent. He must have worked himself to death. That's all I could think of. And Rianata proved me right.

She said, 'The brightness suddenly went from him. The lightness suddenly went from him. He looked at me and frowned. When I touched him he was cold. He shook his head, then turned away and walked away. Something inside him had stopped. Whatever he was doing to protect us, it was too much. It broke him. Go on, Merlin, go down and find your answers. The time to remember Cathabach will be later. And I must wait for Urtha, and for what happens next.'

She touched a finger to her lips, the finger to mine, then turned and ran quickly back along the path.

I followed the whisper through the crack in the stone, along the earth channel that ran deep into the hill. In the first chamber were the bones of horses and weapons stacked against the stone-lined walls. Their blades were the colour of blood. There was no light here, but I was now beyond caring: I used light-of-image to see clearly. Just a trick, really. Swords, spears, shields, a thin horn-and-leather breast-plate of exquisite design; five horses; five human heads. A trophy room.

The second chamber was so small I had to stoop. It was an empty place, reeking of rot and ruin, open only because of the careful use of timeless stone, creating the chamber, shaping the chamber, maintaining this hollow space. There was nothing here but masks, four masks, slung from the ceiling on cords of leather and beaten metal. To touch them would be to shatter them. The masks were wood, covered with painted mud, and when I looked at them I recognised the older men that I had once met as youths in a narrow valley. Cailum was there, and Vercindond, and Orogoth. But the fourth mask, though shaped for a face, had no features. This would have been Radagos.

What had happened to Radagos?

What a strange room this was. It hinted at the past pleasure and vibrancy of youth; it resonated also with the anticipation of the gloom of later years. It was without imagination; yet it suggested everything that had been imagined and which imagination could summon for the future. Lifeless, yet powerful.

This was a room of pause. Of the small death.

Perhaps it was meant to reflect the experience of all men when, for a brief time, the sense of wonder of life abandons them; when they are caught in that middle realm between the earth and the stars. When they are unsure of themselves. When they need to shape themselves again, recognising that an eagle's eye – sharp, *sharp* as honed iron – sees only what it wants to see as it looks for it, its easy prey – and that there is a vision that is wider than the narrow focus of the hunter, be it winged raptor or wise, hungry youth.

Four masks – what had happened to Radagos? – to show that four friends, four brothers, had been the key to life at its beginning. Perhaps the blank mask was to say, in Durandond's understanding and in the way he had been buried, that everything in life is an unmarked stone before it is shaped by the encounter.

I felt at peace in this room and stayed there for a long time.

But as with the passing of a day, one must always eventually shift, stretch and move on.

It was a crawl, then, round the maze of the shaft before entering the burial room itself. No one had been here since Durandond had been placed on the bier in his four-wheeled cart. By light-of-image I saw the corpse; it was covered by his cloak, a garment now little more than threads held together by threads, draping a body no more than bone held together by sinew. The remains of his dogs lay at his feet. The room was packed with his favourite things, and I summoned charm-of-memory to make them glow again, to shine again with an echo of their old life. Pots, jars, helmets, weapons, barrels of meats, herbs, fruits and grain. And boxes; and the images of children; and the carved images of women and older men; and the beautiful image in beech wood of an especially handsome woman, and this I guessed to be his wife, Evian.

I summoned Morndun then, and raised the dead king, applied charm-of-memory to the desiccated brittle-bone of the once proud man. A forgotten spirit-of-life glistened.

He rose from the cart, looked at me, quite angry, I suspected, but then, as if he remembered me, he gave me a sallow smile.

He stood up, head bowed (the ceiling was low, though why this should have mattered to him was not apparent, since he was insubstantial in this form), and walked to the oak bench at the eastern wall of the chamber. He sat down and leaned forward, hands clasped, breathing hard.

'So: you again,' he whispered.

'Me again.'

'How long has it been?'

'Long. Very long.'

He was silent for a while. 'It's a strange life, this life of sleep and dreams, then life and action, then sleep again, and dream again. Eternity is an odd thing. The brightness of life in the otherworld has an insubstantial feel to it. Too much glow, not enough shadow. A land decorated with light, but false light. I like sleep the best. Death sleep. And for most of my death, my dreams have been good. Until recently. In fact, you have woken me from one of the worst of my recent dreams. I've been dreaming of the Rieve. Is that why you've called me back? To ask about the Rieve?'

'I want to know about the Daidalon. I want to know about how you came to Alba.'

He looked up at me, strong face dark with curiosity. 'The Daidalon?'

'Very important.'

He thought about that, then nodded quickly. 'How long will you give me?'

'Not long. I'm sorry. Holding you here is very expensive. I have to conserve life as much as I can. I have to conserve strength. My shadow stretches far away into Time. You know this. You sneered at me for it when we first met.'

'I wasn't sneering. Why would I have sneered? I'd come a long way to find you. I was probably teasing.'

'Teasing, then.'

Again he sighed. 'The Daidalon. By the sour breath of the Dismemberer, yes. That was something of a mistake. The Daidalon. I remember, now. And the Rieve. And Alba. My dreaming self must have known you were here. Because my dream is breaking: I was dreaming of my father. The loss of my father …'

'I'm listening.'

'Such a terrible time …'

31

Breaking, they Face the Setting Sun

To the far north the sky was black with smoke. Durandond and his father watched from the top of the Eagle Tower. The glint of light on metal told of the movement of an army south. They spilled through the valleys and across the plains, racing towards Eponavindum, the royal citadel of the Marcomanni.

They were not the enemy. This was Durandond's friend Orogoth, running from the destruction of his own stronghold in the heart of the territory of the Ambiarisci.

The messenger had arrived earlier with the warning. The Savage Rieve had swept eastwards during the night, overwhelmed the walls, and set Orogoth's citadel of Trigarandum to the fire. Orogoth had fled, with his father's corpse on a wagon, as many of the treasures of Trigarandum piled into chariots, carts and slung across the horses of his companions as they had had time to gather.

Arcandond was pale and shaking. He had been ill recently, and his sight was failing. He seemed older than his years. But he could see the destruction to the north; and he knew of the reports of the overwhelming of the Vedilici and Ercovisci as well. The old kings were dead, their sons fleeing to the west, taking whatever they could, running for their lives.

Durandond comforted his father, but Arcandond would have none of it. 'I'm not so old.'

'Forty-four years. That's not so young.'

'My father lived to sixty. He died fighting.'

'Not this sort of fight. Time to go. Omens and common sense dictate it. We won't stand against the Rieve.'

'You won't. I will.'

'Then I'll stand with you, and we'll ride to Ghostland together.'

'No.' Arcandond's voice was strong. 'I can't allow you to die. You must take your courage and fighting instinct and take it in a different direction. Deny the battle. We can't win. We're broken. But you can take our name to another land.'

'West?'

'There is nowhere else to go.'

Arcandond was well aware of the prophecy his son had received, scant years before. He added, 'I can stall them at the Pass of Olovidios – at the Great Tree.'

Durandond spoke anxiously. 'They'll take your head. Parade it on a spear. Stick it in a niche in a tall stone, outside their gates.'

'The head will smile in an arrogant way,' his father murmured.

'The head will shrivel,' Durandond protested. 'It'll become a skull.'

'I've always admired the skull's smile,' Arcandond said with quiet amusement to his son. 'So much said for so little effort.'

'Then this is goodbye. And with great effort. But with not much to say.'

Father and son embraced. The wind brought the harsh sound of shields being struck, the beat of approaching slaughter. Arcandond suddenly shivered, glancing into the sky. 'The crow is trying to take me already. But I'm *not* ready!' he shouted. With a last glance at his son, he turned away, to find his arms.

Durandond descended from the tower and made his way to the high gate that opened into the *scrying* groves, the orchards where the Speakers practised their craft. Already the gate was open and two men stood there, hands and short black robes bloodied. The crude wooden masks on their faces were blank-eyed and expressionless, but the knives with which they had performed the sacrifice were being held by the blade, bone handles pointed towards the king's son. Durandond felt a moment's shock, even though he had been expecting this.

It was over. The reading of the victims confirmed it. The citadel would not last the onslaught from the east, nor the gathering forces from its own land, the restless, angry population whose recent starvation in the famine had turned them from reluctant subjects to the citadel to a forest and farmland army of discontent.

He had seen it coming.

Ever since his first feat had been accomplished, in his tenth summer, and he had been invited into the sprawling, opulent hall that was the Hall of Kings and Champions, he had sensed the mood in the lands that paid their taxes to the king. The hall shone with statues in gold and marble. It vibrated with shields and silver; it growled with the finest hunting dogs; it stank of rich wine; it glittered with crystalline stones, beautifully shaped, carved into animal forms, some large enough for a small child to ride. No straw on the floors here, but thick, colourful rugs brought from countries so far towards the rising sun that Durandond, as a boy, could hardly imagine the distance.

The traders came by road and river, train after train of them. The roads were separated from the land by palisade walls and garrisons of armed men. There had always been two worlds in existence at once. The world of the road and the hall; the world of the field, the forest, and hunger.

Towards dusk, Orogoth rode along the north road, two hundred men behind him, all of them battle-weary. Behind them came wagons driven by women, and women on horseback, children clutched across the saddle. The last of the Ambiarisci climbed the winding road to the high gate and came inside the vast enclosure, into the city.

'Radagos has already gone west. He hopes to meet Cailum at the sea-coast, near the white cliffs. As for Vercindond, I have no news of him, except that he escaped with fifty men, a handful of family, and two carts of the dead. All of us have taken our dead. The Rieve is destroying the tombs, dragging the earth from the mounds, breaking into the chariot chambers and throwing the honoured bones to their dogs. They are distributing the wealth of the death road, selling everything that our ancestors needed for their journey. They are defacing the memorials. These people have come from the pits and cauldrons of the underworld. My father said they come from Hades, a Greek Land monstrosity. Hades killed him, then.'

'Greek Land has mostly supplied us with our comforts,' Durandond said quietly.

Ororgoth eyed him carefully. 'Transformation. Our Speaker of Land has been warning about it since he wailed his first *scry*. Our fathers were not as strong as the first kings.'

'I agree. They were idle. But we are not kings, not yet. Just princes.'

'You're wrong. *Kings*, now. All of us but you. And that will soon change.'

Orogoth's words were harsh, but he was exhausted and bowed his head in apology. Durandond shook his head: no apology necessary.

'This place will fall,' Orogoth said.

'I know. That's why I intend to go west. To find another hill.'

'That old wanderer was right after all. Remember that day? By the Sky Shatterer, I could have killed him, he made me so angry. But he was right.'

'I never doubted him,' Durandond said. 'But he gave me a vision. And it's a vision we can all share. I suggest you feed your clan—'

'What's left of it,' Orogoth intoned gloomily.

'—rest the horses, and be prepared to travel with us at first light.'

'The Rieve moves fast. We may not have until first light.'

'That fast?'

'That fast.'

So Durandond made his peace with his father. He visited his mother's tomb in the company of his two sisters. When he had finished, Arcandond himself came and rode around the decorated mound, inside the royal grove, where his wife had lain since her last childbirth.

He had refused his son's request to take her body with him.

'We have until first light?' Arcandond asked.

'With luck, and the indulgence of Taranis.' Durandond pointed to the storm clouds gathering to the north.

'Then we have time to hide your mother's tomb. Your mother will be safe. But take the verses of her life and make sure your sons and daughters memorise them.'

'Sons and daughters it is, though I have other things on my mind at the moment.'

Four hundred men went with Arcandond out onto the plain, by torchlight, to line up against the wild horde coming from the north. Already the night began to rumble with their war-wagons, and the din of their shield striking. Towards dawn, the distant air was shrill with the sounding of horns and the cries of men at the gallop. They sent a pulse of hatred ahead of them, and the stink of smoke and ruin.

Around Eponavindum, the land began to stir. It was as if the fields and woods gave birth to screams, but the screams were of triumph and vengeance. Ragged, rough and ready-armed, the tribal territory of the Marcomanni transformed into a bitter net, to catch the king.

Durandond had prepared for this. The wagons were ready, his own two hundred horsemen heavy with weapons, the children and women armed and hidden, ready to spring to the attack if the net closed too soon.

Arcandond's army had painted their faces grey and red, the red running in a single vertical stripe dividing their faces. On his saddle, each man carried the head of an old enemy, reeking of cedar oil, and the carcase of a hare strapped to the withers of his mount. The hare could fight, the hare could run, but the hare was favoured by the Moon, and would never run scared.

As Arcandond led his troop to the north, to meet his fate and his death, Durandond rode south to where the hills became clustered and the valleys turned to the west through deeper gorges, protected from all but the most determined hunter of royal bounty.

The last gift that Arcandond had given his son to treasure and protect was the small box of oak in which the fifth part of the Daidalon was kept. The two Speakers, still stained with the blood of omens, stood on either side of him, their grim faces telling all that Durandond knew was to be their own fate. They could never leave the sacred groves. The Rieve would find them and remove everything from them that had ever been used to *scry* the future.

As Durandond accepted the box, his father said, 'I have never used it. Nor did my father. And nor must you. When it was used, it turned against the user. Nobody knows how, or why.'

'I know the Declamation,' Durandond assured his father. 'I know the misfortune it contains.'

'This is the fifth part. Neither the fifth part of a man nor the fifth part of a god. It's the fifth part of something beyond knowing. You know that it must never be reunited with the other four parts.'

'Yes. I remember the Declamation! I must never use it, I must never destroy it.'

There were tears in his eyes. His father, battle-harnessed, stood before him, eyes as strong as the iron he would soon be wielding, but heart and body as frail as the man he had become in these long years of luxury and untested spirit. Durandond felt love for him, and shame for him.

Arcandond didn't need to say the words to his son: I could have been a better king. I could have been a better man. Be that king in my place. Take the pride we once had as a clan and settle it on another mountain.

As if the words had been spoken, Durandond whispered, 'I have every intention of doing so.'

He embraced his father, cheek and chin, knelt before him, then stood, smiled a last goodbye and turned from him.

Later, entering the low hills to the south, safe for the moment, Durandond rode up into a ridge and looked towards the citadel. Flames rose from the walls. Dark shapes tumbled from the towers. Death moved chaotically among life running with frenzy and despair.

'We should have listened to the Wanderer,' Orogoth observed sadly.

'As I said before: I *did* listen to him.'

'Then why did you do nothing about it?'

'I thought we *were* doing something about it,' Durandond said with a wry glance.

'Travelling west?'

'That's what he told us to do. There was no escaping the prophecy, in my opinion. That's why I'm prepared, whereas you were not.'

Orogoth accepted the criticism. 'Cailum rode with his father against the Rieve. At least he sounded his war-cry, even after his father was cut down beside him.'

'He's still going west, though. A messenger brought the news.'

'He has his father's body with him.'

'Good. West is where the Dead live. West is where we make our mark.'

Orogoth laughed for the first time in this encounter. 'By the dawn shout of Taranis! Your confidence flows as full as the milk from Brigantia's breasts.'

Durandond glanced, amused, at his foster-brother. 'A good thing?'

'I'm not complaining. We need to invoke as much confidence as possible, now that we live in the shadow of our fathers' humiliation.'

'Then take my advice: stop invoking gods and start riding.'

'West. To lands unknown,' Orogoth agreed.

'No,' said Durandond. 'Home!'

The hunched and melancholy ghost of Durandond drew on my

strength as an unborn child in times of famine draws upon the body of its mother. Draining, desperate, drawing the vitality that it needs to survive, a desperate clawing and clinging to life that weakens the mother, but leads to the expulsion of a living, healthy infant. This shade, aroused by my need, now milked me for sustenance as it remembered for me.

I aged. I had given up the struggle. Something in me had changed, giving in to fate, just as something had happened to Durandond in that long-ago when, instead of rallying his retinue of champions and fighters to ride with his father against the Rieve, he had obeyed the wisdom of the older man and abandoned his kingdom to the wasteland that would follow:

To go in search of a greater land, to continue the dynasty of kings.

Durandond had acted with wisdom, even thought the act must have seemed cowardly. But I knew something that this shadow of the king might not have known: that what Durandond had put in place was a new clan kingdom, and a kingdom based around the land, not the citadel. Yes, Taurovinda was central to the land. But greed was not central to the stronghold.

Such a simple change. And yet it meant that one day Pendragon would inhabit the territory, with his own gutsy and lusty spirit.

Do these things matter to you who perhaps read this long after the events? I have no way of telling. All I can tell you is that in those days, these things mattered.

Watching through Morndun's mask, it was clear that Durandond was remembering the time of the fall with some anguish. He had died, I was certain, with thoughts of his father on his mind. He sat on the bench in his tomb, slumped forward on his knees, looking around at the goods in his mortuary house, his gaze lingering longest on the shield and helmet positioned at the head of the bound and sleeping corpse. A mask of tarnished silver covered the face, but Durandond's thick white hair still lay spread on the wood of the bier.

After centuries, this mortuary house was still spacious, the rot only visible in certain hangings, and in the tarnishing of the metal, and in the form of the bones of his five hunting hounds, curled at his feet. The wooden bier, strong layers of oak, and the oak pillars holding up the heavy ceiling were still intact.

Durandond had not been buried with his wife and children, which surprised me, but then I was not aware of any fate that his family might have suffered.

'Eventually we came to the sea,' Durandond went on. 'We were scattered along the coast, and sent messengers between our forces. The last to arrive was Vercindond of the Vedilici. An enclosure was constructed for the five kings and their families; a second was constructed to contain the wagons with the honoured dead, those that we had managed to raise from the earth before the Rieve swept across us. A hundred carts were placed in circles within that enclosure, and it was guarded night and day.

'We set to the task of building boats. So many boats! They lay like an ancient fleet along the strands below the cliffs. Some were designed for horses, some for the wagons, some for supplies. There is a skill in building ships, but we had built them for the river Rein, not for this unpredictable grey sea.

'By the summer, though, we had boats enough to cross to the land we knew as Alba. We did not anticipate a friendly reception. Those first weeks after our landings were bloody and furious. The people used chariots and horses in ways that astonished us. They seemed to have mastered the power of stones, great rocks flew at us. Their priests were more warrior than healers. They did us damage.

'But we forced our way west. We were a great force against the occasional war band from the older inhabitants of Alba. We took over their mortuary grounds for camps and fortified them. We drove them this way and that. Many of them retreated into the deep valleys and dense forests, out of sight, but not out of our thinking. They watched us constantly as we scoured our new land for the right places to settle.

'And one by one my foster-brothers found a place to stop, consider, then to make a decision to settle. First Orogoth, then Cailum. A moon later, Vercindond had a vision of his fortress to the east and turned back the way we had come. Radagos went deeper into the west, and though messages came from him for some days, there was a moment when they ceased, and our young Speaker *scryed* that he had stumbled into the Otherworld, and been consumed by it. A dreadful fate.

'As for me,' the shade glanced at me, frowning. 'I found your hill. The hill as green as the cloak I gave you. I swear that it grew before my eyes, one mist-shrouded morning when I stood with Evian, my wife, lost in the wild land, unable to sleep, feeling the pinch of cold and hunger. We seemed to be heading towards a great lake, or sea, some expanse of water scattered with islets just visible through the fog. I remember saying, "We will never find a place to start again."

'"Nonsense," she said. "We can stay right here if you want. The mist will clear. It feels firm below our feet. I can hear the belling of stags. This land is rich. And I'm tired of wandering. Make a decision."

'There was an uncompromising sort of challenge in her voice, the first time I'd heard it. She was tired and finding me tiresome. I didn't know it, but our firstborn was already flexing his muscles inside her.

'As the fog cleared, we saw the illusion of water was just dew on the plain, and the hill was there, forested, bare-topped, stretching away from us, but steep from our point of view. We were looking at it from the east, and in my mind's eye I could see the shimmer of gates and walls.

'On the top of the hill a bull was grazing. The grass there was bright. The bull was white. I had never seen a bull like it. By evening, four of us had crept up through the wooded flanks of Taurovinda and captured the beast. It was immense, and it gored one of us badly. But we caught him and tethered him, and then we took possession of the ground. The next morning, as trees were felled to make a roadway, I drove the first stake of the palisade wall into the earth. I felt it open the hill below me. I sent down roots and here they'll stay.

'I sleep below that mark.'

I let the spirit pause for a while. As with Tairon's mother, time spent in this resurrected state was short. Immediately after death: the 'ephemera', or the 'twilight time'. Long after death, the 'returning dream'. But like all dreams, this time of imagining would quickly corrupt into chaos.

Eventually I prompted him. 'You took a fifth part of what you call the Daidalon. The others also took a fifth part?'

'Yes. The Daidalon. A man, brought to the Rein as a curiosity many generations before my birth. He had been captured on a southern island, in the southern ocean, by mercenary traders, men more used to dealing in gold-dust, weapons and the skins of sheep, I was told. Daidalon was their name for him. He had been traded as a weapon in himself. My ancestors thought of him as a trickster. He was dragged between the citadels and made to perform.'

Durandond looked up at me. 'This was before my time, long before my time. But some of what he created still hung in the great halls of our kingdoms. Carvings, masks, discs and monstrous, tiny forms, attached to wings. Sometimes when a storm raged outside the hall, the winged statues would actually struggle to fly. This was not just the wind on the delicate frames, the butterfly wings. They truly seemed to struggle to escape the leather thongs that suspended them. They had life in them.'

'And this Daidalon?'

Durandond pointed to the casket in the corner of his mortuary house. 'A fifth of the part of him was kept in there. The heart and lungs of the man. That's what I was told. The heart and lungs of the man. Made out of gold, beaten thin, two layers with a code inside them. But they were taken soon after my death.'

Made out of gold.

I urged Durandond to recall everything he had been taught as a child about the Daidalon. He sighed. The spirit was weary. The house was becoming gloomy, earth closing in, the smell of dank suggesting that not everything was as pristine in this mortuary as perhaps it looked. Durandond was becoming agitated. He needed to re-inhabit the corpse; to return to whatever island in the Realm of the Shadows of Heroes he rode with vigour. He was, after all, no more than one of the Dead, though he was not party to the vengeance that the Dead seemed to be wreaking on this land that he had claimed as his own.

Which was perhaps why he kept apart.

But this presence of memory was fading fast.

'When he died, in one of the citadels, he began to show what lay beneath. Flesh and bone, yes, but struts and tendons made of metal. And organs that were not blood-filled but metal-sheened. Bronze and silver and gold and copper; and there was amber in him; and hard stone that gleamed with colour when looked at in different ways, though it seemed at a glance to be as pure as ice. And other stones, shaped carefully, that bled rich colours, from scarlet to the blue of a summer sky; from twilight green to the dark purple that oozes from belladonna.

'The skin and flesh was just the mask. Some god, some forge of the gods, had filled the carcase of this man with moving parts.

'My ancestors cut him up and divided the parts. Five parts. Each had its own power: small gold discs from the eyes that opened a whole new world to those who knew how to look through them. His hands were bronze bones, but they could summon elemental forces that no Speaker could manage. The gold and silver plate that they found in his skull brought dreams and visions that have no meaning, but induced madness. In his tongue there was a golden comb that vibrated with sound, the sound of languages that no Speaker could comprehend. Some of the languages were in song form, so I'm told. When the comb sang – and it took only a touch of the metal to make it sing for a moon or more – the night sky changed.'

'How,' I asked him quietly, 'do you know that the fifth part was stolen?'

'It happened during the twilight moment, shortly after I had died, when I still saw the world around me. I was making ready to ride to the river, to the Hostel of the Fine Red and Silver Horses, to select my steed for the other world. The mortuary house had been prepared at the end of a shaft, deep below, but I was still on the high platform, covered in my cloak and shield, in front of the doors to my hall. Speaker for the Land came furtively to where the grave gifts were being gathered. It was night. Though I was guarded by the High Woman and my surviving sons and their hounds, he must have entranced them. He opened the casket and removed the gold. He tied a cord to it and slung it round his neck. There was nothing I could do.'

'How was it shaped? The heart and lungs.'

'Like a crescent moon,' Durandond said. 'The blood and breath of the man.'

I let him rest then. The spirit was not just weary, it was expended. Apprehension filled the mortuary house. Perhaps it was protected against whatever possessed the hill, but this long-dead king was aware that his founding nation was in great danger. Whether he knew, in that spirit-sense, that Ghostland had already claimed his kingdom, I didn't know. I had disturbed a rest that was already disturbed. I would disturb it no longer.

I dismissed Morndun and summoned Cunhaval the hound, and

with Cunhaval's aid scrabbled my way along the winding shaft, back to the surface.

32
Discarded Dreams

I was weary by the time I reached the upper chamber of Durandond's burial shaft. I could feel the fresh air from above and took two deep breaths.

The next thing I knew, a small shape had launched itself at me from one of the corners, and draped her arms around my neck.

'Did you find him? Did you speak to him? Did you raise him from the dead?'

Niiv was nothing if not exuberantly curious.

'Yes. I did.'

In the darkness, all I could see was a strange glow from her eyes, a hint of light coming from deep within her. Her breath was sweet. She brushed her lips on mine, a cursory acknowledgement of being glad to see me, before she persisted, 'Did you use Morndun? To raise him?'

'Of course I did. And it hurts to do so.'

'Teach me how to hurt like that. Teach me the death mask.'

'You never give up.'

'I'll always give in!'

Again she kissed me, but now she felt the tiredness in my bones and ceased her unsubtle fingering of my weary carcase in search of any pattern, inscribed on the hidden ivory, that might give her that extra little bit of 'charm'.

'You need to sleep,' she said.

'Yes I do.'

'Did you get answers? The answers you were looking for?'

'Yes I did.'

'May I share them?'

'Yes you may.'

'But not now!' she insisted, to my surprise. 'Time for that later.' She was fussing at me, concerned for me. 'Get some food, get some sleep. The hounds don't seem to worry about us moving around the orchard, just as long as we stay inside the fence.'

'That's good.'

'You didn't really subdue the metal monstrosities, did you!' She was teasing me in the dark. Her voice gave her away.

'Didn't have to. They were set to stop you leaving the orchard, not the lodge. And they didn't see me coming in because I'm good at that sort of thing. But they're powerful. All of Shaper's creations are powerful.'

'He transformed the land.'

'He transformed himself!'

'Can *you* do that?' We had started to crawl up the shaft.

'No. The summoning of the shadow-masks and possession of beasts – my talents – are not the same.'

'He's more potent than you. Is that what you think?'

Her question caused me to shiver. Indeed, what *did* I think? I had never experienced anything like this Daidalos. For some time now I had been wondering whether or not he was one of the original *nine* who were sent to walk the Path. The nine children selected for a task whose design and outcome were facts withheld from them. I didn't remember him from childhood. And I was sure that only Medea and I had failed, as yet, to return to that starting place; to return home after all the millennia. Daidalos, then, was perhaps from a second home. The past was almost as mysterious as the unknown, unfathomable future. More profound and wiser minds than mine had shaped the world, then, and I was perhaps a far smaller rock in the mountain than I'd realised at that time.

'He's ... different to me,' I replied to the eager Niiv. 'He draws his strength from a place I don't understand.'

There was silence for a while as we found the grips and steps that led us up to the grove and the fallen stone and small light. Then Niiv whispered. 'Take care, my Merlin. Be careful. I want to find you again after – after everything is finished.'

There had been a strange look in her eyes and a wistful note in her voice. Had I been aware of both these things at the time? I imagine so. Her words, ambiguous, haunted, gentle, had struck me like a dart. But I had brushed them off, as I would have brushed off the stab of an insect's sting. Noticed, but not allowed to be notable.

I remember thinking only that I did not want to leave the girl; that I did not want to lose her, not yet. And that yes of course I would be careful.

She made her way into the shadows of the orchard. A breeze blustered for a moment, a whisper of nature that seemed to speak words: it was my imagination of course. Wasn't it? To hear the breeze whisper: *don't go back to her.*

Whatever it is, it has transformed the hill.

Cathabach's words: but had they been said as warning? Or as guidance?

The old shaft will take you down, Cathabach had said. The old shaft? It took me a moment only to intuit that he had meant the sacred well.

I made my way through the stone maze. It was a small shock to discover the shrivelled, shrunken remains of the three young women who had guarded the place. Each was seated, arms folded, head thrown back, mouth gaping. They looked exactly as if the very spirit and air had been sucked from them in a single instant.

I had descended into the hill by way of the well before. There is a feeling of drowning, then of intense cold. The walls contain you, the waters spin you, icy liquid forces itself into your lungs; the deep earth itself seems to be pulling at your feet.

And then you are on a damp ledge, by a flowing river, illuminated by streaks of phosphorescence in the cavern walls. This is the place where the waters of Nantosuelta feed the labyrinthine currents of the hill, channels that flow between the rocks, and spill in several places onto the land as simple springs.

Taurovinda had always been connected with Ghostland, and this watery, placental link was proof enough.

Shaper had been here, though for how long, I couldn't tell. Long enough, however, to have left his mark on the walls and ledges. His symbols were everywhere; the stone had been shaped into figures; he had played, here, played at animating the rock itself. Discarded discs, pressed from poor metal, lay scattered everywhere, but it seemed to me that for a while at least they had functioned.

He had made Taurovinda into a Shaping Chamber. How long ago? Not that long. Perhaps he had probed here from the Otherworld over the years, before establishing his first foothold in Urtha's land, across the river, an advance camp preparatory for the full invasion.

He had listened to the life above him. He had viewed the land. He had directed his attention to the East, away from the setting sun. East. Home. His birthplace.

His life, his mind, his fury resonated here, fresh in the ancient place of smoothed rock and flowing stream. Discarded dreams, echoes of new challenges, still sang from the surfaces. Wherever Shaper went, he left a trail of desire. I was reminded of the eerie after-presence of Queller, in the cave above Akirotiri, another entity so old, so close to the embrace of earth and forest, that her scent lingered wherever she journeyed, like a distant cry caught on a spiralling wind, fading slowly, never to vanish completely.

What are you doing? I asked of the slick faces marked on the cavern. *Where are you going?* I whispered to the freezing water. The earth rumbled, a mournful movement, the echo of a storm.

I didn't need to answer my own question. But I needed to find Shaper. And he was still at the river, at the ancient boundary. Why had he not crossed by now? Was he still searching for a way to extend the boundaries of Ghostland? What was holding him back, this man, this creation, who could reassemble his own being, his own life, from the machinery that he himself had fashioned from the ores of the earth and the dreams from the stars?

Shivering in the cold of the underground, staring at the discarded bronze discs, the crude figures on their dulled surfaces alive with the phosphorescence, a thought arose: vengeance. And a name: Jason.

And thinking of Jason, of the last moments I had seen him, crouched and anxious on the river's edge, preparing to cross to Ghostland, I felt suddenly afraid for the man.

We should not have gone our separate ways.

I should have told him who was crossing the Winding One in the second boat, entering a forbidden realm, drawn there by the dying mother, the mother out of time.

Rather than risk Niiv attaching herself to me again, insisting on coming with me, I eschewed the easy ascent by which I might return to Argo. I slipped into the freezing water and let Nantosuelta carry me through the hill and below the plain, to where this snaking limb of water joined with the main river, in the heart of the evergroves.

After I had wrung out my clothes and shaken myself back to

warmth, I went to find the ship. It came as a surprise and yet no surprise at all to find that she had gone, taking with her the honey child.

I could have laughed had it not been for the fact that I now knew what was to come.

And Jason? This is what I learned – later – of Jason.

33
Shade-Magic

The moment Jason launched the boat from the bank he tried to take control, using the slim paddle to push across the flooding water to the darkness opposite. The river itself snatched the paddle from his grasp. And when he flung his weight against the hull, to try to make the small craft spin, he might as well have been striking the wall of a cliff.

The boat turned at its own pace, lulling him quiet, progressing to Ghostland in its own time, in its own way.

Lying back, gazing up at the stars, Jason smiled as he surrendered to the river. Then he laughed out loud. The heavens moved around his gaze, a restless farm of images, but he could not see the 'archer' – the Centaur! Chiron. This river was too far north, he knew.

Nevertheless, he invoked his old friend:

'I tried, Chiron. All my life I tried. And for most of my life I succeeded. You gave me good advice. Can you send a horse for me now?'

Nothing stirred in the night sky.

Chiron had told him that should he ever need help he need only look to the heavens. 'There I am,' the self-proclaimed "centaur" had teased his young charge, indicating the constellation known as the 'Man-Horse Hunter'. 'That's where I get my strength.'

'That's a goat, not a horse.'

Chiron was amused. 'The goat dances in Cornus! Over there.'

Jason was dismissive of this elemental magic. 'You see shapes where I see directions. I see stars that one day I'll need to sail by. Useful signals. That's all I see.'

'Well, yes. But sailing is about more than ships and seas – at least, when it comes to being a king. You don't need to believe in the heavens. But you ought to understand how others believe in them ...

'And hopefully not to confuse goats and horses.'

Jason had laughed at that. 'I'll try not to. So those stars are a man and a horse, an archer on four legs.'

'It's a man who holds close his animal nature. Wit and strength, Jason, young Jason ... wit and strength.'

What was the river doing? The water flowed past him, but the boat was still, caught, as it were, in an eddy, its low prow pointed towards the narrow darkness between thrusting willows, whose night arms reached to embrace him. Fires burned beyond that dark crevice of gloom. And there was movement there.

Jason wanted to leap into the river and swim. But the fight was out of him, and he lay quite still, alive in starlight, embraced by the river, ready for life, death, vengeance or release. Anything.

He thought of his father, Aeson, and of his childhood, and his growing years when he had been sent north, to that country of horses and wild riders, to die or survive, taken into the care of Chiron. Foul-breathed Chiron. Moon-howling, self-immolating Chiron. Chiron – supposedly a Dacian – who spent so much of his day strapped to his dust-grey steed, grey with dust himself, disguised with leaves and dressed in the drab colours of his plains-roaming people, that he might easily have been confused with a centaur.

Even Chiron joked that when he dismounted, he had to tear the skin of his thighs from the horse's hide.

The man had been saved from death by Aeson at the battle of Xenopylas – no poet had been there to record it – and had in turn saved the king, who had never forgotten that saving grip and the rescuing grasp of the horseman as they'd fled the field, never abandoned the memory, kept contact and sent favours to the *wild man* in return for a single horse every summer, a gift appreciated.

Chiron had trained Jason in everything he needed, but most especially in the use of his wits and cunning. 'There is a difference between a foot-soldier who fears the sudden thrust of a spear through his guts and a king who fears an omen. The first strides forward to meet the fear, survives or not; the second lets fear root him to the spot. Easy to chop down.'

As he floated gently in the middle of the Winding One, Jason laughed again and cried out to the stars, to the memory of his old friend: 'Grant me at least that I proved *that* point, old horse! Never rooted, always restless!'

The boat nudged the gravel of the bank, between the drooping fronds of the willows. The second craft was there as well, but waterlogged, its lowest strakes hacked by an axe.

Jason scrambled ashore, drawing the boat behind him, securing it. Around him, the land was alive with sound, not of voices, but the low droning of beasts and the heavy movement of machines. There was no brightness in this night air.

He had had no expectations of what he would find on this side of Nantosuelta, except that Medea would be close. He unbuckled his sword belt, wrapping the leather around the sheath and carrying the weapon in a way that would make it hard to use. He found moist leaves and wiped the mud from his boots. He wondered whether or not to remove one of them, to walk one-booted into whatever was waiting for him.

For a while he was caught on this new shore: he stared at the scuttled craft, wondering who had been its occupant. He gazed at the distant fire on the land, listened to the world that was beyond his comprehension.

Rooted to the spot.

Enough of that!

He made himself comfortable, used the cold water to refresh his skin, then ascended the narrow path between the trees until he came to a structure in stone and wood that framed the distant fire. Not a temple, not a sanctuary, but a small and welcome hostel, hollow, in that he could walk through it to the land beyond, but secure, in that it gave protection from the stars, the rain; a shelter, with dark rooms leading off from its rough-hewn walls.

He came to the far exit. Urtha's land stretched out before him, glowing with fires, mysterious with movement. Jason was briefly disorientated: it seemed that mountains rose before him, but he could see clouds and stars through the slopes. The mountains faded and there were the hills, the woods, the fires.

If he had intended to walk out into the open of the night, he hesitated, and in that moment of caution a voice whispered from behind him:

'Step back. Don't cross.'

The voice had been Medea's. He saw her now, black-clad and pale-faced. Like a wraith, she slipped into one of the openings and he heard her running.

He followed, finding himself in a dank corridor, the flagstones slippery, the walls stinking with slime that seemed to ooze from the fissures between the rocks.

'Is this the passageway to Hades? Where are you taking me?'

Ahead of him, the woman's footfall sounded hesitant. Then her laugh came, low and brief. 'Not to Hades. I would have thought you'd have enough of Hell.'

She was off again. For an instant Jason glanced back at the still-lingering light at the end of the passage. But tugged by tiredness and helplessness and not a little curiosity, he slipped and slid on down the road, steadying himself with his hands, breathing the air that, though tainted, at least seemed to flow towards him. He became a creature similar to a bat, seeing by sound and smell rather than by eyes.

'Where are you taking me? Is this your idea of vengeance?'

Again, that pause in the darkness. Again the low, sour laugh. 'No, Jason. No. Not vengeance. I no longer have the capacity for such poison. A jar of wine, unused for many years, breaks in the winter and spills its soured contents. Anger is like that. Better to throw the clay jar far away before it breaks.'

'Well ... thank you for the lesson in temperance. But where in the name of Cthonos and his pale, blind sons are you taking me?'

'Here! Open your eyes.'

'My eyes are already open.'

'Try again.'

She was standing by a tall, narrow window. Daylight illuminated one side of her face as she stood with her back to the wall. The sudden light was harsh, stark; it burned the age from her, softened her skin, her gaze.

'I remember this place well,' Jason said. 'Your private room, looking out over the harbour.'

'Looking down at Argo; at your drinking friends. At the way you wasted your years with me.'

'This is not Iolkos. This is a dream.'

'Clever, clever. I made this place to keep me warm. When the Otherworld of these barbarians spread across a king's land to the river, I came with it. I had no choice.'

'You were dragged here? Is that what you're saying?'

'I was uprooted. The land flowed east. I had always lived at the edge of Ghostland. I came forward with that sudden growth.'

'Uprooted ...' Jason echoed quietly, and they both laughed.

Medea whispered, 'Yes. Not for the first time, eh?'

'Not for the first time.'

He walked over to the window. Medea smelled of a fragrance he recognised, with its hint of rose and cinnamon, and the musk of an animal. This is how she had oiled her body when he had met her in Colchis, before they had become lovers. As if to keep him waiting, to frustrate him in his ambitions, she had then worn nothing by way of scent except the odour of a ram. Foul and filthy, he had embraced it without question, knowing that she had been testing him.

In Iolkos, again she was rosewater and musk. And for a while he had basked in a paradise for his senses.

In this nowhere-place, this edge of the Otherworld, Jason stared at the empty harbour below with a sense of nostalgia. Argo had been moored there for many years. He had used her almost as a second home, her deck covered with canvas, the quayside littered with barrels and ropes and crates and jars. And yet she had been a restless vessel. Many times he had gone to find her at night, only to discover that she had slipped her ropes and prowled out onto the ocean.

She had been a sad ship all those years, but she had stayed loyal. Each dawn, she was there again, a little fresher on her decks, the wind from the open sea still fragrant in her sail.

Now Jason glanced at Medea, who was watching him closely. 'Who crossed in the other boat?'

She shook her head. She wouldn't answer. 'Why were you laughing as you crossed? What memory brought that unusual sound to your voice?'

'You were watching me?'

'Of course I was watching you. I've been watching you since you returned from the dead.'

'Not a comforting thought.'

'I don't mention it to give you comfort. What made you laugh?'

'What made me laugh ...' he repeated, then shrugged, leaning on the marble sill and staring into the false light of his past. 'I was thinking about how very clever I'd been as a youth, and how quickly that wit was stolen from me. I was thinking of Chiron. And my father Aeson; you never knew him. Only that bastard of an uncle of mine who killed him.'

'Peleas. Yes. The man who teased you into searching for the fleece. But without him, you and I would never have met.'

Jason's laugh was so spontaneous he almost choked. 'Well: romantic though that sounds, it couldn't have been for the worse, all things considered.'

'Sour man. Sour mind.'

'Yes. The murder of his sons does that to a father.'

'I didn't kill our sons. I took them away from you.'

'You took them away from their world. You killed them as you killed me. Spite spoke through your hands, not protection.'

'Spite blinded me to the needs of my sons. I don't disagree with you, Jason. It was a shocking thing to do, to displace them so far in the future. Though I kept with them, I stayed with them. I watched over them ... as best I could. It exhausted me. I have no time left, now; days at the most.'

'Don't look for pity or forgiveness from me, you witch.'

'I don't. I'm not.'

Suddenly angry, Jason spat on the floor before Medea. 'Watched over them? The last I saw of Kinos, my Little Dreamer, he was dead from his own madness, stretched on a bier in a childish, Shadeborn palace of his own creation.'

'I was there. Remember? He had followed me to this place, this northern Ghostland. I was there. I saw him die.'

'You were a shadow, hugging shadows, too ashamed to confront me, too dead to shed a tear.'

'Oh, I shed tears, Jason. Don't ever doubt that! To watch your youngest son die so wretchedly is not a play to be visited twice.'

The silence that hung so heavily, then, seemed to whisper another name: the eldest boy, Thesokorus. The Little Bull-Leaper.

Jason whispered, 'Who was in the other boat?'

'Yes,' Medea said knowingly. 'Yes it was.'

'Thesokorus? He's here?'

'Thesokorus is close.'

'The last time I met him was near an oracle, in Greek Land. Dodona. He had been hunting me. He opened my guts with a single blow and left me for dead. The wound still hurts. But then, you know that: you've been watching me since my resurrection.'

'Are you afraid he's come to finish the task?'

Jason smiled thinly, wearily. 'I'm not afraid of anything. I'm *rooted to the spot*. I'm taking no further part in my own actions. So strike your bronze shields and summon your shade-magic.'

'Sad man. Sour man.' Medea came over to him. 'You poor "Shade" of a man.'

Her skin was old but her eyes and her lips were young. She kissed Jason on each cheek, then on his own lips, touching his face with fingers that shook slightly. She held his gaze with hers.

'The last time I saw you,' she whispered, 'which was not so long ago: you were full of life again. I remember hearing your words, as you guided Argo out onto the river, to seek, to find, to strive for the last years of your life ...'

'You were watching. Of course.'

'Always watching,' she teased. 'Let me remind you of what you said:

'I have ten years, Merlin, and I won't waste them. Ten years at least, ten good years to sail this good ship on strange waters and find strange places to ...

'... and you paused. And you laughed when Merlin suggested: "To loot?"

'Yes. Loot. It's what I do best. Ten years, Merlin. Listen out for my story. Now get off my ship, unless you want to join the adventure.'

Jason nodded, remembering. And he said, 'Merlin expressed the wish that I would find what I was looking for. I answered that I was looking for nothing; but that I hoped "Nothing" wasn't looking for me.'

'I know. I heard it all. By the Beard of the Ram! you were your old self again, that young man, less wit than ambition, more strength than care for his own safety, drawn to the unknown. I could have loved you again, right there and then.'

They held each other; lost lovers remembering lost love.

'The unknown *consumes* men like me,' Jason whispered. 'We are born in that place. We can never know its limits. In the end, we disappear there.'

Medea sighed, a small, sad sound as she held her face to his chest. 'I knew that from the moment I met you. Do you imagine that I didn't? I fled Colchis with you, on Argo, because I wanted to be a part of that unknown. To share it.'

'I let you down,' he murmured after a moment.

'No, Jason. Our paths were different. They always had been. All paths run together for a time. They always separate.' She brightened then, catching his gaze and smiling. 'But when you left Taurovinda, only a few seasons ago, I still celebrated your new passion; when I watched from hiding; when you seemed so exhilarated with the thought of adventure.'

Gently, Jason pressed his lips to Medea's forehead. 'Well. It didn't last. I was looking for something that had gone. Long gone. I slowed down. And Argo slowed down too. These Celts, Urtha, the king of this land, he and his Speakers talk of "wastelands". They talk of three wastelands that drained the kingdom over the generations. Well, I've come to know all about wastelands. It became a wasteland on that ship after a while. There was something desperate in Argo's heart. An unhappy ship – she put us into hibernation; like winter foxes. Until we came back to Alba, and I found Merlin again.'

'Argo brought you back here for a reason.'

'It has something to do with that business on Crete, a thousand years ago, or whenever. Something to do with my wedding gift to you.'

'It has everything to do with your wedding gift to me.'

There was something in the way she looked at him; expectant, testing, waiting for him to respond. The light from the window seemed to flare, then darken, and his gaze was drawn again to the harbour below.

A ship was moored there now, and he recognised Argo at once, but not Argo as he and the shipwrights had reconstructed her in Iolkos. This was an older ship, its hull painted in an intricate weave of blue and red, the shapes of the creatures of the sea familiar to him, the eyes that watched from the strakes familiar to him, the gleam of polished bronze bringing back an echo of the day he had pirated the vessel as she sailed close to his own sea-channel, killing her crew, abducting Argo to refashion her, to make the vessel he would need for the perilous journey in pursuit of the fleece; in his hunt for Medea.

A figure was standing on the quayside, looking up at the small palace. The light on its face was golden, though the eyes were dark. The skins that clothed the man were grey and brown, the hides of wolves and goats, stitched together.

And the quayside was no longer the familiar haven of Iolkos.

'I recognise the place, but I don't remember it.'

'The harbour on Crete, where you came ashore as an angry man, challenged by your uncle to steal the ship before you searched for the fleece.'

'Of course. But ... then this is not your creation. This place is not yours.'

Medea smiled thinly, barely covering her sadness and desperation at this final betrayal.

'It's his,' she agreed. 'I have nothing left to offer. Not even protection. The flame is out. Yes, it's his. The Shaping Man. He's shaping the edge of the world as he remembers it. As he shapes, so he moves, and he must cross Nantosuelta. When he crosses the river, he will leave nothing but wasteland behind him.'

Jason was almost amused. He glanced at the sky, searching for the dark wings of scavenging birds, waiting – as he knew they waited in this northern land – to drag the dead to their own Hell.

'Argo brought me here to be killed.'

'I don't think so,' Medea whispered. 'She loved her captains.'

'What, then?'

But before she could answer, if indeed she had an answer to offer, the world of the palace shifted and dissolved around them. The sweet smell of rose-oil was replaced by the sharp smell of pine, and the crisp freshness of mountain air. They fell apart from each other, Jason sliding down the scrub-covered hillside, Medea tumbling after. The sky was an intense blue. He struck an immense grey rock, its scarred form rising from the hill like a petrified tree stump. Grey trees grew from where the rock had split. Their branches played like a dancer's hands above him.

The next he knew, a flash of tarnished bronze had leered at him, a face like a Gorgon's. A hand had pushed him roughly. Several shapes reached for him and dragged him away from the rock and onto open hill. He tumbled again, his legs weak from being kicked. The last thing he saw was that he had reached the edge of a river.

The last thing he heard was Medea's mournful cry, somewhere above him. All power had gone from her. She had exhausted herself completely.

Now the sun, beginning its descent to the west, framed a figure, and again, bronze shone dully from its face and from its hands.

34

Edge of the World

I was halfway across the devastated land that had been Urtha's realm, halfway to the river, walking among the ruins, when I finally heard the distant song, Argo's song of summoning. She was mournful. She was urgent. The song was a cry, a memory of her first building, of the bone pipes and stone whistles that we had used to signal across the distances when I had been a child, and when nature, and things created out of nature, had moved and shifted to the simple tunes we had created.

I was resting in the remains of a village that Ghostland had scoured of life, slumped quite comfortably on the stone hearth of a lodge, behind a screen of fallen thatch, indulging in the remnants of memories of the fled, flayed and dead. The shouts and echoes of those shouts were strong. The fields and enclosures were open graves for crows. The invasion force had not treated the people of the villages and farms kindly. They had made images of them, hanging them from trees, grotesque offerings to the carrion hordes.

They would not be the honoured dead.

And yet among this horror, there was beauty. The world of the Shadows of Heroes had flowed into this land, and to cross one ridge that smelled and looked like Crete, rough terrain and strong, vibrant vegetation, was to descend towards an island, hazy in sunlight, its surrounding waters moving in patterns as if with a life of their own, neither waves against the shore, nor ripples, more the chaos of unseen movement below the surface, creating refractions and reflections that were absorbing to watch.

Distantly, the armies of the Dead were camped in their groves and valleys, waiting for the next shift east. I could have chosen to run among them as hound, or deer; or flown as crow or hawk; but

I had chosen to cover the ground by way of the chariot of gold, gift of Nodens, great god of the Sun, uncle to the two wild sparks who for me, and for this time, represented everything that was urgent and reckless. They were strong and death-defying, attributes that can only, truly, be mined like precious ore from the young of the world.

It was Conan who carried me. He curled up in his chariot, dozing lightly. He had been appalled at what he had seen as we had made our journey.

I was glad, too, that we had left Niiv behind; and Kymon and Munda. It would fall to the children to pick up the pieces when things were finally resolved. And there would be horror enough for them at that time.

Argo's summoning song drifted on shifting air. This is how I remembered it from the mountains of my birth. The valleys carried the song, but the sound was broken by the breeze; it came in code; so the verses were repeated, and gradually the whole melody could be pieced together.

As a hound follows the scent trail, a wolf the blood trail, so I followed the song trail. I became increasingly aware of the urgency behind the haunting tune, of how Argo was communicating sadness to disguise the fact of danger.

Soon Conan reined in the horses, turned the chariot side-on and peered to the east. We were just crossing a ridge. It was dawn, and the sun was glowing ahead of us, brightening the sky but plunging the land into a final shadow. The horses were nervous, as was the Sun Prince.

'We're almost there,' he said, 'but we have to make our way through a legion. The good islands are behind us, I'm sorry to say.'

He tied his long hair into the tight knot on the top of his crown that signalled battle-readiness. With his knife, he scraped the scruffy beard from his cheeks and chin, leaving only the hair on his upper lip. Blood oozed from the clumsy shave, but clearly this was intentional, as he wiped it with both hands, pressed it to his face, then went round to the horses, making them smell the raw iron of his life. They bucked and bayed, but he spoke quiet words and they soon calmed.

It was a weary look he cast as he passed by, returning to the chariot. His features, lean and strong, were beginning to be marked by unexpected age and unwelcome experience. I noticed that his lips were dry and cracked, though everything else about him spoke of athleticism and the readiness for combat.

'My brother is out there, somewhere in that mass of death. I'll have to find him; and if you spot him, tell me; but don't worry, I'll deliver you first. To your ship. There is a little of Mercury in me that must be obeyed,' he said with a grin. 'The message must get through!'

As the sun lifted and the shadows dispersed, I saw the hordes. They filled the eastern horizon for as far as the eye could see: tent-cities, enclosures, fields of practice, fields of games, the whole view was of a waiting army, restless, feeding, furious, a frustrated and festering mix of the great, the good, the desperate and the savage of many times and many lands.

'They don't know what they're doing.'

Conan looked at me curiously. 'What do you mean?'

'They inhabit a world where the past is a memory, and activity is a dream. Their existence should be splendid, and spent in the game of life, not the pursuit of death. They don't belong here, pressing against the edge of the world, iron-handed, blood-lusting, like a curse waiting to be cast.'

Conan thought about what I'd said. He agreed. 'Like water, draining into a well. A force attracts them. A downward force. They've been drawn here, but are helpless.'

'Water from the well,' I mused.

Conan was in full lyrical flow. 'The tears of children and old men. Shed without understanding. Uncontrolled.'

'Helpless.'

Conan drew his burnished sword, passed it to me, carved bone- and leather-grip first. 'Take this. You might need it.'

'I won't need it.'

He stared at me for a moment; laughed. 'What a confident man you are. And not even the son of nature. No relation to a god. Merlin. Antiokus. I must try to remember you. Merlin. Like the bird. Do you have wings?'

'That's not overly demanding enchantment. I can arrange for it.'

'I believe you can. Here. You can have the scabbard as well, if you're afraid of cutting your fingers.' He offered me the patterned sheath for his sun-gilded blade.

'I told you. I won't need it.'

'Confident.' He was approving.

'Old. Unwise,' I corrected. 'In fact, more a creature of nature than even a son of the Sun. Let's go to the edge of the world, Conan. An old friend is waiting for me.'

He gave me a curious look, then shook his head. 'You're a strange man. I would enjoy walking in your dreams.'

He whipped the horses then and we were off again.

I might, myself, have opted for a slow, gentle, discreet approach, but Conan suddenly uttered a high-pitched cry, leaned forward, striking the rumps of his steeds furiously with the reins, urging them to a run that seemed impossible even for young horses. I held on firmly, if not for my life, certainly for saving the bruises that would accompany any fall from the chariot.

The Dead became interested in us. As we ploughed through their lines, so bands of them rode down upon us, some armoured heavily, some lightly, some with spears, some carrying no weapons at all, even standing on their horses as they inspected us at the gallop.

A train of chariots appeared around us, wild-haired drivers laughing as they tried to outpace us. Fifty or more, I counted, and they were competing as much against each other as against the son of Llew.

He outran them easily, and they dropped behind, crying a chant that made him smile. They were complimenting him.

We rode past fires and tents. Occasionally arrows hissed about us, some striking the car's flanks, a few lodging in the horses, which seemed unbothered by the stone points.

Through woodland, onto meadow, through a dip in the land, along a river, a tributary flowing into Nantosuelta, the Dead stood to inspect us, chased us, fell back, shouted at us and were soon lost against Conan's wild run.

They were a blur of colour, a field of faces, a fading howl of curiosity.

When at last we came to the line of bronze, he slowed slightly. The eastern horizon was brilliant with the sheen of Shaper's inventive mind. There were hundreds of giant men, all crouched on one knee, weapons and shields held before them, the metal forms an echo of the oak men who had risen in the land of the Coritani, the land they now watched and coveted. As we approached their ranks, so those ahead of us stirred, rising to their feet and turning slowly to watch us as we came towards them.

They moved to bar our way.

Conan, shouting above the roar of wind in our faces, asked, 'Did you say you could summon wings?'

'Yes.'

'Well, watch this!'

He called to Nodens, invoked his uncle in a howl of challenge and compliment, a mixture of curse and respectfulness. He was grinning as he shouted.

Nodens seemed to hear, and not to mind.

The two chariot horses became two among a hundred, all white, spreading out ahead of us, held by harnessing that radiated from the chariot as a web of rippling silk. The chariot appeared to swell. It took on a blaze of light, a sun-glow that was astonishing even to a well-travelled, time-travelled man like me. Did it rise from the ground? I don't know. It consumed the space ahead of us. It set the land alight with its blaze of gold. The bronze warriors drew back, bowing low, crouching to avoid the fire.

We flowed through them, gliding effortlessly. They watched us pass into the distance, their strange, dead eyes continuing to hold a gaze that might have been surprise.

'Now do you understand why my brother and I steal chariots?' Conan asked with a mischievous smirk.

'I'm glad your uncle was in a good mood.'

With the metal car and the horses back to normal, the charm removed, we raced towards the river. A hostel loomed ahead of us, a dark hall with several doors cut out of the rough wood. No beauty here, not on this side. Conan drew the sweating animals to a halt. He was as exhausted himself.

'I get confused about the hostels,' he explained.

'Why is that?'

'They can be so easily manipulated.' He gripped my arm and smiled his farewell. 'This is where I leave you. I have to find Gwyrion. I can smell the river, so you don't have far to walk.'

'Thank you for the ride.'

'I hope it works out for your friend, the king. Urtha. A fine man. The descendant of a fine man.' Conan winked at me. 'My father and my uncle go back a long way. They knew Durandond very well. And all the others; all those sons of broken kings. They couldn't save the kings from their excesses, but they tried their best. My father rules in the west, my uncle across the sea-channel in the east.

That creature, the Shaper, has upset them. I think you can count on my father, should you need to.'

He had gone. I entered the hostel and passed through its corridors without difficulty. The place seemed as dead as the men and women who sat moodily in the rooms and galleries. They watched me through vacant eyes, these once-heroes who had been drawn into a new and unwelcome game. I gained the impression they were uncertain as to which way they were travelling.

Perhaps the instinct I had shared with Conan had been correct. Though behind the hostels the life of the dead still seemed full of the joy of death, here at the edge of the world there was fear of the unknown!

Beyond the hostel the land brightened, the air smelled sweet again, a memory of Greek Land, the fragrance of a more romantic past. Argo was moored there, distantly and below me. She watched me from her bow-eye. I saw the single tear that had been painted in blue, just that hint of emotion in the steady gaze that had always been carved and illuminated on her hull.

But the echo of Akirotiri was sinister. I realised that my view of the harbour was from the cave where Queller had watched us in our journey between worlds. I could see The Winding One through the illusion, the old river and the forest that bordered her. And beyond her, a land now coveted by a force of the Dead impelled to this invasion by a creature out of the past.

I made my way to Argo, allowing the illusion to keep me on the downward track, to the stinking quayside, to Daidalos's place of safety.

Argo breathed softly; no song of summoning now, no song of welcome, no whisper of greeting; just a silent warning. I climbed the ladder slung from her hull, stepped into Daidalos's reconstruction of my ancient little boat, my boyhood dream. He had fitted her out well for sea-passage, yes, but not so well that she could have made the sort of ocean voyage that Jason would later undertake. This was a smaller ship, designed for a smaller crew, for coastal journeys. But there was somehow more magic in her.

Was the Spirit of the Ship still there? Of course it was. That part of Argo had not altered, no matter how many times she had been rebuilt. It simply changed with the change of her captain.

I went aboard and, after a moment's hesitation, stepped through into the world that Daidalos had made.

I entered the labyrinth.

It was not Daidalos who prowled those dark corridors, of course. It was the memory of the man: the *shaping*, the sentience that had drawn itself together because of the skill in science and enchantment of that ancient inventor. Its thoughts were loud echoes in the passages. Its needs, its fears, its anger, its urgency, all were flights of mind-song. I was reminded again of the echoes of Queller, the fading manifestation of Lady of Wild Creatures who could not move, during the *dying of her light* on Crete, without shedding anguish.

I followed the thought-trail deeper into the complex. Perspective shifted, disorientation occurred, but Shaper could not disguise the soft breath of his own anticipation. He drew back from me, unseen, as I stepped forward. When the walls crowded in, or the passage became so low that even a crouch was painful, the 'sense' of his watching presence was somehow magnified.

He comes closer ...

The creature's curiosity was a stink in the confined airways. The entity did not understand me. It knew humans, ghosts and shades. It did not comprehend the young-old man who worked his way towards the confrontation. It was not hard to hear those fragments of its thinking.

He comes closer.

Familiar. Old. Why do I know him?

Why remember him?

This labyrinth was a crude memory of the original chamber that had been scoured from the deep rocks of Crete. It was enclosing, confusing, stifling; it was sinister. But it did not possess the distorting power, the feeling of endlessness, or evoke the morbid sense of hopelessness I knew had been experienced in that original creation. Despite this, I knew I would be wrong to underestimate the powerful shade that was drawing me closer, spinning his trap.

Yes! That was precisely what Daidalos was doing; he was spinning this labyrinth as he moved, weaving the stone around us, winding us towards the centre. And it was a strong weave. I felt unskilled, here. The smallest exercise of enchantment would have been a major effort. He had drawn on Ghostworld. He had garnered strengths over many years, fashioning them to his own needs, layering his shadow with the tricks and talents of the dead of ages.

And yet he was still anxious about me.

Why do I know him?

And why did I feel the same?

And then Medea walked towards me through the labyrinth. She came towards me out of the darkness, pale in complexion, sad in her look, walking as if in a dream.

For a moment I felt delight, then realized the painful truth: that she was dead. Though she glowed and gleamed, and came to me with brightness and affection, she was in that hinterland between life and death that the Greeklanders call the *ephemera*.

Her arms reached out and took me into her embrace, a fleeting moment, a last cradle of affection.

'I have to go.'

'What happened?'

'I have to go.'

'What *happened*?'

'I'm used up. Protecting my son has used me up. I'm in transition. I'm sorry. I will see you back where we began. I have a path to walk.'

I was surprised to find that she was warm to the touch. So small a woman, so slender. My arms embraced her and she was like a ghost. She was crying, but then looked up at me, dark eyes full of the love we'd known in an age gone by, the frown, the creases of despair that now governed her face those of a woman who knows that her time is finished.

'We'll find each other again,' she whispered. 'Sooner or later.'

'Either sooner. Or later. But yes. We'll find each other again.'

'In the meantime you have your Niiv.'

'For a while. I'm sorry, Medea.'

'Sorry for what?'

'For the lost years. When we were young and the world was young.'

She sighed into my breast. She laughed quietly. 'Our paths were different. Our paths parted. Trails take on different hills and different valleys. They all come back to the starting point. We didn't miss years, you and I. We had many years. That was our problem, being as old and as interminable as we were born to be, two people who could escape the clutches of Time ... '

Looking up at me, she touched a finger to my face fondly. 'It's a shame we are not fully immortal. Our problem was that we had too many years to use, and too many lovers to use them on. We didn't waste a moment. We felt the need to find different loves for different seasons. All of this in a span of Time that no one can understand. And now I'm dead; and you're not. But you *will* be dead. One day. And we'll find each other again, and perhaps understand what our purpose was.'

'Wanderers.'

'Wanderers.'

She tugged my hair, pulled my face down to hers, pressed her mouth against mine. A last kiss. Her lips were as moist, soft, as fragrant and as yearning as a spring flower opening after rain. Everything in that kiss was the joy of remembering.

Then she whispered, 'My son will kill his father, unless you intervene. They're out there now, and Thesokorus is angry. Spend a little of your life, Merlin. Please. For me. For your sister. Out of love.'

She had gone from me as quickly as she had appeared in the gloom of the labyrinth. I stood there shaken and shaking, trying to suppress tears, tears for a woman whom once I'd loved and whom I had come to hate, and who had been a constant torment in my life. I could think of none of that now, none of the pain, none of the pursuit, only of that idyll of play and teasing, and affection that had been our first years. The time of love and joy, so long ago that it might have been the play of gods unknown.

I became angry then: a red rush of rage. I looked at the cold stone and saw only a man's greed. Daidalos was walking home, and dragging a world with him. It occurred to me, as I hammered hands against that cold rock illusion, that the man, born in the past, born to understanding and brilliance on that remote island, could not cross the river.

It was a moment of inspiration. Nantosuelta, the often calm, sometimes raging flow of water that defined the edges of two worlds, would not let the man cross. He was incomplete, and the river knew it.

And yet, he had savaged a land. Urtha's land. The land of my friend, and of my friend's family. The Dead had come willingly with him. They were legion, lining the banks of the new river. The Unborn were restless, unhappy at this unhappy outcome.

Daidalos had power. He had sucked power from the Otherworld. He had shrouded himself in the strength of ghosts.

Well. At that moment, in the blaze of fury, losing my sister from the beginning of Time, my lover, thinking of Niiv, who could not tame Time as could I, who would not last the distance in the days that I wished her to stay with me: in that moment I decided to age.

This is how it felt.

My bones seemed to shatter inside my flesh as the charm was scraped from them. My blood congealed in my heart, but flowed from my skin. My hands became red, and I cried tears of blood, unable to hold back the flow of anger. I shattered the labyrinth, shattered the stone, exposed the man who stood at its centre.

For a moment Daidalos was shocked. I stepped towards him. He looked strong. He gleamed. His eyes were hollows. His face coated with dark hair, his arms, naked, bruised and powerful. He began to weave again.

Stone formed around me.

I shattered the stone.

Stepping away from me, for a second time I sensed his confusion and fear. I picked up a shard of rock and ran at him. I struck him and brought him down, straddled him and struck at him again.

'Brutal. Brutal,' he gasped with a laugh. 'But in the valley, your friend Jason is about to die. Don't you wish to see it?'

And rage was gone. I looked around. This was not the edge of the river, it was not the mountainside where Daidalos had been ensnared by Jason, lifetimes in the past. This was a place in Greek Land. We were on the slopes of the valley of the oracle at Dodona, and below me, beyond the bleeding creature who lay so compliantly at my feet, as if waiting for me to make one move so that he could counter it with equal strength, there, by the stream, Jason was backing away from his eldest son, Thesokorus; the bull leaper; the man who had come to be known as King of Killers.

'What am I witnessing?' I whispered to the man.

'A touch of vengeance before I find a way to get back to my own home.'

I let the stone fall. I felt ashamed. I could not at that moment understand from where this sudden rage had come, nor why this half man, half machine, had allowed me to beat him without defending against the blows. Perhaps he knew that I was mourning the passing of an old friend, one who had become a haunting enemy. I looked at Daidalos. He did not seem to be enjoying the situation. Rather, he was waiting for events to unfold.

For a third time I realised how confused he was. But now, something else: fear.

I walked away from him in this illusory landscape, down the hill to where father and son faced each other in the Greeklander way, preparing to do combat, but uncertain as to the moment at which to commence the fight. Each leaned forward on his left knee, right hands held loosely on the hilt of their swords, fingers outstretched, not yet gripping the leather-bound ivory, not yet pulling the iron from its scabbard, to make the assault.

As I approached, I heard their conversation. It was the son who was speaking.

'I thought I'd killed you at Dodona. I smelled your shit, your blood. You couldn't have survived that strike.'

I'd witnessed the contest. It was after the Great Quest had failed to sack Delphi, and the Celtic armies were dispersing in dismay. Father and son had found each other in the valley of another oracle, and the encounter had not been warm.

'I survived,' Jason said cautiously. 'I see you've inherited the same tendency. Unless those scars on your face and arms are for decoration.'

'My life has been short, but not without its difficulties. That's neither here nor there. That strike I gave you went deep.'

'Not deep enough. Not in the flesh, at least. It wounded me though. All I had done was come to find you again, you and your brother. My two sons by Medea.'

'I didn't believe you then, how would you expect me to believe you now?'

Jason's grin was grim. 'I have no answer to that. I want only for a final voyage in Argo, with Thesokorus at my side. Leaping over bulls, if he wishes.'

'I no longer recognise that name. I am Orgetorix.'

'My son, nevertheless, under any name.'

'And Kinos? What about my brother.'

'Dead. I'll say it bluntly. He didn't have your metal. He had a mind that was wonderful, imagination that was intriguing, but when it came to character, he was not a killer of anything, and certainly not of kings. He was broken from the moment he first learned to think. Thinking broke him because his dreaming broke him. Do you remember how we called him 'Little Dreamer'? He broke himself in the underworld, in a place of his own dreaming. And not even his mother could help him.'

Thesokorus reached down and stroked fingers against the moist earth by the stream. He was breathing hard, and I noticed that he was shaking, one hand on the earth, the other on his sword. He looked up at Jason, his face narrowed and hard, older by years than the years that had been shaping him. 'Tell me about my mother. I saw her moments ago, and she was nothing but a ghost. Did you kill her?'

'No.'

'Then who killed her?'

'*Time* killed her,' Jason responded without pause. 'And you. And Kinos. And me. And places and times, and events and circumstances that none of us were privy to. She had lived a long life. I was just a flutter in her breast, a moment's touch of desire and fondness. She had more time for the man you call Merlin. She was Merlin's sister, I know now. And they are older than forests.'

'I am not that man's child.'

'No. You're not.'

'She had children by other men?'

'I never thought to ask the question.'

'But! Let me get this clear. I am your son. Medea is my mother. *Was* my mother. I am shaped by you. I must live and eventually die by the way you shaped me.'

'Yes, you must. And now I have a question for you.'

'Ask it.'

'Concerning the life that is left to you, a span that is longer than the life left to me, or certainly I hope so, though your scars and intemperance give me some cause for concern ...'

'What about that life?'

'Will you live it with rage or without rage; with affection or with notions of vengeance? I betrayed your mother. I don't deny it. I paid a high cost. Higher than you ever knew, because before I could speak to you, my guts were bleeding, my shit spilling out, your knife the cause. None of that matters now. I have a new chance, a brief chance, and if I could find now those gods that once gave me the strength and confidence to live my life in the only way that life should be lived ...'

'What way is that?' asked Thesokorus quickly.

'Life upon life. Upon life. Upon *life*! Until there is no *longer* life!'

Thesokorus beat his fist against the earth, but with enthusiasm. He met his father's gaze again. 'I like that thought. I like it very much. The one thing in my life that has been missing since I surfaced from such a strange dream, of being sacrificed and hidden ... the one thing I have missed is what my brother, by your words, had in abundance: dreams; and purpose; I have had action. Scars prove it. Battles! Scars prove it. I scarred my father. My father's scar proves it. I have missed my father all my life. But I can't think of you as my father. I can only think of you as Jason.'

When Jason didn't respond, Thesokorus gave a wry little sigh, then said, 'But now I think *Jason* is enough for me. You found men and women, heroes and half-gods, and formed them into a crew for that little ship, you, a man, no more than a man, and you tamed Herakles, and Theseus, and Atalanta, and you found the fleece of gold! And I grew up with those stories, and those stories are all I have of you. Oceans, rivers, creatures, rocks that clash, spaces that open in the cliffs and draw you in. And all of that with the constant presence not of gods, advising those heroes, but of a man who had no direction except forward. You found my mother by going forward. You came home to Iolkos by going forward. And you found rivers and streams, and hauled that ship over dry land, and you knew yourself, and you knew your direction. You knew a simple truth: that a small stream, if followed, must always end in Ocean, and by following the coast of Ocean, you can always find the shore from which you had once set sail.'

He paused for a moment, still dragging his fingers through the earth. Then he shook his head. 'What was it that happened to me that these simple truths were denied to me, when they would have been so important to me? Why am I a wanderer, like that strange friend of yours, Merlin?'

'You are what you are because what happened, happened. I betrayed Medea for another woman. In her fury she took her sons by me and killed them. Or so I thought. In fact, she flung you into the future, and in so doing brought herself close to death herself. Fury never makes fools of the wise; it makes fools of fools. Medea and I were fools, though there is no denying our lust. Why were we fools? Because love was never mentioned. She wanted children. She created many, spared only two. I will tell you this, Thesokorus. I will never, I doubt any man or woman will ever, understand what was going through that woman's mind when she abandoned you to time, in hate for me, in fury at me.'

Were they aware of me, standing just a few paces away? It seemed they were wrapped in their own world.

For a few moments I couldn't tell whether they were about to strike at each other. Certainly Thesokorus was still as tense as a cat about to spring.

Then slowly both men straightened. I glanced round to see Daidalos watching from the top of the slope. Light glinted on him as he turned quickly away, a disappointed man.

Jason unbuckled his sword belt and slung it over his shoulder. His son did the same. Both men nodded to each other, each without smiling. Then they went to the water's edge, crouching down, and after a moment sitting down, side by side, staring into the distance in silence.

I left them alone.

With a roar like thunder, the land again transformed, but not back to that half seen vision of Crete; this was the eastern edge of Urtha's realm, and Nantosuelta flowed violently past, curling round this bulge of land from south to north. The army from Ghostland was spread out in the forest, restless spirits on restless horses, waiting for the way to cross to the realm of the Coritoni, where only the Unborn had been allowed to travel. It was dusk, here. Fires burned on the hillside across from where I stood. A grim hostel rose before me, the rear door a narrow wedge-shaped space framed by massive lengths of round oak. The carving of an elk's head glared from below the eaves, spade-shaped antlers stretching five men's lengths in each direction; the muzzle of the beast was not elk: it was snarling wolf.

Beyond it, moored, was my Argo, in the last true form she had taken: part Greek Land, part North Land, fine oak and hard spruce lashed together, fit for high Ocean as we had discovered.

Daidalos had clearly used his garnered influence to ready his army for the crossing, getting them to hammer on shields, shouting out their war cries from whatever age they had come, and hurling a storm of sling-shot onto the opposite banks; I doubted their iron arrows could cross the water.

The fear was: if they couldn't cross either, they would turn back and finish the pillaging of Urtha's land that they had begun in their dash to go east.

'Daidalos!' I shouted, then. 'Daidalos!'

There was no reply from around me, so I entered the hostel. It was a massive space, almost as dark as night, polished metal shields hanging on wickerwork partitions, reflecting the dim light that crept through the eaves, and the shadowy movement of those who moved about the hall.

'Daidalos!'

A shield was struck by iron, then a second, and the hall rang with the sound. As it faded, I sensed the presence of the man.

'Who are you?' he asked from his hiding place.

'I'm the boy who built Argo. I built the first little boat. When you fitted her out, in your island harbour where you had your Shaping Chambers, you would have experienced the Spirit of the Ship. All her Captains have their echoes there, and so I would have been there.'

But why did I know him?

Daidalos prowled this gloomy hostel. Sometimes a silvered shield caught the gleam of bronze, sometimes the pale reflection of his face.

He was silent for a long time. Then he said, as if he had heard my question, 'You put a small image on that boat. The image of a man, the receptacle of your own captaincy. You built a boat and you built a sailor.'

I *hadn't* remembered. But it came back to me now. Of course! The little figure, what the Greeklanders called *kolossoi*. A life in wood or metal. My small figure had been roughly hewn from the fallen branch of an oak, whittled to perfection (or so I'd thought, being only a few years old at the time) polished with oil, painted vibrantly, hidden after that, in a small, secret compartment in the back of the crude, simple vessel.

Now I understood. It was as if insight into that other world 'where charm rules rather than learned knowledge' was flooding me with understanding.

'I made you,' I whispered, still struggling to understand the process by which that tiny figure had matured into the man and then this creature.

'Every time she was rebuilt, I grew stronger,' he said, as if again sensing my question. 'I stayed with Argo until I was strong enough to leave, to make my way in the new world. I found an island, perfect for my dreams, perfect to develop and refine my skills. And later, when I was exploring the Middle Realm and fighting unnatural forces, Argo came back and I made her even stronger - only to have her *pirated* by the man who should be dead by now, as dead as the woman who just departed. But that's now a task for another time.'

'You helped build Argo. Do you believe she wants such vengeance?'

'I have no love for that ship. She betrayed me.'

'And grieved about it.'

'By aiding my abduction, she helped kill my children. Only Raptor survived. He was already beyond the boundary of sky. But Argo has been helpful since then. She is trying to make amends.'

I said nothing in response to that. I couldn't read the meaning. And Daidalos, this re-born man, was still challenging me, perhaps because of his anger at my coarse and primitive assault upon him.

'When I find the other part of this,' he raised half of the gold lunula amulet, Munda's half; I could see it clearly reflected in a shield, Daidalos's shadow looming behind it, 'I shall cross and open the way for the army. I will take an army with me across the world and back to my mountains. With their help, I'll destroy the Woman of Wild Creatures who made my life so hard.'

'And everything in your path.'

'It won't be that wide a path.'

'You are rotten to the bone with vengeance.'

'On the contrary. I am bright with new creation. I'm missing only the fifth part. Four were enough to let me cross the first shore of the river. But I could only exercise a slight influence further east. I made oak idols out of two hundred warriors; I summoned the Oldest Animals. I even stole the spirit of a man, a slave from the south, to bring back newly fallen discs from the island, when I heard the whisper from Argo that she would be voyaging there—

Talienze! So that had been his function ...

'—I knew, then, that I had the same range of strengths, but only in a very small measure.'

'He would not have been able to bring back new discs. Your stolen spirit; Talienze. You know that in your heart – or in the space where your heart should be. You know the fact.'

There was silence again. 'Raptor is still in the Middle Realm.'

'There's no Middle Realm. It exists only because you desire it to. You created it just as you created the discs, flying down to your mountainside, with their gibberish and those facts among the markings that you longed to know and have confirmed.'

Something struck one of the shields, sending it clashing to the floor and spinning even as the striking object itself spun around it. A second flying disc passed so close to me that I had to bend with a swiftness that my body hated. I was feeling old. This one also struck a shield, fell at my feet and I picked it up. It was hot and inscribed with patterns and symbols.

I could feel Shaper's confusion, as tangible as sweat.

'You see?' he said uncertainly. 'Even here the boy can reach me.'

'Why do you say that?'

'Because the origin of those discs was not from me.'

'No. It was from me.'

It was not an easy charm, not as easy as animal possession, because it involved metal. But it could be done, and Daidalos had been doing it for years – years in the past, that is. That was a strong talent.

'The mistake you made,' I said to him quietly, 'was not that you strove too hard for the impossible, but that you failed to realise that you were born too soon.

'When you were desperate to explore a place that may or may not exist, and sent your sons and daughters to their deaths, you betrayed your own mind. You started to draw on the unnatural. The unnatural exists, but it exists to keep the natural under control. The moment you sent Raptor to your fabled Middle Realm you were lost. Only the unnatural could have got him there. You betrayed your intellect.

'You forgot, or you denied, that you were a man born too soon to see his dreams come true.'

'All of us can face that particular reality.'

'I agree.'

'Some of us fight against it.'

'To what end?'

'The triumph that comes with glimpsing the unknown.'

'A life, the lives of all you love, are worth a glimpse?'

'You tell me. You're the man who walks with all of Time as his lover, hanging on to her every word, soothing her and stroking her.

A boat gently drifting. Argo was your cradle and your shroud. I went beyond the boundaries!'

'You failed.'

'I tried! I sent my life to the boundaries. Two beautiful sons, three beautiful daughters ready to follow them. I sacrificed life for understanding. Isn't that the whole reason that we are given the power of imagination?'

'Imagination is to be used to envision. You used it to create false understanding. You dreamed beyond the boundaries. Many of us do. Nothing wrong with that. How much we'd like to achieve an understanding of the incomprehensible. We have to accept that all we can put in place is a small part of future time, a small addition, a little help for the time when you don't have to stitch wings into sons to make them fly.

'You shaped your own world of dreams for yourself, Daidalos. You are an *adept* at shaping, there's no denying it.'

'You shaped me first. Yours was the life spark.'

'You used it well. Until Crete.'

'I've used it again to bring this river back to her ancient bed.'

'But she won't let you cross over.'

'She will. Just as soon as I've found the other half of this.' Again, the flash of gold. 'Argo has told me that it lies close to the other side of the river, where the king's son dropped it.'

Now he showed himself again, a shadow, passing swiftly to the riverside door of the hostel. I followed him, but found he had vanished again, though I could sense his watching, eager presence.

And something was happening to Nantosuelta.

Between hostel and farther bank the river was slowing! What had been a raging flow, scouring at the banks and the overhanging foliage, was now calming in the rising moonlight. And as the flow ebbed, so she gradually exposed the gentle slopes that led to the stone-strewn bed itself.

How the army thundered! They surged forward, leading horses. Shield-din and voice-din sounded furious and rhythmic in the fresh night air, the blood-roar of gathering courage. Torches made a wall of fire on our side. Torches made a stream of retreat from the other.

The bronze hounds bayed. *Talosoi* moved down the very edge of the water, dropping to their familiar crouch and watching and waiting.

Argo had slipped her moorings, slipped away, prow towards us. There was a gleam in the water below her, a sun sparkle in the pale moon. A figure slithered across her side, eel-like, small and slight, dived down, surfaced, holding the lunula. The figure came aboard again lithely and Argo returned.

The din continued. The rain of stones continued. Slingshot was returned from the scant forces of Vortingoros's defensive army, but from behind us, no sign of Urtha or Pendragon, or the others.

Now Daidalos appeared, a slinking form in his greying rags of clothing. He went down to the mooring place. The *Talosoi*, those that I could see, some ten among forty, turned to watch him. The figure slipped out of Argo like an eel from its mud shelter, lithe, swift and sure, and as she passed Daidalos she tossed the golden fragment towards him; he caught it; Munda ran from him, ran to me, threw herself into my arms.

'I *had* to do it. Trust me!'

Daidalos held high his 'heart and breath', then looped a cord through each piece and slung them round his neck.

Nantosuelta was now a low, slow-flowing river, through which the hordes of the Dead began to wade at chest height, leading horse, dragging chariot, each formation preceded by a squad of spearmen, lightly armed and clothed, shields held before them to repel the stone shot.

The river was clogged with men and animals.

And then the river surged!

For the second time that I had witnessed, a bole of water, a great wave of destruction, poured along the course, flowing powerfully up the confining hills, throwing boulders and trees before it, coming towards us at such pace, faster than Conan's chariot, faster than young dogs chasing a flight of game birds, it was on us in a moment. It had brought with it the great trees of another forest. Their broken trunks crushed the hostels, the *Talosoi*, scoured the bank of the river itself. Both sides suffered. The army of the Dead was swept away still howling, away to the north. Even as ranks of them arrived to see the chaos, they seemed incapable of turning back. They lunged forward, plunged, sank, drowned and screamed their way back to a new darkness.

I had a feeling that the river would later turn in its flow and take them west, to where they belonged, rather than to the sea.

I cowered in the Hostel of Shields, Munda wrapped in my arms, as if I could have protected her from any of the danger at that moment. Daidalos stood in stunned astonishment at the river-entrance, watching the destruction of his final dream.

Argo stayed at berth, protected by some older charm, her painted eyes staring at her two once-Captains. She rose on the surge, but was not dislodged by it, even when a massive tree, torn from four hundred years of life, branch-whipped the area, a lost life flailing in anger as it was borne away from its rooting place.

Only the Hostel of Shields and its inhabitants, and Argo, survived the deluge. On our side, that is. As fast as it had come it had ceased, and the river calmed again. Munda and I stood up and stared towards where the storm had raged. The backs and skulls and raised arms of the *Talosoi* were, for me, a grim reminder of the approach, so long ago, to Ak-Gnossos on Crete.

Daidalos was standing, staring down at the broken lunula around his neck. He had imagined that this last of the five parts he had fashioned, through amazing skill and great insight, to protect his body through time, would have been the way to open the passage home, for himself and his army of forlorn mercenaries, the unquiet inhabitants of the world where there should only have been tranquillity and pleasure.

I was not surprised. The dying are always greedy for life; why should things change later in the event? Not even the natural can control *that* unnatural aspiration.

I looked down at the girl. 'Talk to me. About what just happened.'

'I went swimming again. After you'd left. The river whispered to me. I've often been swimming in the Winding One, despite the *geis* on me not to. She often whispers to me.'

'And what did she whisper?'

'She is protective to the dead and to the living. She is the barrier. She is the edge of two worlds. My father's kingdom is now and always will be vulnerable, because it is half between each world, and a man like Shaper, a stranger, a dead man brought from a different world, can have a great effect on how she flows. But at the end of it all, she won't contemplate extending her boundaries. Her task is to *protect* life on the other side. It was wrong to try and cross her. The man called Shaper would never have succeeded. She'd never have let him succeed.'

She was shivering. I gave her my deerskin coat. 'Where's your brother?'

'With my father. With my mother. Tidying things up at home. Niiv is missing you, by the way. It's quiet now, but they are making preparations for war against the invader. Sending out the signal for recruitment. And finding our cattle, scattered everywhere. Finding our horses. Calling council to discuss the new Speakers. My father is considering a campaign to the north to recruit fresh warriors.'

'I thought he was tired of fighting.'

'He is, but he mustn't show it. And a king without hostages of importance is not a strong king. He must have royal hostages to bargain with if he's to have mercenaries, and horses.'

I would have laughed out loud, but didn't. 'You begin to speak like the daughter of a king.'

'And learn!' she agreed, still shivering from the river. Then she nodded towards Shaper. 'What about him? When do we kill him. How? I want my lunula back, preferably blood-ripe.'

'The lunula is his. It always was.'

'Why?' she asked, irritated.

'A little piece of his life, in bronze, is hidden inside it. It was stolen from him. As were his daughters. All save one. Wait for me.'

I started to walk towards Daidalos, and then a thought occurred to me and I glanced back at Munda. 'I'm pleased you think of Ullanna as your mother.'

Munda smiled and nodded.

'And learn,' she repeated softly.

I couldn't bring myself to touch him. I walked past him, but genuinely felt a moment's pause, a moment's sadness. His eyes, when he turned to look at me, were filled with dismay and loss. He held the two halves of the simple ornament as if they had betrayed him.

Perhaps they had.

I whispered to Argo; she whispered back. I told her what I was going to do. There would come a time, recently as I write, when I would question why I did what I did next. It took so many years from me. It took so much life from me. It changed me.

I went aboard Argo, found the Spirit of the Ship, crossed the threshold, greeted Mielikki and her lynx (in summer form) and sat down.

I summoned one of the ten masks, the ten tutors from my

childhood, the ten ways of moving through and summoning the world. I had had enough of Morndun, *Death moves through the world* and Skogen, *Shadow of unseen forests*. I had summoned the memory of Moondream, *Woman in the world*, and Cunhaval, the *Seeking Hound*. These were far more powerful interactions with the charm that was instilled within me than just shape-shifting and occupying wrens.

Now I wanted Sinisalo. *The child in the land.*

Mielikki moved away. The air was summery, the wild grass tall, flowers abundant. Even here, in this memory of childhood when the masks had spoken to me, teaching me, even here I could feel the slight movement of Argo, my boat, on the water that flowed between two kingdoms. I summoned the past.

—Where are you Sinisalo?

After silence for a while, I called again.

—Sinisalo?

—I'm here. You've been a long time walking your path. Do you have any plans to finish and come home? All the others are home. All eight of them. We've just welcomed your sister.

—How was she?

—Sad. But that will pass. She did her time in her own way. The only lazy one is you. The boy who wouldn't bother to tie his laces. The boy who liked life too much to use his great powers of charm, enchantment, manipulation, call it what you will. You have a lot left to give. So I suppose we shall be a long time waiting for you.

Sinisalo was cheeky. A small, white face, a smiling child's face, a flop of unruly copper coloured hair, watching and listening with a child's intensity.

But this was no child, not really. Just the representation of the child in the land.

—What do you want me to tell you? The child asked.

—How many years will be taken from me in exchange for a year for Daidalos's dead daughter.

—The honey child?

—The child killed and preserved in a crystal jar of honey, yes. Killed by a creature of the wild. Dragged here by me. To be found at this moment in the hull of this ship.

—How many years can you spare?

I told Sinisalo.

—For that she can have ... ten. Is that enough?

—I can't afford much more. That will have to do.

—Well then. We'll see you sooner than we were expecting.

Sinisalo laughed sweetly, waved goodbye, seemed to disappear into the long, wild grass and pink and purple flowers.

'I don't know her name,' I said to Daidalos as he stood in Argo's stern, staring at the girl, 'but you have her for a while, and I suggest you disentangle her from the wings.'

Yes, though *I* forget her name now, he cried *out* her name, and she cried out to him, and in the shadow of the Hostel of Shields, on the quiet river, they embraced. I noticed how his hands stroked the clumsy wings and their awful struts and straps, the tendons that linked a child to a man's madness, a daughter to a father's misplaced love; perhaps, at the end of it, just a tie that needed to be broken.

And they had ten years to enjoy that separation. Together.

Gods, I felt old, now. Even Daidalos noticed it.

'Why did you do this? It's taken a lot from you.'

'Go home. On Argo. She'll take you. I have a path to walk, but before I can do that, I have the rest of a life to live here! And I'd like to live it without the Dead howling at my backside.'

'Why did you do this?' he asked again.

I didn't answer him as I left the ship. I glanced back only to see the gleam of life and joy in the child, her happy bewilderment at where she now found herself as she emerged from what terrible dream I cannot bear to think.

It might have turned out differently if it hadn't been for remembering that small piece of oak, shaped into that small piece of man, kissed by a child and set adrift after near disaster on that old river by the child who had wished it captaincy and long life.

The river took the old ship in her bright new form, Jason's Argo, passing away from me, taking Daidalos and his daughter home on wings of Ocean.

But before she slipped away, she whispered to me.

I didn't know who Shaper was until he called to me from Ghostland. Everything I had done, all the betrayal, surfaced again. Thank you for helping me.

'I hadn't known you were feeling such pain.'

You couldn't have known. I kept it from you. Before you came back to Taurovinda. But every time you were on board, I felt courage. I needed you to see what had happened. I needed your strength.

'It's over now. Nothing to concern you but storm seas. And finding a crew to help you with the winds.'

Yes. It's over now. But you will sail in me again. You belong in me more than Jason, or any of the others. But we will all gather for the Deep.

Across the river, men were gathering in the night, torches burning fiercely, shouts and questions and confusion as bad a din as the shield-din of earlier.

A small hand suddenly took mine. Munda looked at me curiously. 'You look a lot older in the moonlight. You're not ill?'

'Not ill.'

'Good. Because there's a man on the other side of this hostel with two white horses, a sparkling chariot, and a brother. And he says that taking us to Taurovinda will cost you nothing. His father said so. I have no idea what he's talking about, but it's time to go.'

I laughed quietly as I followed her to where Conan and Gwyrion were arguing about who should hold the reins, because they needed to drive fast, since their father – from whom they'd stolen one too many chariots, but who was for the moment rather pleased with them, though was irascible and erratic of mood – was likely to find some excuse to imprison them again at the next phase of the moon, which was very close to arriving.

And indeed, they drove as fast as a falling star, and we all arrived bruised.

The death of vengeance is the most beautiful death of all.

Anon

I am a part of all that I have met.

from *Ulysses*, by Alfred Lord Tennyson

Coda

Niiv had been with the women at the well, chattering and laughing. She had spent most of the day there, something she had not done for some time.

At dusk I was taking a breath of air, outside the King's hall, where a council was being held. They were discussing cattle, the Coritani, and the construction of a new sanctuary at the place where, a few years ago, the Hostel of Shields had finally crumbled into the stone-strewn river bed, exposed again as the river had retreated, as the Winding One had wound back to old courses.

Niiv called out and came running up to me. She pecked me on the cheek, squeezed my hand. She was elfin-eyed and as mischievous as ever, and had clearly enjoyed her day at the well.

'I'm suddenly very tired,' she said. 'I can't think why. I'm going to ride down to our lodge in the evergroves.'

'I shan't be long after you. This meeting is very tedious.'

She found her grey pony and rode through the east gate, down across the plain to the sanctuary of trees and mounds, where we had built our small home.

I returned to the meeting, sitting close to the door, feeling the welcome warmth of the central fire. Winter was in the air, the first sharp signs and scents of it. A brisk touch on the cheeks, a swirl of darkening cloud, moving from the north.

Kymon was on his feet, addressing an issue agitatedly and strongly. He was a tall, rugged man now, his grey cloak pinned at his midriff, the fire making a golden sheen of the sweat on his chest. His right arm was horribly scarred from a raid, as was his cheek, the white scar cutting through his full moustache. Urtha sat, listening with an air of impatience, as his son took him to task on some matter of protocol.

Colcu, King of the Coritani and a guest at this council, sat with his legs spread, his arms crossed and his face fierce, listening to his friend, unhappy with what he was hearing, but respecting the courtesy of the Hall.

Recently, relations between Kymon, Urtha and Colcu had become strained; over what issue? I could never tell. Horses, hostages, hunting. Always something.

After a moment Urtha caught my eye and frowned. I shook my head slightly, raised a hand, and he nodded, giving me a grim, sad smile before staring down at the ground as I left the hall again for the chill evening.

'Merlin!'

One of the women at the well was beckoning to me. She was carrying a small bag and when I reached her she passed it to me nervously. 'Niiv left this behind. I don't know if she meant to.'

'I'll take it to her. Goodnight.'

It took a moment before I remembered what it was: the small sack that Niiv had been carrying when she had clambered, screaming abuse, onto Argo, as we had departed for Crete. There was an object in it, something she had guarded very carefully at all times, except when she had run with the swarming crowds of Tairon's town.

When the woman had disappeared behind the trees, back to the water grove, I opened the bag and took the object out. I was sure Niiv had meant me to look at it. At least, that's how I rationalised my invasion of her property.

It was a piece of grey slate, not metal as I'd thought, on which she had scratched words using her own language. It came as a small shock to realise that she had made these markings, expressed the thought, at a time of great hazard. She had been preparing for the worst during that voyage, and this had been then, and was now, a promise to me:

I have put aside enough of my life to find you again in times to come. I long for that future time. Please be sure you recognise me when our paths next cross. All of this for an affection I felt for you from the moment we skated on the ice, in my own country, in the shadow of my father's death. My Merlin. Your Niiv.

I placed the bag gently in the corner, trying not to disturb her as

I entered our home. But when I crept into the bed, Niiv was still awake, lying on her side, away from me. She turned to look at me. Her eyes were wide and happy, bright with life and affection, her smile warm. 'Tell me something.'

'Anything,' I assured her as I pulled the furs over us, shivering with the cold.

'Did you truly come to love me?'

The form of her question startled me, saddened me. I couldn't speak for a moment. But then I kissed the tip of her nose, held her close, feeling the way she pressed her back against my body, curling into me. I brushed my lips on hers as she gazed at me. 'I love you. You know I do.'

Now her lips touched mine, a teasing kiss. 'I asked you: did you *truly* love me?'

Again, it took me a moment to find the words. I spoke softly. 'You irritated me at first. You even scared me on occasion. You know this. We've talked about this before. But things have been different for a long time. You must know that too. I love you very much.'

She sighed, smiled at me once more before turning her head away, to rest on the pillow. 'I believe you do. I believe you did. You loved me. This is not the end, then. We will have a future together. I'm so glad of that.'

She snuggled into me again, trying to catch my warmth. 'You're not going to leave me, are you? Not tonight.'

I closed my eyes and listened to her soft breathing.

'No, Niiv. I'm not going to leave you.'

She shuffled and sighed, then settled.

'Hold me tightly, Merlin. I need to sleep, now. I need your arms around me. I have to brave the dream.'

'What dream is that?'

'The Swan Dream. I have to dream of swans. They're so beautiful. I love them. So did my father.'

I held her very tightly. I talked to her quietly. And quite soon she went to sleep.

My arms did not tire of holding her.

Came the dawn, came Urtha. He pulled back the deer-skins of the doorway and sharp winter light spilled into our small house. Urtha was a dark shadow in that frame of brightness. Brusque and brash, he was suddenly humbled when he saw the scene. He didn't speak for a moment, then asked, 'Am I disturbing you?'

'No. You're not disturbing us.'

He looked at Niiv, then at me. 'I can see from the dried tears that this has not been the easiest of nights.'

'A very long night.'

'Shall I wait outside?'

'No. No – please. Stay where you are. I'm ready to feel the day.'

I eased my arm from under Niiv and kissed her cool brow. I remembered again her scratched promise.

I have put aside enough of my life to find you again in times to come.

Yes, I thought. And you'll be young and I'll be old, and you'll make my life a challenge again.

But there was pleasure in the thought, and joy, despite this silent moment of loss.

Her grey hair was spread over the goose-feather pillow. Her hollow cheeks seemed younger now, all creases of concern and age in her old woman's skin relaxed. 'I told you not to squander your charm,' I whispered. 'But I'm glad you don't want to lose me.'

Urtha sighed from the doorway. 'I suppose I'll lose you too, now. You'll be walking that Path you've been missing for so long.'

I left the bed and pulled on my winter clothes. 'I have no other choice. I'll be on my way again.' They were hard words to say to a man who had become a great friend.

Urtha nodded, resigned to the inevitable. 'I know,' he said quietly. 'I've always known. The day always comes. By the way: someone's back again. Our friend: Argo. She's moored very close to here. Are you surprised?'

What could I say? His words made me feel melancholy, but for a moment only. I was moving on and there was a thrill in the thought of it. I was more than ready for change.

'No, I'm not surprised. I knew she would come. I've been feeling her presence for a few days, now. I'm going with her too.'

'Where?'

'North, of course. Where else? I have to take Niiv home to her father. Then I have to pick up the journey where I left off, when I met Niiv and Jason and you, three encounters that led to a good few years of change in my life.'

Urtha smiled at the memory. 'I'll miss you. Especially with winter coming, and this place confined within its walls.'

'You'll find plenty to do. You always do.'

Beyond him, the light was winter-harsh, an odd sort of light. The light that comes from a heavy snowfall.

'Has it been snowing?' I asked. 'That *will* make it a hard season.'

'Not snow, not yet,' Urtha said with a knowing shake of his head. 'You have to see this to believe it. It happened overnight.'

He held back the skins for me and I stooped below his arm and stepped into the evergroves, looking with astonishment towards Taurovinda.

The land for as far as the eye could see in all directions was white with swans.

Notes on the Text

The Codex: The 'Merlin Codex' is a set of writings, on parchment scrolls, found in several sealed, hollowed lengths of petrified wood in a cave in the Perigord region of France in 1948. They are fragmentary. Other such containers may yet be discovered.
The Codex has been divided into three parts: *Celtika*, *The Iron Grail,* and this third volume, *The Broken Kings.*
The three volumes represent different periods of writing over a very long span of years. The style changes; details are not consistent. Nevertheless, they are an insight into forgotten history and legend, written by a man who is legend himself, although we have come to much misrepresent and misinterpret him.

Merlin: known by many names, including Antiokus (see *Celtika*), Merlin was a boyhood nickname meaning, according to the text, 'cannot tie his laces'.

The Oldest Animals/the Ten Masks: There are several references to the 'Oldest Animals' and the 'Ten Masks' in the Merlin Codex. They are a Western European form of what the Australian indigenous people refer to as The Dreamtime. The Oldest Animals of Western Europe's ancient mythology were the Owl, the Salmon, the Stag, the Bear, the Beaver and the Wild Hound. The masks are: *Moondream*, the woman in the land; *Lament,* sorrow in the land; *Sinisalo*, The Child in the Land; *Skogen*, the Shadow of Unseen Forests; *Hollower,* the Hollowing Man (able to access the Otherworld); *Morndun,* The ghost in the land (who walks in the underworld); *Gaberlungi*, the Storyteller; *Cunhaval*, the Hound that runs through the land; *Silvering*, the Salmon that swims through the rivers of the land; and *Falkenna*, the Bird of Prey that hunts from the skies of the land.

Crete: I have used the modern form of the name for the island, rather than Minoa. The Egyptians of the Sixth Dynasty may have known the sea-farers of Crete as *Ha-nebu* or 'northerners'; another name was *Keftiu*, 'those from the hinterland'. In the Old Testament, Crete is referred to as Caphtor.

Druid: literally: 'oak man'. Druids were men (sometimes women) who were trained in memory, medicine, wisdom, poetry, and magic. They were called by various titles – rarely referred to as druids – and I have adopted Speaker for Kings, Land and Past.

Talienze: The Codex is unsatisfactory on the nature of the Speaker, Talienze, who was from Vortingoros's kingdom, but had certainly been brought there, perhaps as a child hostage, or perhaps as a wandering man who chose to settle. It may be that part of the Codex is missing, or that the boys who described the abrupt end of the man (see text) gave an incomplete picture.

Pendragon: this man is clearly the Arthur of later legend, as yet Unborn. His ease of movement between the Celtic Otherworld and the 'real' world contrasts with the difficulty of such movement by the Dead. Merlin occasionally attempts to explain how these differences are controlled, what rules they obey, but his descriptions are confusing, referring to an older understanding of magic, and I have chosen to omit them.

Daidalos: I have used the older form of the name, Daidalos, rather than the more familiar Daedalus, as this is how it appears in the Codex. The Dyctean cave referred to in the text is the cave where Zeus was born on Crete. It is not clear from the Codex whether Daidalos had adapted Zeus's birthplace to a shaping chamber.

Honey children: The Codex suggests that Daidalos had three daughters, but the fate of two of them is unclear. What is certain is that Lady of Wild Creatures – a form of the Earth or Mother Goddess – used the child or children for her own ends, perhaps 'stealing back' the caves that Daidalos used as shaping chambers, but an account of their fate, if it was known, is missing from the Codex.

Argo: When Jason refitted Argo, he used oak from a branch of the Dodonian oak, an oracle, a grove in Greece dedicated to Hera, Zeus's wife. Athena was Hera's daughter. Though they often argued (ferociously), they each took a turn, in Jason's time, in protecting Argo.